THE DAEDALUS KEY

BRIAN SHEA
RAQUEL BYRNES

Copyright © 2025 by Brian Shea and Raquel Byrnes.

All rights reserved.

No part of this book may be reproduced in any form or by any electronic or mechanical means, including information storage and retrieval systems, without written permission from the author, except for the use of brief quotations in a book review.

Severn River Publishing
www.SevernRiverBooks.com

This is a work of fiction. Names, characters, businesses, places, events and incidents are either the products of the author's imagination or used in a fictitious manner. Any resemblance to actual persons, living or dead, or actual events is purely coincidental.

ISBN: 978-1-64875-723-5 (Paperback)

ALSO BY THE AUTHORS

<u>Memory Bank Thrillers</u>
The Memory Bank
Retrograde Flaw
Aurora Fragment
The Daedalus Key

BY BRIAN SHEA
Boston Crime Thrillers
The Nick Lawrence Series
Sterling Gray FBI Profiler Series
Lexi Mills Thrillers
<u>Shepherd and Fox Thrillers</u>
Booker Johnson Thrillers

To find out more, visit
severnriverbooks.com

1

California, Channel Islands, ten miles off Santa Cruz Island

Bobby Khan stood on the bow of his father's dive boat, his legs shifting with the swells, as he fiddled with the remote control to the undersea rover. Crisp January winds swept across dark ocean waves, bringing the scent of salt and minerals. The sun had set, leaving a band of orange light hovering on the horizon. Overhead, a silvery moon floated among clouds in the dimming sky. The California mainland sat in silhouette against the ocean before him, the cliffs of Santa Cruz Island behind. In the near distance a horn sounded, the unique patterned tone of a drone ship. Bobby glanced up and caught the ghostly form of a freighter cutting through the thin fog. Its running lights glowed purple, a warning of its unmanned status.

"I think we're too close to the shipping lane," Bobby said over his shoulder.

"We're fine. We're fine. It course-corrected on its own, see?" His father pointed at the drone ship from the forward cabin. "What about our own hull? See anything?"

They'd taken the boat out for a test run after repairs, but his dad swore he could still feel a drag on the rudder. He'd asked Bobby to drop the submersible to take a look. So far, he'd found nothing but barnacles. Bobby brightened the headlamp strapped to his forehead and tried to redirect the ROV's camera back toward the hull, looking for the damage. The submersible was acting off, losing communication intermittently. Losing the forward lamp. A mess. Sure, it was refurbished, but Bobby knew what he was doing. It had worked fine yesterday for what they normally used it for. Scuba groups paid a lot of money for underwater shots of them spotting a juvenile shark during a dive. He'd made sure it was in top shape. So, what was the problem all of a sudden?

"I think I have to pull her up and take a look." Bobby adjusted the contrast on the controller's screen and squinted at the images. Something was wrong with the signal between the submersible and his controller. He peered over the railing down at the cables trailing into the water, searching for movement from the rover. Nothing. What he needed was his workshop back on campus, not a freezing dive deck. The temperature had dropped, nearing fifty now, and his flannel wasn't cutting it anymore.

His father poked his head out of the cabin. "Don't worry about it. We'll check it out back home."

"Yeah, I lost the signal again anyway." Bobby tapped the controller screen with his fingers. Then he stood and hit the lever to retract the tether cables to the submersible camera. "I'm bringing her back up."

His father shuffled across the deck with a metal mug of steaming coffee. Gray spiky hair over dark, hooded eyes. He waved absently out toward the sea. "We should get going. The problem might not even be the rudder, anyway. Might be a strut."

Bobby nodded, gathering his equipment while the tether wound onto the spool next to him. "I'll get in the water tomorrow morning and take a look up close."

"That'll work." His father checked his watch. "The scuba group is scheduled for seven a.m., and we still have to fill the tanks—"

The water shifted suddenly under the boat; a reversal of flow rolled underneath the vessel, sending it listing to one side for a moment.

"What was that?" Bobby asked, a little nauseous.

His father held onto a nearby tank rack, leaned over the side, and stared down at the black sea. "Whales?"

"Yeah, I don't think so." Bobby's breath came in puffs of vapor as he scanned the water. It felt wrong, the swell of the waves. Off-kilter somehow. He hit the pulley controls and stopped the rover from rising. "Dad, maybe you should go grab the binoculars. They have that, uh, starbright lens, right?"

His father nodded, heading back to the cabin. "I'll check the radio too."

"Don't drop the signal. Don't drop the signal." Bobby licked his lips, concentrating on the submersible's controls, directing the front lamp of the camera outward. His fingers shook, but he got it pointed right. A form slipped past his view. Fast and dark. His gut twisted at its speed. It wasn't natural. Not animal, anyway. Not that big. He blinked, not understanding. "What the hell?"

Panting, adrenaline soaring through his veins, he adjusted the dials, fighting for a clear picture. The drone freighter was closer on his right, its lights pulsing as it sliced through the water. His dad ran back with the portable radio, tension pulling at his tired eyes.

"I've got dead air."

"Like, nothing?" Bobby asked.

"Nothing. My phone too."

Bobby reached into his flannel and checked his own phone. No signal. "What is going on?"

Then his father handed him the digital binoculars, his gaze flitting along the darkening vista. "We're getting out of here—"

A hollow clang resonated across the water, and they both froze. Full and rolling, it moved through Bobby's chest like the ring of a giant bell. It faded to an even tone that hung in the air.

"Did that come from under—"

"Yeah, it did." Bobby lifted the binoculars to his eyes and panned the near distance. He adjusted the smart lenses to offset the dying light, casting the seascape in light blue. "But from what?"

The only thing out there was the drone freighter. It was almost in front of him, and the lights flared in the low mist. He traced its journey across his field of vision for a few minutes, but nothing seemed amiss. Bobby looked away when a muffled explosion rocked the boat, throwing them to the deck. The vessel shuddered as if thrashed by violent wind; the cacophonous rattling of the surrounding equipment seemed to go on forever. They stumbled on the deck, grasping for a hold. The submersible's control console slid past him on the deck, and Bobby grabbed it, yanked the memory disk from its side, and stuffed it in his pocket.

"Was that a mine?" His father held onto a safety bar on the bulkhead for balance, his lip bloody. "Did we hit something?"

"No, it came from the freighter." Bobby braced his hip against the railing and lifted the binoculars to his eyes, adjusting for stability and low light with digital filters. Something was happening to the freighter. The lights flashed off completely. And the sea...it churned around the hull as if boiling. "Dad, you have to see this."

"Tell me about it after we're out of here," his father shouted as he ran for the helm. He fired the boat up just as the shaking subsided. They started to pull away, but then the waters shifted, pulling their boat as if on a chain. They went backward despite the gunning engine. His father glanced back, his eyes full of fear. "You feel that?"

Bobby nodded, his heart ramming as his mind reached for an explanation. They drifted faster and faster toward the center of the shipping lane.

"Throw off ballast!" his father yelled. The engine roared as he pushed the throttle. "Get us lighter."

Bobby tossed everything he could reach, his eyes on the drone freighter. It loomed large in the shadowy mist as they floated inexorably toward it. A hard object hit the hull, and he chanced a look overboard. Strange shapes in the water scraped against the side. It was getting dark, but he would swear it was ice.

His father tried to accelerate out of the pull of the water, the boat's engine revving with the effort, the lurch of the craft toppling Bobby to his knees. And still the ocean pushed them toward the freighter as if magnetized. They crested a rising swell, towering over the sea, and Bobby looked down at the freighter. It sat in the center of a rippling depression. The dummy ship rattled, intense vibrations wracking it apart as the signal mast, steel containers, and navigational towers toppled with the force of the shaking.

"Hold on!" his father yelled from the helm.

Bobby clutched onto the railing. "What's happening?"

The screech of tearing metal sounded from the freighter below. The ship listed to starboard as something ripped through the side of the hull. Jagged and hard, the sound of breaking glass filled the air around him. Their boat tilted backward, losing ground, sliding sideways toward the center of the whirling trench. Bobby fought to get to his father at the helm as first aid kits and other safety equipment tumbled past. He slipped and slid on the wet deck as the vessel tipped further backward. Roaring filled his ears, and Bobby peered overboard. The ocean poured into a vast void surrounding the dummy freighter, falling like a waterfall into the abyss. His logical mind, the engineer in him, tried to understand. To give meaning to the moonlight reflecting off the sheets of frozen ice streaming past the boat. Then everything seemed to stop.

The motion of the water, the shaking of the ship, the sounds around them. Bobby's breath came in hitches as he glanced down at the waterfall locked in a moment of stillness. A high, piercing tone hung suspended in the air like a final note. And then it all crashed apart. The sea shattered into a million pieces, and a giant maw opened up, devouring the freighter as the walls of the trench surrounding it collapsed.

Bobby's boat cantered backward sharply, throwing his father from the helm. He toppled down the deck of the boat, screaming, reaching for Bobby, who lunged for his father. Too late. His father fell, mouth wide with terror, into the black of the sea. The boat tipped, teetering on the edge of the chasm. Bobby scanned the water around him, panic gripping his chest. The sea beyond the vortex, past the front of his vessel, churned with less violence. Bobby ran straight for the helm, leaping for the edge of the chaos. He hit the water, feeling the pull as he swam with all his might away from the collapsing ocean as it took his boat behind him. Gasping for breath, his mind fractured with panic and grief. A moment later, the depths broke free of their spell, dissolving into angry waves that spit up pieces of his life. A bucket. Some oil from the engine. A life vest. Bobby waited for his father to surface. He never did.

2

Backstage Party Bus Rentals – Seattle, Washington

Former detective Morgan Reed sat in the back of a stuffy party bus watching a glitching hologram of a dancer strut around a real pole. Thumping house music and flashing laser lights gave the impression they were in a dark, neon-kissed club instead of barreling down the interstate. It was nearly ten at night, hot, and the air conditioning leaned heavy on the deodorizing filter that couldn't quite cover the smell of sweat, beer, and grease. Not a great mix. About fifteen finance bros partied in their casual Friday outfits, sang drunkenly with the music, and chatted up the few actual women on board while drinking out of plastic cups. Except for his virgin screwdriver, Reed looked the part as he eyed the driver. She was distracted, on her phone as she drove, her voice sharp. She was arguing with someone. He made a note in his leather sketchbook. Out of nowhere, a shiver worked through him. Despite the heat of the bus, he felt cold.

Reed had started taking investigation jobs from his longtime friend, Coyote, as soon as his PI license came through. Now, months later, he found himself on the trail of an elusive thief. Someone was somehow stripping Backstage Party Bus Rentals of their liquor, gas, and various food items, and try as he might, the owner, Bohdi, couldn't figure out who it was.

"I tapped the booking office phone," Bohdi had said during Reed's walk-through after hours. "Nothing. He's taking calls, offering our standard packages, upselling like a pro, and putting the event on the calendar. It's not him."

"I'm going to need to speak with former customers."

"Why?"

"I have a hunch." Reed pointed to the plans of the facility Bohdi had laid out in the bus depot office. Surveillance video of the bus depot and parking lot played on a nearby laptop. "And I need to talk to you about your cameras. You don't have full coverage."

"I don't know, man. I had the security system professionally installed." Bohdi had argued. "How do you know there are blind spots?"

"Watch the video again. Do you see me loitering around your storage building?"

"No."

Reed nodded to the surveillance feed time stamp. "This was taken after our first consult. I did a walk around your property looking for security lapses. I strolled right in via the alleyway between the buildings."

"Well, that sucks." Bohdi shook his head. "That company charged me an arm and a leg."

"We'll close up the gaps." Reed ran his finger in a line from the depot to the storage building. "I want to place hidden cameras in a few more spots..."

Reed had set up additional surveillance in the booking office, the bus depot garage, and the cold storage building. In the parking lot leading away from the bus disembarking area, Backstage offered snacks from a food truck for customers returning from their night out. Chicken wings, French dip sandwiches, loaded fries, pizza. Bohdi believed the food truck cook was stealing food, but he'd never seen him take anything. Reed had planted a mini camera near the food service window. With the traps set, all Reed needed to do was watch and wait. Which was how he'd been spending the past two hours in the back of the bus. The music thumped through him as he tried to look like he was having fun.

His phone rang, and he plugged his ear with his finger to block out the music and answered. Reed's former partner at Seattle Homicide, Nat De La Cruz, raised her voice over the noise.

"How's it going so far?" Nat asked. "Catch any robbers yet?"

"I used the time before tonight to talk to former customers. Turns out a coup has been going on right under Bohdi's nose. And you'll like it. It's all techy and slick."

"Ooh, can't wait to hear about it." She sounded amused. "You know this is your first official case?"

"Coyote has been kicking me jobs for months."

"I meant it's your first as a bona fide private eye. I should buy you a fedora. You know, make it official."

He smiled at that. "Please don't. Besides, odds are one of Bohdi's employees is screwing him over. I'm not exactly chasing down master criminals here. They stole beer bottles and junk food."

"You're finding a bad guy, aren't you?"

"I should be tracking down Pierce Rexford," Reed grumped and pulled on the collar of his black polo. "Not babysitting frat boys."

"You're still pissed about the Rexfords?"

"They're killers. All of them." The last time Reed had heard from Jacoby, a Homeland agent he'd met while hunting Slater, was back in January. Nat was just stepping back into work after she took a bullet. She'd been antsy, cooped up, so she and Reed assisted Jacoby with surveillance. They followed Pierce Rexford, the scion of a powerful political family. He was fresh off a book release about a family tragedy in Alaska and was on a speaking tour in Seattle. Reed and Nat worked with Jacoby's task force, Gray Zone, for a week tracking Rexford on his tour, but it was an uneventful surveillance. Since then, nothing.

"Have you heard from Jacoby at all?"

"Nada." Reed stood as the party bus pulled off the freeway. He craned his neck to peer through the heavily tinted windows. As he turned away, out of the corner of his eye he caught the figure of a man sitting on the other side of the dancer. Reed looked through her transparent body, and his gut knotted. Michael Slater stared back at him from the seat. His face bloody from the explosion he died in, vitals vest still registering a flatline, he looked at Reed with crazy eyes as he lifted a finger gun to his temple and fired. Reed twitched when a shiver ran down his spine, but he shook it off. The hologram flickered, and Slater's figure disappeared. Nat's voice in Reed's ear caught his attention, and he shook the images from his head. "Uh, sorry, what were you saying?"

"I said, screw him." Nat snapped her gum. "Listen, you're working. I know it's small potatoes or whatever, but you're working."

"Yeah." Reed had been trying to control the intrusive scenes with meditation, VR work, etc. The injected memories popped up less and less, but they were still there. Roiling at the center of his mind.

"You okay?"

Reed rubbed the hair-thin scar that ran from his left eyebrow to just below his lashes. A gift from a youthful offender, it itched when he was tired. "I've just been preoccupied planning this sting."

"How *are* Coyote's finance bros working out as undercover operatives?" Nat asked.

"They're drunk and rowdy, which kind of sells this whole thing." The day before, Reed had spoken with former customers and had learned of a special VIP section of Bohdi's website that offered several "hidden" deals available only to repeat customers. When he'd explored the site, he'd found a cash package of two hours' bus time, hologram included, as well as refreshments, which turned out to be hot sandwiches and other food sold from the truck. The owner confirmed there was no such deal, and so Reed booked the bus for the cash package. He set up a time for him and his "office buds" to get picked up. And they were now on their way to an indoor skydiving venue. "I still don't know how the code is getting passed around. The people I spoke with all got it from other customers that were in their party. I haven't met with all of them yet. Someone had the initial code."

"Sounds like you're angling for another night on the party bus," she teased. "Don't get spoiled by the job perks."

"Believe me," Reed said, moving to avoid a stumbling finance bro on his way to the can. "It's every bit as glamorous as it looks."

He rang off and waited for the bus to stop at the light at the end of the off-ramp. The brakes hissed, and Reed checked himself in the window's reflective surface. Dark hair cut back to office-worker length, clean shaven, he made sure there was nothing in his teeth before making his way forward. Reed purposely leaned in too close, speaking over the group of guys arguing over fantasy football. "Hey—Ashley, is it?"

"Ashlynn." She glanced at him with a slight curl to her lip. "I don't know where to get drugs."

He forced a rich-guy laugh, shaking his head. "No, my buddies and I had such a great time, I was thinking I might rebook one of these discount trips for my brother-in-law. Soon-to-be, anyway. Sort of like a pre–bachelor party. Do you know how I can get back on the VIP section of the website? I lost the code, and I can't find it on my computer."

Her demeanor softened, and she smiled. She hooked her thumb toward the minibar area where the cooler of food sat. "The code is on the food wrappers."

"That's smart." Reed grinned. "And the booze and food are included in the two-hour deal, right?"

"Just like now." The light changed, and she took the bus left toward the skydiving place. "Remember, there's a fifty-mile limit on the distance."

"That's okay." Reed grabbed a French dip sandwich as they pulled in front of their destination. "Plenty of ways to get in trouble around here."

She dropped Reed and the faux bros at High Five, a skydiving facility that offered wind-tunnel sessions. Coyote knew the owner and had arranged for everyone to hang out there as thanks for helping Reed out with the sting. They bellied up to the check-in counter, yelling about dive-bombing and drawing askance looks from the serious divers. Reed put some distance between him and the drunken mob, slipping to a quiet area near a display of historical equipment. He was waiting for the bus to leave and used the time to check the surveillance footage of the bus and cold storage area.

"Aw, man," Reed muttered when he watched the recorded feed on his phone.

The camera caught what Bohdi had been missing. Earlier, Ashlynn had parked the bus at an angle to the cold storage door. Reed's camera had a clear shot of the food truck cook, Darren, coming in early, seemingly preparing for the day, only to exit the food truck struggling with a heavy cooler. He walked to the bus and came out empty-handed. A few minutes later, Ashlynn went into the cold storage room and walked out with a crate of beer. Then she went back in, only to exit a few minutes later with bottles of hard cider and other wine coolers.

Reed dialed Bohdi's office. "I know what's happening to your supplies."

"Am I going to hate life?"

"For a little," Reed said, sending Bohdi the camera feed link. "But you won't be getting robbed blind anymore. I'm on my way back to you."

Once Ashlynn drove away from High Five, Reed walked out to the parking lot where he'd left his motorcycle earlier and returned to Backstage's rental office. When he got there, the party bus still hadn't returned. He spotted the owner right away. He stood in the doorway, arms crossed, looking sour. Hair in a nineties shag, Bohdi Dubois wore a faded band T-shirt stretched over his ample gut, black jeans, and biker boots. He nodded at Reed as he walked up.

"I take it you reviewed what the camera picked up from the walk-in cooler?" Reed asked.

"Yeah, I did." Bohdi sighed heavily. "The cook too? I just hired that guy."

"Where did you find him?"

"Ashlynn, ah, crap...she said she worked with him before. I trusted her judgment."

"Well, you thought it was just Ashlynn because the gas and booze point that way, but she has to be working with the food truck guy. We just didn't know how they were bypassing the booking office to make the side deals." Reed handed Bohdi the wrapped French dip sandwich. He tapped the QR code on the foil wrapping. "This is a link to a website that looks almost identical to yours. It's not. It was created about four months ago by Ashlynn. She tried to disguise the ownership, but a friend of mine traced it to her." He brought up the recording of his conversation with Ashlynn and handed the phone to Bohdi. "She knew all about the website. Offered me the cash deal. She and Darren are doing this together."

"I don't understand. She's been with me for years." Bohdi shook his head.

"I think I know why. They're getting married." Reed had followed Ashlynn the day prior and had beautiful shots of her and Darren making out at the movies, a burger joint, and while walking into her apartment.

"I had those idiots over for New Years."

"I wouldn't tear myself up about it." Reed reached into the neck of his polo shirt, disengaged the button camera attached inside, and shoved it in his pocket. Then he swiped over on his phone to show a website to Bohdi. "You caught them. Fire them. Hire new people. I'd run a thorough background check next time. I looked up the food truck guy, and he's on parole. Be careful when you go to fire him."

"He's busy right now getting more supplies from cold storage. After your call from the skydiving place, I called the cops in case things get messy with Ashlynn. Guess it's good they're coming if Darren's involved too."

"That was smart."

"Well, crap," Bohdi murmured. He handed back Reed's phone, disgusted. "Thanks, I guess."

Reed clapped him on the back once. "You can press charges with the video. I'll show up in court if you need me to."

"Thanks," Bohdi said absently. "Oh, there's someone here for you."

Reed stopped mid-stride. "Who?"

"Didn't give his name," he said and nodded toward the eating area set up for patrons of the food truck. Little round tables and foldable chairs sat café style underneath a portable awning. "He said he was a friend from the station."

"The station?" Reed thanked Bohdi and headed toward the food truck parked just outside the bus depot. He didn't see anyone at the tables, but he did catch movement inside the truck. Reed wracked his brain wondering who from the Seattle PD would need to talk to him. It was eleven at night. What couldn't wait?

He walked up to the order window of the food truck and stilled. "Bad Moon Rising" played softly on the radio speakers. Not the police station, Reed thought. Pilsner Radio Station. The one Gray Zone controlled. A figure appeared at the small order window, and Reed smiled ruefully. "Speak of the devil—"

"And he will appear," Jacoby answered. He stepped down from the food truck's rear door and hopped onto the asphalt, half-eaten pizza slice in hand. "We gotta talk."

3

Jacoby wore cargo shorts, walking tennis shoes, and a T-shirt that said *I love LA* on it. A well-worn fanny pack was strapped to his waist, and Reed spotted a bedazzled letter *D* on the front. Crooked and unevenly spaced, it looked like a child's doing. Jacoby could easily pass as a tourist, nothing more. Plain brown hair, unremarkable brown eyes, an average white guy's slight pudge at the neck. He was perfectly forgettable, which was Jacoby's tradecraft.

"You look better than the last time I saw you," Jacoby remarked. "Been boxing again?"

"What do you want?"

Jacoby took a huge bite of the slice. He chewed, considering Reed, a smirk on his face. "Stop pouting. I didn't need you until now. Things had to fall into alignment first."

"Nope. I'm not some benchwarmer at your beck and call," Reed said. He turned and strode toward the staff parking lot, but Jacoby followed.

"Benchwarmer is a little reductive, don't you think? I'm playing spy games over here. Kings and queens, realms at stake. I didn't forget you. How could I? You're one of my most dangerous weapons."

"Yet you cut me out of the Rexford investigation."

"The Rexfords?" He looked at Reed like he was a stupid child. "I've got a lot of irons in the fire. You think Danzig and the Rexfords are the only bad actors out there?"

"One of them almost killed my partner," Reed snapped. "Danzig *did* kill people close to me. So yeah, I'm stuck on those particular 'bad actors' paying for what they did."

"There's a lot of moving parts to all of this. It goes past Aurora and the Sound Corridor project."

"Then tell me how."

"I can't right now."

"Then you wasted a trip." Reed sped up his pace.

"You think getting clearance for you is easy? You're compartmentalized, for now."

Reed paused, staring at him under the streetlamps, unsure what to believe. "Clearance for what?"

"You know what I'm going to say, right?"

"You can't tell me. Convenient."

"Not really." Jacoby finished off the pizza. "For now…I want to put you on this." He wiped his fingers on his shorts, reached into his fanny pack, and pulled out a small digital tablet. Handing it to Reed, he asked, "What do you know about rogue waves?"

"They're rare." Reed swiped through the photos on the tablet. He stopped on one with a team of rescue ships on some kind of search. There were also two driver's license photos in the file. An older South Asian man and a younger one who bore a striking resemblance to the first. "What am I looking at?"

"While you and the formidable Detective De La Cruz were helping me track Pierce Rexford in Seattle, a very important ship was sinking off the California coast. Specifically, it sank halfway between mainland California and one of the Channel Islands. About ten miles out." He pointed to the rescue video. Boats circled around floating debris. "It was a drone freighter carrying a ton of medicine, textiles, industrial items. No one was aboard. The Coast Guard investigation said it was a rogue wave."

Reed looked at him askance. "Really?"

"The voyage data recorder recovered from the wreck bears out third-party reports of a large disturbance in the ocean near Santa Cruz Island."

"But...you don't buy it?"

Jacoby shrugged. "Rogue waves *have* been reported in that area before. In 2009 and 2023. Another few years later. So, not out of the question."

"Why do you want me on rogue waves and sinkings?" Reed blew out a frustrated breath. "Look, unless Pierce or Bunny Rexford were on that freighter—or better yet, Danzig—I have no idea why you're telling me this."

"Someone saw the alleged act of the weather gods, and they're saying it was something else entirely. They say it was a deliberate sinking."

"Who?"

"A father-and-son business team, Sami and Bobby Khan, owned a charter boat that they ran out of Ventura Harbor. They were out on the water that night near the sinking." Jacoby nodded at the tablet. "Their boat stalled near the shipping lane. According to the son, Bobby, they saw the freighter go down. And then, according to him, whatever sank the freighter took his father's boat as well. What he describes doesn't sound like a wave to me."

Reed looked at the files again. "Is he credible?"

"Their charter boat did sink on the same night the freighter went down. Bobby was fished out of the water by the Coast Guard, so he was there. They didn't find the father's body, but Bobby told anyone who would listen that he didn't drown. He was instead 'sucked into an endless dimension of ice and darkness.'" Jacoby shook his head. "The kid is traumatized for sure, but I still need to talk with him."

Reed narrowed his gaze. "He sounds like he's had a mental breakdown. Alternate dimensions? Why would you need to talk to him?"

"Some aspects of his story, however mislabeled by Bobby, sound a lot like technology I've heard about before."

"You're joking." Reed stared at Jacoby, and when his face didn't change, he shook his head. "What aspects, exactly?"

"Listen, all you need to know is on that tablet. Take it. Read it."

Reed shook his head. "Nuh-uh. I need more."

A police cruiser pulled in front of the Backstage office behind Jacoby, and they moved over to the far tables.

"Okay, look. About a month after Bobby lost his father in the sinking, he started a podcast. *Outpost of the Abyss*. Given some key words he'd posted on several conspiracy forums, I had him monitored loosely. He talked about the sinking often, described the phenomenon he saw that night, and mostly fought with people who left comments. Some of his videos were going viral in some watched sectors, but not much else was happening. I was going to cut him loose, but then he said the magic words. 'I have proof.'"

"Why didn't he say anything about this proof until months later?"

"No idea. But as it stands, two weeks ago, he started talking about video and photographic evidence of what he saw out there that night. He described a large object that moved faster in the water than he'd ever seen. He said it was big, smooth, and it set off a wormhole. He mentions getting the proof back from having it 'cleaned up,' and he promised to post it."

"And you believed him?"

"Some parts, yes." Jacoby buried his hands in his pockets. "I believed he saw something he wasn't supposed to. If he had proof, I wanted to see it."

"Did you?" Reed swiped to the end of the data file. "Get the proof?"

"I had an agent make contact with him via his podcast, posing as a popular news streamer interested in pushing his story to a wider audience. He bit. We arranged a meeting. He didn't show. When I sent someone to his apartment, we found evidence of a struggle. Bullet hole, blood, broken glass, but no Bobby. That was three days ago. No one's seen him since."

Reed nodded. "Of course he's missing."

"Gives weight to what he was saying, no?"

"Or the aliens took him."

"His podcast is down. We're not sure if he did it or if it was someone else. But some of the transcripts are there."

Reed read a few paragraphs. The descriptions of ice and glass and the way the water behaved made no sense. "This kid sounds like he's sick, not a threat to national security." He tried to hand back the tablet.

Jacoby wouldn't take it. "You ever wonder what a Civil War soldier might think if he saw a weaponized drone on the battlefield?"

"Are you saying he's not nuts, he just doesn't know what he really saw?"

"Yes, and not only is he spouting information he shouldn't have knowledge of, but he's also apparently caught someone's attention who takes him serious enough to pay him a visit."

"Cool story," Reed tossed the tablet onto one of the plastic tables, "but it doesn't have anything to do with me."

"This kid is running out of time."

"I don't see how I could help. You said he went missing in California. I don't have any contacts there. I'm not even on the police force anymore."

"Even better. Private investigators have more leeway out there."

Reed pointed toward the city lights in the darkness. "I'm not leaving Seattle, not with Nat and Coyote finally recovering from the last time I ran after ghosts in another state."

"Fine. Take the tablet, see what I've got and let me pick your brain. How can you say no to that?"

"No." Reed started toward his bike in the employee lot. "I'm not pulling my friends back into the black hole that is chasing down Danzig and his maniacal plans. I'm out."

"I've seen you hunt down people, Reed."

"Yeah, I'm the only one, right? The military trained *one* guy to do what I do and no one else." Reed stopped walking. "You know what, I looked you up. You created Gray Zone and peopled it with tier-one operators. I'm sure one of them can find Bobby Khan."

Jacoby stared at him. "You're the only one with Slater's memories."

"Lucky me," Reed said as he pulled out his key. "And stop popping up in my life out of nowhere. It's creepy."

They strode past the office and the police car where Bohdi spoke with two patrol officers. His wild hair backlit by the neon Backstage sign. Reed recognized the older patrolman as he passed. Someone he'd worked with before he left the force. Reed nodded to him but was met with a hostile glare.

"I read your psych report," Jacoby said, seemingly oblivious to Reed's rant. "The army's and the SPD's. You don't stop. That was the main thread through everyone I spoke with about you. Relentless. You aren't capable of walking away from a case like this."

The older patrol officer leaned toward the other. The word "burnout" floated Reed's way. Ignoring them, Reed said, "People change. I'm not a soldier anymore. I'm not a cop. I'm a civilian moving on with my life."

"That was in the file too," Jacoby said. "The whole normal-life thing."

"Yeah?" Reed got to his bike, pulled on his helmet, and started the engine. "What'd it say?"

Jacoby looked at him with fascination. "Do you really think that's in the cards for you?"

4

Holden House Apartments, South Lake Union – Seattle

Reed's childhood friend, Coyote, was a savant of both money and people. That combination garnered him a small apartment complex, which he won in a high-stakes poker game. Six units around a courtyard pool. Fenced, locked, and private. With Coyote's associates often under the scrutiny of the law, Holden House offered discretion and security at a premium. Everyone kept to themselves, and the fact that it was in the industrial area of downtown next to a fabrication plant was the best part. No foot traffic. Coyote had offered him a unit in exchange for keeping the peace among the guests who might get rowdy. Given that Reed was already built like a bouncer and had done a little "persuading" for bookies in his youth, it was an easy decision.

After getting home from the Backstage rental place, Reed showered off the stink of the party bus and ordered some Indian takeout. He tried to watch a show, but he couldn't shake the hallucination of Slater he'd had earlier. It spooked him. He'd been trying to convince himself he had a handle on his symptoms. But over the months since the Aurora case, every time one symptom of the foreign memories lessened, another ramped up. It was like he couldn't escape the killer. In fact, they seemed even more inextricably linked than before. Slater and his murders had launched Reed straight into Danzig's world. Long dead, the mercenary continued to haunt his waking life.

The side effects of using the MER-C system were at best still the same, but even Reed admitted that wasn't really true. He had to do something, trying meditation, breathing exercises, even yoga for a brief, painful few days. Nothing seemed to move the needle on the false memories, lost time, sleepwalking, and sudden-onset flashbacks. He read books on mapping the brain and organizing intrusive thoughts, but mind palaces and mnemonic devices didn't make any sense.

The labyrinth idea came to him one night as he sketched out the connections he'd uncovered between Danzig and world events. He'd fallen asleep, and the dream he'd had was so vivid, so clear, that he startled awake and began working out the idea in his notebook. It made sense, Reed thought at the time. He'd taken plenty of humanities classes for his philosophy degree and often used his art skills to sketch ruins, draw sculptures, and note details for a field dig class. An elaborate maze was a natural fit for his skill set. With the help of a used biofeedback machine he'd bought on a medical surplus website and some research, he figured out how to use the system to induce a meditative trance. He could go deep into his mind with the sound cues and reach a place in his imagination in which he could both explore and lock away the troubling memories within the labyrinth.

Reed adjusted the lead wires on the feedback machine, attached the sticky electrode patches to his scalp, and placed a sensor band around his chest. Respiration rate, pulse ox, breathing activity, and temperature registered on the display screen. A soft voice from the machine's speaker told Reed to relax, and then the tones began. Low and steady, they reminded Reed of the warning sounds from a racing video game. One, two, three low tones followed by a higher one. Then again. Over and over, like a metronome. Reed concentrated on the sounds, slowing his breathing, ignoring outside stimuli. The feel of the couch beneath him fell away, the smell of the room, the light behind his lids. All of it darkened as he went further into his own mind. And then he heard only the tones of the feedback machine. His breath. A light in the far reaches of his inner vision pulled him. And then he was there. He knew by the scent of old, wet stone wafting around him.

Reed fought to stay with the scene, focusing his concentration. Out of the darkness, the ancient, craggy walls of a labyrinth rose from the moist ground at his feet. Their dark and twisted paths lit by the pale blue flames of the torches mounted at intervals along the walls. The maze had no ceiling, yet the walls rose impossibly high, piercing an indigo sky. Like a mouse hunting for cheese, Reed took the path left. He strode purposefully down the flickering passageway, his gaze searching the surface for a specific cluster of stones. In the distance, faint as an echo in the wind, the repeating pattern of the machine's tones drifted to him. Reed wandered the corridor until he found it.

A grouping of colored stones marked a place on one of the walls. Licking his lips, he reached out to the central stone. It had a fracture, and when he touched it, the crack grew until it split the wall asunder. The jagged rock of the labyrinth fell away, revealing beyond its borders a chasm of black, endless emptiness. Reed's pulse pounded in his head as the abyss grew to encompass the entire rock wall before him. Time stopped, the cadence of the feedback tones ceased. His icy-cold breath suspended mid-exhale before him. Reed froze, waiting for what came next. Bloodcurdling screams and desperate cries echoed from the void in the labyrinth, but it was Slater's maniacal laugh that flooded Reed with dread.

He reached for the void, willing to fall forever into it if it meant ridding himself of the memories. But the chasm changed before he could touch it. The interior going dull as the opening sloughed off the wall like a sheet of dark sand. It fell in a pile at his boots, the emptiness disappearing. Frustration welled in his chest, and he punched the stone wall. Pain seared through his hand, and the labyrinth dissolved around him. He gasped, snapping out of the trance as the machine beeped loudly with respiration and pulse warnings. Reed blinked, staring at the hole his fist made in the drywall.

He flinched when he spotted Nat sitting at the breakfast bar of his apartment. Her gaze went to the ragged hole in the drywall he'd just punched.

Mahogany hair framing her heart-shaped face, dark eyes amused as she sipped from a can of soda. "You're going to wanna ice that."

He put his hands up, slowing his breathing. "I really need one of those arena things that keep you from walking into walls."

"Yeah, it looks like VR can't hold a candle to your imagination." She looked at him, her gaze narrowing. "What happened with the Backstage case? Did the sting go wrong?"

"What makes you ask that?" Reed peeled off the electrode patches, avoiding her eyes.

"The boxing gym is your usual practice on Fridays, but you went straight home and hopped on your janky brain scan machine to fight the wall instead."

"It's not janky, it's 'previously loved.'" Reed gave her a faux insulted look as he quoted the description from the woman he'd bought it from. "The wall was an accident."

"Whatever. You're avoiding my question."

Reed wound up the wires from the feedback machine, thinking. "Okay, you're right. In the bus earlier, I saw something."

"Slater?"

"Just a flash, no big deal," he admitted. Her face showed she didn't think it was "no big deal." She'd been with him from the start of the whole ordeal and knew the effects. "You know what, I ordered food. I'll fill you in on everything that happened with the Backstage case over midnight dinner. It's Indian…extra naan."

"My favorite, nice touch." Nat considered him for a moment and then finished her soda. "Did you run into the void again? Is that what this wall-punching thing is?"

Reed nodded. He'd told her about it. "I don't know why it's there. I didn't imagine it on purpose. I don't understand."

"After I lost my family, I saw someone for a while to get through it. I told you this."

"You did." Reed wondered where the conversation was going.

"Parts of the night were…difficult." Nat slipped off the stool and walked around the counter to the fridge. She pulled out some frozen corn and handed it to him, eyes sad. "It came to me in bits and pieces. Waking up. The fire. Looking for my parents, my sister. The fireman pulling me out..."

"Nat, you don't—"

She waved his comment away. "My point is that sometimes our minds don't reveal everything all at once for a reason."

Reed tossed the frozen bag up and down in his palm, unsure. "You think the void is my messed-up brain's way of protecting itself?"

"I think your particular situation is extreme, but I don't see why normal trauma defense mechanisms wouldn't work the same way."

"Yeah, maybe."

"What's wrong with leaving it alone if you don't know what's in there? At least for now." Nat rounded the counter, caught the bag of corn, and took his hand. She placed the bag on his bruised knuckles. "Maybe you're not ready for what's there."

Reed shook his head. "I need to know what it is."

Nat opened her mouth to argue, but his phone dinged. It was the food delivery.

"I'm not saying ignore it," Nat said, heading for the door. She held his gaze, worried. "I'm saying get a better idea of what *could* be in there before you unleash something that might make your symptoms worse."

He grabbed the plates and sodas, watching her deal with the delivery robot at the door. He suspected she knew more than she let on. She was one of only a few people who knew what the MER-C system had done to him. Despite the Glycon-C patches that Jacoby had given Reed that took the trauma out of viewing a foreign memory, the symptoms of having used the system persisted. Maybe Nat was right. Maybe he should leave things alone.

When they'd settled in to eat, she pointed at him with her naan. "So, tell me what happened with the party bus that had you all twisted? Did the report to the client go bad?"

Reed shook his head, chewing on his butter chicken. "Well, kind of."

"Spill it. Start with the missing booze and go from there."

"Well," Reed began, "It turns out Bohdi Dubois had an employee problem..."

He relayed the outcome of the sting. The double-crossing employees. The police showing up.

"That doesn't sound so bad, to be honest," she said between bites. "At least not enough to take out an innocent wall."

"Yes, I thought so too until Jacoby showed up at the party bus place. He wants me to look into a case for him." As he described their meeting and told her about Bobby, she set her food down, listening intently. When he was done, she looked at him with a blank expression. Unreadable. "What? You think I should say yes?"

"Whoever this Bobby kid is, he's in serious trouble if Jacoby is looking for him."

"A million dollars says he's running from Jacoby, not some mysterious killer."

"You don't trust him. I get it."

"Trust him?" Reed almost laughed. "Jacoby is problematic at best. You know how little we've been able to dig up on him since Aurora. Almost nothing. With *your* skills?" Jacoby was a man-made ghost working behind some very dangerous scenes, and he wanted to pull Reed back into the fray. "He ran Slater even though he knew he was cracking apart, maybe even sent him after me. The guy was neck-deep in everything that happened up in Aurora. He's everywhere and nowhere. Plus, I have no idea where this guy's loyalty lies, and he tells me nothing. I don't even know what Gray Zone actually does."

"Don't forget what he did in Alaska."

"That's what I'm saying. And now, after months of silence, he wants to keep playing his cloak-and-dagger games, talking about compartmentalization. I'd be going in blind. Behind someone who might already have the kid —" Reed shot up from the couch, pacing in front of it. "I can't ever get a straight answer out of him. Half-truths, vague rumors of plans, it's all vapor." Reed shook his head. "No thanks."

"Okay, so you tell him no." Nat stood and walked over to him. "But let's be honest. You're miserable doing these PI cases." She put her hand up at his protest. "Don't even act like you haven't been all broody."

"Your point?" Reed grumped, knowing she was right.

"This kid disappeared in California, right?"

"Yeah, and I told Jacoby I'm not leaving the state again to chase down shadows. Going after Danzig has already cost too much." His gaze settled on the thin surgery scar just beneath Nat's collarbone. She almost hadn't woken up. "I think going down that road again, diving back into Danzig's world, would be stupid and dangerous."

Her deep gaze bore into him, searching. "Yeah, you keep saying you're out, but that's not how you're built, is it?"

"I don't get what you're saying."

"I hear all the reasons. But what I'm getting from you is you would help Jacoby and go after Danzig…if it didn't put me or Coyote in danger." She shook her head. "Don't make decisions based on fear for us. We knew what we were doing going up there to help you. Hell, it's literally my job to run toward bullets. What happened in Aurora isn't your fault. It was just another case."

"That's stretching it." Reed flashed on the blood leaking between his fingers as he'd tried to keep her from dying up on a mountain.

"I've been back on active duty for months. I'm fine. I wasn't even shot, really. It was a ricochet—"

"I already told him no, so…" Reed said a little too sharply. He walked away, rounding the couch. Not letting her see the dread. "Sorry. I mean, it's the smart thing to do. To walk away from all that. Jacoby doesn't need me. He has a whole task force."

She regarded him for a moment and then nodded. "Okay. I'm letting it go. You still have one problem, though."

"What's that?"

Nat pointed behind him, and Reed followed her gaze to the digital tablet on the table by the door. Retrieving it, he stared at the screen, taking in the photos he'd seen earlier. It was the tablet Jacoby had told him to keep. "Where did this come from?"

"It was leaning against the inside of your door when I got here. I think someone shoved it into the mail slot."

"That son of a—" Reed waved the tablet at her. "I told him I wasn't interested."

"Jacoby doesn't seem to take no for an answer, does he?" Nat wiped her mouth with a paper napkin. She had a weird look on her face. "What're you gonna do about it?"

5

The Geek Lair – Seattle

The defunct mall near the nature reserve had been a popular place once upon a time until a bigger one with a fancy movie theater and an ice rink was built closer to the city center. For decades, the old building sat abandoned near an equally forgotten duck pond bordering a ragged patch of protected land at the edge of town. After some vandalism, the city cemented all the entrances shut to keep out teens and the homeless. Plans to demolish the eyesore were derailed a couple of years earlier when Seattle PD's cybercrime division found a use for it.

More specifically, Nat, while undercover, had found out that a couple of homeless hackers had taken up space in there. They had spliced into existing power lines, set up satellite links on the roof, even renovated parts of the stores to accommodate an entire virtual reality lab. When Reed had first seen it, he'd called the setup "the geek lair." It stuck. Nat admitted to Reed the two guys were using their system to jack into the dark web for nefarious reasons, but the unit was getting actionable information from the setup, so it remained untouched during her investigation.

After, the SPD ordered the closing down of the location, and on paper, it had. Someone had mysteriously changed the status of the mall grounds to "protected status" within the city's system, and all talk of demolition stopped. Reed wondered if it was Xanadu, one of the hackers who'd remained loyal to Nat, or if she had done it herself. They both had the skills to infiltrate a system like that. He suspected the latter. Xanadu stayed around to help Reed and Nat on a couple of cases involving Danzig. He lived there still, and Reed called ahead and asked him to leave the hidden entrance unlocked.

The morning after his meeting with Jacoby, Reed strode down the promenade as his eyes adjusted to the muted light coming in from the mall skylights. The space seemed larger somehow now that it was empty. Some of the security gates still hung in front of the empty stores. Graffiti and signs of squatting were old, faded from age. Broken windows lining the upper level let in wind that stirred the trash on the floor and made it skitter across his path. Old signs hung from peeling walls, cracked and caked with grime. But where the rest of the mall was a wasteland, what Nat and Xanadu had created in one of the larger stores was a remarkably functional computer lab.

An irritated voice sounded from down the dark hallway as Reed approached the entrance to the work area. Reed squinted against the flashing lights flaring out from the VR system.

"Xanadu?" Reed shouted as he navigated the cables running along the floor. Squeezing between tables with dismantled electronics, he headed toward the bank of display screens on the wall and spotted him. Pudgy, bald, with a penchant for wearing ugly sweaters, Xanadu flailed with haptic gloves while strapped to a circular virtual reality treadmill. "Hey!"

"Who goes there?" He pulled off his goggles with a grin. "Oh wow, you got here fast."

"I finished the Backstage case. Thanks for looking up Darren's arrest record for me, by the way."

"No prob."

Reed watched the realistic-looking Viking battle raging on the wall screens for a few seconds. "Still playing Red Lars?"

"*I'm* Red Lars." Xanadu rolled his eyes as he stripped off the equipment. "The game is Sails of the North. My clan...is Frostwolf. I've told you this before."

Reed nodded like he understood. Xanadu was deep into video and tabletop fantasy games. The more swords, ships, and sorcerers, the better. The vernacular and style of speaking tended to slip into his speech.

"Well, if you're done conquering the high seas," Reed said, and held up the tablet Jacoby had left for him, "want to try some spy games?"

Xanadu copied most of the information onto the system he and Nat had created. Reed used VR goggles and haptic gloves but not the entire suit and helmet like before. The last time he totally submersed himself in the virtual world, it brought on a seizure. Xanadu locked him into the vitals vest attached to a stabilizing arm in the center of the omnidirectional treadmill. That way Reed could move freely in virtual space without walking into walls. The vest would signal any biometric abnormalities and indicate if he needed to disengage from the system.

Standing in the vast black emptiness of virtual space, Reed used the white schematic gridlines of a virtual workspace to orient himself. Xanadu had also tapped into the program, and his avatar appeared next to Reed as Red Lars. Long red hair, scars from battle, he nodded at Reed and then swiped a large hand between them. The uploaded information from Jacoby's tablet converted to the VR platform, letting them sift through the virtual information much faster as well as check information online. They spent the next few hours going through the data Gray Zone had amassed on Bobby Khan and his father, Sami Khan.

Mostly in report form, the file detailed a thorough review of Bobby's social media accounts, job history, his posts while he was at university, everything. An agent had interviewed several of his fellow students, but they didn't really seem to know him that well. He'd left halfway through his junior year. Family business, they said he told them. Not much. Financial reports showed that Bobby hadn't used any credit or bank cards since Jacoby said he went missing.

"No movement on the financial end. So, either he's dead or he has some way of surviving out there without money," Reed said, flipping through the virtual documents. "Maybe he's couch surfing."

"I've done that." Xanadu's voice came out of the Red Lars avatar. The burly warrior wiped his eyes with a dirty palm. "He was barely making it. Looks like he used to give the equivalent of half the rent for the apartment he shared with his father. These last few months, he had to fork over the whole amount. He must've been strapped for cash all the time. So sad what he was going through."

Reed pointed to a large check cashed a couple of months before Bobby disappeared. Sliding the virtual bank statement across the space to Xanadu, he said, "I'm guessing that was an insurance payout for the boat? He didn't deposit it, though."

"No, he didn't. Not at that bank, anyway."

"Where'd the money go, then?"

"Not sure. I can chase down the name on the check. Manafort Underwriters sounds like a soulless corporate entity that would cover a boat, though. Oh, check this out," Xanadu said. "I know Jacoby told you Bobby's podcast was down, but I found his archive. Want me to download it?"

"No, they pulled all the episodes. I have the transcripts in the tablet."

"This is his *archive*. There are drafts and unedited versions he might not have posted."

"Okay, that's good. Can you send the files to my phone? I'll listen to them later." Reed sifted through some random findings the web crawler spit up. There were more Bobby Khans than he'd imagined. Aside from the podcast and his comment fights with listeners, Bobby hadn't posted much in months. The website for the Khans' dive boat charter business was also shut down.

"Oh, man, I found a memorial page for his mom. It was a fundraising one that was deactivated years ago." Xanadu kept digging and then turned to Reed. Red Lars's scarred lip pulled down in a frown. "I feel so bad. He was just chugging along in school, and then his life fell apart when his mom got sick. I think he had to quit."

"Show me." A series of photos appeared next to the document floating in front of Reed. One of Bobby at his university mixer popped up. He stood with a group of young men and women behind a foldable table at what looked like an outside college fair. A hand-painted sign in front of the table read *Engineering Club*. Reed enlarged the photo with a gesture from the haptic gloves. Chubby cheeks, too-big glasses, Bobby held up a peace sign as he smiled for the camera. Reed flipped through the images. Bobby in an engineering lab working on a robot of some sort. At a birthday dinner in a restaurant, his mother wearing a headscarf, cheeks gaunt. Finally, one of him and his father on a handsome dive boat named *Mariah's Spirit*. Both of them were trying to smile but not quite getting there. "He's just a kid."

"Hey, you want me to look into the other members of the engineering club? It can't be too hard to break into their system. Universities, even tech ones like Bobby's, are notoriously bad at securing student information. It's literally criminal."

"Nuh-uh. I don't want you digging anywhere you'd garner attention. No black hat stuff. You're probably not even cleared to see what's on that tablet."

"I was just thinking that maybe we can talk to a few of the other members. See if that can help at all."

"*We* aren't talking to anyone. You need to be crystal clear on that, you get me?"

"Yeah, okay." Red Lars's broad, animated shoulders drooped. "You guys said I could help out in the field soon. Like, I'm ready."

"I know, man." Reed lifted off his goggles. "But whoever was hunting for Bobby shot at him in his own home. There was blood on the walls. You're too valuable to put in that kind of situation. Who would drag me out of cyberspace when I get lost?"

Xanadu nodded, clearly disappointed. "Next case, though, right? Nat told me about the hologram stripper. I would've paid to see that."

"Believe me," Reed said, pulling the goggles back up. "Whatever you've got going on in that massive brain of yours is better."

"What if I found out who his friends were on campus another way?"

"No hacking?"

Xanadu held his hands up. "No hacking, I promise. What I have in mind is totally analog."

They spent another hour watching video of the area near the Channel Islands where Bobby's boat went down. The VR enlarged the view of a kayaker filming his venture into the sea caves on the leeward side of Santa Cruz Island. The swell and fall of the kayak gave the recording an unsettling feel, but the island itself was beautiful. Craggy rocks, crystal-blue water, lush vegetation dangling from the cliffs. Ideal. Nothing about it suggested what Bobby claimed he saw out on the water that night.

"I'm going to check some deep web forums," Xanadu said. "If he was an engineering student, he might have been more tech savvy than most. Maybe Jacoby's team missed something."

"Be careful." Reed pulled out of the VR program and peeled off the gloves. "We're not the only ones looking."

6

The White Lion

He'd demanded an industrial space that could be counted on to remain undisturbed, and his client obliged. Of course he did. No one else could do what he does. He surmised the facility used to be for making candles. The smell was not unpleasant. It masked the rot of rubbish permeating the rusting building. Dank and prone to leaking pipes, it was cold, dark, and home to some kind of animal who only came out at night. Nevertheless, it sufficed. He'd needed high rafters for his cables, and the space had a soaring, five-meter-high ceiling. He sat on the highest crossbeam at the roof, peering down at the ground.

A locked safe sat in the center of the cement floor below. It was lit only by the dappled sun streaming through the broken windows above. He wore tinted goggles, and the instruments strapped to his chest rattled as he checked them. The harness strapped to his torso squeaked when he leaned forward. About to drop down, he paused when a tone sounded in his earpiece. He tapped it to answer.

His client didn't wait for a greeting. "There's someone on your trail. Time is running out."

"I'm not alarmed."

"You should be. I told you about this man. I have no idea how he knows about Bobby Khan, but you must find this witness. Reed cannot get his hands on him."

He glanced across the floor to the table holding his laptop. It ran several trace programs he'd designed himself. And he'd paid a data tracker a bounty on Khan. No one ever remained hidden from him. "The detective will not get to the witness first. I'm closing in."

"When you do find him, the plan has obviously changed significantly," the client spat. "This was supposed to look like a suicide. The tragic end result of a fractured mind. Instead, it looks exactly like what it was."

"You said your contacts in the LAPD thought it was a robbery gone wrong."

"For now. If Reed starts digging into it, there will be a problem."

"Then Reed will have a problem as well. It's hard to investigate while trying not to die." Leaning forward on the balls of his feet, he teetered on the edge of falling. "The other situation, I am working on."

"I know your record. What you're capable of. But do not underestimate Reed. That mistake has been made before."

These men. They order mayhem and then clutch at their throats like old women. "Is he not two of your states away at the moment?"

"Distance won't stop him."

"How do you know this man is in fact looking for Khan?"

"One of his known associates acquired some information I had my people watching. He's looking."

"Okay, I am aware." He was tired of this man's meddling. "I will contact you with news."

Before the client could answer, he ended the call. Taking in a deep breath, the White Lion tilted his head and judged the distance to the floor in the flickering light. Then, silent as the shadows, he leapt.

7

Bangkok Kitchen, Belltown – Seattle

Bright yellow serving robots slid quietly across the polished linoleum floor of the automated all-you-can-eat restaurant. Their friendly digital faces smiled as they navigated the full house with polite offers of refills. Cheerful music played overhead, and the general vibe of the restaurant's opening night felt like a party with locals. Reed sat in one of the corner booths with Nat and Coyote, reveling in the scent of Thai food as another serving bot pushed through the kitchen door. The food moved efficiently from table to table within self-propelled covered chafing dishes. Nat waved at one, and it rolled over to their table. An androgenous, calm voice warned her of possible allergens in the dish as the lid rose.

"This is a cool idea," she said to Coyote as she pulled out a bowl of pad thai. "So now you're a restaurateur? I thought you hated robots."

"I'm more of a silent partner," Coyote said in his lazy drawl. He nodded at the owner, who stood by the register, speaking with departing guests. Older, gregarious, he seemed to remember everyone's name. "That whole business in Aurora, the agricultural robots, kinda warmed me up to the whole automation thing."

Reed chuckled. "One shot at you."

"Water under the bridge. Especially when there's business to be had." Coyote gestured toward the owner. "Mr. Suwan over there had the same idea, though he lacked the necessary finances. I was looking to expand my business, but I'm no restaurateur. An associate of mine who knows Suwan's family put us in touch."

"Wow, from cybercafé to speakeasy..." She held up her bowl. "To excellent Thai food."

They bantered back and forth, Reed working on his cashew chicken as he half listened. His mind wandered back to Aurora, to the revelation of Danzig's scheme for the area. The Sound Corridor project, something called Resonance, and his plans for Pierce Rexford. Reed was lost in thought when his phone dinged next to him. It was Xanadu. He'd sent a message with an attachment.

"What's that?" Nat asked. She'd seen the text.

"I went to the geek lair earlier today. Xanadu helped me go over what was on Jacoby's tablet." Reed put his phone down. "I'll check it later."

"I knew curiosity would get the better of you." Nat smirked. "You almost lasted twelve hours."

"I checked out what Jacoby had so I could tell him I looked in case he ambushes me again, that's it. I already told him no, anyway."

"I get that a kid in trouble is not a situation you can just brush off, but Jacoby tracked you to Alaska based on a search for your prints, remember? You need to be careful."

"What's this, Morgan?" Coyote cut in. He was the only one who called Reed by his given name. "You're talking to that Jacoby guy again? I wouldn't trust that man farther than I could chuck him."

"I wanted to verify some of the things independent of Jacoby's files. Nothing I would need a warrant for." Reed leaned back, full. "This Bobby kid really did lose his father, his livelihood, and maybe his grip on reality in that sinking. It's sad."

"Xanadu said you guys did some digging." Nat sat up straight. "Oh, that reminds me. He's on his way to a tabletop game conference later this week. I promised to feed the shop cat. I'm gonna call him really quick."

She got up from the booth and wandered toward the entrance. Coyote tilted his head, scrutinizing Reed. "What're you two talking about?"

"Xanadu fed a stray over at the abandoned mall, and now he's its human." Reed shrugged. He snagged one of Nat's spring rolls and popped it in his mouth. "I warned them."

"No, the Jacoby thing."

Reed and Coyote had been through a lot of dark situations over their decades-long friendship. They'd survived together in the bayous of Louisianna as kids and fought together in the deep deserts of their military deployment. Coyote knew about Danzig, the MER-C system, and what the foreign memories had done to Reed's mind, all of it. There was no reason to keep him in the dark. Reed told him about his conversation with Jacoby at the Backstage bus depot and about Bobby Khan.

"The things you get yourself into." Coyote chuckled. "A missing kid who might have been abducted by aliens?"

"More like he maybe fell into an endless space portal." Reed finished off his soda. "And I'm not 'into' anything but this next case you were telling me about. You said it was in Tacoma?"

They talked about the new case for a minute before Coyote said, "You know, the problem Jacoby's team is having is probably what's keeping this Bobby kid alive. No digital trail to track him with. If your partner over there or her hacker friend couldn't find him, there's only one other way to locate the dude."

"I know, someone needs to knock on doors. It's just not going to be me." His gaze settled on Nat, who spoke on her phone outside the restaurant window. She caught him looking and smiled, nodding at whoever was on the call. Reed shook his head. "I'm not going to California."

"You sure about that?"

"Jacoby has a whole team at his disposal. They don't need me."

Coyote finished off his milk tea with a giant gulp. "Famous last words, as my mama used to say."

A couple of days later, while working on a surprisingly interesting purebred dognapping case, Reed realized that he was being followed. He first clocked the man with the scraggly goatee when he was at the grooming place. Reed had borrowed a neighbor's dog for cover, offering to pay for the shampoo treatment so he had an innocuous reason to chat up the receptionist about a client. It was while he was fussing with Waffles the Chihuahua's treat situation that he noticed him.

The guy hovered near the fancy shampoos, trying to look casual. Reed saw him again at the vet. Not inside, but in the parking lot while he was leaving. And now, at the dog park. The guy had no dog and didn't seem to be watching the obedience class out on the grass field. He sat on a bench and kept glancing in Reed's direction. Reed pretended to record Waffles, and though the dog didn't do much more than sit on the grass and shake, the angle did prove useful in capturing video of the goatee guy. After a few minutes, the man got up and left without looking back.

Later that week, Reed was at the grocery store when he caught sight of the guy again. He wore a hat and kept his distance, but it was him. Out of the corner of his eye, Reed saw him walk past his aisle. The guy paused long enough to glare but moved on. Pissed, Reed strode to the end of the aisle, spotted the guy loitering near the eggs, and cut across the linoleum toward him. The guy took off again. Reed didn't want to run him down in the dairy aisle, so he hung back, but something was weird about the whole thing. What was the guy trying to do? If he was spying on him, then he sucked at it. Reed had spotted him easily. Intimidation? He sucked at that too. Uneasiness squirmed in Reed's gut.

Reed had switched from his motorcycle to a plain black rental sedan for his surveillance case involving Waffles, and he called Nat when he got to the car. He waited to see if his stalker would exit the store through the front doors or slip out the back. Nat picked up, and he heard shouting in the background.

"Are you at the station?"

"No, hold on." She muffled the phone, shouted an order, and came back. "Sorry. No, I'm at the Technology Tower right now. There's an issue with a pipe in the bathrooms. It's a whole thing. People are acting like we're all gonna get electrocuted. What's up?"

"There might be trouble."

"Not a great way to start a conversation, Reed." She moved to a quieter area. "Tell me."

"Remember I told you about the guy at the dog park?"

"You saw him again?"

"He was at the grocery store just now."

"What do you think is going on?"

"No idea." Reed kept his eyes on the people flowing in and out of the entrance. "But it's something."

"You think it's Jacoby?"

"What would be the point of hiring an average-looking dude to stare at me from afar?"

"Maybe he thinks it'll piss you off enough to get you to look into the Bobby Khan kid."

"No, this feels..." Reed scratched at his sideburn, thinking. "Amateurish? Which doesn't mean it can't be dangerous. But...the guy seems off somehow."

"Could he be from one of your cases?"

"I doubt it." Reed racked his brain for a possibility, but all of his cases so far were run-of-the-mill civil annoyances. "I don't put people away anymore."

"So, a guy who isn't really intimidating stared at you in public places and you felt compelled to call me in the middle of the day?" She clicked her tongue. "That's suspicious. Why the alarm?"

"The thought occurred that I may not be the only one being watched. We're all working on the Bobby thing."

"Nuh-uh. I would've spotted a tail."

"I don't know, Nat. There's a lot of ways to watch people without them knowing." He debated his next sentence, knowing Nat's tendency to run toward a fight instead of away. "I'm thinking of tapping Coyote for a couple guys to sit in a car outside your place for a few days. Mine too. We've been here before, and it's probably nothing, but..."

Silent for a few moments, she then asked, "You sure it's necessary?"

The image of paramedics carting her away flashed behind his eyes. "For my own sanity, yes."

"Fine." Nat sighed. "You said you got video of goatee guy at the dog park. Why don't you send it to me, and I'll see what I can find when I'm done here."

He relaxed against the car seat. "Are you still coming by?"

"Yeah, but I might be late. The water destroyed some of my custom equipment, and I want to save what I can." Her voice went quiet. "What if it's Danzig? He's sent thugs your way before."

Reed's conflict with technology titan Everett Danzig had attracted all kinds of dangerous individuals. But guilt over his friends getting hurt because of his battle to bring the billionaire down weighed on him, and he dropped the investigation after Aurora.

"He knows I backed off. There'd be no benefit for him to come at me again. And the guy trailing me was not one of his Spectre mercenaries." While he spoke, the goatee guy exited the grocery store and walked across the parking lot to a lifted red truck. Not exactly subtle, so not a professional. "I'm betting this is related to the Bobby Khan case."

She was silent for a moment, then, "Okay, I'll talk to Xanadu when he lands. He left for his conference an hour ago. I'll ask him where he poked around and how it might lead back to you, but he's good at what he does." Someone spoke to her, and she came back sounding a little annoyed. "I have to go. We'll talk later?"

They ended the call, and Reed felt a little better now that she knew the situation, but not by much. There was someone else he had to talk to. Taking a circuitous route back to Holden House, he checked for a tail but didn't see one. The guy was finding him somehow, and he made a mental note to do a sweep for trackers. Reed called Coyote when he got back to his apartment and told him what he'd told Nat.

"What's he look like?" Coyote didn't sound surprised.

"Medium-build white guy, dark hair and eyes, goatee."

"Yeah, mine looks different. Started yesterday."

"Why didn't you say anything?" Reed peeked out of the living room window to the parking lot, watching for movement.

"You're not the only reason trouble comes into my life, Morgan. And though it's true that you are the most consistent source of it, I wasn't sure it had anything to do with you."

"I think the trouble is mine this time, brother."

"Give me an hour or so, and I'll be by."

Reed spent some time working the punching bag in the apartment gym.

His shoulder, once pierced with a round during a case, ached, but felt looser. He jogged around the complex, took a shower, and did some work on his maze sketches. Sitting on the couch, he ran his charcoal over and over the void, making himself endure the dread that pooled there. There had to be a reason he couldn't see what was inside.

Nat buzzed his phone with a message and a data packet. She'd managed to match the goatee guy's face to a mug shot. Rodney DeVry, aged thirty-two, plenty of charges for being an ass to everyone around him. The most recent, an aggravated assault, was for getting into it over a football game the year prior. Rodney skipped bail, but stayed in Seattle? Not a stellar decision-maker. Other than that, he had no military record and did some light time ten years back. Nothing to suggest why Danzig or Jacoby would hire him to stalk Reed.

He wondered if Nat was right in thinking that Rodney might be from one of his recent private investigation cases. Maybe he should take another look at his files after lunch. Coyote showed up a half hour later, pushing through Reed's front door without knocking. Mohawk tied back, long sleeves and heavy jeans despite the heat, and combat boots with spikes. Fight clothes.

He looked at Reed sitting at the table eating a sandwich and hooked a thumb over his shoulder. "I got an extra bat in the trunk."

8

Belltown

Rodney DeVry strolled down Foster Drive, his hands in his baggy jeans, hoodie pulled over his head, eyes sweeping the sidewalk. The late afternoon sun burned near the horizon, casting a warm summer glow along the city block. He passed several of the newer places, the gourmet gelato shop, the truffle oil tasting room, peering into each store as he went. Pulling his phone from his pocket, he glanced at the screen. His gaze snapping up, he scanned across the road, and then he took a turn toward the recreation area at the end of the block. Gray metal fencing enclosed the city park, directing visitors to the entrance on the right.

A group of people with dogs talked near a stone bench, and he gave them a wide berth. Rodney wandered the grounds, dropping candy wrappers and cigarette butts until he spotted the yappy Chihuahua and the dude in the familiar black outfit. Hiking his jeans up against the weight of his gun, he circled around his mark. Rodney kept his gaze on Reed, skirting the picnic goers, the running kids, and other people enjoying their warm evening. When the guy stopped walking, Rodney settled next to a lamppost, slipped a flask out discreetly, and sipped while watching him fuss with the dog.

A few minutes later, the guy and the dog started walking again, and Rodney followed them down a side trail. He had trouble keeping up. Stumbling on the uneven ground. Wheezing a little at the pace. Reed turned off the path, pulling a doggy doo-doo bag out of his pocket as they veered behind a stand of bushes. Rodney's hand went to his waistband, closing around the handle of the Glock as he paused. He craned his neck around the hedges, creeping forward, his hand coming up. He pointed the barrel at the back of the mark's head as the man leaned over the dog. Rodney's finger slipped to the trigger, and then he froze.

Reed shoved the barrel of his gun harder against the back of Rodney's skull and whispered, "Surprise."

Rodney stood ramrod straight, his gun still aimed at the man with the dog. "Dude, this isn't what you think."

"Oh, so you weren't just going to shoot my buddy in the back?"

"I...what?"

"Turn around."

Rodney did, and his eyes grew wide when he turned to face Reed holding a gun on him. "Who is that, then?"

"Not me." Reed glanced at Coyote, who held the shaking Waffles inside Reed's jacket. "Drop the gun."

"I thought..."

"You really need to look back once in a while, man. I was practically waving at you the whole way." Reed pointed to a boulder near the edge of the clearing. "I will not ask you to drop the gun again, Rodney."

"Oh, shit. You know my name?" He dropped the gun.

"He knows your whole life, dumbass." Coyote kicked the gun away and patted him down. Turning to Reed, he said, "I'll be on the lookout. Make it quick. Use the silencer."

"Silencer?" Rodney's voice broke.

Coyote walked away, and Reed motioned with his own weapon. "On your knees."

"Whoa, whoa, whoa," Rodney said, crouching with fear. He wore knuckle-less driving gloves. "We can work this out, right? You're a cop. You can't just shoot people."

"I'm not a cop anymore. They fired me." Reed gave him a stony look. "For shooting people."

"It's not personal, okay? You're just a job!"

"Who hired you?" Rodney hesitated, so Reed checked his watch. "You have ten seconds."

"Okay, okay." Rodney nodded frantically. "There's these people I owe money to, and they said if I did this...thing for them, they'll wipe out my debt."

"This thing being, you kill me," Reed clarified.

"I have no beef with you, dude, but they threatened my mom."

"Who did?" Reed heard a woman's voice on the other side of the tall bushes. She was talking to Coyote about the dog. "I need a name."

"No way." Rodney cowered, but his face was set. "They'll feed me to the fishes, man. But I *can* tell you the hit came from outside."

"Outside what?"

"The organization that sent me." Rodney licked his lips. "It was a chit. Someone called in a favor."

"How much do you owe?" Reed asked. The woman sounded closer, like she meant to enter the clearing.

"A hundred thousand, dude." Rodney's gaze went to the hedge, his eye twitching. "They really, really want you dead, man."

Reed grabbed him by the front of the hoodie, getting in his face. "Not good enough. I need a name."

"Look, the guy who called in the chit isn't even from—"

A fat English bulldog loped around the hedges, and everything went sideways. Reed spun, hiding his weapon, stepping into the path of an old woman who chased after the dog. He "accidentally" bumped into her. She was old and rickety and bounced off Reed's chest. Her glasses went flying, and he caught them midair.

"Whoa, ma'am," Reed said as he stopped her from toppling over. She looked to be in her seventies. Gray hair in a bun, lipstick the color of flamingoes, large dangling abalone earrings. "Are you okay?"

"Oh, my stars," she breathed in an English accent. "I am so sorry. My little Winston ran back here..." Her voice trailed off at the sight of Rodney running away at full speed. She squinted. "Have you seen my glasses?"

"They're right here." Reed smiled winningly and held them in his opposite hand, pulling her gaze from his escaping would-be murderer. "Not a scratch."

She smiled nervously, squinting back toward where Rodney disappeared, but he was gone. It took a few minutes for the old woman and Winston to take care of business before they wandered back out to the park. Reed rendered Rodney's gun safe and threw it in a storm drain near the walking path. Coyote fed a steady stream of treats to Waffles as he and Reed stood watching a bunch of kids kick around a ball.

"Well, that was a bust," Reed said. A chill moved through him despite the balmy evening, and he crossed his arms. "I feel like the silencer comment sealed the deal."

"I'm glad he bought it." Coyote pulled his mohawk from the ponytail and scratched his scalp with a gloved hand. "Did you learn anything before he took off?"

"Rodney was paying off a debt to an unnamed organization that was also apparently paying off a debt to the nameless person who wants me dead."

"And that is not a short list," Coyote said with a chuckle. He held up a burner phone between them. "Good thing I picked Rodney's pocket."

"Old habits die hard?" Reed grinned as he held open a pocket for Coyote to drop the phone into. "I owe you."

"Take it off my tab."

Reed called Nat and filled her in. He told her about Rodney and what he'd said, and she told him to bring the burner phone. She'd look at it after a meeting. An hour later, he went to see her in the cybercrime forensic data lab. He slipped in, avoiding anyone who might recognize him, and made it to the elevators without incident. Cybercrime's main work area looked very different from the Homicide floor. It resembled a flight deck for a futuristic battleship. Unfamiliar equipment lined the workshop walls, ergonomic chairs sidled up to high-tech work consoles, and blue light illuminated a hallway of inaccessible labs.

He walked past the updated wall of floor-to-ceiling display screens that scrolled the details of various cases across the glass. The technology continued to process data far past the end of shift for most of the department's officers, so the area was relatively empty. Night Crawlers, as Nat called them, the team that trolled dark web spaces and engaged with online criminals all night, worked in a separate, noise-controlled room at the end of the hallway or in the VR units at the Technology Tower downtown.

It was late, past nine. Reed had stopped to grab takeout for the both of them. The skeleton crew on the cybercrime floor meant no one noticed him as they settled into one of the equipment rooms. Nat walked the bagged burner phone through forensics, getting her friend to scan for prints. They found none. Both Rodney and Coyote had worn gloves. Reed hadn't touched it outside of an evidence baggie. So, nothing there. Back in cybercrime, Nat worked with the burner phone, fiddling as she picked at her fries. By dessert, she'd pulled the numbers from the contacts list and ran them. They led to unlisted numbers going to burners. The texts proved more fruitful. Someone had been watching Reed like a hawk.

"They're tracking your bike," she said and pointed to a text conversation. It detailed his various trips to and from the apartment. They'd tracked him to Nat's home, stores, everywhere. "When you switched to the car to drag Waffles around, you tripped them up. But they sent a guy to the rental place who paid the clerk to look at your account."

"They have trackers, talk money, and at least two guys that we know of following me." Reed scratched at his sideburn. He told her what Rodney had said about who hired the hit, including the promise to forgive Rodney's hefty gambling debt. "There's a lot of money floating around this."

"Lemme ask you something...if someone put a hit out on you through a local criminal element, that means they aren't from around here, right?"

"I would think. Rodney seemed like he was going to say something to that effect."

"Who could do that? Call in a favor worth enough to pay off Rodney's debt and pay off the rest of the expenses. By your count, it's over a hundred grand now. Who has pull like that from afar?"

"I know what you're getting at, but Danzig doesn't work like this. He'd just send one of his Spectre mercenaries to gut me during the night."

"That's a nice picture." Nat frowned. "Then we need more data. Names that can make things happen like this."

"Maybe we should bring in someone with information like that," Reed said. "Someone like Parker."

Nat's boss at Intelligence had a checkered history with Reed, but they'd been better lately.

"I'll ask around," she said. "Someone over there might know who would have the juice for a hit on a former detective."

Reed leaned back in an ergonomic chair and tossed a few of the last pieces of crunchy fry bits in his mouth, mulling things over. "What about the app?"

When he first inspected Rodney's phone, he'd noticed an unfamiliar icon on the home page. It had a four-digit passcode that was locked. Nat said she could break it.

"It's weird..." She brought up the phone's home screen on a larger monitor and typed in four asterisks. "I had Ada, the SPD's AI, run a series of brute-strength programs. It cracked the passcode in a few minutes. Turns out the icon is for a medical app."

"Medical app?"

"Weird, right?" She navigated the menu, showing him the various features. It looked consumer grade.

"What's it for?"

"That's what's interesting. The app is for tracking medical equipment telemetry. So, if you have a relative with a fall risk, all you have to do is slap a medical smart sticker on them with gyroscope capability, program it to talk with the app, and you can get an alert if grandma takes a header down the stairs while you're at work."

"The compassion is thick with this one," Reed said with a grin. "Can we track down the account holder via the app?"

"It goes to a dummy account. The whole thing is about as secure as the solitaire game you play on your phone." She shrugged. "You can get the smart stickers at pharmacies, big-box stores, even your general practitioner. They're readily available to the general public, so nothing there either."

"The guy didn't have anything like medical stickers on him. I double-checked with Coyote." There'd been a lighter, a flask, some candy, and nothing else on Rodney. Not even a wallet or a set of keys. "What other kinds of things can you use with the app?"

"Uh..." Nat poked around in the program with the monitor's touch screen. "Those nonprescription blood sugar trackers work with it. Some alcohol skin tests, the over-the-counter kind parents get to test their teens, stuff like that."

"What was Rodney's app tracking?"

"I'm not sure." Nat showed him a section of the app that showed what devices were connected to it. She pointed to a string of numbers. "I'm betting that's an item number or a serial number for a medical device, but I don't know what. I have the AI working on it." They sat in silence for a few minutes, and then she said, "Maybe you should call Jacoby and tell him about what Rodney said. He might know who could order a hit on you like this."

"I didn't want this. I told him I was out."

"Yeah, well, someone didn't get that memo."

Reed shook his head, feeling the air around him grow heavy. "I should never have looked into Bobby Khan."

That night he dreamt of deep, dark water and biting winds tossing him on an icy sea. Waves came at him in droves, crashing onto his head as he gasped for air, rolling him beneath the depths until his lungs burned. He thrashed, fighting the shards of glass that flew with the driving rain. In the distance, lightning lit up a sinking vessel. Strobing it in and out of existence. The howling winds tore at the masts, and then the screams hit him. They were frantic, staccato, shrill. He covered his ears, unable to block out the sound until it shifted into a repeating tone. Reed woke with the fourth ring of his phone. A familiar number flashed across his screen, and his palm went instinctively to the empty bed next to him. It was cold. She'd been gone for hours.

"Reed?" Nat's voice broke as it floated to him in the dark of his room. "Can you get down here right away?"

"What's wrong?" Reed rose, already pulling on his pants. She didn't sound good. "Where are you? Are you all right?"

"It's not me. It's the geek lair." Nat sniffled, and the sound of men shouting in the background set Reed's pulse going. "It's...there was a fire, and he...I thought he was already..." She couldn't speak, her voice cracking. "I can't—"

Reed rushed for his keys, grabbing his wallet, weapon, and jacket as he strode out the door. He'd not heard her like this. "What happened?"

"They killed Xanadu," Nat whispered. "Th-they burned him alive."

9

The Geek Lair – Seattle
4:00 a.m.

Reed spotted the black cloud of smoke roiling over the abandoned mall way before he arrived. Meager light burned at the horizon, promising another hot summer day, but the misty air that hovered above the road left a watery residue on his helmet's visor. Roadblocks kept out civilians, but patrol waved him through as he pulled up, clearly told to do so by Nat. He drove along the side road through the marshy reserve, his gut churning. Charred tree trunks and bushes lined the way toward the broadside of the building. The mall looked gutted. Black, gaping holes where windows had been glared out from underneath the dawn sky. The bulk of the fire was out, but a group of firefighters worked the hoses, directing the powerful spray toward a still smoldering roof. The fire marshal chatted with Tig, Reed's former boss, who stood with a Styrofoam cup of coffee in his hand. They talked animatedly, gesturing to the mall's listing structure.

Reed parked and headed over, nodding to a patrolwoman who lifted the crime scene tape to let him under.

"Detective De La Cruz is over there," she said.

He ducked beneath it and spotted the lone figure under a weeping willow tree. Nat stood with her back to him, hugging herself as the wind shifted her dark hair around her shoulders. She turned at the sound of his footsteps and held out her hand. He took it, pulling her into a quick hug.

"Are you holding up?"

Nat nodded, her eyes rimmed with red. She looked destroyed. Ash marred her thin T-shirt, and she shivered in the morning air. "I'm fine. I just want to find who did this."

He draped his coat over her slumped shoulders. "What have you learned?"

"There was an anonymous tip to 911 about a fire at the mall last night around ten. A few hours later, firefighters clearing the area discovered a body in a section of the mall that appeared lived in and called Homicide. They did a quick-ident with the scanner in the field. When the identity came back on the victim as James Faulk, also known as suspected hacker Xanadu, it led them to me. Police records show him as my confidential informant on several undercover cases for cybercrime. They didn't know we were still working together off book." She wiped her eyes with a sooty palm, leaving a smear on her cheek. "He said he was leaving for the airport. He sent me a text he was walking out the door. I should've—"

"This isn't your fault."

"I *knew* he wasn't ready, you know? It's why I kept putting him off when he asked to help with investigation outside the geek lair." She took a heavy breath, watching the firefighters. A group of them moved to another section of the mall, attacking a smoldering area of the building. "He role-played a Viking warrior...he made lemon bars. I mean, he was more normal than any of us! I can't believe they left him in the f-fire to die like that!"

"Nat, come on. Let's get out of here. Have you eaten?" Reed reached for her, knowing her family's similar passing must be playing in her head, but she pulled away.

"The fire marshal won't let anyone in until it's safe, but I talked them into giving me a quick look." She handed him her phone. "I took pictures."

The images were brutal. They found Xanadu duct-taped upright to a pillar near the VR area he and Nat had built. The body appeared singed, and Reed didn't know how she did it, but she took up-close photos of

Xanadu's face, his hands. His fingers bent at wrong angles, broken. His lips and nose bloody.

"They worked him over." Reed flipped through the images.

"I told Tig and the fire marshal I thought this could've come from his private life. He was into some light smuggling. Mostly collectibles for the rich-nerd set. They suggested it also could've come from the work Xanadu did for me and Intelligence around Christmas last year. We took down a ring of fentanyl smugglers three months ago. They had connections to the Middle East."

"Why didn't you tell them we were digging around Bobby Khan's life a few days ago? You know that's more likely."

"I know."

"Nat—"

"Look at him! They did everything but pull out his fingernails!" Her voice broke as she pointed to the mall with a shaking hand. "The one door, the one way to get out was wedged shut with wood shoved in the crack. They *wanted* him dead. In fact, whoever killed Xanadu proved it. With this..." She pulled out an evidence pouch from her pants pocket and held it between them.

A charred, thick medical bracelet sat in the plastic bag. "What is this?"

"It's a medical device. Specifically, a vitals bracelet. It registers a patient's heartbeat, respiration, temperature, oxygen, and other information. Sound familiar?"

Medical grade, Reed thought. It looked expensive. "Like the app on Rodney's burner phone?"

"Yeah, I checked the ID number on the app. It doesn't match Xanadu's bracelet. Which means it corresponds to a second vitals bracelet." Her gaze went dark with anger. "Rodney had one for you."

"Rodney..." Reed pulled out his phone, dialing. There'd been a second man. One who didn't look like his own stalker. The one following Coyote.

"I can't even tell where the danger is coming from at this point," Nat railed, pacing in front of Reed. "I was so worried some deranged mercenary was going to jump out of the shadows and fry my brain with that damn MER-C system. Or catch you on a run. I didn't even think Xanadu might be in danger. He wasn't with us during any of the confrontations with Danzig."

She sniffled, watching him dial his phone again. "I was glad you told Jacoby to kick rocks. Between worrying about you and—" Nat froze, caught Reed's gaze. "Coyote."

"He's not answering calls or texts," Reed said, motioning for her to follow. "I'm calling Camille."

Coyote's sister answered as they got to Nat's car. Her soft drawl as familiar to him as the smell of beignets. "Why, Morgan Reed, how are you, mon chér—"

"I'm sorry, Milly, but it's an emergency. Where's Coyote?"

"He's working late doin' books." She sounded concerned. "Why?"

"Where?"

"I don't know. His office, the cybercafé..." Her voice cracked. "Why do you sound so worried?"

"He might be in trouble. If you can get ahold of him or any of his men, do it. Tell him we got hit."

"Yes. I will. Call you back." She hung up as Nat pulled into traffic.

"Where are we going?" Nat honked at a package delivery truck. "Holden House? His speakeasy?"

"They're both south. Drive in that direction." Reed turned up her police radio, listening as he dialed again. "Come on, brother. Pick up."

Camille called back, her voice shaking. "No one is answering at the café or the speakeasy. I called the front office of his apartment complex. He always checks in if he's going to be on the grounds. I can't get ahold of anyone!"

"I'm on my way to find him." Reed braced himself on the dash as Nat took a turn wide.

Dispatch came over the radio as they tore down the freeway, the AI's computerized voice serene despite the message.

All units, be advised, we have a 10-71 at 7269 Katarondex Road, Belltown. Shots fired from a moving vehicle. Possible casualties reported. Suspect vehicle described as a dark blue sedan, heading eastbound on Cedar. Approach with caution. EMTs en route. Secure the scene, over.

"That's him, right?" Nat asked, throwing on her lights.

Reed nodded. "That's the address for Apocalypse."

She grabbed the car radio. "Dispatch, this is Detective De La Cruz, I am en route to the 10-71 at Katarondex." She glanced at her dashboard navigation screen. "ETA fifteen minutes. Requesting status update and current unit positions. Over."

10-4, Detective De La Cruz, copy that, the dispatch computer answered and was gone.

"He's okay," Reed said under his breath. He checked his weapon. Made sure he had his concealed carry license ready.

Nat nodded, her eyes on the road. "He's always okay."

Coyote's cybercafé, Apocalypse, housed a speakeasy in the back where plenty of shady characters gathered, Reed included. Hacker collectives, bookies, the kind of people who wanted a secure server and no cameras in a coffee shop. He checked his watch. They were night people. That was good, Reed told himself as they arrived. The lights of the first responder vehicles flashed in the morning mist as they turned onto the right block. A slew of patrol cars and ambulances clogged the street. People crowded against the crime scene tape pulled across the sidewalk cordoning off the café.

"I'll see what's going on," Nat said as she parked, and they got out. Reed stayed by the car as she flashed her badge at the patrol officer guarding the scene. He pointed toward a group of men in suits by an ambulance, and she strode over.

Reed scanned the area, spotted a figure watching the whole thing from across the street. Coyote leaned on the brick wall opposite the café, partially hidden by a digital advertisement kiosk, a trail of smoke rising out of his mouth.

"They're looking for you," Reed said, walking over. He nodded at the police presence.

"Well, they're not finding me till my lawyer gets here." Coyote's face bled from several cuts on his cheek and forehead. He took another drag, and Reed saw his hands were steady.

"Were you inside?"

"I was."

"Did anyone else get hurt?"

Coyote shook his head. "Last customer went home around two in the morning. I stayed to do some bookkeeping. Everyone else clocked out."

"Were you in the back? In the speakeasy?"

"Yeah. No lights up front. If anyone was watching, it looked like we were closed. Hours on the door say we're open from two p.m. to two a.m."

Reed scanned the onlookers. Searching for anyone a little too excited about the scene. No one stood out. "They knew you were in there, and that you were alone."

"Looks like." Blood seeped out from beneath his hairline, and he wiped it with his shirt sleeve. "When I called Camille just now, she told me you got hit."

"It was Xanadu. He's gone."

Coyote's gaze went across the street to Nat. "And the force of nature?"

"She's pissed. Wants blood."

"I know you didn't want us pulled into anything, but it's personal now, Morgan. You ready to fight back yet?"

Reed took in the shattered front of the café. Stained glass littered the ground like jagged confetti, bullet holes pocked the brick walls, blood, likely his friend's, stained the sidewalk.

"I have to make a call," he said and walked away, dialing a number from memory.

An operator picked up on the first ring. "Pilsner Station. What is your request?"

"This is Reed. 'Bad Moon Rising.'"

10

Jacoby did not call back right away. Reed instead received a text that sent him to Pike Place Market. It was noisy, crowded, and hot by ten in the morning. Summer tourist season was in full swing. People strolled leisurely along the sidewalks, visiting coffeehouses, the multistory farmers market, and other landmarks. He'd been told to wait by the famous brass pig where people gathered for photos, but he sat off to one side on a cement bench under a Wisteria tree. Its delicate blossoms made a carpet of lavender at his feet. Their sweet scent reminded Reed of honeysuckle as he stared at the last message Xanadu had sent him. He'd received it a few days ago, when he was with Nat and Coyote at Bangkok Kitchen. With everything that happened over the past week, he never got around to checking it. Pulling it up, he downloaded the attachment and read the message.

Hey Reed, I've annotated interesting passages in the most recent blog posts Bobby Khan posted on his podcast site. They mostly follow up questions on the podcast, but there was also commentary and more detailed notes about his experience. Thought you should check out what I found. ~X

He opened the attachment. Excerpts from Bobby Khan's blog flashed onto his screen, and he swiped through them. The young man wrote well. Organized, clear, obviously educated. And yet the contents of the blog called his sanity into question. The way he described the water, the "frozen waterfall" and "glass shards in the sea," seemed otherworldly. Images flashed behind Reed's lids. A memory, not his own, spread out before him, graying out the bustling market. Shock knifed through him, Slater's fear in the moment. Muffled screams filled with the cold of the sea. A cloud of red blooming in deep water. Light glimmered on a crystal edge, and then a sound that made his heart stutter. The crackle of—

"You're Reed." A young lady in a smart suit with a weapon bulge under her jacket stood in front of him. She handed him a phone and turned away, scanning the crowd.

It was Jacoby. "Get in the van. We'll talk there," he said and ended the call.

"What van?" Reed asked, getting to his feet. Images of the memory burned geometric shapes in his vision, as if he'd stared at a neon sign for a moment too long.

"Follow me." She led him down the main sidewalk, along a series of private stairways that wove through apartment complexes and flowering trees. Finally, she veered down a pathway that led to an alley where they waited in silence for a few minutes. A blue panel van with a telecommunications setup on the top and a generic logo on the door slid up to them.

Reed climbed inside, took in the electronics, the communications equipment, and the mesh embedded into the cabin walls, and understood. A surveillance van. She directed him to sit in the seat facing the monitors. As he did, the driver exited the van, and the woman closed the door. They both stood in the alley, waiting.

Reed pulled on the headphones just as a video call came through. Jacoby appeared on the screen, wearing a snow parka with fur surrounding his red-nosed face. The metal fuselage of the cargo plane surrounding him rattled like a freight train.

"I heard about your friend. I'm sorry about Xanadu," Jacoby said, his breath turning to clouds of vapor. "They're telling me it was a hit?"

"That's what it was. I started looking into Bobby Khan, and within a few days I'm being followed, Coyote as well. Then they do this to Xanadu." Reed held up his phone and showed him the photos of Xanadu Nat had transferred for his meeting.

"He was interrogated." Jacoby squinted at the photos. "Would he know anything worth this kind of enhanced interrogation outside of you and your partner? He was a known hacker, if I was told correctly. Black market data."

"He wasn't a saint, sure. And yes, he probably knew some bad people. But the odds of the guy following me and whoever killed Xanadu having a connection to the same medical app to prove death are astronomical."

"We received Nat's detailed report. My people are looking into the vitals bracelet they collected from Xanadu as well as the app. We might get lucky following the purchase trail. What else do I need to know?"

"This Rodney guy who followed me, we have his burner. Nat didn't find any prints, but she got into the messages. They were about tracking me. No mention of Xanadu on the phone. At least not on Rodney's. But another guy was following Coyote." Reed fleshed out what Rodney had admitted about his gambling debt. "Someone called in a favor to a local criminal enterprise and ordered a hit on me, Coyote, probably Nat, but she was with me. At first it looked like Xanadu might've gotten hit in the crossfire, but I don't think so."

"Why is that?"

"Because I would have gone after him too. He's a soft target, the heart of our information system, what he knows is valuable. I should've seen it coming. We dug into Bobby just an inch, and now someone close to the investigation is not just dead. He was tortured."

"More than one hit in the same city during the same time period is telling. Expensive. It takes some influence to convince a third party to take on that kind of heat," Jacoby said, reaching for his phone and tapping something in. "We'll get access to any computer equipment seized at the mall fire. Maybe we can figure out what Xanadu was last looking at. We might see what tipped them off."

"Nat has information on Rodney, but it's limited. I need to find out who he owed. They're the ones who know who ordered the hit."

"We'll get going on things. I'll pull his police records, see who his known associates are. That'll probably give us where he likes to lose his money," Jacoby said. "Take down this code…"

Reed wrote down the alphanumeric sequence in his notebook. "What is it?"

"It gives you access to Gray Zone's files on the Bobby Khan case. More than what you had access to on the tablet I gave you." Jacoby held on through some rough turbulence, then, "The link also allows you to share data securely. Send us anything you have. The phone data, what your partner dug up, everything. We'll start drilling down on what happened in Seattle. Meanwhile, start packing. I'll have a plane waiting for you in an hour at Sea-Tac."

"Listen, you wanted me in. That means Nat and Coyote, too."

"Detective De La Cruz isn't a problem. I'll have Homeland request her for a task force. You can come on as a consultant. That means modified credentials and weapons clearance, given you already have a concealed carry, but Mr. Doucet—"

"Coyote doesn't need anything from you," Reed cut across him. "Just don't give him trouble if he happens to vacation in the area around the same time I'm there."

"I can do that," Jacoby said, signaling to someone off camera.

"Bobby's notes, his blog. Everything you gave me has him talking about lattices and matrices." Reed considered Jacoby for a moment, then, "I think Slater knew about what Bobby saw. That or something similar, because I'm starting to get flashes of things."

Jacoby stilled. "How do you know you're not imagining what you read about in Bobby's rantings?"

"Because it was a memory. As if I'd seen something, firsthand, in the water. All of it completely unfamiliar. I've never seen crystal lattices in the ocean before, but when I saw them, I also thought about what Slater had said to Hazel the night he ripped her memory. He asked her about something I didn't understand at first. The Sound Corridor—"

"You know that's Danzig's plan to take over the Alaskan region. Where are you going with this?"

"Slater also asked her about Resonance."

Jacoby's gaze turned stone-cold. "What did you say?"

"When Slater was in Aurora. When he ripped Hazel's mind that night in the woods, he asked her about something called Resonance."

"And she said..."

"Nothing. She didn't seem to know anything apart from that she was dying. But someone involved in that whole mess does, don't they? That's who Slater was trying to find." Reed shook off the memory of Hazel's last moments. "I'm betting it's a Rexford."

Jacoby rubbed his face with his palm. "And you didn't mention knowing all of this because?"

"Same reason you didn't, I expect." Reed leaned toward the camera. "What is Resonance?"

They sat in silence for a moment, and then Jacoby got up, moved to a darker, quieter part of the plane, and said, "Two days ago we got wind of a police report out of Tacoma. It was filed in March by a man named Dr. Oscar Kernigan against Bobby Khan for stalking and trespassing."

"What does he have to do with the sinking?"

"According to the complaint, Bobby wanted to talk to Kernigan about a paper he had written nine years prior when he was a physics student at California's Pacific Institute of Technology and Science. The paper he wrote had similar wording and imagery referring to crystalline formations in nonfrozen water."

"Bobby must've found the paper in an archive and thought Kernigan could prove what he was saying."

Jacoby nodded. "This was early March. Dr. Kernigan withdrew his complaint a few days later, which is why it didn't pop on our first pass."

"Did Kernigan know what Bobby was talking about?"

"That's what we wanted to know. After getting his PhD in physics, he worked at various labs and universities researching quasiparticles. I sent someone to ask him what the hell that was and found out Dr. Kernigan went missing just a few weeks after he withdrew the police report against Bobby."

"I can't see Bobby killing anyone. Not from what I've learned so far."

"He didn't. Bobby was online arguing with someone on a live session of his podcast when the physicist went missing. His financials show him ordering from a delivery service as well."

"I'm guessing whoever was tracking Bobby killed Kernigan."

"We're leaning that way despite the official report. Kernigan's body was found at the bottom of a ravine along a jogging path he was known to run daily. He was single, and his parents live in Miami. No one noticed he was gone over the long weekend. It was also during storm season. Almost a week went by before a dog walker found him. It was ruled an accident. Between the weather and the time...add a tumble down a rocky ravine to that...not a lot of evidence to connect his death to Bobby in any way. His manner of death would also hide some serious injuries. Like broken fingers."

Reed ground his jaw. "You think Kernigan was questioned like Xanadu."

"At the time of his death, Dr. Kernigan was working with collective excitation phenomenon for the government."

"*Please* speak English," Reed said, the heat of the enclosed surveillance van getting to him.

"Let me put it this way. He was a high-level researcher for ASTRA. You know what that is?"

"No."

"The Advanced Studies and Theoretical Research Agency is the scarier, more clandestine big brother of DARPA. Kernigan was working there on something that had to do with his field of study. Matrices, structures in nonfrozen fluids."

Reed stared at the screen in disbelief. "What the hell did you drag me into, Jacoby? This was a missing person's case."

"It still is. That's your part. It's all you're cleared to know, right now." The lights in the fuselage behind Jacoby flashed red, and a strapped cargo pallet slid past him on tethers. "Just know, if Kernigan was questioned by people who know what Bobby saw, that's a problem."

"What kind of problem?"

"One you don't have clearance to know about yet."

"Explain something to me. Slater didn't ask Hazel *what* Resonance was or *when* it was or even *where*. He asked if it was in play. That's how you talk about—" A slow dawning moved through Reed, twisting his gut. "Is there a weapon in play? Is that what you're saying?"

Wind whipped around the fur hood shielding Jacoby's face. "What I'm saying is get your asses to LA."

11

The White Lion

His client strolled along the perimeter of the dark space, the hologram flickering with warehouse dust. He watched Everett Danzig pace angrily and saw the predator still in him behind those pale eyes. He wondered why this Reed didn't kill him when he had the chance in that hangar. Many wondered this. Perhaps he didn't have it in him to take a life in cold blood. A chink in the armor, the White Lion thought.

"You should have told me you were going after Reed," Danzig said with cold anger in his voice. "I would have advised you not to send an amateur."

"I didn't go after Reed. The men I sent were a distraction. A professional was in the mall with their information man, Xanadu. I got what I needed."

"And you gave Reed what *he needed* to jump on the case by killing one of his team. Was the drive-by your idea as well? Perhaps the mall fire was not flashy enough?"

"One of the men sent as a distraction unfortunately had a cocaine problem. He 'improvised.' I had him taken care of."

"You've made a gross error in judgment. Given what's at stake for you, I wonder if you're thinking straight."

"Then tell me what I want to know," the White Lion said with barely contained fury. "Time is of the essence—"

"Enough! When you do what you've been hired to do...on schedule, I will give you everything you need. Until then, Reed is not to be disregarded."

It was the White Lion's turn to pace. He circled the holo-disk, wanting to crush it beneath his heel. Forcing a calm expression, he said, "He is an unfortunate complication but manageable. Xanadu told my man he believed that Reed was on the cusp of taking the case and going to California. He would be out here hunting regardless of what I did. By your own words, he's relentless. It was a calculated risk, and it was worth it."

"How? What did you learn?"

"You questioned how Reed found out about Bobby Khan. According to my man who questioned Xanadu, he was brought in by someone named Drake Jacoby. He's an agent with—"

"I know who he is." The hologram of Danzig paced a circle around the mobile projector on the floor. "That treacherous bastard."

"You know him, then?"

"We've had dealings before."

"Why would Jacoby do this? Bring in an outsider like Reed?"

"Because he's smart." Danzig's bright blue figure flickered in the dark of the warehouse. "Reed is a serious threat. To my plan and to your mission."

"I have what they have now. And the distractions worked. They haven't made much headway. I'll make sure they don't make any here."

"And the safe?"

"It's crackable."

"Even under the conditions I described?"

"The trial run pointed out pitfalls. I'm correcting for them."

"Just be sure that this time, no one survives."

12

Santa Barbara Airport, California

It took a while to arrange things with Seattle PD and work out logistics with Coyote, who was traveling separately. It was nearly five by the time Reed and Nat landed at Santa Barbara Airport. The late afternoon sun hovered bright and stifling over the city as they walked toward the private parking lot. Heat waves shimmied up from the asphalt as shoebox-sized security robots skittered along the pavement between expensive cars, their ever-roving cameras searching for thieves. Santa Barbara, a beach town about ninety miles north of Los Angeles, had strong historical ties to European explorers. The airport looked designed with an eye toward Spanish Colonial Revival, with smooth white walls that soared into arched entrances. Open-air spaces and natural lighting gave the sense it was supposed to resemble one of the many missions that dotted the California coastline. Reed wished he had time to draw it.

A warm breeze brought the scent of the ocean. He and Nat wore plain clothes, and somehow, she looked like she belonged there, dressed in light colors and fabrics. Reed's perpetually dark wardrobe seemed out of place in the resort town.

"I came out here with my family in high school. This whole city looks like a vacation spot," Nat said, stretching her arms as they stood at the curb. "I thought we were flying into LAX."

"This is closer to Ventura Harbor, where the Khans kept their boat," Reed said, scanning the landscape.

Tall, curved palm trees bobbed over a twinkling coastal sprawl. A black town car with tinted windows pulled up in front of them, and a woman pushed out of the passenger seat. She was tall, lanky, with a neat dark brown bob. She wore three shades of gray, sensible shoes, and was thoroughly ordinary. Definitely one of Jacoby's.

"Reed and De La Cruz?" she asked as she held out her hand. "I'm Luna. I'll fill you in on the way."

They said their hellos, loaded their luggage, and climbed inside the car. The custom interior bench created enough space for all of them to sit comfortably, facing the front. She silently handed Nat and Reed each a sealed padded envelope as they sat down.

Nat ripped hers open and rooted around inside. "Is Luna your first name or your last?"

"Just Luna." As they pulled away, she tapped on a remote, and the glass divider between their seats and the driver lit up as a display screen. Files appeared and ordered themselves on the long surface. Schematics, documents, videos, scrolling updates. She used a laser pointer to highlight a drone video. The craft executed a flyover of townhouses near the harbor. The date stamp read yesterday. "This is Bobby Khan's residence. Gray Zone has it on ice. It's sealed, and we have a man inside the building in case the residence gets any visitors. No one has shown up. If you would like to take another look yourself, the key fob is in your envelope, Agent Reed."

"Agent?"

"Both of your credentials say Special Agent. Jacoby doesn't want jurisdictional issues when you're investigating," Luna said, nodding at Nat. "You'll get used to it."

Nat grinned. "You know, I think I could."

"Speaking of jurisdiction, I'm your liaison with local police, so keep me in the loop," Luna continued. "Jacoby directed me to set up a Field Ops site close to the Khan residence. We're doing a drive past the townhouse neighborhood for you to get a good look on our way, but here's a preview to get your bearings." Luna nodded to their envelopes. "You have credentials, a secure phone preprogrammed with numbers you'll need, including each other's, Jacoby's, and mine. Please try to contact me first if you need something. He'll just call me to make it happen, anyway. You've got money, a couple of vehicles, and other supplies you'll need to get settled. There is also a boat available if you want to visit the site of the sinking."

"Is it worth visiting?" Nat asked, flipping through her credentials. "I mean, it's been months."

Luna shrugged. "I was told to accommodate whatever you might need for your investigation. For reference, the sinking of both ships occurred off the mainland-facing coast of Santa Cruz Island. I've uploaded the Coast Guard's report to the database. Including information on any labs, conservation programs, and research projects active in the area at the time."

"Any of them report a disturbance that night?"

"One. A whale-breeding project indicated they had 'abnormal harmonics' on the night Bobby saw the phenomenon. We've got people looking into the readings. They apparently have to translate them for us."

"Speaking of research, what's out there, exactly?" Reed asked. "I looked it up online, but all I really found were tourist sites. Would there be campers there? Possible witnesses to the sinking?"

Luna brought up some videos and other information on the island chain. "We checked. There were three campers. A solo and a couple. They were on the leeward side of the island, so they wouldn't have seen anything but the open ocean even if it wasn't dark. No one was on the mainland facing the shore. Remember, the incident took place in January. Tourism slows significantly around that time."

"Anything shifty going on at the other islands?" Nat asked.

"Officially, other than wildlife, there's not much out there to cause trouble."

"Unofficially?" Reed asked.

"We'll get back to you on that." Luna navigated the Channel Islands information with her tablet. A zoomed-out photo of the chain of islands appeared. "There are technically eight islands in the archipelago, but five are part of a national park and marine sanctuary." She used her laser pointer on the screen. "This one is Santa Cruz. It's the largest landmass in the island chain and about twenty miles from California's shore."

It was lush by California standards, mostly brush and tall grasses, rolling hills, and jagged cliffs overlooking the ocean.

"What kind of civilian population are we talking about out there?" Reed asked.

"There are universities with satellite research centers for marine biology, conservation efforts for wildlife like seals, otters, and other animals. They have botanical studies of rare plants only found on the islands as well as anthropological programs studying the island's indigenous people. Add to that, two of the islands, San Clemente and San Nicolas, are owned and managed by the government."

Nat reached out and swiped through some files. "Any chance Bobby saw military activity beneath the water?"

"None we could confirm, but that's not conclusive," Luna said. "We're checking back channels. However, the bases are a significant distance from Santa Cruz Island."

The map of the islands showed structures along the coast and some inland. Reed reached for the divider and manipulated the image on the screen, trying to zoom in. "Students and possibly soldiers. Anyone else out there we should know about?"

"Most of Santa Cruz Island, the entire west side, is The Nature Conservancy, which is privately owned. The rest of the island, the smaller east end, is managed by the National Park Service. You can camp, hike, et cetera, in the east end, but not in The Nature Conservancy area. They host research stations and private labs, and they close off parts of the island for annual migratory nesting. It's very controlled for scientific research."

Reed jotted down notes in his sketchbook. "As far as you know, nothing on the island could cause what happened to the two ships that night?"

"We aren't sure." Luna tapped the tablet, bringing up an image of a proposed research facility on the divider screen. Clearly a rendering for the public, it blended into the side of the island with dark colors and organic lines. "When Congress passed the Ocean Innovation Plan, a lot of money poured into the California coastline. Small-project programs from universities and startups with little more than proof of concept flocked for their share of the money. Research out there includes cutting-edge hydroelectric technology, water temperature effects on wildlife, conservation efforts—anything having to do with the ocean and technology got approved."

"Like Silicon Valley, essentially," Nat said. "Very little verification or oversight."

Luna nodded at the building on the view screen. "That building is a facility owned by Deep Wave Dynamics. They're supposed to be studying the effects of shipping traffic on underwater ecosystems."

"Supposed to be?" Reed asked.

"During our investigation of Bobby's claims and disappearance, Deep Wave popped on our radar as a possible source of data for what happened that night. They study what the noise of all of those passing ships does to marine life. According to their website, they essentially take marine acoustic and seismic equipment out to the shipping lanes to gather data. But when we reached out, we got nothing. We asked around the university and private research community about them, but they seemed shrouded in mystery. According to public records, Deep Wave lab wasn't yet operational and had no data to share. Their secrecy coupled with the location of the Deep Wave lab grabbed our interest further."

"What's wrong with their location?" Reed asked, staring at the digital map.

"It's way over here." Luna pointed to the other side of the island facing the open ocean. "They study the shipping lanes between the mainland and Santa Cruz Island, but their research lab is nowhere near that."

"That *is* weird," Reed agreed. "Most research stations set up near their subject of study."

"Why build a lab on the other side of the island?" Nat asked, leaning in. "Did they give an explanation?"

"We didn't ask. We decided to dig instead. I did hear that the Deep Wave research location is constructed on an older, defunct research station's ruins, and in an effort to minimize our human presence on the preserve, it made sense to reuse already disturbed land rather than make a mark on conservation land."

"But you don't buy that?" Reed asked.

"Maybe I would have if they weren't being cagey."

He nodded. "If Deep Wave Dynamics did have something to do with the sinking, it makes sense they wouldn't do it in their own front yard."

"I agree, Agent Reed," Luna said. "And, when we looked deeper, it became clear we were on the right track because of where Deep Wave gets some of its money."

"Always follow the money," Nat said, fiddling with her new phone.

"We did, and it piqued our interest." Luna manipulated the on-screen files to show them. "It's funded by an endowment to California State University, Channel Islands, by something called Blue Horizons Trust. It's a nonprofit conservation charity with murky ties to several tech power players that Gray Zone is watching. Our interest lies in the fact that it's a *restricted* endowment. Which means it was created for a specific kind of research. Danzig's High Rock Holdings has a tangential connection via charitable donations. It's weak, but it's a thread to him."

"It's weird they're not operational yet," Nat said, peering at her phone. "The press release for the endowment says it was created five years ago."

Reed nodded, realizing what she'd caught. "So why isn't it built yet?"

"That was our question. Ostensibly, it's been mired in red tape and permit hell for those five years," Luna said and passed them some eight-by-ten photographs from her folder. "According to Deep Wave's official statement, the facility hasn't opened yet. They haven't even started internal construction. But we took a peek at power usage on the island, and they're using a lot. More than a fully constructed lab would, even. Naturally we took satellite images of the location at several points in time over the past week. We spotted the required construction machines and their operators, but we also saw this..."

The surveillance stills showed several figures arranged on the dock area of the facility. Another showed men, clearly armed, patrolling the grounds. A series of Zodiac inflatable boats appeared to come and go over time.

"That's a lot of security for an empty building." Reed tilted his head, thinking. "What about thermal imaging?"

Luna dug out a few more prints and handed them over. "Take a look."

Reed raised a brow when he did. The internal heat of the facility indicated the presence of more than empty space. "What are they doing?"

Luna closed her file. "Something we'd like to know, for sure. But for now, Jacoby's orders are to stay on task. Find Bobby Khan, ASAP."

The ride back along the coast to Ventura Harbor took forty-five minutes. They passed the typical beach city businesses. Tattoo parlors, surf shops, psychic and natural medicine offices, and the like. Bright, candy-colored storefronts with striped awnings where one could sip a power smoothie after a yoga class drifted by as they drove. Nat talked about San Diego, her hometown, and how it was better than Santa Barbara while Reed watched the city flash by his tinted window.

It wasn't until they were pulling onto Spinnaker Drive that Reed spotted the dark form of Santa Cruz Island from across the beach. They pulled into the boomerang-shaped Ventura Harbor Village, a collection of tourist-friendly shops that housed art galleries, wine-tasting venues, restaurants, and other boutique stores.

"Bobby and his father frequented this area. We've conducted a canvass of the employees. The interviews are in the database," Luna said as they drove through the retail spot. "In your packets are business cards with your name and a scannable code. You can hand them out to people you speak with, and they can use the code to get in touch with us if they have information."

Nat peered at her stack. "I'll bet scanning that code registers a lot of personal information from their phone as well."

Luna smiled. "We like to be efficient."

Out in the harbor, soaring masts of yachts shared the water with rusty fishing trawlers. The small stretch of beach running along the outside of the harbor village hosted both vacationing families as well as locals. From roller-skating couples to laughing children to street performers painted with garish grins, everything bustling beneath a bright blue sky. It reminded Reed of Venice Beach if it had gotten sober and had a posh makeover. They passed a street of condos and townhouses just off the beach.

"This whole area used to be a motor home park, but the city put in affordable housing units. The Khans lived in that building there." Luna pointed out the window. A row of thin townhouse buildings stood butted up against a sidewalk lined with flowers. "We clock it at a ten-minute drive from the area where they kept their boat."

"Was it ever recovered?" Nat asked. "The boat."

"It was not," Luna said. "Nor was Mr. Sami Khan's body."

They left the shore area and drove deeper inland to a manufacturing area about five miles from the Khan townhouse. A row of several empty industrial buildings sat on a private road. They pulled in front of a corrugated metal warehouse, and Luna led them to a side entrance, where she used an electronic fob to unlock the door. Once inside, the sheer size of the space made Reed pause. He'd stood in similar command centers on foreign soil. Large display screens, workstations with cables snaking off into shadows, a seating area with a big-box-store couch-and-loveseat combo surrounded by a few small tables. Upstairs, a makeshift barracks and a decent bathroom setup built into the second-floor loft offered long-term comforts. The rest of the warehouse ground floor held two nondescript black sedans parked next to the rolling metal doors.

"You can enter the code Jacoby gave you here. It's one-time use, and I need to scan your face, but then you're in. You'll get real-time updates from the Gray Zone network." Luna walked around the control center, turning on the screens and computers. She pointed to the far wall where a fridge, cooktop, and dining set sat. "We'll bring you food supplies and anything else you need. If you require medical attention, we'll cover that too."

As she continued the tour, Nat leaned close to Reed and whispered, "Field Ops?"

"I think the whole game just changed," Reed said.

Once they settled in, Nat got to work rooting around in the Gray Zone network. She wanted updates on the vitals bracelet they'd found on Xanadu as well as any data they'd managed to salvage off the geek lair's computers. Reed knew she dealt with grief by attacking what caused it. He left her to do what she needed. Coyote called. He was driving down from Seattle on his bike and would be there the next day.

"I have to make a stop to talk with an old intelligence buddy," Coyote drawled, the sound of highway traffic in the background. "He has some connections to a group of shippers out that way."

Reed grinned. "You mispronounced 'smugglers.'"

"Tomato, to-mah-to," Coyote said easily. "At any rate, they use Ventura Harbor now and again. I'm gonna see if they've heard any rumors about what went down the day the Khans' boat sank. I also have some feelers in about your buddy, Jacoby."

"Why?" Reed frowned.

"Because you always had me check out people we were working with. This is no different, Morgan. I told you I don't trust him."

Reed thought for a few seconds, then, "Don't get caught."

13

Seafarer Suites – Ventura, California

It was still early evening, and the days were long, so Reed decided to start at Bobby Khan's last known residence. The consensus was that no one could find him because he was likely couch surfing. On his way out of field ops, he'd asked Luna for a list of Bobby's friends, known associates, former coworkers, and fellow students. Moments later, she sent it to his phone. He updated Nat and left with one of the sedans.

The Seafarer Suites were small, white clapboard Cape Cod–style townhomes with little porches and built-in flower boxes. Designed to resemble East Coast beach cottages, they looked more like dollhouses to Reed. Bobby Khan's neighborhood sat sandwiched between a Sheraton Resort and a housing development. Reed parked and nodded at the agent sitting in a similar sedan parked under the tree across the street. The guy lifted his hand in acknowledgment as Reed passed. Reed's secure phone from the envelope was larger than his own, enough so that he didn't need to bring a tablet. He unlocked it with his print and pulled up the file from Gray Zone detailing the crime scene as he made his way to the residence.

It was one of five along a small side street. Delicate gingerbread-style filigrees decorated the modest home. A warm breeze pushed wind chimes around somewhere in the distance, and the golden sunlight sliced between the trees. Knotted pieces of crime scene tape still encircled the railing though the rest had been torn off. Reed used the keys Luna provided to unlock the townhouse and then pulled a foldable blade from his pants pocket. He slid the edge along the crime scene sticker sealing the front door.

The stale scent of old food and stuffy air flew at his face when he pushed through. Reed entered slowly as he swiped through the files, holding up his phone to compare the photos taken by the detectives and what was in front of his face. Nothing seemed off. Fingerprint dust and other signs of the investigation paled against the apparent physical fight that knocked over lamps, broke chairs, and left blood smeared on a wall. Reed wandered the first floor, taking everything in. It was a bachelor pad. Ratty recliners sat facing a large display screen on the wall. It hung over a cheap cabinet that held dusty stacks of mail and a bowl of random detritus.

He toured the living room, the half bath with a sink and toilet, and the galley kitchen. He checked the fridge. A large burgundy soup pot shared space with still wrapped discount menu tacos, stale fries, and some takeout containers. The cabinets were bare save for instant noodle bowls and some mac-and-cheese cups. Jacoby's file on Bobby's financials indicated that the condo was paid for through the end of the year by an overseas account. Reed realized it must be the missing insurance money from the boat.

Some sort of dried food marred the middle of the kitchen floor. Reed knelt, inspecting the oily residue. The scene report on his phone said it was soup, possibly ramen. He rose and ran his finger over the bullet hole, head height, in one of the cabinets over the sink. Forensics report stated the bullet had changes in its striations and a slight residue—possible suppressor use. A killer with a suppressor, a professional, wouldn't miss. Reed wondered if Bobby somehow knew they were coming for him or if he'd been tipped off. Yellow sticker indicators marked blood drops on the floor. Bobby's blood type. It led away from the kitchen to a window in the living room. The forensic team had found blood smeared on the bricks outside the window as well as droplets in the grass leading away. A minimal amount of blood, according to the medical examiner.

Reed stood with his back to the bullet hole and looked through the kitchen. Raising his hand in the shape of a gun, he followed the line of sight. It led to the bathroom door across the floor. He moved to the small half bath, pushed open the door, and glanced at a cracked window. Reed remembered Bobby's height was five eleven. The height looked right, so why just a graze? Reed opened the bathroom window and peered out. Soft grass below a low window made footprints unlikely. The lock was broken, the screen cut. Reed let his gaze take in the mix of developed neighborhoods, resorts, cruise line businesses, and other buildings. Plenty of places to hide and wait.

The second floor of the townhouse held the bedrooms. Bobby's father, Sami Khan, had kept his bedroom neat and tidy. A sliding door leading onto a small terrace lent a beautiful view of the harbor. Various books arranged by size lined a wall shelf above a made bed. Dust covered much of the décor, which consisted mainly of photo frames. The pictures were of Bobby as a kid building a puzzle at the kitchen table. Sami and a teenaged Bobby stood with arms around each other's shoulders at the rim of a canyon. Their tired smiles and sunburnt noses spoke of a long hike. A few other moments in time from long ago. Reed took photos with his phone of each.

A ceramic frame sat by itself on the dresser across the room. Angled away, it practically faced the corner of the room. The picture was of Sami and a woman standing on the deck of a boat, smiling. She was his age, slight and pretty in a refined way. Her glossy dark hair styled with a cut meant for easy maintenance. Short and pixie-like, it suited her face. Reed remembered Mrs. Khan's face from Jacoby's files. Reed glanced back at the bed. The nightstand next to it had a clean surface. No books or reading glasses. Plenty of room to have a photo of your late wife close by. The sentiment was as common as finding toothpaste in someone's bathroom. It's what most people did. Why not Sami? Why push it out of sight? Reed chewed on that while he kept wandering.

Bobby's room was another story. Movie posters decorated the wall, and piles of books were stacked in the corners of the room. Engineering texts and notebooks sat open on the small desk in the corner. As if Bobby expected to return to school and didn't want to fall behind. A college kid. Clothes littered the floor and bed, hangers strewn everywhere. Reed didn't see any luggage, and most of Bobby's electronics were reported missing by the forensics team. It appeared he'd fled. But the bullet hole bothered Reed. The scene dictated a scenario that didn't match the evidence. If Bobby was taken by surprise enough that he dropped his ramen midway to the table, how did he pack his things and run? Was he already packed? Did he return to the townhouse later under the nose of Gray Zone surveillance? He jotted down his questions as he walked.

Reed switched to listening to Bobby's podcast as he walked the house a couple more times, looking for anything out of place. Halfway through the introduction, he stopped the recording. Even with the windows closed, Reed could still hear construction noises, the occasional horns of ships, barking dogs. None of which was on the recording. He hadn't seen anything that resembled a makeshift recording studio in the townhouse. No foam egg carton tiles on the walls for soundproofing, no recording equipment, nothing. Reed sent Nat a text asking if it would be possible for her to tell if Bobby used a software filter on the recordings to clean up the noise or if he recorded in a soundproof booth. If he did go somewhere else to record, he might be hiding out there. She said she'd get back to him.

Reed searched the police report once more. All of the neighbors interviewed by the detectives reported only knowing Sami and Bobby enough to nod in passing. The Khan men kept to themselves. Didn't have visitors. Reed walked to the terrace door off of Sami Khan's main bedroom, sliding the door all the way open to let in fresh air, then stepped out to look around. The sun rested lower in the sky, and the blue of twilight crept along the streets. Scanning the landscape, Reed wondered if Bobby needed medical attention. There wasn't much blood, but he would need the bullet wound cleaned. Depending on where it was, he might need help especially since his truck was still in the parking lot.

The report from Luna stated they checked local pharmacies for someone buying wound care products. Nothing popped. Where would an unconnected kid, possibly hurt and scared out of his mind, go? Cheap hotels, veterinary hospitals, the ER with a fake name…the minimal blood suggested Bobby survived and left the townhouse. The question was, did he escape a killer or leave as a hostage?

Reed shoved his hands in his pants pockets. He was cold again. A wave of shivers moved through his body, and he gritted his teeth to keep from chattering. Residual issues from using Jacoby's treatment for the foreign memory symptoms made it hard for Reed to maintain his temperature. The sea breeze coming off the cooling water chilled him more than it should have. A soft tinkling in the corner of the terrace caught Reed's attention. Wind chimes dangled from the eave. A beautiful collection of bone china teacups and gilded shards, antique silver spoons, and polished sea glass trimmed with silver. Pieces of delicate stained glass were strung on a gold filament down the center.

It was a piece of art, not something you'd get at a beach novelty shop. Judging from the décor inside the house, the Khans hadn't spent what little money they had on expensive handmade wind chimes. The strings still had the sheen of newness, the pieces unchipped from gusts. They couldn't be more than a few months old even in the steady California climate. Reed had a feeling they weren't Mrs. Khan's. She'd passed a while ago. This was new. It had to be a gift.

Reed straightened up with a start. Something had bothered him about the fridge. He hurried back down to the kitchen and opened all the cabinets, looking for other pots. He found cheap stainless steel and black plastic-handled pots and pans. Nothing like the fancy enamel Dutch oven in the refrigerator. Reed pulled it out, set it on the cabinet, and looked inside. Beef bourguignon. Covered in mold, but unmistakably the famous French stew. Couldn't be older than a week. He put the lid back on, thinking, then checked all the drawers.

Not a lot of spices past onion and garlic powder. He found soy sauce and chili oil in the fridge but not much else. Plastic spatulas and spoons. Not a cook's kitchen. He'd seen the price of those fancy enamel pots. They were in the hundreds. The person who made that stew was a gourmet cook at least. None of the neighbors interviewed said they'd had any recent interaction with Bobby. Most of them hardly knew the Khans, but someone cared for Bobby. They'd delivered a time-consuming stew in an expensive pot. That suggested at least a minimum of trust. And the wind chimes, they suggested something more. Bobby had been gone for a week. The soup was about that old. Whoever brought it to him might be the last person to have seen him before he disappeared.

Reed strode back upstairs to the terrace and inspected the wind chimes, looking for a maker's mark or some indication of origin. He found it on a wooden disk dangling from the central cord. It bore the name of a store. *Windsong Creations.* He looked up the name on his phone and got an address. It was just down the street. He took a photo of the chimes and closed the townhouse, then headed back out onto the street. He paused, getting his bearings. Across the street to the east was an older housing development where a row of five or six old-style Victorian beach cottages lined the shore of the beach near the harbor. Converted into boutiques, the small homes offered specialty art and keepsakes, resort wear, and other tourist favorites.

Flickering in the front lawn of one of the homes caught Reed's eye, and he walked over, strolling as if on a pleasant beach walk, glancing around to see if anyone seemed interested in what he was doing. The shimmering he'd seen was a reflection off of a spinning metal lawn art piece. The wind sent the circular design whirling as he walked up to the front of the small gallery. The name, *Windsong Creations,* was carved into an artfully refinished piece of driftwood. Sinuous shapes of glass and metal sat on shelves just inside the front window. The frosted window in the door obscured Reed's view. A sign over the doorbell announced that the private gallery was by appointment only, but Reed spotted movement inside. He rang the bell, reaching for his credentials and holding them up to the window in the door.

"Agent Reed," he said and smiled. The silhouette behind the frosted glass stilled but didn't answer. He held up his phone to the window. "I think you gave either Sami or Bobby Khan these wind chimes because you cared for them. I need your help."

The figure moved closer, and then the door opened with a chorus of tinkling bells overhead. A woman, sporting long gray hair with strands of beads braided in and faded tattoos on her arms and fingers, opened the door with a smile. Paint splattered her overalls and T-shirt along with some kind of powder. She had blue eyes that reminded Reed of the sky over cornfields. A soft sixty, he thought.

"What's this about?" she asked with a faint Midwestern accent.

Reed stepped back, giving her room. "Ma'am. I'll just say it straight. I think Bobby Khan is in trouble, and I was hoping you knew how I could find him."

Her gaze narrowed at him. "What makes you think I know this person?"

"If you let me see your kitchen, I can tell you. I think he still has your soup pot."

She eyed him for a moment, then, "Well, I *would* like that Dutch oven back." The older woman pulled the door all the way open, letting Reed into the gallery. "I'm Marla Jenkins. And yes, I do know Sami and Bobby Khan. In fact, I was starting to wonder if you guys were ever going to come find me."

14

Reed found Marla's gallery interesting. A combination of high-end oil paintings, nautical watercolors, and local crafts. Glass cases with blond wood frames held jewelry made with shells and sea glass. A few larger, more intricate wind chimes dangled from the ceiling, their soft tinkling soothing. Dream catchers and hand-painted tarot cards shared space with towering chunks of crystals and bundles of incense. It smelled of sandalwood and lavender. A real hippie-dippie place, as Coyote would say.

Reed followed her to the back of the gallery, where they settled onto an overstuffed couch. She brought him iced tea and laid out a plate of vegan cookies that looked like compressed sawdust. He stuck to the tea.

Marla raised a brow. "You're telling me you found me with a pot and a set of wind chimes?"

Reed smiled. "To be honest, the wind chimes and the Dutch oven were the only two expensive items in that home. They suggested someone cared for the Khan men. So, it was a good bet they were related. Are the wind chimes your personal work?"

"Yup. They were a birthday gift to Sami. He'd said once that the sound took him back to his childhood."

Reed took in her barely trembling lip and sat back. "Can you tell me how you know them?"

Marla blinked away tears. Reed sipped his tea quietly, waiting.

"We were seeing each other, Sami and me, about seven months when he—when the boat sank..." She hugged herself. "We started out as friends. I met Sami at a local bookshop event, and we got to talking. Before I know it, we're having coffee and commiserating about our dead exes."

"Come again?"

"I'm a widow, and I think just wanting someone to talk to was good for both of us. Our relationship evolved from there, but like I said, it was new. I hadn't even done his star chart yet, but we were getting serious. The problem was he hadn't told Bobby about us."

"Mr. Khan kept the relationship from him?"

"His wife died of cancer three years ago. Bobby quit school to help care for her and then stayed on with Sami's charter business to help pay off the bills. They still lost the house, that's why they moved to the townhouse. With so much change and loss, Sami said he just wanted to give Bobby a little more time before he hit him with his father dating."

"You never met Bobby?"

"Not formally, I never got the chance." Marla shook her head, looking away as she nibbled on a cookie, dropping crumbs everywhere. "I think Sami felt guilty for being happy."

Reed thought of Nat and how they'd met right after the tragic death of someone he'd loved. "I know the feeling. He would've come around."

She smiled sadly at that. "After Sami passed, there wasn't a funeral. I don't think Bobby had it in him to plan anything, and they were so tight with money. Sami said his wife's end-of-life care cost them everything."

"They were struggling, I saw that."

"I wanted to help but, but Bobby didn't know about me, and I..." She shook her head and sighed. "I didn't know what to do, and my psychic was away in Aruba, so I didn't do anything until I saw Bobby walking past my store. He and his father used to take walks around this area some evenings. He looked horrible."

"What do you mean?"

"Just drawn, thinner. His hair hadn't been trimmed. You know, unkempt." She nodded out of the front window toward the harbor. "He walked by at the exact moment I went to close up the gallery. I *knew* it was a sign. I met him out on the sidewalk one time he passed and introduced myself as his father's friend. He seemed...lost?"

"Grief will do that."

"He started stopping by the gallery on his walks. He'd poke his head in the door to say hello. Sometimes we'd have a sandwich, and he'd talk about how he was getting work from fellow charters, but not enough, I think. That's why I started dropping off dinners here and there. Before that, he probably hadn't had a proper meal in months."

"And you never told Bobby about your relationship with his father."

Marla shrugged. "I had no idea how to go about it, actually."

"I get that." Reed nodded. "When was the last time you saw him?"

She told Reed about delivering the pot of stew about a week before Bobby disappeared, but hesitated, stumbling over her words. Finally, she pressed her lips together, thinking.

"Listen, I saw someone with Bobby a few days before he went missing."

Reed sat forward. "Did you recognize him?"

"No, he was a stranger." She gestured with her cookie. "It had been a few days since I dropped off the beef bourguignon, and I saw Bobby's truck parked outside the townhouse. The lights were on, and given that he looked so forlorn the day before on his walk, I thought I'd pop in. I walked up to the door, but it was a little ajar, and I heard talking. Two male voices."

Reed sat forward. "Bobby?"

"Yes, and another man. And then I saw movement in the crack of the open door. A tall, thin fellow. Definitely not Bobby."

"Did he see you?"

"No..." Marla relayed how she'd seen a flash of him walking in Bobby's home. She couldn't tell what he was doing, but he was moving around quickly, talking while Bobby walked out of sight. "I didn't want to interrupt, so I decided to come back later."

"Did you hear what they were talking about?"

"No, and they didn't sound heated at all, which is probably why I forgot about it." She hugged herself.

"Why didn't you tell anyone?"

"Two reasons. One, my husband, Trevor, was a defense lawyer. You know what his mantra was? *Never talk to cops.* And his brother was a policeman. Can you believe that? Trevor said never, ever volunteer to be a witness, especially if it's attached to violence." Marla sat back with a sigh. "And two, when I saw the police down at the townhouse a couple of days later, I went to see if I could find out what was going on. They were saying Bobby ran off. That his equipment and his clothes were gone. No one mentioned he'd been hurt. So, I didn't even think of the stranger until later when Gale, she sells candles a couple of shops over, said there was a rumor the police had found blood in Bobby's place. Is that true?"

Reed nodded. "It's complicated. It appears someone broke in. There was gunfire and what looks like a struggle inside."

"I-I didn't know." Marla's hand went to her mouth, brows furrowed. "I didn't know what I'd seen could help Bobby."

"Why don't you help him by telling me now?" Reed pulled out his sketchbook and ink pen. "Can you describe the man you saw at Bobby's apartment?"

She paused. "I'm not sure I want my name attached to something like this. What if he finds out I saw him?"

Reed pulled out his phone and selected a photo of Bobby from his gallery, showing it to her. "He's just a kid, Marla. And he's in trouble."

Her gaze settled on Bobby's smiling, sun-kissed face. "I only just saw a flash of a figure, I mean..."

"As an artist, you must have taken in more than you consciously realized. Your mind is trained for details, right? What about impressions. What did the stranger *feel* like? His—"

"His aura?"

"Uh, sure." Reed sketched out a door, ajar, on his page. "Let's go back to the moment you first glimpsed him through the crack..."

He talked her through creeping up to the door, peering inside, sketching quietly as she talked stream of consciousness about what she'd seen and felt. A tall, lithe man. Caucasian by the look of his hands. How she thought the stranger moved wrong until she realized his hair was throwing her off.

"It was white."

"White like bleached? Blond?" Reed outlined a figure passing the doorway.

Marla shook her head. "No, it was blank white. Like he'd seen a ghost. And sort of long. It touched the collar of his trench coat. I realized I'd originally assumed the stranger was old because of his hair, but his movements and voice were young. Although even that was off somehow."

He stopped sketching. "Tell me."

"His voice was youthful, like Bobby's, but different. He sounded not quite harsh but like he was used to being obeyed, if that makes sense."

Nodding, Reed jotted down notes, taking her critiques as he worked the image. Sharp cheekbones. Sloe eyes like a Scandinavian. White brows. He pulled what he could from that moment, talking her around the details, and then turned for her to see his sketch. It was a side profile of a tall man with severe bone structure in his face and white hair. The collar of a black trench coat obscured some of his face, but the *feel* was right, she said. It was the stranger.

"That's good, Agent Reed," Marla said with a satisfied smile.

"Have you ever seen this man around Bobby or the area before?"

Marla shook her head. "I'd notice a guy like that."

Reed asked her about Bobby's podcast and the missing recording equipment.

"Do you know if he made the podcast at home, or is there another place he'd go?"

"I didn't know he was doing that," Marla said, rising from the couch.

Reed followed suit, and she led him back toward the front door. Her vibe was a little off, as if she wanted to get rid of him all of a sudden.

"Would he store his equipment somewhere other than his home?" he asked.

"Well, they had a storage locker at Ventura Harbor. He kept most of the gear he recovered from his father's boat there."

"Is he still paying for that locker?" Reed hadn't seen any charges for that from the bank statements.

"I don't know, honestly," Marla said, stopping by the front door of the gallery. "Sami paid for things in cash, though. He didn't trust banks after they took his house. If he had a big charter, he'd pay for a couple of extra months ahead of time in case business dipped. He was savvy that way. Always thinking of how to keep the business going for Bobby."

"Did Bobby tell you what happened that night out on the water?"

"Bobby is a brilliant kid, but he's also been through a lot. Just because his story sounds out there, it doesn't mean it isn't true."

Reed smiled. "Do *you* think that Sami Khan fell through a subsea portal?"

Marla shrugged. "I think they never found his body."

They talked for a few more minutes, Reed asking if anything weird had happened recently, even if it seemed unrelated to Bobby. Marla tugged on a lock of hair, thinking.

"Would a break-in count?"

Reed stilled. "Here?"

"No, at the townhouse...sort of. Bobby said that the main office on the property had sent a memo to the homes in the development that there'd been a break-in. Petty cash was taken, graffiti on the walls, someone peed on the plants."

"Vandalism?"

"Yeah, apparently the email was just a general update that they were going to hire a private security officer to patrol the area at night. He seemed relieved, actually."

"When did this happen?"

"That's just it. It happened about a month or so before Bobby disappeared. And it didn't even happen to him. The main office is five houses down from his unit." She shook her head, her lip quivering slightly. "It's just that now that someone broke into Bobby's place and..."

"I understand," Reed said softly.

He talked with her for a few more minutes, gave her one of his scannable business cards, and went to leave, but she stopped him, her face worried. "Agent Reed, can I tell you something?"

"Not if it's my future," he joked.

"I told you I can't divine the future, silly, but I do see something interesting." Marla tilted her head, looking at Reed strangely. "Your aura is positively pulsing with red."

He paused. "Is that bad?"

"It can mean passion, leadership..." Her mouth pulled to the side as she glanced at the air around him.

It kind of creeped Reed out. "Or..."

"Depending on your chakras, sometimes it means a transition."

"Transition?"

"Relationships, work, sometimes even life itself."

"I don't understand."

"Like I said, I don't see the future. I don't have that gift," Marla said, but her hand went to Reed's forearm, her gaze going behind him. "But I can tell you this. Be aware, death follows you close."

He had no idea how to respond to that, and so he thanked her for both the tea and the dire warning and told her to go and visit a friend for a few days to be safe. Then he headed back to the Khan townhouse. The agent from the watch car was still there when Reed got back to his own car. He slid into the driver's seat, navigated the unfamiliar phone, and called Nat.

"Whatcha got?" she asked after one ring.

"Sami Khan had a girlfriend." Reed flipped through the pages of his sketchbook. "Marla Jenkins. She owns the *Windsong Creations* art gallery, where I was just at. I need what you can get on her, ASAP. I think she's the last one to see Bobby alive."

"What'd she say?"

"She was helpful, struggling emotionally. But I got the feeling there was more, so I'll take another run at her later. She saw something, Nat. We need to tell Luna to sit an agent on her home and gallery for a while."

"I'll let her know. She stepped out for supplies. What else?"

"Two things. Marla told me that there was a break-in at the property's main office about a month before Bobby disappeared. I don't remember seeing that in any of the Gray Zone files. Do you?"

"Nope. You think it's related?"

"I have no idea."

"Okay, well, if the owners of the townhouse complex had security cameras around the office that got broken into, I bet I can ask Luna for a warrant for the recordings. She is amazing, by the way. Did you know she's Austrian?"

"I would think Gray Zone already did that," Reed muttered, wondering if he was chasing shadows. He shivered again in the warm air, and a sliver of worry pushed through him.

"The report did say that they pulled recordings from the complex's cameras around the time of Bobby's disappearance," Nat continued. "They didn't see anyone suspicious on the property during the attack or in the days prior. No one looked like they were watching Bobby's area. I'm pulling up the recordings." She typed quickly on a keyboard. "You said two things. What else did Marla see?"

"She saw someone in Bobby's home, talking with him a few days before he was attacked." Reed took a picture of his sketch and sent it to her by text. "I know it's not much—"

"This guy looks like an anime character."

"Yeah, it's the best we have for now. How far back does the security footage from the townhouse complex go?"

"Lemme see...two weeks before Bobby was attacked in his home and a few days after."

"See if we can go back further. The break-in is bugging me. I want to see if the cameras caught anything."

"I'll talk to Luna about getting the earlier recordings. Are you done for today?"

"Yeah, the last twenty-four hours are catching up with me. I'm heading in."

After the call, Reed leaned back and stared out the windshield of the car at the evening sky. Seagulls complained as they soared over the sand. He thought about what Marla had said about death and auras and change. He didn't tend to believe in that kind of thing, but Xanadu's death and coming out to California seemed to shift things. Pushed them onto a path toward something he wasn't sure he could see before it was too late. Outside, the palm trees leaned lazily toward each other, crisscrossing like a scene from a postcard. Pink cotton-candy clouds hovered over a lavender horizon. It really was a beautiful place to die.

15

Coyote called the next morning, rousting Reed out of bed at seven. He answered while looking around for Nat or Luna. The loft and bunks were empty. A modular wall separated the sleeping area from the kitchenette, but he smelled coffee and heard voices on the ground floor.

"I'm at Ventura Harbor right now. They're about to open the gates. Come find me at the little food shack thingamabob they have out there. They have breakfast burritos here with bacon and fries in 'em."

Reed sat up, blinking against the morning light coming from the high windows of the warehouse. A ship horn sounded in the distance. "Who eats fries with breakfast?"

"Don't knock it till you've tried it, Morgan. I'm going to be walking about by the boats, seeing what I can see. Give me a shout when you finally drag your lazy ass out here," he said and hung up.

Reed texted Nat the invite, heard her phone chirp downstairs, and then he jumped in the shower. He threw on some black work pants and a dark work shirt, rolled at the elbows. He nixed the tie and wore his work boots, going for California casual. He walked downstairs and found Nat and Luna sitting at the consoles in front of the big screens. Luna hadn't stayed the night at Field Ops like he and Nat, so she was staying elsewhere. Probably a nice hotel. She looked rested.

"Jacoby is impressed, Agent Reed," Luna said, looking up from her keyboard with a smile. "You managed to uncover an unknown witness and a possible suspect in less than a day."

Reed walked over to the coffeemaker and poured himself a mug of consciousness. "The question is, did it gain us any ground?"

"It did." Nat typed on the console, bringing up some documents. "We followed up on Marla's storage locker suggestion, and she was right. There *is* a storage locker, but it was under Mrs. Khan's maiden name, Mariah Lodi."

"It's why it didn't appear in either Sami's or Bobby's financial statements, and it wasn't under their names when we did our search." Luna shook her head. "We missed all of this because we never found Marla in our initial sweep."

"We know about her now." Reed glanced at Nat. "Tell me what it knocked loose."

"Plenty. I cross-referenced the name of the Khans' charter boat, *Mariah's Spirit*, with places that offered storage within a ten-mile radius of the harbor." Nat pulled up the website of a storage place next to Ventura Harbor. "Turns out the locker was under her father's name, who first leased it. Mrs. Khan continued to pay by cash after his death. When she passed, either Bobby or Sami continued to do the same."

Reed sipped his coffee. It was glorious. "They never changed the paperwork."

"Exactly. The boat was the same deal," Nat added. "With the boat gone and Bobby no longer pulling charters, the idea of storage fell through the cracks. But it's there."

Luna brought up some older-looking documents. "The vessel was originally registered to Cosvo Lodi, Mariah's father. Mariah inherited the boat and the locker from her father about twenty-five years ago when she married Sami. He took over the business, paid a stipend to the father for his retirement, and planned to pass the business on to Bobby, I presume. Sami made sure the boat was in Bobby's name in part."

Reed pointed at the screens with the wooden stirring stick. "Marla mentioned Sami would pay cash because he didn't trust banks, and I think that mistrust extended to Bobby. According to Jacoby's information, Bobby deposited a check we think was the boat's insurance payout into an offshore account. He could be drawing cash. That's a decent amount of money to stay hidden if you know what you're doing."

"I guess we know why he hasn't touched his bank account," Luna mused.

"The question is, does he have the nerve? He's injured and scared. Would he hide out or run for it?" Nat asked.

"I listened to his podcasts," Reed said. "At their core, they're Bobby screaming into the void that he believes his father was a victim of something other than Mother Nature. He's angry. Convinced his father's actual cause of death was covered up. I don't think he'd leave. I think he'd try to prove what happened to his father."

"Even after being attacked? Shot at?" Luna didn't look convinced.

"*Especially* now," Reed said. "The attack proved he was onto something. Why go after him if he's wrong?"

"Also, this proof Bobby said he had of what happened that night hasn't shown up," Nat added.

Reed nodded. "Yes. I'm thinking he still has it or knows where it's hidden and is working on releasing it."

"Or he's dead already." Luna shrugged. "They've proven they're willing to kill."

Reed's gaze shot to Nat, who stilled at Luna's words.

"Maybe he is," Reed said evenly. "And if I find proof he's gone, I'll stop looking. Until then, he's out there, and he's got a target on his back."

"All right, you two. I seem to be outnumbered." Luna jotted something down on her tablet with a digital pen. "I have agents working the friends, students, and coworker interviews. They're nearing the end of the list I gave you. Not a lot of people knew Bobby very well. He was shy and very busy with school, but I can have them double back on those interviews if we find this person of interest from the video."

Reed's brows shot up. "What video?"

"Oh, this one," Nat said and pointed to the center display. She'd cued up a video, and a facial recognition program ran its digital tendrils over two images: an uploaded copy of Reed's sketch from Marla's description of the stranger and a data window with a single frame of video taken at night, comparing the two. The program used measurement lines to pinpoint brow ridge angle, eye tilt position, and nose length and slope, crawling over the frame of video like a digital spider. "By the way, Homeland warrants get shit done. We have the full surveillance package from the townhouse complex. It came twenty minutes ago. Luna and I have been running it through some programs."

"Agent De La Cruz's sifting program is incredibly efficient," Luna said from her seat at the console. She was typing into a command line interface, the black box for coding that Nat often used. "I think Gray Zone might be interested in how she built it."

"I'll bet." Reed leaned on the console next to Nat, gave a subtle wink, and watched the facial rec run its data. "This is the guy? Where'd you find this image?"

Luna tilted her head side to side, uncommitted. "It's a preliminary estimate, but the data is leaning in that—"

"It's totally him," Nat cut across her. "Marla told you that there was a break-in about a month before Bobby was attacked, right? I didn't find anything at the four-week mark, but I did at the five." She pulled up the video from the townhouse complex security cameras. It showed a shadowy figure sliding across the asphalt, then the sound of crashing glass. "That's the window in the back door of the office."

When the figure passed back and was gone, Reed sighed, frustrated. "That was a whole lot of nothing."

"It wasn't, because check this out. First of all, we think we found the purpose of the break-in at Bobby's townhouse development. Whoever pretended to vandalize the office also inserted a RAT—a remote access Trojan—into the townhouse office's computers. It's a malware program that creates a back door, enabling someone to have administrative control over the system."

"He was watching Bobby," Reed said.

"Right," Nat said. "So, I went even further back, just to be sure, and saw this..." The security camera had recorded two figures standing on the side of the main office, talking in close proximity. They were in a small alleyway between the building and a fence; trash bins sat against the wall. A pillar, part of the main office's design, partially blocked the view of the camera.

Reed leaned in, narrowing his gaze at the figures. Bobby stood, arms crossed, defensive, his brows furrowed. He was shrugging as the other figure appeared to be speaking, but the upturned collar of his trench coat obscured the bottom half of his face. A pop of stark white hair peeked out from under a knit cap. "That has to be the guy Marla saw in Bobby's home, right?"

"When was this?" Reed asked.

"Three days before the break-in. Last week of April." Luna held up her phone. "I checked the almanac. It was unseasonably warm that first week of April, which is when this was recorded."

"The large coat and winter cap bothered you too." Reed nodded. "Marla said he was wearing it inside Bobby's townhouse in June as well. He was hiding his face."

Nat pointed at the two top screens. "He knew where the cameras were too. See how he avoids each one like he knows their range?"

"Yeah," Reed watched the tall man. Marla's description was right. He moved like a predator.

"Oh, you asked me if I could tell if Bobby recorded his podcast at the townhome and then used a filter to smooth out the sound from the boats and stuff."

"Right...did he?"

"No. Everything I looked at on the podcast's metadata indicated he'd been using recording equipment and maybe a sound dampener on his microphone. No filter, though. He made those podcasts somewhere else."

"A quiet place."

"Yeah. A studio or maybe the library?" Nat shrugged, her eyes rimmed with red like she'd been crying earlier.

"Coyote is meeting us at the harbor if you want to come," Reed said. "I bet there's a donut shop between here and there."

A wisp of a smile crossed her lips. "Enticing, but no. You go. I just got the rest of what Homeland could recover from the geek lair's computer system. I want..." She cleared her throat. "I need to see what he was up to when he was killed. It could give us another direction to look."

Reed wanted to argue that someone else, someone not so close to

Xanadu should do it, but thought better of it. He smiled instead. "I'll bring you back something."

Ventura Harbor was a sea of meandering concrete and ice plants with bursts of purple flowers butted up against the aqua-blue water of the Pacific. Sleek yachts, rusty trawlers, sports boats, and the like shared space. Reed walked along the sidewalk leading to the front gate, past stacks of canoes and kayaks for rent. A group of paddle boarders circled some sea lions sunning on a buoy. He checked his watch. It was past eight thirty in the morning, and yet no one seemed in any hurry to get to a job or anything. Coyote sat on a stack of crates next to the chain link fence surrounding the harbor entrance.

He tossed his cigarette at some ducks and rose to meet Reed, handing him a hot breakfast burrito. "I found the locker area, if you want to hit that first."

"We don't need a warrant, according to Luna, but we should hit the front office anyway. I want to talk to the clerk."

"Luna?" Coyote fell in step with Reed as they headed that way.

"She's Jacoby's babysitter for us," Reed explained as he ate. He filled Coyote in on what she'd told them about Santa Cruz Island, what's out there, and the video with the white-haired stranger.

"You've been busy."

"Luna's got us wired in with Homeland," Reed said, tossing the finished burrito wrapper in the trash and pushing through the glass entrance to the office. He shot a look at Coyote. "Keep her informed, but not as much as we are, you get me?"

Coyote nodded. "Does Nat know this?"

"Nat never tells anybody everything."

The counter guy's name was Chet, according to his faded name badge, and he looked like he crawled his way to work with one hell of a hangover. He had a messy mop of dirty-blond hair and a sunburnt nose. The collar of his blue polyester polo shirt curled up at the edges as if melted by an iron. "Can I help you guys?"

Reed flashed his Homeland badge and nodded at the file cabinets behind the counter. "I'm following up on one of your clients, last name is Khan. They had a slip and a locker. We want to take a look inside the locker."

"Gotcha," Chet said, eyeing the badge and then Coyote with confusion. "Is he really a Homeland agent?"

"Him?" Reed shook his head, amused. "What do you think?"

"I'm his bodyguard," Coyote said with a smirk.

Chet gave them both a weird look, then turned and rooted around in one of the filing cabinets. "Is Bobby in trouble or something?"

"You know him?" Reed asked.

"Everybody knows the Khans. They're good people." Chet pulled out a manila folder and turned, opening it on the counter between him and Reed. "Terrible what happened to his dad."

"The sinking?" Reed asked, reading the contents upside down. The locker's lease had expired a week ago.

"Well, yeah, that, and also how bad Bobby took it. He was talking crazy." Chet pushed the papers toward Reed. "He was so smart...I guess his mind just couldn't, you know, take it."

"Did anyone touch the locker?" Reed asked, flipping through the paperwork. "It says here Bobby's lease expired a bit ago."

Chet shook his head. "No. We sent out snail mail notices that his locker lease was ending. We didn't hear back. Toby, the harbor maintenance guy, was supposed to clear it out this week, but his kid is getting married in Boca Raton. He's out until next Friday." He glanced at Coyote. "By the way, uh, do you all need a warrant or something? It's Bobby's private stuff now, I guess."

"What was the maintenance guy going to do with the contents of the locker?" Coyote asked.

"You know, I never asked before." Chet shrugged. "I think he just throws everything in the dumpster."

"Then what's the harm of us taking a peek before it goes in the trash?" Reed asked.

Chet agreed with his reasoning and handed over the management's master key to the locker building's front security door. "Listen, I heard Bobby might be missing. Maybe on the run?"

"Where'd you hear that?" Coyote asked.

"Just scuttlebutt around here. You know, rumor. Is he okay, though?"

"That's what we're trying to find out," Reed said. He handed over one of his cards and told him someone might be back to take his statement.

As they headed toward the locker building, Reed navigated his new phone and shot Luna a message about sending someone to speak with Chet. She answered back immediately.

Someone will be there in an hour.

Coyote was silent while he texted, then, "You think this kid is dead or what?"

"Fifty-fifty at the moment," Reed said, and told him about Marla and showed him the drawing of the stranger she'd seen in Bobby's home.

He glanced at it, unimpressed. "So, we're looking for Jack Frost now?"

"Something like that…" Reed slowed as he walked toward the locker building. The heavy metal door stood ajar. A smell of melted metal fumes wafted toward him as he approached. He leaned in, squinting at the corroded security deadbolt. "Someone used acid on the lock."

"Man after my own heart," Coyote said with a grin. "Guess we're not the first ones to find out about this place."

Inside the locker building itself, rows of floor-to-ceiling cages lined the walls. It reminded Reed of his equipment locker in the forward bases. He glanced inside each one as he strode down the center path until he found the correct space number from the file. The lock on the cage door also appeared melted. He nodded at the other cages. "None of the other ones are broken into."

Coyote nodded. "Went straight for Bobby's. Whoever did this has to be the guy on the video you were talking about."

"And he got here first."

Reed pushed through the ruined door, and they both walked around inside the cramped space filled with old boat detritus, life jackets, tackle boxes, ropes, and buoy floats. Reed didn't find the submersible Bobby spoke of in his podcasts. He seemed to also be using the locker for personal storage. Boxes presumably from their old house stood stacked against the far wall. They'd been searched. Some of their contents lay scattered on the floor.

They sifted through Bobby and Sami's life before the death of their beloved Mariah. A photo in a tarnished silver frame sat atop the contents of the last box. An older Asian man and a young girl stood in front of a brand-new-looking boat. *Mariah's Spirit* scrawled across the stern behind them. Bobby's mom and her father when she was a child.

"Seems like your suspect left no stone unturned," Coyote said after about an hour of searching.

"Yeah," Reed muttered, disappointed. "We should go."

"Hold on, now," Coyote said and crawled underneath one of the tables near the cage's front wall. He pulled out a plastic milk crate filled with wires and other equipment. "What do we have here?"

Reed walked over, peering at the thin square of black netting in Coyote's grasp. "What the hell is that?"

"I believe it is the spit screen for a standing microphone," Coyote said and tossed it to Reed. "The kind one might set on a desk while recording a podcast."

"I thought Bobby might have been recording here, but..." The harbor sounds still came through the heavy walls and door. The ting of chains, horns, seagull calls, and traffic nearby. "Nat said he made the podcasts in a quiet place, like a studio. This isn't it."

"But it would be close."

Reed shook his head. That wasn't enough. Shops, office buildings, restaurants, and hotels all fanned inland from the harbor.

"Listen, I talked to some guys out on the water as they were rigging their boats to go out. I got an earful about how nice and smart Bobby was, but not much else. Some of them said they tossed him work here and there. There is one guy I think is willing to talk away from the crowd."

"Oh yeah?" Reed caught the flash of a red light out of the corner of his eye. A softball-sized object sat atop one of the beams of wood that crisscrossed the ceiling. The red light in its center mass steady, unblinking. Could be a smoke detector, Reed thought, but something ticked at his senses. His hand slid to his waist holster.

"I heard most of the locals go to a dive bar about a mile from here called the Sea Shanty. I think we should check it out."

"Yeah," Reed said, squinting at the device. His gut squirmed, and he motioned for Coyote silently. Putting his finger to his mouth, he then pointed up at the ceiling and mouthed, "What is that?"

When Coyote looked up, the device moved, and flexible blades snapped up from the inside of the drone fuselage and whirled like a tiny helicopter. It dove at them, pellets blasting out like firecrackers. Blindingly fast, Reed drew and fired on the drone, blowing it out of the air. It landed in a hail of shattered plastic on the cement floor. Actuators whirred as the drone continued to try to fly. He strode over to it and leaned above it, peering into the camera. He stared for a second, muttering under his breath. The red light flickered as the device's lens struggled to focus on him. He fired again.

"Are you okay?"

Coyote rubbed an angry red mark on his neck but nodded. "Yeah, but I'm getting damn tired of those things shooting at me every chance they get."

Holstering his weapon, Reed called Nat.

She answered after one ring. "What's up?"

"I need your help here at the harbor."

"Who'd you shoot?"

"Not a who, a what." He described the drone as he moved the shattered camera with his boot. "I think I just let the killer know we're onto him."

16

The White Lion

Flashes of the job burned behind his eyes as he leaned over the soldering iron and wires. The television flickered in the background, playing a recording of a newscaster at the scene of a political rally. That day played over and over in his head. The snap of the curtain a moment before he fired. The certainty he'd hit his mark. Screams from the crowd in the distance. Through the scope, beneath the fluttering flags of the speaker's country, the audience scattered, the target's security piling on top, too late to save his life.

He'd moved quickly, smoothly, breaking down the rifle and assembling it back into the crutches he'd used to conceal the weapon from hotel security. Everything was going as planned. Halfway through, a noise at the door made him freeze. A young woman dressed in a maid's uniform had snuck onto the closed floor. It was under construction and locked. She shouldn't have been able to enter, but there she was, a lit cigarette in her hand, shock on her face. She turned and ran, screaming as the White Lion went after her, but the building and the surrounding area were soon choked with *polizei* as they searched for the assassin.

She escaped the White Lion that night, but not the men looking for him. They'd found her. Questioned her and dumped her body on the same spot he'd taken their leader's life. And then they'd come after him. He wished they'd killed him, because now...

A soft tone broke through his reverie, and he glanced at the surveillance feed on the screen next to him. One of his drones was offline. The camera had sent a data burst stating it sustained damage. A last message before it went dead. The White Lion played it back, watching with fascination as Detective Reed stared straight up at the mobile camera, his movements jerking like a flip-book animation as he aimed for the drone. He said something. His lips moved as he fired, but the damage had corrupted the audio.

The White Lion paused the feed, staring at the look in the detective's eyes in that moment. Leaning back, he regarded the man he'd been warned about and finally saw it. No fear. No surprise. Just the look of a stone-cold killer as he peered down the barrel at the White Lion. He hit play again, watching Reed's lips, and then frowned when he got it.

I've seen you, too.

17

Ventura Harbor

The Sea Shanty was a hole-in-the-wall bar with actual saloon doors and peanut shells on the floor. Dim lighting from fake lanterns strung along the ceiling lit up burgundy vinyl booths and dusty netting tacked to the walls. Blown glass spheres and foam buoys seemed to be caught in the tangled strands. When Reed and Coyote walked in, the customers in the dark corners glanced over, then looked away. Dockworkers, fishermen, the rough set. No tourists. The scent of old fry oil and greasy burgers hit him as they surveyed the place.

Reed texted Luna about the drone and told her he'd asked Chet at the front office to post one of the harbor security guards there. Coyote elbowed Reed and nodded at the bar. A guy sitting at the end waved them over. He wore his long curly hair strung through the back of his cap, dark brown waterproof bib overalls, and rubber boots. He was working a rum and Coke when they walked up. He said his name was Pitch Williams.

"Rich?" Reed asked, sliding onto one of the stools next to him.

"Pitch. As in pitch and roll. My dad was a fisherman and a moron, apparently," Pitch said and took another sip of his drink.

Coyote put some bills on the counter for the next round of drinks and lit a cigarette, offering one to Pitch, who took it. After it was lit, Pitch took a long drag, as if he hadn't had one in years, and then used it to point at Reed.

"Your buddy and I were talking about Bobby. He said you're looking for him. Is he in some kind of trouble?"

"Not from my end," Reed said, eyeing the cook behind the counter. He didn't seem to care about the smoking. "Someone attacked him in his townhouse."

"Oh shit," Pitch said and sat up straight. "Is he okay?"

"That's what we're trying to ascertain," Coyote said through an exhaled cloud of smoke. "You said you knew him. What do you think he'd do if someone kicked in his door and started shooting?"

"Is that what happened?" Pitch looked at them with shock. "What the hell, man?"

"That's what it looks like." Reed took out his sketchbook and slid the still of the white-haired stranger over to Pitch. Nat had printed it out for him before he left. "Have you ever seen this guy around here?"

"No." Pitch frowned at the image. "He doesn't look like he'd go unnoticed. Is he one of them albino people?"

"That's unlikely," Reed said. "If he's a hired killer, he'd need excellent vision. People with albinism have nystagmus, involuntary eye movement."

Pitch and Coyote both looked at Reed for a beat, then Coyote said, "Either way, where do you think Bobby might have gone?"

"That I don't know. We weren't that close. But, to answer your question about the attack, Bobby was a nerd, sure. But he wasn't a pushover. He worked the boat like a pro. Like Sami taught him. He was a tough kid. If someone went after him, he'd give them a fight."

"Do you have any idea where he might lie low?" Reed turned when a man dressed in jeans and a T-shirt walked in from outside. He nodded at the cook, slid into a booth, and stuck his nose in a menu. Reed turned back to Pitch. "Would you or any of your colleagues offer him berth?"

Pitch finished off most of his drink, glancing around. "Look, we've all let Bobby sleep it off on our boats at one time or another. He took his father's death hard, so we helped him out, you know. A few of us helped him haul whatever was left of his father's boat when it floated to the surface that next day."

"Did you find anything odd out there?" Reed asked.

"You know, I did. The whole area around the wreck looked like it had been chummed. Fish parts floating around everywhere."

"You don't see that every day," Coyote intoned.

Pitch shrugged. "We gave him jobs when we could, but it's been tough all around this season. Charters are dropping off since the park service closed off some favorite snorkeling locations for conservation efforts or whatever. Either way, Bobby was losing friends with that crazy talk about aliens and shit. Sailors of all kinds tend toward superstition. We don't need more to worry about. I told him to cool it. Maybe write it down or something, but he had to stop spouting off in here and on the jobs we gave him."

"Did he?" Reed asked, writing down notes as Pitch spoke. "Lay off the tall tales?"

"He did, actually. Said he was starting some radio show."

"Podcast," Coyote said, dropping his cigarette butt in Pitch's nearly empty glass. "Any idea where he'd go to record it?"

"You know what...Midas might." Pitch made a low whistle, and a guy from the dark corner near the jukebox looked up. He came over. "Midas, this guy is from Homeland. He's trying to find Bobby. Did you know that someone broke into his house and shot at him?"

"What? No." Midas shook Reed's and Coyote's hands but gave them a bit of side-eye. He was almost a carbon copy of Pitch in dress and hat choice. Though his hair was black and short.

"You told me he was talking about recording a radio show, remember? It was a few months back."

"Yeah, maybe," Midas said, eyeing Coyote.

Coyote grinned. "I'm not a Fed. And though he looks like it, Agent Reed's not really one of them either. We think that whoever attacked Bobby also went after a friend of ours. We want to talk to him about it."

"Oh yeah?" Midas said. "What'd he do to your friend?"

"He tortured him for information, then locked him in a building and burned him to death," Reed said evenly. "So, you understand our urgency for Bobby."

Pitch and Midas stared with horror at Reed before Midas finally answered.

"He, uh, he said he was gonna look into a communal workspace thing. That place over on Lexington. Flex—something."

Pitch snapped his fingers with recognition. "That's it. Flex Space."

"Come again?" Coyote asked.

"It's this building with, like, conference rooms and other office-type spaces for rent or something," Pitch explained.

"It's in town?" Reed asked, already texting Nat. "You sure that's the name?"

"I think so." Pitch looked at Midas. "Is that what you remember?" Midas nodded.

Reed handed out his card and turned to leave, but Pitch said, "You're gonna find him in time, right?"

Reed nodded. "I will do my level best."

A few minutes later, while they waited for Nat in the harbor parking lot, Reed looked up the business on his phone. The retail chain offered workspaces to content creators and small businesses. Offices for teleconferences, access to 3D printers and supplies, even a rentable commercial kitchen. Next to him, Coyote fielded calls on his cell, turning and whispering in conversation.

"What're you so busy with?" Reed asked, spotting the long black sedan from the airport.

Coyote ended the call and looked at Reed. "I have to go."

"Something wrong?"

"I need to meet with a guy," Coyote said, already walking away from the approaching sedan. "It's about your buddy, Jacoby."

The car pulled up, and Nat leaned out the open back window. "Where's he going?"

Reed watched his friend hop on his motorcycle and take off. "I'm not sure I want to know."

Nat climbed out of the car, and whoever was driving pulled away. She had a leather messenger bag hanging across her body; the ting of her instruments sounded from within.

"So where is this killer drone you claim attacked you? Maybe I can get some info off of it."

Reed winced. "You should've just brought a baggie."

The most Nat could do with the drone in the storage cage was sweep up all the parts and slide them into an evidence envelope. She said she'd take a look at it back in the Field Ops building. Luna called and told them Jacoby had ordered her to close down the storage building and dust for prints in Bobby's cage. Maybe the guy who broke in left something behind. It was a long shot, but he wanted it done. They were also pulling the feed from the harbor's security cameras to see if they could catch a better look at him.

"I don't care what they said about you, Agent Reed," Luna said with amusement. "You do seem to be worth the headache."

Reed faked a chuckle, wondering whom she'd been talking to. He told her about Flex Space and said he and Nat were on their way. They took Reed's car, deciding to hit the Flex Space property next since it was only ten minutes away.

Nat wanted to inspect some of the drone parts, so Reed drove. Twenty-five minutes and a lot of traffic later, they pulled up to the building.

"If I had to guess," Nat said as they walked in, "I'd say the drone fuselage, if you will, was machine printed. Something about the seams...hopefully the flight controller will have more."

"What can you get from the motherboard or whatever?"

She smiled at that. "If you didn't completely decimate them with your sharpshootin' back there, the electronics, or brain, of the drone could give us input it processed. Data from obstacle avoidance sensors, the pilot's commands, if it was run off a light AI and making its own decisions, we'll get the logic flow, stuff like that. Also, there might be GPS data used to adjust the drone's behavior. So, not nothing."

"If I didn't kill it."

"We'll find something."

Nat said it with such finality, Reed didn't dare doubt it.

The front lobby reminded Reed of one of those chain coffeehouses where people go to sit and work at long uncomfortable tables. Dark colors with textile artwork gave it a warm, organic kind of vibe. Spa music played over the low din of people working at booths and small tables. Patrons came and went, dressed in business suits, workout clothes, jeans and tees.

There was even a guy in pajama bottoms, though he had a man bun, so it figured, Reed thought. Something about the crowd prickled at the edges of his consciousness, but he couldn't snag it.

They found an information desk at the side of the space and wandered over. Reed signaled to the attendant, a middle-aged man with alien-green hair worn in small spikes all over his scalp. He came over with a friendly smile, swishing as he walked because everything he wore was made of jute or burlap or some kind of natural fiber. He gasped audibly when they showed him their credentials.

"Are you for reals from Homeland?" He leaned forward, whispering, "Is this a raid?"

"Why, whatcha got back there?" Nat asked with a grin. "Anything good?"

"Oh—" His eyes grew wide.

"Just kidding," Nat cut across him as she squinted at his photo dangling from a lanyard. "Owen, is it?"

He covered it with his hand subconsciously and nodded. "Should I call my manager?"

"No one's in trouble," Reed said, pulling up Bobby's photo on his phone. "This man was attacked recently, and we're trying to find him."

Owen blinked at the photo, then glanced up, worried. "What does Bobby have to do with *Homeland*?" he hissed.

"You know him?" Reed asked, slipping his card across the counter. "Was he a client here?"

"Yes, uh..." He pointed at a door to the side of the counter. "He rented one of the mini recording studios for a while."

"Did you ever talk to him?" Reed asked. "About anything outside of his business here?"

"Oh, crap, is this about the aliens? Was he telling the truth?" He looked from Reed to Nat with terrified curiosity. "You know what? I think I'll call my manager."

While Owen did that, Reed called Luna. Inside of a half hour, Owen got a call from the owner, who'd just spoken with a very convincing woman from Homeland. He told Owen to cooperate. According to the account that Owen looked up for them, Bobby used the phone-booth-sized recording studios for a few months, but the records showed he hadn't been back since March.

They checked out the room. Reed searched the booth for something Bobby might have hidden there but found nothing.

Back at the front, talking to Owen, Reed said, "You never answered my question. Did you ever speak with Bobby?"

"I don't want to give federal agents the wrong idea about him. He was a great customer. Came in on time, cleared out of the room on time, paid up front without hassle. A really nice guy." Owen gazed out at the sea of worktables. "One time, he brought in a pastry and I commented on how good it smelled, and the next time he came in, he'd brought me one, too. He's a nice guy."

"Yeah, but you already said aliens, man," Nat said. "No going back from that one."

"Okay, look, I heard from some people here about what he was saying. Time portals and other dimensions." Owen shrugged. "I thought he was just quirky. You're saying he was right?"

While Reed continued with Owen, Nat slipped behind the counter and rooted around in the system. Luna told her she should have access to Flex Space's security cameras.

"Who told you about the aliens?" Reed asked.

"No one. One of my jobs is to check out the equipment before and after use. You know, for damage and stuff. I went into one of the sound booths after Bobby one time and found some notes. I think they were for his podcast." Owen touched his palm to his chest. "I honestly thought people had the wrong idea. I thought he was doing, like, a story hour. You know, fantastic tales. Are you saying he was onto something real?"

"I'm not saying anything. I'm *asking* if you ever saw Bobby talking with anyone else here?" Reed pushed past Owen's question. "You must have a lot of regulars that get to know each other. Would he have confided in one of them if he was in trouble?"

"I didn't see him talk with anyone more than chitchat by the coffee bar or whatever."

"Anyone counts. Did he spend time with the person who refilled the coffee machine? Maybe he talked with the previous sound room renter about something. Did he use one of the spots at the table and bother his neighbor at length?"

"He was kind of a loner." Owen leaned against the front of the counter and stroked his chin. "Though he did ask for the Job List one time. Maybe he met someone there?"

Reed paused his pen over his page and looked at him. "Job List?"

Owen explained that it was a list of regulars and their skills for hire. It was available only to people who paid a membership fee. So, a vetted clientele for them, and a discount for regulars who needed work done. Bobby had asked to see the list with audio/visual professionals.

"Did he connect with anyone?" Reed asked.

Owen shrugged. "Not that I know of, but I can send you the link."

"I want the master list," Nat said from behind them. "The entire file, Owen. Unedited."

"I wouldn't—"

"I don't care what kind of sketchy stuff you guys are peddling off the books," Nat said. "Hackers, forgery experts. I talked to a friend of mine at LAPD Cybercrime before we got here. My partner and I don't care about any of that right now. We're looking for a missing person, so if I find out you held back, I'll make you regret it."

Owen stopped arguing and got them the file. Reed leaned against the counter while Nat updated Luna about the list.

"Who do you know at LAPD Cybercrime?" Reed asked.

Nat gave him a dazzling smile. "Jealous?"

He smirked, looking away. "Too cruel."

About an hour and a half later, Luna assured them that Gray Zone was in possession of the security camera data from the harbor and Flex Space, as well as the master list of jobs. Reed left Owen his number in case he remembered anything, and they headed out for lunch.

Nat had somehow talked Reed into trying something called boba, which seemed to be sweet, milky tea with choking hazards. He concentrated on the cookies they'd also bought as they sat in the cat-themed café.

"What do you think?" Reed asked as Nat swiped through the list on her tablet.

"I think being this close to LA isn't working to our advantage. There're more than five hundred names on here offering audio/visual services."

"Is there any way to tell if Bobby accessed the list? Or better yet, which names he clicked on?"

Nat shook her head and held up the tablet. "Not with this."

They decided to head back, with Reed waiting for her to turn her back before dumping his drink in the trash. They had just slipped into the car, when his phone rang.

"Agent Reed," he said, feeling like it sounded dumb.

"This...this is Fiona. Owen called me and said Homeland is looking for me...is that right?" Her voice broke with stress. "He said I might be in danger."

"In danger?" Reed signaled to Nat and mouthed, "Fiona." She turned down the air conditioning to hear better. Then he put the call on speaker. "Why would he say that?"

"Because I did some work for Bobby back in April, and it was...weird."

Nat held up the tablet to show three Fionas on the list.

"What's your last name, ma'am?" Reed scribbled notes in his sketchbook.

"Fiona Wells. I do digital rendering work. You know, for like indie films and stuff."

"And you worked with Bobby on..."

"On a recording he'd made with a submersible...he called it a rover. Anyway, he wanted me to clean it up. Is he okay?"

Reed stilled and locked eyes with Nat. "Wait, you've seen the recording of the night his father's boat sank?"

Fiona let out a little snort-laugh. "Yeah, like a thousand times."

18

Invision Effects and Engineering – Los Angeles County

Reed was surprised at the dramatic change in weather when they drove inland from Ventura Harbor. The ocean breeze grew hotter, if that was possible. Eventually, the sand and palm trees gave way to skyscrapers and sprawling venues. It turned out that Fiona had moved since working with Bobby. She'd followed a job an hour and some change south to LA County. She worked for a small audio and visual engineering company about seven miles from downtown LA. Fiona agreed to meet, but they had to come to her workplace because everyone was on deadline, and the producer said no one was allowed to leave until they finished.

"I can take, like, a long break, though," Fiona said on the call. "Frank isn't a monster."

She gave them the address and asked them to text when they arrived so she could go out to meet them.

Nat drove since she was familiar with the area, and Reed wanted to think. Something was bugging him, but things were moving so fast he couldn't put a finger on it. Maybe it was how differently people in LA seemed to dress and move. Pulling out his notebook, he chewed on his inner cheek as he sketched out one of the large crystals he'd seen in Marla's gallery. There was something there...

Nat told him that the geek lair's servers hadn't yielded much. Xanadu had opened the file they'd used to store information on Bobby about twenty minutes before the fire was reported, but he couldn't get into the Gray Zone files because it needed Reed's face to unlock them. Everything they knew about the case, their strategy, and Reed's notes had all been downloaded.

"He's so far ahead of us," she muttered. "He knows how we think. How we break apart cases."

Reed closed his leather notebook. "Then he knows he should be worried."

Multistory hacienda-style buildings with arched entries and wrought iron accents shared space with metal and reflective glass high rises along the industrial area. Everything seemed to be dusty, as if blasted by the annual Santa Ana winds. Traffic sent the smell of hot rubber and sizzling tar wafting along the gritty breeze. Reed rolled down the window, and it felt like a hair dryer was blasting in his face. The taste of dirt and smoke lingered in the air as they moved past the traffic from the nearby Los Angeles Zoo and skirted Glendale but made good time.

The address Fiona provided took them to an area with large warehouse-style studios and vast parking structures. Further down the street, they passed rows of smaller three-story buildings that resembled business offices.

"I think that's it," Nat said as she veered toward the entrance gate.

Invision Effects and Engineering was a modest studio that catered to indie films. The visual and audio effects were their bread and butter, according to the website Reed had dug up on them, but they also offered software support for practical effects, like animatronics. Black metal bars cordoned off a building set back from the street, and one had to pass a guardhouse at the gate to enter the lot. Nat pulled up to the window.

"Help you folks?" A young man, skinny in a too-big security guard uniform, leaned out of the guardhouse. His hair was styled in a long shaggy wolf cut, as if he'd stepped off an eighties heavy metal band album cover. His name was Laken. He showed them where to go in the parking garage and warned them the elevator was broken. "The offices you want are on the other side of the parking garage, not this front one. You gotta park, walk through the garage to the east entrance, go out that door, and the engineering department is across the courtyard."

Reed texted Fiona and told them they were there. She said she'd meet them in the courtyard. Nat found a spot on the first floor, and they parked. At nearly two in the afternoon, the heat from the ambient air prickled his face when he stepped out of the air-conditioned car. The structure was dark and stifling, but as they walked out the door on the other side of the garage, they found themselves in a courtyard between the buildings. Old valley oaks lined the central sidewalk, providing dappled shade that helped the heat considerably.

"Might want to rethink all the black there, Dracula," Nat said with a grin.

"I think I should've brought more biodegradable-looking clothes to LA."

A street vendor with a brightly colored kiosk sold fruit cups with spicy sauce near a group of people doing tai chi underneath a large tree. A man in a Hawaiian shirt strummed softly on a ukelele, humming to no one in particular as he sat lotus style in a spot of sun. Reed shook his head. It was a different world out here.

Fiona met them at a plastic picnic table near the entrance to the building. A redhead with a wild mop of curls, a dusting of freckles across her nose, and a huge smile, she leaned a hip on the table while sipping from a dewy can of soda.

"Ms. Wells," Reed greeted her.

"Fiona, please. And I'm sorry you had to come out here. It's crunch time, you know?"

"Not a problem," Nat said with a friendly smile. "We're glad you called."

"Thank God for Owen. He's a sweetheart for letting me know. I had no idea what was going on. I've been on a digital diet." She looked at Reed. "Have you ever tried it?"

"I don't know what that—"

"You know, dig in with work and creativity. Avoid the negativity of online stuff." She glanced at Nat. "You should totally give it a try."

"Mmm, I'll think about it," Nat said and shot Reed an amused look. As if she would ever intentionally disconnect.

They all took a seat at the table, and Fiona explained she did mostly foley or sound procurement but had been pulled onto a project at the last minute. It was a film about AI and the director "absolutely hated" the graphics for the character's digital interface, or something to that effect. "So, you know, even though I'm mostly a sound engineer, I've done a lot of visual work in college, and when I was on small films."

"That's what Bobby needed?" Reed steered her focus. "Your help with his recording?"

"Yeah, yeah," Fiona said. "As you know, he got my name from the Jobs List via Owen. He said when he contacted me that he needed help cleaning up artifact noise and blurry visuals for a camera used underwater. I thought it was like a 'swimming with the sharks' kind of deal. Bobby mentioned he did charters, but this was…not that."

"How so?" Reed asked, scratching out notes with his fountain pen.

She explained that he'd had trouble finding someone with a data lens reader. That kind of storage choice was unusual for a consumer-grade underwater camera setup, but Bobby told her he'd refurbished the machine from a scientific research program that had gone belly-up.

Reed was familiar with the storage device from a previous case. Data lenses were layered glass circles that resembled clear disks. The size of a silver dollar, their etchings and facets made them ideal for bulk storage, according to Nat. Though they were not commonly used, as they needed a specialized reader.

"So, it was a lot of data," Nat said. "More than images and sound?"

Fiona nodded. "I think so. There were other readings, like for scientific study or something. You know, water temp, current readings, uh…I think there was GPS pinpoint on there. I told Bobby I had a reader because I worked on large data projects for studios, but that's all I had. I said I could maybe do something with the audio and visual static, but the other stuff was not in my wheelhouse. He seemed to be okay with that and told me to do what I could."

"And what did you do, exactly?" Reed asked, writing down as many of her terms as he could while she explained.

"I removed the ambient sound, sharpened the images, but it was dark, and it was underwater. There was a shape, but it was distorted. It was fast, though. I was surprised. I heard a sort of metal clang, like a gong. And then a while later, a definite blast. When I first talked to Bobby about the job, he said he'd heard an explosion on the surface. Like a boat backfiring, but I don't think so. What I heard sounded much louder than that." Fiona's eyes grew wide as she spoke. "Anyway, I think it damaged the data. There were gaps in the recording. It went full-exposure white at one point. The current readings went haywire, like the water was going in all directions or something. Like I told you on the phone. It was a weird recording."

"Did you say anything to Bobby?"

"When he offered me the job, he said he'd caught what he believed was evidence of an underwater collision, possibly with a vessel or large animal. Again, I was thinking marine mammal gets hit by jet ski or something. But honestly, I've never seen anything move like that. A torpedo, maybe…" Fiona's brows pulled down. "And it definitely didn't move like an animal. Too fast. It changed direction weird, too."

Nat shot a look at Reed. Bad news. It was likely Fiona had seen something she wasn't supposed to.

"What kind of software did you use?" Nat asked.

"That was a pain because Bobby was adamant that I promise not to upload the video to any online filters or programs. So, I was limited and had to do the cleanup with programs I already had on my system or cloud. We all use AI for the details. It saves hours, but Bobby was almost scared about it. Like someone was going to steal his recording or something."

"He was afraid of someone finding out what you were working on?" Nat asked. "Were you careful?"

"Yeah, I did everything manually with equipment I had at home, or I stole some time here at the studio. I did manage to sharpen the main acoustics, and I swear, it sounded—" Fiona shook her head as if clearing her thoughts. "Never mind."

"Tell me what popped into your mind just now," Reed urged. "Believe me, nothing is too weird for this case."

She looked at him with doubt. "Seriously?"

"What did you hear?"

"It was muffled, of course, it was in the ocean, but I could've sworn I heard...glass cracking?"

"Did Bobby tell you that's what it was?" Reed asked.

"What? No. I didn't get a chance to talk with him about the contents of the data lens recording. Not really. He was super antsy the last time we met."

Reed showed her a photo of the white-haired stranger, but she didn't recognize him.

"My roommate does hair and makeup," Fiona said, tilting her head to gaze at the photo. "I really feel like the hair on this guy is fake...right? It's too stiff."

"Stiff?" Reed stared at the photo.

Nat leaned forward. "Listen, when I asked if you were careful just now, I didn't mean the job. I meant, did you tell anyone else about what you saw on the recording or your connection with Bobby?"

Fiona was quiet for a moment, the gravity of the situation hitting her. "I *am* in danger, aren't I?"

"Someone attacked Bobby in his home. I think you should stay with someone for a few nights. Go out of town," Nat answered. "Just as a precaution."

She started to hyperventilate a little, and Reed softened his tone. "I know you're frightened, but I need you to think, Fiona. Who knows about this recording and that you did it for Bobby?"

"I mean, I might have mentioned working on a side job to some friends before I moved, but I don't think I said what it was exactly. Bobby was really paranoid about it not getting out."

"Okay, that's good. Walk me through what happened. Bobby called and hired you. You guys met, I presume, at Flex Space?"

Fiona sniffled. "Yeah. When he first contacted me, I quoted him two grand, and he said he'd not be able to pay until April. He mentioned insurance money that was coming. Once April came around, I met him at Flex Space...well, outside it by a coffee cart."

"And how long did it take you?" Nat asked.

"Well, that's just it. Not long, really. I called Bobby, set up a meeting in early May to hand it back to him and get the second half of my payment.

He cancelled at the last minute. He said it wasn't safe. Which freaked me out."

"Did you ever connect with him?" Reed asked.

"Yeah, uh, a week or so later, we met back at Flex Space, and he even gave me a tip. I made twenty-five hundred on the job."

"And that was it?" Nat asked. The tone of her voice made Reed glance over.

"What do you mean?" Fiona's face flushed.

"Now, I'm on the tech side of things, and I always, *always*, make a copy of the original before I even start to work on anything. Especially if it's going to court or someone is acting super sketchy about it. You know, for insurance."

Fiona's eyes slid from her guiltily. Nat leaned across the table. "I'm going to need your copy, Fiona. No argument. No denials. Just the data lens."

"You don't want any part of what Bobby was mixed up with," Reed added. "Let us help you get clear of this."

There were in fact denials and some First Amendment protests until Reed reminded Fiona that she had just admitted to using Invision company equipment for her side-hustle job for Bobby. When Nat got up to go and speak with her boss about a subpoena to seize the equipment, Fiona suddenly remembered the data lens was at her apartment.

"Look, I can't leave, though," Fiona said with a wince. "If I leave, I lose my job. They're not kidding. I can't afford to get fired. Can I please just have like two hours? And then I'll go with you guys."

"You understand you're in possible danger," Nat asked, her look incredulous.

"I'm safe here." Fiona waved her hand around the serene courtyard. "There's a guard gate, and I'll be inside a sound studio the whole time."

She finally agreed to forty-five minutes, which would give her time to hand off her tasks for a few days. Reed told her not to leave the building without them or a security guard. Meanwhile, they went to speak with her boss, Frank, in his office, who turned out to be a pretty cool guy. He looked like he taught literature at a liberal university and was understandably concerned for his employee. They kept it vague. Telling him that Fiona may be a witness to a crime and that her leaving was not really her choice.

He assured them her job was safe. Nat emailed them a photo of the white-haired suspect to circulate with the staff, telling them to call the police immediately if he was seen.

They got directions from Frank to Fiona's office and made their way up to the third floor. Posters of various movies, commercials, and other productions lined the hallway. When they got there, a woman sat at the desk, but it wasn't Fiona. This woman was a skinny blonde who looked up, surprised.

"Who are you?" Nat asked.

"I'm Willa. I'm taking over for Fiona for a few days. What are you guys doing up here?"

"We're looking for Fiona," Reed said, his gut checking him. "Where is she?"

"She was supposed to wait for us here," Nat said, picking up his concern. "Is she in the bathroom?"

Willa stood, confused. "*You* told her to meet you in the garage."

The hairs on Reed's neck rose. "When?"

"Like a few minutes after she got here." Willa's gaze went from his to Nat's, worried. "She was explaining something, and she got a text. She said it was from Agent Reed, that there was a problem, and that you wanted her to meet you at her car right away. She was scared—"

Reed took off running back down the hallway. He slammed through the stairwell door, Nat a step behind as they raced the two flights down. Nat called it in to Luna while Reed dialed Fiona.

"We have a possible situation," Nat rasped as they took steps two at a time. "We think the suspect lured Fiona Wells away from her building. We need backup at 21347 Baxter Keith Road, Burbank. Possible abduction in the parking garage on premises. Be advised, there is a guard gate."

Reed tried calling a third time as they pushed through the ground-floor stairwell door. They rushed across the lobby, across the courtyard to the garage entrance. A bloodcurdling scream tore out from within, followed by a sharp popping sound. Reed's jaw ground at the noise as he and Nat flanked the door, pressing their backs to the stucco wall.

"Fiona?" Reed called out.

Another scream, weaker, and Reed moved. They cleared the floor, calling for Fiona. The garage looked empty. Reed signaled to Nat, and they searched the cars. The smell of pepper spray lingered in the air, and a bejeweled canister sat on the floor next to a little red coupe. He waved Nat over, and they crept up on the vehicle on both sides.

"Oh no," Reed holstered his weapon. "Call an ambulance!"

Fiona sat slumped in the driver's seat of her car, her purse upended on the concrete floor just outside the open door, the contents scattered. A ragged wound tore her abdomen open, and blood pooled beneath her blouse, spreading quickly. Reed grabbed a sweatshirt draped over the passenger seat and used it to apply pressure. The blood, warm beneath his palms, saturated the material, and his gaze found Nat just outside the passenger window.

She paced, her gaze roving the area as she spoke on the phone with dispatch. "We need a bus at Invision Engineering and Effects. Parking garage. Possible stab wound. Suspect is still at large..."

Barely breathing, Fiona looked pale, crimson spatters dotted her delicate chin and neck. Her pulse fluttered frantically at her throat, trying to keep up with the loss of blood. In the distance, the sirens wailed.

Nat stepped in with a first aid kit the security guard, Laken, had given them. The young man stared, wide eyed, as Nat stuffed Fiona's wound with roll after roll of gauze.

"Is she going to be okay?" he asked with a shaky voice.

"Where the hell are the paramedics?" Nat muttered. "Can you go and make sure to wave them in?"

He nodded and ran back to his gatehouse, looking like he might puke.

The patrol officers arrived a minute later, swarming the garage and cordoning off the entrances from looky-loos. The blood on Reed's hands cooled, got sticky, and he paced a few feet away, anger burning through him. Reed wondered how the attacker could do that—how did he fake his number to Fiona?

A noise in the garage level above caught his attention, and he strode up the rising path to the second floor. He wandered the rows of vehicles, listening. And then he saw it. Furtive movement near a parked truck. Like someone climbing out from underneath, then a sliver of light as the rear emergency exit door of the garage eased open. Reed took a step forward, then another, and spotted him. A tall man, thin, but with jet-black hair and a medical mask.

Reed moved through the cars in a crouch, his gun coming out, then he popped up and yelled, "Homeland Security, move and you're dead!"

Shots exploded in the garage, the windshield next to Reed shattered with a round. He ducked, getting his bearings as car alarms blared. Reed rose, spotted motion, and ran toward it. More shots blasted off the cement pillars of the garage, a car hood, going wild. He raised his weapon to fire back, moving forward, trying to flank him, when the emergency door slammed open and the figure slipped through. A glimpse of steel flashed in the assailant's hand before he was gone. Reed ran to the door and glanced out. The suspect leapt down the flights of metal emergency stairs, taking four at a time, then jumped to the ground. When he landed, he turned and fired at Reed, who ducked back into the garage door entrance. A moment later, Reed chanced a peek back out. There was no one. The shooter had vanished like a cat in the night.

Panting with adrenaline, Reed pulled his phone and called Luna. "We need a net, now. This guy is in the area." He gave her the description and told her what happened. She said she was in touch with local PD, had informed them of the task force operating in the area, and would ask them to mobilize.

Back on the ground level, the paramedics had arrived. While arriving officers searched the rest of the garage floors, the paramedics worked on Fiona, trying to get her onto the gurney. She had saline and oxygen, and a paramedic fought to apply a pressure bandage. Nat stood by a pillar, wiping her hands with a sanitizing cloth, watching them work. Reed walked over, and she offered him one from the package.

"He slipped away," Reed said, taking a wipe and cleaning off his hands and wrists.

"Did you get a look at his face?"

"He wore a mask, but I think Fiona was right about the hair. It was too black."

"So, the guy does disguises?"

"Maybe he does now." Reed told her about what he'd mouthed to the drone he shot.

She nodded. "You must've gotten to him if he changed his appearance."

A sinking feeling settled in his gut. "Or the images we have of him with the white hair are also fake, and we don't know what this guy looks like at all."

"How do we run this scene?" Nat asked. "Did you get a shot off?"

"He was too fast."

Luna called Reed back as the paramedics loaded up Fiona. "I'm liaising with LAPD, but I'll get you out of there as soon as possible."

Nat spoke with one of the paramedics. They had no idea what kind of wound Fiona sustained, but it was bad. When they drove off, Reed showed a photo to her on his phone. It was an image of a large hunting-style knife.

"The assailant had this on him. I saw it when he ran out of the exit. It's an injection knife," Reed said. "It's called a Reaper. I saw them working undercover on a weapons-smuggling case. They're from South Africa, I think." He swiped to show another photo. "Their hilt holds a canister of CO_2 that discharges an explosion of freezing, rapidly expanding gas into the wound through a hole at the tip of the blade."

"What the hell?" Nat looked at him, horrified.

"Yeah. They're modeled after those shark-deterrent spears that scuba divers use." Reed glanced at Fiona's car. He needed to get inside, see if the shooter found what he was after. "I heard that distinctive pop of the pressure release, and then I saw her. The knife leaves a very distinctive wound. The pressurized gas causes a kind of freezer burn to the surrounding tissue."

Nat looked at him, her face pale. "She looked like her middle just... ruptured. Like a split watermelon."

Reed glanced around. "Maybe just keep that description between us."

"You think she'll make it?"

"I don't know. I already sent this to Luna. Maybe they can trace the weapon."

Nat nodded at the photos. "That's spy craft. This guy is like a movie villain."

"He's just a man that—"

A low buzzing sound outside the garage entrance pulled Reed's attention. He turned to see a small round device, like a large hockey puck, zip into the garage. The sight was familiar to Reed in a déjà vu kind of way. Detached, out of place. The device skidded across the floor, and a flash of memory burned through Reed. Sand and smoke and burning asphalt. The smell of death.

"Bomb!" Reed yelled, diving with Nat behind a nearby car as Fiona's coupe exploded in a thunderous blast. Debris slashed through the garage, the sound deafening. On the floor, his ears ringing, he looked across the cement underneath the car and stared right into the fearful eyes of Slater.

"Reed..." Slater lay on the ground, dirt beneath him turning scarlet, military boots passing behind as troops scattered, the blast of return fire resonating in Reed's ears. Slater reached out to Reed, the skin of his trembling hand covered in raised, prickly goose bumps, the fingertips charred. "Find the key."

19

Two more ambulances arrived a few minutes after the explosion, followed by LA Fire, then the LAPD Explosives Unit, who took over. A paramedic checked Nat and Reed for concussions. Reed's ears still rang. Both he and Nat sustained cuts from flying shrapnel but otherwise escaped unscathed. Not so for the police officers who'd been closer to Fiona's car. The paramedics were loading them up as Reed and Nat headed out to review the security cameras. Luna was en route to Fiona's apartment with some agents. Reed filled her in about the explosion.

"Yes, I heard on the scanner," Luna said, a siren in the background. "Are you and Agent De La Cruz still operational?"

Reed grinned. She made them sound like robots. Maybe that's how she saw them—as tools. "We're scuffed up but fine. I'm headed to review the footage from the cameras in the garage. Maybe we'll get a better view of the assailant than we have so far." He told her he'd get an updated sketch of the assailant ASAP. "The hospital should know about the CO_2 weapon."

"I'll make sure they do. What else?"

"He shot at us and left spent casings. LAPD has them."

"We're in contact. Speaking of which, Mr. Doucet has still not activated his phone or checked in at Field Ops. But I understand he was with you in Ventura at the harbor storage. Is he with you in Los Angeles?"

"Yeah, he won't use your electronics, and I'd be surprised if he shows up at the Field Ops. Coyote does his own thing in the background," Reed said. "He'll be around when it counts."

"Very well. Keep me posted." Luna sighed and disconnected before Reed could answer.

As they were walking over to the security office, Reed told Nat about seeing Slater.

She listened silently, nodding slowly as he spoke, then, "You told one of the first responders you knew it was a bomb because you'd encountered it in the field. But I get the feeling that's not true."

"No. It's not. Slater faced that device before, not me. I think the sound triggered a latent memory inadvertently transferred from him."

"That's a scary thought." Nat looked up at him, her dark gaze worried. "What else is in there that you don't know about?"

"That's what I'm trying to find out," Reed said as the image of Slater's hand flashed in his mind. He'd had chicken skin. "It's why I need to see what's in the void in my head."

"I don't think you should be screwing with any mind mazes or thought castles at *all*, to be honest."

"Oh, you've been honest," Reed said, a little heated.

Nat stopped walking, and Reed turned to see why. She looked at him, her mouth set in a thin, tense line. "Did it ever occur to you that something destructive might come out of that void in your memory? That maybe it's the only thing keeping you from going off the deep end like Slater did?" She watched his face and nodded. "Yeah, didn't think so."

Reed didn't have an answer to that, so they walked the rest of the way in silence. A few minutes later, he and Nat stood in the security office with the head of the LAPD Explosives Unit and a security guard from the studio named Melissa. Multiple screens displayed recordings of the last hour. The head of the bomb squad, a silver-haired, veiny-nosed fireplug of a man named Captain Gene, pointed at the middle display.

"Go ahead and play it for them," he said to the guard.

Melissa was young and fast with the system, her neat ponytail shifting as she navigated the recording. She hit play seconds before the explosion, running it back at a quarter speed. The puck-shaped bomb raced into the garage, slid under the coupe where the paramedics had just removed Fiona, and exploded. Melissa froze the frame.

Reed narrowed his gaze at the screen. "Kind of small, isn't it?"

Lt. Gene nodded. "It was a focused blast to take out the car, I think. There's nothing left of the coupe. It's charcoal."

"Is there any way to trace the components?" Nat asked, tapping on her tablet. "Does this particular device have a name? Like Claymore or Bouncing Betty? It might give us some dealers to check out."

Lt. Gene shook his head. "Nah, unfortunately, fabrication plans for a simple guided grenade like this are available if you know where to look on the dark web. The housing can be made cheaply with an at-home 3D printer, and the explosive can be connected to a simple gaming remote control."

"You're saying he made it himself," Reed said, eyeing the damage. Limited mostly to the car itself, this was destruction of evidence. "He was covering his tracks."

"Well, we definitely can't get DNA or fingerprints from that mess," Nat said, eyeing the charred coupe on the screen.

"Also, it was a hell of a distraction," Lt. Gene said. "I heard the perimeter went up late because of it. These devices can be either on a timer or remotely detonated once navigated to the target as well, so you'd just throw one and take off during the chaos. Like one of those magicians disappearing in a cloud of smoke." He pressed his lips together, anger flitting across his features. "I saw them used in Syria by rebels fifteen years ago when I was in the military. They're not new and are getting easier to manufacture with consumer 3D printers. Hell, we ran across similar devices here in LA a few months ago at a packing center for drugs. The dealers put slots in the wall with these hockey-puck bombs in them like booby traps. As soon as the crash team entered the apartment, the devices swarmed out and started exploding. It was a mess."

Nat shook her head. "These homemade weapons are getting out of hand."

"Is there anything distinctive about the explosives?" Reed asked. "One of your team ran it through a preliminary sniffer."

"It was made from readily available ingredients at your hardware or garden store. This was a down-and-dirty weapon. Nothing sophisticated."

The security guard, Melissa, glanced at Reed, her ponytail swinging about her chin. "Do you want to see the altercation?"

Lt. Gene motioned to another display screen. "Show 'em."

A high-angle shot of the parking section played on the screen. It showed Fiona's red coupe sitting in a mid-range parking spot. The camera picked up movement in her front seat, though the lighting was bad. Shafts of sunlight filled with dust split across the view, obscuring half of the image. Melissa zoomed in on Fiona sitting in the front seat, and they could see her tapping on her phone. Behind her, a silhouette emerged from the darkened corner of the garage, walking slowly. He was tall, lanky, and moved like he was stalking prey. Fiona didn't seem to see him. She was talking to her phone as if on a video call. The assailant's hand swung, throwing something in the distance, and Fiona's head whipped right, away from her door. In that moment, the figure emerged, he ripped open her door and grabbed at her. He wore a watch cap over black hair, and a swath of material covered the lower half of his face. Same long dark coat with a high collar.

"That's gotta be him," Nat whispered.

"It's him." Reed recognized the eye shape, the pale skin, the long, narrow nose bridge...those he didn't disguise. "I watched the recording of him speaking with Bobby at least a hundred times. This guy moves the same."

On the monitor, Fiona screamed, yanking herself back into the car. She flailed, reaching for something as the assailant tore her purse from her hands. She turned, sprayed him in the face. He reared back, pulled something from his coat, and lunged at her. Then, a sharp pop of the CO_2 knife that sounded like a firecracker, followed by Fiona's second, weaker scream. A few seconds later, Reed and Nat ran into the garage in the recording, but Melissa paused the scene.

"That's why he missed me," Reed said. "He couldn't see because of the pepper spray."

"You lucked out," Nat said, looking at her buzzing phone. "Luna said to call her."

Reed and Nat thanked Lt. Gene and headed back out of the security office. They stopped in a breezeway leading off the courtyard to call Luna. He put her on speaker phone when she picked up.

"Anything new on the camera feed?" she asked without greeting.

"Not much. There's a better angle of the assailant in these images, but not a better look," Reed said. "He's using disguises."

"Gray Zone will acquire the feed from LAPD and see what can be done," Luna said. "We'll run it through the databases."

"Did you find anything at Fiona's?" Nat asked.

"We're at Ms. Well's apartment right now. We haven't found the data lens you spoke of," Luna said. "The residence looks ransacked. Someone did a thorough job of looking before we got there. Sliced couch cushions, panels torn off walls, every photograph stripped to see if the data lens was in the frame. We'll continue our search."

Reed wasn't sure if it was even there. Fiona had lied about making a copy in the first place. She could've lied about stashing it at her apartment as well. If she had it on her, there was a good chance the attacker took it.

"What about the perimeter? Were there any sightings of this guy?" Nat asked.

"Unfortunately, the perimeter disintegrated with news of the bomb. There's press at the gates right now."

"She's right." Nat showed him a news streamer's feed just outside the parking lot. "There's a big crowd."

"Also, I had another sweep of Bobby's townhouse done with more of a fine-tooth comb. They found scratches inside the front room smoke detector."

"Scratches?" Reed asked. Nat looked over at him, her brows pulled down with confusion.

"Yes," Luna said. "And the plastic insulation on one of the wires had markings as well. My techs believe it could indicate a surveillance device was attached and spliced into the power line. I believe he'd been listening to Bobby for quite some time. Weeks, maybe even months."

"The break-in at the main office of the townhouse development could have been a cover. Do the real damage to the office, hide the fact you shut off the cameras to break into a townhouse," Reed said.

"That's not a far-fetched scenario," Nat said. "He could've been scoping out human security coverage as well."

"I bet that's how he knew about Fiona," Reed said. "Bobby could've spoken to her on the phone while in his home. The timing is interesting."

"Yeah," Nat said. "What are the odds he moves on her at the exact moment we were there to speak to her?"

"Someone tipped him off." Reed remembered Rodney, the guy hired to stalk and shoot him in the park up in Seattle. "This man coming after Bobby hires people. One of them put a tracker on my car and motorcycle."

"I'll have a tech do a sweep of your vehicles. Your burners are encrypted. My guess is there are already images of you and your team circulating, Agent Reed. You need to be careful."

"Circulating, as in a bounty on our heads?" Nat asked. "That sucks."

"I'll give Coyote a heads-up." Reed glanced out at the courtyard.

"Hiring out surveillance makes sense if you're in a city with no connections," Luna said. "I'll get a cybercrime team to check out the local clearinghouses."

Reed looked at Nat, confused.

"They're like wanted ads on the dark web. If you need cash and have a casual relationship with the law, you can make good money," she explained. "Kind of a less sophisticated and much cheaper version of the Night Market."

Reed had been to the virtual auction house with Nat once. It nearly killed him.

"I will let you know what we learn," Luna said. "What are your next steps, Agent Reed?"

"I'm headed to the hospital to see about Fiona. If they bagged her property, I'll look through that as well. Maybe she hid the data lens in her clothes."

"I sent a two-man team to the hospital already. You can trade cars with them. Leave your key fob with the front reception. I'll have them acquire the victim's property and anything else that came in with Ms. Wells. Hold on." Luna spoke to someone, but it was muffled. Then she was back. "I'm told they found her phone. We'll need that ASAP. We're set up here to break in, and we could use Agent De La Cruz's help on that. I believe she worked on a program for Seattle PD's cybercrime unit... is that right?"

Nat grinned. "You just know everything, don't you?"

"I know more than most," Luna said. "Anything else?"

"From what we saw on the security feed, she might've recorded the attack," Reed said.

"Then we definitely need you, Agent De La Cruz. I'll send a car."

Nat turned to Reed. "While I'm there, I have an idea about getting in touch with Bobby with it."

"See you soon," Luna said and was gone.

"I guess I'm off to Field Ops. I need a shower anyway." Nat sighed, leaning back against the stucco wall of the breezeway, eyes closed. Fiona's blood stained the edges of her sleeves. "Maybe Luna has chocolate stashed somewhere."

Reed stood opposite her, relishing the cooling wind, watching it rustle her dark hair, splaying strands across her throat. "How're you holding up?"

"I feel like I should be more upset about getting blown up." Nat pushed up from the wall and stroked her hair into place. "I'm just angrier now. About everything."

"Shrapnel will do that." Reed's gaze rested on the minute cuts at her cheek. She carried her anger in her shoulders, and they were up by her ears. "What's going on?"

"Nothing, it's just Bobby is just a college kid, and he's up against full-on assassins with robot bombs. What chance does he have?"

"He's done pretty well so far. And he has you. He has me and all of Gray Zone."

"Yeah," Nat said, her gaze slipping from his.

Reed tilted his head, trying to catch her eye. "Don't forget Coyote."

She rubbed her eyes like she did when she was tired. "I'm going to work out a message for Bobby and use Fiona's phone to get it out there."

"What do you mean?"

"Just because he isn't posting online doesn't mean he isn't checking on things. Maybe talking to friends. His phone is a no go, but maybe not his online spaces."

"What about whoever's after him? They'll be looking too."

She nodded. "I have to think about how to go about it without tipping off whoever else is looking for Bobby. They'll be monitoring his socials too, but—I think I can get at least a warning out to him." Nat pulled out her phone, flipping through the contacts. "You know that friend I mentioned at LAPD Cybercrime? I asked them to schedule some time for me with their deductive AI program. I wanted to see if I could enter the descriptions Bobby used on his podcast of that night, along with the other data we've gathered so far, and see if it can extrapolate what the Resonance device really is."

"Okay, I think I understand most of what you just said."

"She happens to also be really good with malware. I think I can work with her on a way to get in touch with Bobby without anyone knowing."

"She?"

A wisp of a smile pulled at Nat's lips. "Did I not mention?"

"Must've slipped your mind," Reed said, but again, her mood felt off.

Nat seemed lost in thought as they walked back to the parking lot together to wait for her ride. She wanted to grab her things from Reed's trunk, but the key fob wouldn't work. She tried it again, getting more agitated before she let out a frustrated growl and slammed her palm on the top of the car.

"Nat, I know you're worried about the void thing, but—"

"That's not it. I mean, yeah, I think you're being an idiot about that, but..." Nat paced a little circle in the parking space, agitated, then pointed out at the street. "Luna wants me to go and help her work evidence, but I don't even *care* about justice anymore. I just want my friends and innocent people we talk with to stop dying. I want it to end, all of this. Danzig, the Rexfords, whatever the hell Jacoby dragged us into. I want to just—" She strangled the air in front of her. "You know? I want them to pay for all this chaos and pain."

"They will," Reed said, looking out at the sea of brick and steel and glass. "We aren't chasing behind Bobby's attacker anymore. We got to Fiona *before* him. Spoke to her about what she saw before he could stop us. I nearly caught him in the garage."

"He...mangled her."

"But she got him too, hurt him. He's not a ghost or a movie villain. He's a man who can be caught, and we're getting close."

20

Burbank Unified Hospital

Reed headed out to check on Fiona at the hospital. He'd missed lunch if he didn't count the boba place, which he didn't. He hit a drive-through on the way for a burger and fries, then pulled into the hospital parking lot to eat. Traffic had taken its toll, and it was already six thirty in the evening, but still warm. The ice-cold soda from the meal hit the spot as he sat in the parking lot with his windows down. He stared at the towering hospital with its tinted windows reflecting the peach sky and thought about what he'd seen in that garage. Slater's terrified gaze burned behind his eyes, only Reed never saw the man afraid. Not even when he was dying. Where was that memory coming from? What Slater said in that moment rattled him. What key? What was he talking about?

Reed finished his food and headed up to the hospital entrance, calling Coyote as he went.

"Boy, I can't leave you alone for ten minutes," Coyote answered with amusement. "Did you really blow shit up already?"

"Wasn't me this time. Where are you right now?" Reed wiggled his earlobe in an attempt to quell residual faint ringing in his ears.

"I'm at my meeting with a guy at LAX." The sound of overhead announcements cut through his voice. "I'll tell you about it later. Nat said the white-haired guy tried to kill y'all with a remote car bomb. That's a new development. You sure it was him?"

"He had on a black wig, but it was him." As he entered the main lobby, Reed gave Coyote the details on Fiona, the missing data lens, the car bomb, and almost catching the assailant. A couple of detectives stood over by the reception desk. They looked over and nodded like they knew who he was. Interesting.

Reed nodded back and continued to the counter. "I'm at Burbank Unified Hospital now. I called before I left, and they said Fiona will be coming out of surgery in a couple of hours. I'm going to stick around to see if her attacker comes by. They're sending some patrol officers to watch her door when she comes out."

"I'll meet you there. I'm close. Besides, I don't like talking on government phones," Coyote said and hung up.

A reception clerk walked over, and Reed showed him his badge.

"Oh, I have something for an Agent Reed." He reached below the counter and then slid a small bulging envelope toward him. It was the key fob for another sedan. "Someone named Luna said to tell you they've distributed a photo of Ms. Wells's attacker to the staff."

Reed nodded as he switched fobs and then asked about Fiona. The clerk sent Reed to the surgical floor, where another clerk told him to wait for someone over by the doors leading into the surgical suites. A few minutes later, a short, older woman in scrubs and a head covering pushed out of the double doors and led Reed to a side room for families. She was older but sinewy fit, like she ran marathons. The tip of her nose moved when she spoke. Her name was Aaliyah, a surgical nurse sent out by the surgeon to speak with Reed.

"Ms. Wells's condition has changed. There's been a complication, and we have no idea when she'll be out of surgery."

"Changed how?"

Aaliyah looked at him with sympathy. "She had extensive damage to her abdomen and massive blood loss, Agent Reed. Her surgeons are doing everything possible to help her."

"It was a Reaper blade. CO_2 blast." Reed showed her the photo on his phone.

"We were made aware before she arrived. Thank you for that. We adjusted care accordingly, but I have to tell you, even if she does survive the surgery, she'll be unconscious afterward for some time. You might want to leave your number with the surgical desk, and we'll give you a call when you can speak with her."

Reed thanked her, left his card, and went to look for the cafeteria, texting Coyote to find him there. The cantina offered the usual fare. Most of it prepackaged. Salads and fruit cups encased in shiny cellophane. Bagels wrapped up with packets of cream cheese. He wanted a dessert and wandered the snack area, tried to get excited about dehydrated banana chips, but finally decided on a caramel-and-chocolate bar.

He found the coffee machine, tapped out his order on the screen, and stood there listening to the sound of piping hot coffee sputter and stream into his biodegradable cup. Twenty-four hours ago, he was walking off a plane from Seattle. Tired, his gaze roamed lazily along the cafeteria crowd. He glanced at the people standing in front of the kitchen watching robotic arms make their simple meals. Behind large plexiglass windows, the automated kitchen flipped burgers, grilled hot dogs, poured soups, cut pizza, and prepared other hot meals with crushing efficiency.

Someone caught Reed's eye among the crowd. He wasn't watching his food being made or paying at the display screen. He was holding an empty tray and staring right at Reed. Jeans and a pale gray T-shirt. The guy looked away. And then it clicked. Why he'd been troubled all day. Reed realized now that he had a closer look that he'd seen the guy before. At the Sea Shanty, walking in when he was speaking with Pitch and Midas, at Flex Space in the crowd of workers at the tables, and now…an hour away from Ventura in an LA hospital. Not a chance that was coincidence.

Pretending he didn't see him, Reed took out his phone and called Luna.

"There's a guy here who's been following me since Ventura Harbor. I want to question him, but it could turn into a scene."

She was silent for a moment. "Is he the one who was in Seattle?"

"No, different guy."

"Get a photo and send it. My agents there will text you when they're ready."

"Ready for what?" Reed asked, but she was gone.

Reed paid for the candy bar at the kiosk, which took him right past the line of people waiting for their prepared dinner. He put the phone to his ear, pretended to talk with someone about the state of the coffee, and recorded every second of his pass by the guy in the gray T-shirt. Once out of the cafeteria, he veered a hard left into the stairwell and stopped on the second landing. He sent off the video, wondering if it would've just been easier to arrest the guy.

Two seconds later, his phone trilled, but it was a text from Coyote. All it said was, *Reflection pool.*

Reed peered out the cafeteria window at the grounds below. Wide-open lawn, nearly empty. He had a better chance of seeing the guy if he followed him out there. He texted Luna his plans and went to find Coyote.

The hospital's grounds offered a place for worried visitors and convalescing patients to sit out in the sun near a fountain pouring into a shallow pool at the far end of an artificial grass field. Low angled sunlight reflected off the coins under the water. Tall, mature trees lost their dry leaves to the parched wind. They tumbled along the grass, getting caught against the fountain's edge. A stand of white oleander bushes lined the fence at the far end of the property, backlit by the deep blue California sky. Swaying in the wind, their sweet fragrance drifted in the hot air. Coyote sat facing away from the hospital on the far side of the fountain, smoking a cigarette. He had his leather messenger bag at his feet.

A text message came through from Luna. Her agents stopped the man following Reed as he tried to use the exit leading to the hospital lawn. The perpetrator became agitated during routine questions and assaulted one of her agents. They arrested him and were now on their way to the LAPD station for questioning. She told Reed he was already screaming for a lawyer and refused to talk, so she'd be occupied for the rest of the night with the suspect. Reed wondered what that meant, since the man refused to talk. Luna texted she would see him, Nat, and Coyote at the Field Ops office the next day but would give updates if anything happened during the night.

"What's up?" Reed asked as he walked up to the fountain.

"That place is crawling with cops." Coyote ashed into the fountain. "How's the computer chick? Fiona, wasn't it?"

"She's still in surgery." Reed sat on the fountain's ledge and drank his coffee. "It looked bad, man."

"What are you thinking?" Coyote asked, his gaze out at the shifting branches of the oleander bushes.

"This killer, he attacks us in Seattle with proxies, and he either has Xanadu tortured or does it himself. Either way, he's been onto us for days. Nat said he has all of our files. He has people out here helping him too, like he did with that Rodney guy we questioned."

"He wasn't just following you either, if I recall. He was sent to take you out."

Reed glanced over his shoulder. "Well, I just spotted a guy in the cafeteria I've seen three times so far today. He's less obvious than Rodney, but not by much. So, there's someone already onto me and Nat...and yet Bobby's attacker *personally* takes out Fiona, almost getting caught in the process? Why?"

"What're you saying?"

Reed shook his head. "There's a desperate...tone, I guess, to all of this."

"Do you think the tail you spotted was feeding Bobby's attacker information on the case?"

Reed ground his jaw with frustration. "He lured Fiona to the garage with a text spoofed as me. He knew we were talking to her *right then*. The suspect Luna's people just picked up for following me was probably giving updates on my investigation in real time."

"And you're going to remedy this how?" Coyote took a long drag.

"I want to stop talking to witnesses for now and go look at where the sinking happened. Maybe check out Santa Cruz Island itself."

"You'll need equipment."

"I'm sure Luna can get what we need."

"You might wanna hold off on telling her anything just yet." Coyote reached into his bag and pulled out a rugged-looking digital tablet but didn't turn it on. "I met with my guy in army intelligence, Stucky, the one who helped us with Slater's redacted file..."

Coyote handed Reed the secure tablet. The documents and reports in the file laid out a clear picture of Jacoby's career. Involved for decades in counterterrorism programs, signature reduction operations, and other missions considered aggressive, but deliberately below the threshold of what would be called open conflict. Jacoby had spent the last twenty years destabilizing, weakening, or exploiting vulnerabilities of a target nation. It was considered a literal gray zone of military strategy. An undefined state between peace and all-out war. Cyber operations against target governments, supply chain interruptions, infrastructure disruption, grassroots funding of political opposition, etc. Jacoby had a hand in a lot of mayhem.

"So, Jacoby was a military spy," Reed said, swiping through the information. "Not a surprise."

"Listen, Morgan," Coyote said. "I know a guy who used to be a mechanist before he got out of government work. He says he's heard about Jacoby, and it's not good."

"A mechanist?"

"They make the mechanisms for covert work. Secret identities, fake faces, online presence, stuff like that. He used to work for what sounds like a special access program with no oversight."

"And what, he just thought he'd share?"

"Stucky got me some information from when Jacoby was active duty, and I found the mechanist's name with some digging. He'd been let go from the program abruptly for undisclosed reasons. When I found the guy, he was retired, in debt, and still pissed. I made it worth his while to tell his tale. That's who I met with at LAX. He's getting out of town." Coyote reached over and pulled out a couple of photos from his messenger bag. One was of a badly injured and sunburnt man, skeletal, vacant eyed. The other one reminiscent of a crime scene. A woman sat slumped in a chair in what looked like an older café. Dimly lit, with dust hanging in the beams of sunlight coming through the shattered café window. She'd been shot in the chest. "Jacoby lost assets in Iraq."

"What was he doing there?" Reed swiped through the file.

"There was an investigation into a breakdown in the chain of command that resulted in the death of two intelligence operatives, a man and woman, under his command. They were undercover, set to make a buy of uranium coming out of Latvia, when Jacoby was made aware of a possible blown cover of one of the assets. Someone figured out he was talking to us." Coyote crushed his cigarette in the grass under his boot. "That bastard sent his intelligence officers into a meet anyway. They killed the woman and took the man hostage. Our government had to send a team in after him. That's what he looked like when they finally got him back. Barely alive."

Reed closed the file. "Did they stop the sale?"

"You're missin' the point, Morgan."

"They *did* stop it, then."

Coyote frowned. "I thought you didn't trust this guy."

"I don't, but I still have to work with him."

Coyote tapped his finger on the tablet. "He plays fast and loose with the people he's in charge of. That's who this guy is, so, in my opinion, whatever you've got planned, I'd keep the details as far as possible from Jacoby."

Reed rubbed his scarred eyebrow, thinking. Coyote knew people. It had saved their lives on more than one occasion. He thought for a moment, then, "We'll need alternative avenues for getting equipment."

"Already got an iron in the fire," Coyote said. "I put some feelers out to the shippers I know in the area. We'll get a bite."

"I might have another idea," Reed said and told him.

"Could work." Coyote nodded.

Reed slapped his knees with his palms and stood. "So, do you want to help me infiltrate a secret government lab, with no backup, tonight?"

Coyote smiled. "Like it's the first time."

21

The White Lion

He stood in a filthy bathroom staring at himself in the scratched mirror, shaking as he splashed more water into his eyes. They burned, and his vision still hadn't cleared. Concerned, he'd tried doing the safecracking again. He reset the equipment and leapt from the rafters. The low light, the goggles, the weightlessness of the cables worked against him, exacerbated by the blurry vision. He'd failed to reach the contents of the safe within the time parameter. It took three tries before he finally succeeded. Not good enough. Certain death would come if he failed.

He shouldn't have missed Reed. He'd had the advantage of surprise, but the man was faster than he looked. Frustrated, he ran his hands through his hair. The pallid color appeared ghostly in the evening light streaming down from a broken window in the ceiling. He palpated the inflamed eyelids and skin, fury rising in his chest. How did Reed find this Fiona woman so fast? He knew Bobby had someone named Fiona "clean up" his recording of the Resonance device but couldn't find out who. The Flex Space information was new as well.

He let his gaze travel his fine bone structure, the pale skin scarred with the ravages of war, and understood why. Reed moved among the throngs easily, an advantage he did not have. He was a watcher, dealing death from the shadows through a rifle scope. Unseen, but feared. This job for Danzig was an outlier, and it put him at risk. Yet he had no choice.

The urgent chirping of his phone sounded from the work area in the warehouse, and he threw his towel down in frustration. It was Danzig, attempting to establish a connection with the hologram feed. The White Lion kept only the lone light on his worktable on, obscuring his visibility before hitting accept. If Danzig saw his face and surmised the vision problem...too much was at stake.

The darkening light offset the bright blue of Danzig's hologram as he walked along the wall of the warehouse. He strode with his hands linked behind him like an irritated professor. "Someone blew up a sound studio in LA a few hours ago. You?"

"It had to be done."

"I was just informed the LAPD is calling it a possible terror attack, given your use of explosives. I hope it was worth it."

"I have the sound engineer's copy of Bobby Khan's data lens now. However, she saw what was on it, so she had to go. All I need now is his original. I've destroyed everything he had in his townhouse and at the storage locker."

"Before you got to her, Reed spoke with the sound engineer, Fiona, correct?"

"Briefly," the White Lion hedged. "Whatever she told him doesn't matter. If she survives the surgery, she won't survive the night. I'll see to it."

"I'm getting tired of sending men out to help you and buy you time, only to still be three steps behind Reed."

"Then stop sending amateurs. If they had done their job, the Khans would not have been out there on that boat in the first place. They would have been nowhere near the detonation that night! Send one of your Spectre soldiers."

"Reed would spot one of my mercenaries from a mile away."

"He's not some obsessive detective, he's an agent leading a task force now. They're closing in. I need more space to work."

"How the hell—" Danzig's hologram glitched for a minute, cutting up the words. "I'll send...to slow them down...must deal with Bobby Khan and get back to your main reason for being there. The timing of...is essential."

"I know this."

Danzig stopped pacing, his face made of blue light sizzling with the moist air. "There's been a development. We have to move the timeline up."

"What happened?"

"You will have a third person to deal with now."

The White Lion shrugged, unconcerned. "It won't make a difference. No one will survive the device within a hundred meters."

"And the time difference with the larger payload?"

"I adjusted my plans accordingly. Speaking of time. Please, I need to know where—"

"You know our deal. You deliver the device and collect what's in the safe first."

"He's my son!" the White Lion shouted, spittle flying from his mouth.

"Then the accelerated timeline works in your favor." Danzig stared back, the cold of his gaze evident through the hologram. "Do your job, and you will get your payment of information. Not before."

Hands curled into fists, the White Lion nodded his assent, imagining how it would feel to finally kill Danzig. "Of course."

"And find that Khan kid. He's the only one who can derail this."

"Reed will lead me to Bobby, and then I'll kill them both."

"You're going to want to make damn sure Reed's dead," Danzig said. "You won't survive him otherwise."

22

Coyote declined to go with Reed back to Field Ops, saying instead that he'd see about Reed's alternative idea to hiring out a vessel. To be fair, Coyote's argument that experienced smugglers might be a better choice wasn't wrong. By the time Reed got back to Ventura County, he was burnt out. The never-ending rush hour had pushed his arrival close to nine at night. He was hungry, tense from all the traffic, and a steady throbbing at his temple put him in a thought spiral about Xanadu and Danzig and now this insane killer who blew things up just to get away. Reed was turning down the street toward Field Ops when Nat called on his personal phone. He put her on speaker.

"Coyote told me to stop using the burners Luna gave us," Nat said. "He told me why. I gotta say, not shocked Jacoby has a sketchy past. Sort of seems like it'd be a job requirement for what he does."

"Yeah, I'm not sure Coyote and I are in lockstep over Jacoby, but it's smart to go private. At least tonight."

"As long as we use the encryption I installed, we're good." Nat crunched on something, probably chips. "So, I heard you spotted another stalker."

"Luna grabbed him. What do you think the odds are she lets me question him?"

"About as good as your odds of breaking into a secure lab at night in unfamiliar waters without anyone noticing. Deep Wave Dynamics may *claim* they aren't operational yet, but we saw images of guards and a heat signature that say otherwise. Seriously, though, you guys don't know what you're walking into."

Reed squeezed his eyes tight, cringing. "Coyote is a snitch. I was going to tell you all of this over late-night Korean food like a decent person."

"Well, you have to get some, now. Oh, he also proudly told me you agreed to do this behind Jacoby's back. Have you lost your mind? You want to try to out-covert the spy?"

"Come on, it'll be fun," Reed said, pulling into the Field Ops inner space. "You probably won't even have to get out of the boat."

"I hate the ocean. You know that."

"You and your equipment will remain dry, I promise."

She was silent for a beat, then, "I mean, were you gonna get short ribs?"

"What am I, an amateur? Of course I was."

She let out an exaggerated sigh. "Fine. What can I do?"

"What you do best," Reed said, smiling. "Data magic. I need a look inside and underneath the lab. Even if it's just an approximation. Can your VR thing do that?"

"It can do that. Luna and her team did a lot of initial research into Deep Wave Dynamics before we were even brought in. I can upload what we need from the Gray Zone network," she said. "So, what's going down, exactly?"

Reed told her about his plan and that Coyote was off finding out if it was viable. "I gave him a wad of cash, so I'm hopeful. I'll need some kind of blueprint, maybe a land survey of Santa Cruz Island, record of structures, what kind of patrol they have, things like that. Luna didn't elaborate much on the island itself."

"Yes, in fact, I remember her saying something about keeping our focus on finding Bobby."

"We *have* to go about this from another angle. The last witness we spoke to ended up in the hospital. My conscience can't take the weight of this case much longer. Not like this."

He could hear her breathing softly on the other end, then, "Okay, I'm going to jump on one of the cleared security networks here at the station, see what I can get on the research facility. I worked out how to move around the network unseen. They really need an upgrade."

Reed pulled to a stop in front of the Field Ops warehouse, confused. "You're still in LA? I thought you left to go help Luna at Field Ops. I'm here now."

"No, I'm at the Ventura Police Department main station. I did manage to get ahold of Fiona's phone. It's a mess, but not completely gone. I still might be able to get something from it, but I needed some tools and programs we didn't have access to at Field Ops. Luna found a spot for me at the forensics lab here."

"Did you get anything from the phone?"

"A video. I think her last. We're cleaning it up now. It should take a few hours. There's a tech here who's a real guru in the making. It's in good hands."

"Okay, that's good. Things are moving fast on my end. Do you need a pickup?"

"They left me a car."

"We're meeting soon, but not at Field Ops," Reed said, staring at the dark warehouse. He suspected Jacoby had cameras installed to keep an eye on him and his team. "I'll figure something out and let you know."

"Call me," Nat said and ended the call.

Reed went inside the Field Ops warehouse to shower and change out of the clothes with Fiona's blood still on them. He called the hospital again but was told she was still in surgery. He wondered how long someone could stay under while that injured. After cleaning up and changing, he grabbed some equipment. Mainly, the portable VR hub and goggles Nat had packed into her luggage. The fire at the abandoned mall destroyed nearly all her custom builds, and she was wary of leaving her equipment anywhere at the moment. He also grabbed some relevant gear, snacks, and water bottles on his way back out. Ten minutes later, he was sitting outside of a Korean restaurant waiting for a large takeout order when Coyote called back.

"Did you tattle immediately after I left, or did you give me a few minutes?" Reed asked, amused.

"I thought it prudent to keep the brains of the operation informed," Coyote said with a chuckle. "Besides, we need Nat on board, and she's less concerned with my personal safety than yours."

"Fair point," Reed said. "What happened with the plan?"

"You were right. Pitch took the money," Coyote said through an exhaled breath. Reed could practically smell the smoke. "We've got his boat and all the excursion equipment he uses for rentals for a week. No questions asked."

"We only need it for tonight."

"I need it for longer. My maritime business associates have a situation that needs attending to."

"Something I should know?"

"Just that it has no bearing on our current proceedings," he said in the most polite, mind-your-own-business way.

"Where'd you send Pitch?" Reed asked as an autonomous waiter exited the restaurant service door. It reminded him of the old, boxy robots in cartoons, like an angular snowman made of metal. The topmost compartment held a camera that swiveled as it scanned the parking lot.

"To see his dad in Omaha," Coyote said. "I offered him a week in Vegas, but he opted to visit the man who named him Pitch."

Reed waved at the robot through the windshield, and it rambled over the gravel parking lot to him. He paid with a flash of his phone, grabbed the bags out of the middle compartment, and started the car. "I'll get ahold of Nat and meet you at the boat."

A half hour later, they all met at the Ventura Harbor gates, used Pitch's key to enter the harbor, and climbed aboard the *Sea Witch*. It had similar specs to the boat Bobby and his father used for their tour groups, though Pitch's had a larger galley and an extra cabin, which helped with all of Nat's equipment.

"You think Luna and Jacoby will find out about what you two are about to do?" she asked and squinted at the controls on the console. They were standing at the helm, looking out at the cobalt horizon through the windscreen. The city lights never let it grow dark all the way. Not like it had in the forests of Alaska.

"Hopefully not until we want them to." Reed helped her set up the VR hub and equipment while Coyote spoke with someone on the boat's radio.

Nat nodded at him. "You've driven a boat, right?"

"Sailed," Reed said and nodded. "I've been on a few."

"Who's he talking to?" Nat asked.

"Harbor master. We needed Pitch to ask for clearance, especially because we're navigating out at night."

Coyote turned, gave Reed the thumbs-up. They were good to go.

Reed and Coyote worked through the prelaunch checklist, securing the gear and the on-deck equipment, inspecting the gauges and instrumentation, and performing other tasks. Nat organized the digital supplies while they worked. By ten thirty, Coyote used the navigation assist to pilot them carefully out of Ventura Harbor toward Santa Cruz Island.

They ate the Korean takeout as they sailed, taking turns reheating it in the galley's minuscule microwave. Reed flipped through information on Santa Cruz Island that Nat had loaded onto her tablet. It was the largest of the Channel Islands and the most visited. It sat twenty miles off the California shore. The Deep Wave Dynamics lab was on the leeward side of the island facing away from the mainland near the center of the landmass. Willows Anchorage, located at the end of Willows Canyon, was a cove-like area protected from the west by hills and stained rock and east by sheer white cliffs that soared to nearly seven hundred feet. Reed zoomed in on Nat's map and saw a series of small structures just off a beach.

"That's practically a fortified location," Reed muttered.

Nat nodded, finishing off her beef short rib. "Those canyons are famous for their violent winds, too. They've been known to blow boats toward the submerged rocks close to the beach."

"Well, we don't have a sail, so the winds aren't the biggest problem. I mean, they're no joke, but..." Coyote held a carton of bulgogi in his hand, chewing thoughtfully. "It's those kelp forests near the cliffs and shore I'm worried about. Pitch said they can be rough to get through."

"Any good news?" Reed asked, studying the small grouping of buildings. Flat and clustered close together, it resembled a marine research campus, not just a small lab. "This is a larger operation than they're letting on."

"They're probably armed to the teeth, too," Nat said with a grin. "So, you've got that going for you."

Coyote chuckled and pointed to Reed. "I'll take care of the water hazards. You figure out how to get us past their guns."

"How much time?" Reed asked, flipping open his sketchbook and setting it near the satellite photos of the lab. "We're crossing through shipping-lane traffic between the island and the mainland, right?"

"The nav unit is plotting a course now," Coyote said.

Luna had explained when she picked them up from the airport that although Bobby's boat sank between the island and the coast of California, Deep Wave's lab was on the other side of the island. Its location had set off red flags with Gray Zone.

"Willows Anchorage, right?" Reed asked, finding it on the map.

Coyote nodded. "We're approaching from the southwest, going around the east end of the island and back west to the location on the other side. If all goes well, it should take us a little over three hours to get there." "When Luna said earlier that the lab's location was suspect, I took a look at the surrounding terrain, and I believe they use this beach to the west of Willows Anchorage to make shore."

They talked about their approach, how Nat would stay back and work comms, their egress plans, and other minutiae. Waiting out the time.

"With the moon full like it is, we might be easy to spot out on the open sea, but marine weather service is predicting heavy fog by eleven tonight. Which is about the time we'll be in the area."

"Yeah, that's common this time of year," Nat agreed. "Not pea-soup thick, but not nothing."

Reed stayed at the helm while Nat walked Coyote through the VR program she'd uploaded with everything Gray Zone had on Deep Wave Dynamics and their research, which wasn't much. He heard them laughing at Coyote's disorientation, watched them flail a little, and then it was his turn.

Coyote slipped off the goggles, shaking his head. "I will never get used to that. It gave me rollercoaster stomach again."

Reed slipped the goggles on, and the VR environment enveloped him in the lined world of a 3D blueprint. Nat's avatar stood next to him in the abyss. Her digital twin looked in Reed's direction, and a virtual breeze played with her hair. She gestured as she manipulated the schematic.

"This is the proposed design of the lab, but when I took a look at the satellite photos of the area, they didn't match. I used a program to merge the two designs for the most accurate probable depiction. I was able to extrapolate a lot of information as to the actual design, but it's not one hundred percent accurate."

"It's close enough," Reed said, using a haptic glove to turn the design on a vertical axis. It twisted like a merry-go-round as he zoomed in and inspected what they had. "I've gone into scarier places than this with less information. We'll need to kill the power somehow."

"I was working on that," Nat said and swiped the schematic away. She pulled up with her hand, and a drone video appeared between them. It was a flyover view of the outside of the building nearest the water. "This was loaded into the Gray Zone files on the lab. It's a few weeks old, but they got great images of the loading dock, the launch area, even a nighttime shot of underwater security lights. You see that big metal box behind the aquarium building?"

"Yes."

"It's the main power station for the whole site. I've got something that can take it down." A small device, the size and shape of a deck of cards, appeared before him in virtual space. Spinning lazily, indicator lines with information popped up beside it, marking various locations. "It's called an EMP device, Thunderbolt class. It's a DIY build from the Night Market, so there's no tracing it. You just slap it on, and it should overwhelm the system. They'll have no cameras, their locks will go manual, the works...theoretically."

"For how long?" Reed asked, subconsciously leaning forward to see better instead of zooming in via gestures. He corrected and used a pinch motion to view the structure.

Nat's avatar shrugged her shoulders. "They've gotta have a backup power supply. I have no idea when it would kick on, though. Systems vary."

"It looks shabby," Reed said, swiping through some photos floating in front of his avatar.

"There's been a lot of effort to appear in disrepair or still under construction, but that wet dock is operational. They're holding something there during low tide. Also..." She gestured with her wrist, and an invoice appeared, floating in front of Reed. It was a large equipment purchase for a lifting arm. She tapped onto a keypad that only she could see, and the paper morphed into an enormous winch system hovering over an open hole in the floor of the dock's wet lab. "This is a telescopic overhead tilting crane with an HFL-certified docking head."

"They have a moon pool?" Reed stared at the equipment. "For what?"

"The grant proposal said it is for the deployment and retrieval of scientific equipment." She moved the winch aside and pulled over the 3D blueprint, then pointed at a section of the lab where a large building stood over the ocean. "Most moon pools are on the bottom of research vessels. The ocean is kept at bay by the pressurized chamber, but this one is above water. It's like a hole cut in the floor of the lab for easy access to equipment, et cetera."

"Or to launch something from inside the lab without anyone seeing," Coyote said from outside the VR environment. "Not even Uncle Sam's eyes in the sky."

Fiona's mention of a torpedo came to mind as Reed studied the winch. What was going on in that lab? Nat and Reed went over the plan to recon the research facility once more. Hashing out the information from the schematic, noting the range of the sensors, cameras, and possible sound detection equipment. Reed went over the schematics, walking through the virtual building before breaking out of VR. Sometime later, Coyote announced from his seat at the helm they'd be at their location in forty-five minutes, and Nat said she needed to go through the data they'd managed to pull from Fiona's phone. She hoped to find a better shot of the assailant's face.

Reed sat at the table in the small galley with his sketchbook and drafted out the maze of corridors in the lab, tracing them with his pencil, memorizing them. Because the Deep Wave Dynamics plans were deliberately incomplete to hide things like the moon pool, there were gaps in the schematics. Reed traced out where the labs would logically be in relation to the loading dock, how the barracks might be hidden, working out the holes in his knowledge. He settled into the rocking of the boat. The push and pull of the waves. In the distance, warning horns from the drone freighters drifted over the water like fog. The dark of the night sea weighed heavy against the cabin windows, almost blotting out sound. It made the ringing in Reed's ear from the blast seem louder. On the instrument panel up front, a light blinked, the scratched plastic cover muting it to soft bursts in the dim cabin. On-off-on-off, like a visual metronome.

Reed closed his sketchbook, letting his head fall back against the wall behind him. Exhaustion moved through his wrought muscles, making them heavy, and the blinking light penetrated his lids enough to irritate the headache brewing at his temple. He breathed deeply, trying to let go of the tension in his arms and aching shoulder. The empty spaces of the lab's blueprints bothered him, and he drifted along the fragile lines of the schematic in his mind's eye. But fatigue pulled him deeper than concentration, down into the dark twilight between consciousness and sleep. The seat beneath his thighs, the sounds of the boat engine, the shifting of the sea all fell away. The blueprint of the lab structure filled out before him, growing heavy with stone and damp as it morphed into the maze walls of his deep memory.

The labyrinth of his making spread around him, enclosing him in the dark passageways of his mind. Ice-blue fire lit the corridor and made shifting shadows along the packed ground. He turned left, looking for the familiar grouping of stones on the wall. A cry of pain flared out from the dark distance of the corridor. Raucous laughter filled with malice followed. Then a wind picked up, snatching the sounds away. Light at first, it grew to a howling wind that tore down the corridor. It whipped cold dirt in his face. Wet, like mud, he slipped and slid on the ground. The walls of the maze moved with shapes that painted themselves across the surface. Familiar somehow, like the depictions of warriors on ancient vases.

But the images changed. The angular poses of the fighting soldiers became the edges of large crystal groupings. Their bodies morphing into columns of rock, piled on each other, reaching for the heavens, only to collapse. The surface of the maze caved in, revealing a chasm in the wall. It yawned against utter blackness. The void pulled at Reed, and he fought it.

Flailing for a handhold to keep from going into the abyss. And then time stopped. The debris in the wind froze in suspension midair.

The only thing that moved was a drawing of a massive bird that flew along the wall of the maze. White-and-gold wings whipped the air as it burst from the surface of the wall in a hail of gravel. Stumbling back, Reed threw up his arms, bracing for the razor-sharp beak of the pale raptor, when it stopped charging. It hovered above Reed, the endless height of the maze tunneling wind through its painted feathers. Its gaze held Reed, and the eyes were wrong. Not bird, but... Another volley of screams warbled down the passageway, and the pace of Reed's pulse jumped.

The bird angled sharply and flew at him, transforming into a winged man as he dove. He moved with the sound of dry paper scraping against itself. His bare feet touched down on the ground, and he tilted his head, staring at Reed. The figure's skin and clothes appeared pale with age, faded at the edges like the drawings in an ancient manuscript. He held his palm out as if expecting Reed to give him something.

"What do you want?" Reed asked, flattening himself against a rock in the wall behind him.

"The key," the figure rasped. His voice like a snake sliding through sand.

Slater's prickled, charred fingers flashed in Reed's mind. He'd said the same thing in the hallucination after the bomb blast.

"What is the key?" Reed asked, fighting to calm his heart rate. Something was wrong. Cold crept along his body. He asked the winged figure, "Is it an actual key? Is it a code? What is it?" Then, a faraway voice floated to him from outside the maze. His name came in waves. *Reed!*

The walls crumbled around him. Desperate, Reed reached for the winged man. The creature screeched, the tips of its feathers bursting into flames. It clutched at Reed's chest with charred fingers, the fire consuming the creature's wings as its furious eyes burned like coal. But the fire was cold, freezing, and it ached through Reed's body as they struggled. The creature ripped, tore like paper in Reed's hands as it tried to get away.

Coyote's voice echoed through the corridor. "Reed! What are you doing?"

A fireball erupted around the winged man, consuming the creature in seconds. Its ashes burst through the air, fluttering down at Reed's feet.

Icy water splashed over him, and he gasped, coughing at the deluge, blinking the memory away. Coyote stood bracing himself against the railing of the boat, his hand gripping Reed as he angled, nearly cantilevered over the edge. He pulled Reed back on deck before letting go. Coyote moved away, a worried, bewildered look on his face. Nat stood with her back against the bulkhead, both hands covering her mouth, eyes wide with fear. An empty bucket sat on the deck next to her.

Reed glanced down at the stretched-out front of his sweatshirt. "What'd I do?"

"You almost dove backward off the deck," Coyote said, his face sweaty, lip bloody. "You fought me to do it."

Nat stepped forward, hugging him like she hadn't seen him in years. Her voice sounded muffled against his chest as she asked, "What the hell, Reed?"

He hugged her back, shaking his head. "I don't know."

They went back inside, and Nat got him a towel. Coyote muttered something about setting anchor soon. They were about five minutes out from the anchorage location, so Reed changed directly into his wet suit. He stood in the head, staring at himself in the mirror, wondering if he'd been dreaming or in a deep trance. One thing he did know, the feel of the paper that had ripped in his hands, the exact faded images, he'd seen them before, and that, Reed thought, was somehow very important.

Nat met him when he walked out of the head and handed him two water-bottle-sized canisters with breathing regulators attached and a pair of tactical goggles.

"I 'borrowed' a couple of emergency oxygen tanks from Field Ops. They hold maybe two minutes of air to get to the surface or whatever. And those are connected goggles for fieldwork. They have a headlamp, camera, and a rolling display that gives you mission information. Weather, temp, stuff like that."

"Where'd you find these?" Reed slipped one of the goggles over his head and let it hang around his neck.

"Luna has a lot of cool stuff in a storage room she thinks is locked. I took some earpieces that connect with my radio handset and a data scraper." She dug around in her jacket pockets and held up a memory storage device. "I loaded up a little creation of my own. A malware program that you need to get onto the facility's computers. It'll give me a way in to their system."

Reed took the device. "What is it?"

"It'll try to connect with the network closest to it using various methods, some of which are unlawful, but we're not going to look at that." Nat nodded to the open ocean. "Once it does, it'll copy everything they have. If Deep Wave is involved, this is our chance to see for ourselves what they've been up to."

The size and thickness of a quarter, the rectangular device felt heavier than it looked. She showed him how and where to place the device.

"If this is Jacoby's device—"

"I took care of that," Nat said. "Whatever information we get is ours alone until we share it. They can't even track it."

"You're a genius, you know."

"Digital goddess, remember?"

Reed smiled. "How could I forget?"

When they were done talking, he walked back up to the deck and strode over to Coyote, who was working with their gear. Slipping Nat's device into a pocket on his belt, Reed sat next to his friend, who shoved waterproof flares in a side pocket of his tactical backpack. The rubberized grip of a gun stuck out of there too, but Reed said nothing. He had his own weapon tucked in his pack as well.

Reed handed Coyote one of the oxygen canisters and a pair of goggles. "Did you somehow smuggle flash-bangs into California too?"

"You know what happened in South America." Coyote gave an exaggerated shudder. "*Always* have flash-bangs."

Reed rearranged his own backpack for a few moments and then nodded at the railing. "Thanks for watching out for me, man. I owe you."

"I'm ride or die, Morgan. You know that. I just didn't realize it was this bad. You sure you know how far you can push it?"

"I let the fatigue get on top of me, that's all." Reed attached a dive knife to the strap of his utility belt. "I'm good. One hundred percent."

"If it happens again when we're on the water, could be bad."

"It won't," Reed said.

Coyote looked at him for a beat and then shrugged. "Just like old times, right? In and out…"

"Silent as a shadow," Reed finished the saying. Then, "Have you ever heard of the story of Icarus?"

"What, now?" Coyote shook his head but smirked. "Never a dull moment with you."

23

Night Swim

Santa Cruz Island loomed silent and massive as they passed around the turtle head of the landmass to the leeward side. Sea caves, too dark to see, let off a mineral scent as they gurgled and hissed with crashing waves. The *Sea Witch* dropped anchor near Willows Anchorage and Reed looked out at the hulking shadow of the island through his Starbright night vision binoculars. Sheer cliffs, white as bone in the moonlight, towered over their boat. An occasional light glittered from the jagged terrain, otherwise the island slumbered in darkness.

Pitch's equipment included an inflatable ship-to-shore dinghy that held six people. Coyote and Reed boarded it with their backpacks and set off from the *Sea Witch* toward Santa Cruz Island. The dinghy's battery-powered outboard motor allowed them to creep in near silence along the surface. Fifteen minutes into their trip, the fog rolled in. It hovered above the black water and muffled the sound of the waves crashing on the cliffs. Reed sat on the edge of the rigid-bottomed boat, going over his equipment. He adjusted the fit and seal of the goggles and inserted the waterproof earpiece, securing it in with an over-ear band.

"Testing," he murmured.

"I hear you." Nat's silky voice came over the earpiece. "And Coyote, I can hear you mouth breathing."

"Always the criticism with this one," Coyote answered back.

Reed's goggles flicked on, and a heads-up display ran along the bottom of his visual field like a news banner, reporting the temperature, his current velocity, and local water currents, among other readings. The nearly full moon washed the area in a soft glow, and the buildings on the shore cut angular shadows against the light landscape.

"Are you getting this?" Reed spotted the indicator light in the corner of his vision.

"It's streaming fine for now," Nat said. "I'm capturing it for posterity."

"Closing in," Coyote murmured, and they veered toward shore.

The wind whipped Reed's face, freezing his cheeks with frigid sea mist. He pulled his face covering up from around his neck, protecting everything up to the bottom of his goggles. They moved at a good clip, taking the last few hundred meters with ease. The surveillance Gray Zone had gathered on Deep Wave's security suggested both waterborne sentinel drones patrolling the surface as well as possible aerial security. No information was available on whether or not they were armed.

The current was strong, and Reed's headlamp beam slid across the undulating masses of the vast kelp forests floating along the surface of the sea. The jagged tops of submerged rocks poked out, dangerously close along their path, but Coyote and the nav unit kept them from getting caught on their deadly peaks. Reed moved with the motion of the speeding boat, keeping his eyes open for movement on shore. Soon the floor of the ocean rose, meeting with the sand bar that marked the beach flowing down from Willows Canyon. Reed killed his headlamp, slipping into the thigh-high water. They pulled the boat to shore, hiding it behind a portion of a nearby maintenance shed. Rising slowly in a crouch, they climbed the hilly beach toward the building sitting to the east, just over The Nature Conservancy border.

A strange sound warbled just beneath the ocean waves and wind. An artificial muffling noise the closer they crept.

"They have sound dampening," Reed whispered as he scanned the property. "I wonder what they're trying to cover up."

The darkened construction zone of the Deep Wave Dynamics laboratory sat enclosed in a chain-link fence covered with ratty, weathered landscape material. It flapped in the wind flowing onshore like a specter's cloak. Reed scoped out the size and shape of each building according to what he'd seen in the architecture plans. A wet dock jutted out from the western side of the grounds, the end of it obscured by another building, which Reed guessed housed the workshop and maintenance.

"Guard." Coyote's voice came from behind.

Reed froze, watching for the silhouette. A man's form crossed the front of the living quarters building, pacing back and forth. Then a faint orange glow flared.

"Smoking. Clock his position," Reed said and kept moving.

Slivers of light peeked out from the edges of some of the blacked-out windows of the facility. Reed and Coyote crept east, approaching the buildings from the side, careful to avoid the pressure sensors they thought might be in the sand toward the front.

"We're ready to kill their power," Reed whispered.

"You're going to want to go behind the aquarium building," Nat said in Reed's ear. "According to Luna's notes, the main power station is located just outside the door. It might be four feet tall, three feet wide, but might be smaller. We talked about where to place the Thunderbolt device, but it was a guess."

"If it's a different size, I'll eyeball it."

"Are you there now?"

Reed patted his chest and felt the mini EMP device she'd slipped him before they launched. "On my way."

They snuck to the side gate of the fence, and Reed inspected the security measures. It wasn't topped with razor wire or even a complicated lock. The remote location and six-foot-high fence were likely enough to keep out curious eyes. They hopped it silently and moved to the rear of the aquarium building. The scent of sea and salt grew thicker the nearer they got.

"Ten o'clock," Coyote whispered, pointing at the furthest and largest building with his gloved hand. "I count two armed guards patrolling the grounds of the main laboratory building."

"I see them." The power station was indeed a different size, and Reed concentrated on where he should place the Thunderbolt EMP. Nat had shown him the wiring plans of the box, and though it looked similar, he wasn't sure he was placing the device correctly. He paused before hitting the detonation button. "Is there going to be a flash?"

"Only if it starts an electrical fire," she said.

"What are the odds of that?"

"Uh...fifty-fifty."

"What?" Reed heard Coyote chuckle in his earpiece.

"Hey, I made it at the Ventura station lab, and they don't have the workshop I have in

Seattle."

"Don't worry, darlin', that's better odds than military equipment," Coyote said.

"You're essentially giving it one hell of a power surge. It should take out the wiring and the main battery," Nat said.

Reed looked around for something to cover the possible flash, decided it was unlikely he could hide an electrical fire, and placed the Thunderbolt. He backed up a bit and slid his thumb over the detonation trigger and pushed it. It had a five-second timer. "Fire in the hole."

Coyote stepped away just as a muffled buzz sounded from within the power box, followed by nothing.

"Was that it?" Coyote asked. "Did it work?"

"Is anything on fire?" Nat asked.

"No," Reed answered.

"Then it worked."

Reed tried the aquarium's electromagnetic lock, and though warm to the touch through his glove, it opened. *Digital goddess*, Reed thought as he pushed through the aquarium door. Everything was pitch black, and the smell of fish permeated the area.

"There are no lights anywhere," Reed whispered.

"Good."

"Uh, Nat, what about the computers?" Coyote asked.

"Oh, the network computers definitely have backup power. They have to preserve memory and offload their data in case of an emergency."

"I need to get to a main terminal, right?" he asked.

"Yes, you have to find one to place the data scraper. An office dummy terminal wouldn't allow you access. I'd check the control center first. It's the operational heart of the program. All the data from their various sensors and instruments runs through there. They'd have a networked computer for sure."

"Copy that," Reed said. "We'll look for one."

Reed turned his headlamp on the dimmest setting, and they proceeded quickly through the building, passing the circular tanks that lined one side of the aquarium. Soft blue light from the skylight illuminated the silvery fish that stirred in their tank. A few wonky-looking sea horses floated listlessly in another. Labels marked other tanks for observation, quarantine for new arrivals, and separate feeding. There were medical stations and tubs of equipment. The whir of compressors, air tubes bubbling in water, and distant dripping surrounded them.

"Let me get this right," Coyote whispered. "We have no idea when the backup power will come on?"

Reed shook his head. "Nope."

"The two of us can cover more ground if we split up."

"No. We have no idea who we're facing here. So far, they haven't been stingy with the security."

"Not gonna matter if the lights go on while we're rifling through their top-secret files, is it?"

Reed looked at him for a moment. The power outage would raise their alert level; they had to move fast. "Nat, where else should we look for one of these main computer terminals?"

"Check the Environmental Monitoring Station. That's where they installed that overhead crane arm. You'd need access to internal commands to operate that."

"That's the far building near the shore, right?" Coyote asked.

Reed nodded. They found the internal door of the aquarium linking it to the main hallway. He glanced down one way, pointed to a map on the wall indicating a path to the Environmental Monitoring Station. "That's where the moon pool would be."

"Got it," Coyote said and went that way.

"I'll scope out the control room," Reed said, veering in the opposite direction. "Coyote's heading to the moon pool area."

Nat hesitated for a moment, then said, "Copy that."

Reed headed to the control center, following his memory of the facility's blueprints. He turned a corner and almost walked into a heavy metal door. He peered inside the wire-enmeshed window.

"I found the main lab." Reed slid the door aside, and it collapsed on itself like an elevator door. "I'm taking a look."

"Sixty seconds since power out," Nat said evenly.

"I'll make it quick." Reed strode into the lab, then deliberately panned the goggle's camera at each section. "Are you seeing this?"

"I am," Nat said in his ear. "What the hell?"

Chemical solution baths swirled lazily in metal vats against the wall. The exhaust lids dappled with condensation when Reed tried to look at what was inside. Some sample vials sat in a glass case on the counter. He picked one up, holding it up to the light of his goggles. It looked like water, but the light gave it a pink cast.

"This isn't equipment for a marine lab, is it?" Reed murmured.

"Hold on, look back at that last station."

He swiveled his head toward a desk terminal. He tapped the keyboard. Nothing. Some files and a few books caught his eye. A clipboard sat atop a strange piece of equipment, and Reed picked it up. He read the printout attached to it.

"There's a weird machine here, and they were running a program called 'molecular collision analysis' on it before we killed the power."

"Okay, good! What else do you see? Record everything."

"There's a book or manual here talking about nucleation site generators...uh...does that mean anything to you? I have some kind of notes about pedestal growth." He glanced at a bank of controls.

"Oh my—stop. Turn back around."

Reed did, and his jaw dropped. "Is that a laser?"

"Luna was right. Something shady is going on out there."

"Pedestal growth," Reed whispered, trying to place the familiar words. He'd read them before. Recently. "I can't—"

Voices in the building caught his attention, and he moved. Shutting off his headlamp, he left the lab in a silent jog toward the control room. He found it quickly and bypassed the large, mounted display screens and instruments gone silent. He wove through the workstations past piles of charts and indecipherable notes toward the computer terminal at the far side of the room. He hit the keyboard when he got there, and the screen lit up.

"I found a main terminal. Placing the scraper." Reed pulled out the small device, peered around the back of the computer station, and found the port with his gloved fingers. It fit, and the scraper's internal LED light flashed as it worked. "It's in, it's doing its thing."

"Reed, I'm seeing activity." Nat's voice had a wire of stress running through it. "I've got some pretty great digital binoculars, and there are sweeping lights out on the beach in front of the main lab."

"Sweeping as in the hands of running guards?"

"As in get the hell out. They know you're there."

"The scraper—" Reed detached it from the computer station and shoved it in his backpack. "Did you hear that, Coyote? Clear out."

"I heard. I'm in the moon pool, and brother, you have to see this—"

Gunfire erupted from Coyote's end, and Reed took off running toward the moon pool.

"Check in, Coyote." Reed sprinted down the dark hallways, relying on his VR walk-through to navigate. "Where are you?"

A tone sounded in Reed's ear. Like an old landline gone dead. "Nat? You hear that?"

"His earpiece is malfunctioning. I'm not getting through to him either."

A distant sound made Reed's blood run cold. It was a powering up, a whirring of the backup system. He slipped his hand to the watertight pouch on his tactical backpack, undid the closure, and pulled out his gun. Breaking into an even sprint, he passed blacked-out windows, unable to see out.

Reed turned the corner and spotted the sign over a set of double doors: *Environmental Monitoring Station*. He paused to listen, peering through the window in the center of the door. Nothing. He pushed through slowly. The emergency lights flickered on, revealing the scuba and submersible equipment mounted on the walls and sitting on shelves. A form caught Reed's eye, and he walked over. A guard, unconscious but with a pulse, lay strewn atop a mess of papers and files that littered the area. Blood trailed out of the open dock bay door to the sand beyond.

"Check in. Check in, Coyote," Reed whispered as he leaned out of the building, looking lengthwise down the side beach. Lights went on in some of the far buildings. A series of broken tones came back. "Say again?"

"What is that?" Nat muttered in the background, her voice tense. "I can't get ahold of him."

"I can't tell."

The seawater within the moon pool glowed with a blue safety light somewhere underneath the shifting water. Debris lay scattered on the cement floor of the chamber, foam and wood splinters. Reed turned back, passing the opening in the center of the floor as he strode back to the corner of the chamber where counters lined the far wall. Set up as a workstation, pipes and electrical bundles wound above the counter. He searched the worktable, making sure to record the reports, laminated charts, containers filled with weird solutions, and other research lab detritus. Moving fast, he counted the seconds since he'd heard from Coyote.

Reed thought he heard voices and froze, listening. A folded map sat underneath a coffee mug. He slid it out and found a handwritten sticky note attached. It said, *Seaward...links?* Another document had a port authority stamp on it. He was halfway through reading it when the tones started again. Reed opened his mouth to speak when it hit him. It was Morse code. Coyote was trying to send a message.

"Give me two tones if you can hear me, Coyote." A couple of answering tones came back, then Reed asked, "Can you get out?"

Reed listened to the answer, while panning the goggle's camera over everything.

Clear. Dinghy. Water sentinels deployed.

"He's out, he's out," Reed said as an alarm blared overhead. Heavy footfalls sounded down the hallway. Through the door window, he spotted several guards running his way. "I'm blown. Pull anchor, Nat, get a safe distance. I'm going dark."

They burst through the door, firing as Reed dove behind a shelving unit full of equipment. He returned fire, glancing at the deck and the beach beyond. It was too far. He lifted his gun and shot out the safety lights overhead. Glass and plastic rained down on him as the moon pool became the only light in the room.

He stilled as two guards entered cautiously, sweeping the room with their weapons, the narrow beams of their flashlights slicing through the darkness. They walked the perimeter, looking for him, checking outside of the dock opening. Reed waited until one of them passed by his shelving unit. Then he threw himself against it, toppling tanks and equipment onto the guard as he climbed over it. The other guard whirled around, firing, but Reed was already falling, dropping into the swirling water of the moon pool, holding the backpack as a shield over his head.

Rounds slammed into it as he knifed into the cold dark waters of the sea. The muffled warble of incoming rounds whizzed past him in the safety light, but he dove, swimming hard and deep into the abyss. White-hot pain seared past his cheekbone, and then everything went black.

24

The White Lion

Gunfire blasted down the corridor, and he ran toward the moon pool. He glanced through the window of the moon pool chamber in time to see Reed escape in a volley of bullets.

Bursting through the door, he shouted at the guard, "Get me a patrol boat, now!"

The guard nodded, running out of the open door to the floating dock. The White Lion grabbed his phone, seething as he strode out and scanned the water beyond. Danzig picked up.

"Reed is here. He infiltrated the lab—"

"Are you certain?"

"He has goggles and his face is covered, but who else would have the audacity?"

Danzig let out a string of curses, then, "*This!* This is why Jacoby brought him in. Reed is psychotic. What does he know?"

A patrol boat engine closed in. The White Lion glanced back inside at the ransacked desk and the files on the ground, his gut twisting. "He went through everything here, and he was spotted in the main lab. The power was out, but it's coming back on, and security says it appears he compromised the computer network. Would he understand what he saw in there?"

"Reed's smart, and he has even smarter friends. He'll put it together. The timeline—"

"Accelerate it."

The guard returned and powered the boat down as he approached. The White Lion ran out onto the dock. "I'm going out on the water. I'll get him."

They piloted the patrol boat in a search grid around the area where Reed would surface. Floodlights slipped across the water as the entire guard detail looked for him. Nothing. Five minutes passed. Ten. How did this man find the Resonance device so quickly? Had Reed tracked him to the lab? Final preparations couldn't be delayed any longer and he had to return, but he'd taken precautions. The White Lion gripped the railing until his knuckles ached. This city detective was wearing his patience thin. He threatened to upend everything.

"Widen the grid and scan a hundred meters in all directions!" the White Lion snapped after a while. "He arrived on something. If you see a boat, board it, detain the passengers. One of them will crack under my questioning."

The guard relayed his message to the other patrol boats. Wind churned the surface of the sea into choppy waves. The fog blotted out visibility to within ten feet. Everywhere he looked, matted nets of seaweed bobbed along the top of the water, obscuring the visual field.

"He has to be around here, right?" the guard intoned, his expression worried.

"How cold is the water? Can he survive?"

"It's June. That'll put it around fifty-eight, fifty-nine degrees Fahrenheit about now. The past ten years the water's been getting warmer earlier in the summer. My guys reported the intruder was wearing a wet suit. If that's true, he's probably damn near enjoying the swim."

Fury burned through the White Lion. Reed was systematically unraveling Danzig's carefully hidden plans for the region. A plan in which his own son's life hung in the balance. It was becoming more unlikely that anything would go smoothly as long as Reed drew breath.

A shape in the distance, black with blunt edges, caught his attention. "There! An inflatable boat. That has to be him."

The engine roared as they veered in its direction. Drawing his gun, the White Lion squinted at the bobbing craft as they approached. It looked abandoned, empty. And then he saw it. The sole of a military boot propped up on the side of the boat. He smiled, signaling the guard to cut the engine. Weapon pointed at the prone form, he lit his flashlight, running the beam along the body. There was blood on the arm, and the head of the figure lying motionless was turned away at an awkward angle.

"I see you are not bulletproof after all," the White Lion said, slipping his gloved finger to the trigger. "Not quite the unstoppable hunter Danzig thinks you are."

The splash of water on the other side of the patrol boat yanked his attention, and he turned just as Reed popped up from beneath the surface of the water. He ripped a breathing mask from his mouth, a grimace of anger on his bloody face.

"Xanadu sends his regards," Reed shouted as he tossed something into the patrol boat.

The White Lion threw himself away from the device a moment before an explosion of light and sound blasted through him.

25

The concussive blast rolled through the water, pushing Reed's breath from him. His goggles buzzed on his face, and he checked the readout. A proximity alert flashed in the corner of the lens. Reed knifed his hands in the water, whipping around. Three waterborne sentinel drones tore across the surface toward him. He stilled, watching to see how they tracked him. It was dark. Couldn't be by camera. Maybe heat? The wet suit might provide cover.

Reed took another breath. The bail-out tank was nearly out of oxygen. And then a sharp pulse of sound hit him, scrambling his thoughts. Sonar round. Like submarines, the sentinels were tracking how the blast came back to them. They turned in unison, their jellyfish-like tendrils churning the water with sparks.

Reed fought the swells of the ocean, and his goggle's headlamp flashed across jagged rocks ahead. He stopped fighting, letting the current throw him against the outcropping. He caught an edge with his glove, whipped around and held on, staying just underneath the surface. Powerful waves caught the sentinels, bashing them against the exposed boulders. Their tendrils whipped past Reed's face as he took a shallow breath from the tank. And then he saw it. A sea lion, floating in front of him, motionless.

The crack of breaking glass warbled through the water, and then the animal split. In perfect slices like a roast on a table. Its body floated apart. A cloud of blood unfurled, thick and crimson in the waves. A disembodied flipper still attached to a piece of flank drifted with the current toward him, and Reed jerked back, not wanting it to touch him. His hand holding onto the rock caught his attention, but then he realized it was bare. The glove was gone, exposing a tattoo he didn't have. He was in Slater's memory of this carnage. Reed yanked himself from the scene. Gasping as he surfaced. Suddenly frigid with cold. Shaking his head to clear it, he spotted the patrol boat. He took the last breath from the tank and dove, fighting the fatigue of hypothermia.

Reed resurfaced a few yards from the dinghy just as Coyote fired several rounds into the transom of the patrol boat, hitting the engine. The boat sputtered, and smoke poured out of the stern. Stunned by the flash-bang, the guard held his palms to his ears and stumbled around the boat. But another man rose from the deck, flailing his weapon in Reed's direction as he tried to see. It was him, the one in the video with Bobby. The white-haired man.

"That's him," Reed shouted as he struggled aboard the dinghy. He pulled out his weapon, trying to aim, but the smoke from the flash-bang and the fog obscured the figure. The guard kept crossing his line of fire. Reed stood, balancing to jump onto the patrol boat, when gunfire cracked through the night. Two more patrol boats sped toward them. Reed growled with frustration. The white-haired man was in his sights.

"We gotta go, Morgan!"

Reed dropped back into the boat, his gut sour. "Get us out of here."

Coyote accelerated the powerful motor away, veering them around the listing patrol boat and into the shroud of fog. Reed turned back, kept his eye on the figure, his jaw clenched with anger. There was something wrong with the man's skin, but he was definitely the one who'd hurt Fiona. Who'd stalked and possibly shot Bobby. And he slipped through Reed's fingers again.

"You all right?" Coyote asked as they put distance between them and the scene. "Your face is bleedin'. Are you hit?"

Reed shook his head, though he did a mental inventory of his current pain. Nothing new. He panned his light over at Coyote. Angry red marks flared across his neck. Signs of a tussle with a water sentinel. Blood oozed from his pant leg.

Reed leaned in to inspect. "Did you take a bullet?"

"A round cut a nice groove along the surface of my thigh. Bled like a stuck pig, but it's not bad. This is what hurts like hell, though." Coyote pointed to the electric burns on his throat. "Did you get a look at those swimming stun guns? Zapped the living crap out of the goggles and earpiece, too. I need me one of those ASAP."

Reed realized his earpiece wasn't working either. He pushed up his goggles, rubbing his face, thinking about the sea lion and the blood. His hands shook with the cold coursing through him. A reaction to the Glycon-C patches he used to combat the side effects of viewing the MER-C system memories. Jacoby had been right, they helped with the worst symptoms, but the formula had thrown Reed's thermal regulation in the toilet. He needed to get warm.

Reed pulled off the wet mask from around his neck. "You were saying before the shooting started that I had to see something in the moon pool area. When I got there, I spotted your handiwork on the guard and some papers on the floor, but that's all."

Coyote's brows furrowed. "You didn't see it? A boat launched maybe five minutes before I walked out onto the sand. Like they were trying to get away. Midsize cruiser, gotta be less than thirty feet. Sounded like a powerful engine. It moved like it had some speed on it, but it sat funny on the water. When the lights hit it...I don't know. The sail was moored up, but it looked...I want to say metal, but that's not right either."

"That sounds unnecessarily complex. I'm mad I didn't see it." Reed scanned the thick mist hovering over the water. He had seen, however, the debris on the floor of the moon pool. Foam, wood—could be from a packing crate, Reed mused. "A long-haul vessel, huh?"

Coyote nodded. "Looked like one of them sailboats Old Man Coop used to take down to Florida back in the day, only tricked out with tech. The fog bank swallowed it up. I couldn't spot it by the time I got to the dinghy."

"I doubt they filed a sailing plan," Reed muttered. "Maybe Nat can get us some imaging of the lab's location right as the boat left."

"Jacoby has likely caught wind about the hullabaloo we just caused. I hope you found something interesting to tell him."

Reed held up the data scraper and a small vial he'd snaked from the main laboratory. "I hope so."

In the distance, shrouded by fog, a light flashed on and off. It was the *Sea Witch*, anchored around the bend of the cliffs. Nat looked down at them from the deck as they piloted close, shook her head, and tossed them a length of rope.

Coyote dropped them back at Field Ops before heading to his own place. He declined to reveal where he was staying, but Reed suspected he was going to bunk out on Pitch's boat. Reed and Nat stumbled back into the warehouse well past three in the morning.

"Go, take a shower, warm up. Your lips are literally blue," Nat said, shooing Reed upstairs. She held up his and Coyote's field goggles. "I need to see what you guys recorded. The stream was interrupted and got choppy. I want to know why."

"You should try to sleep," Reed said, running the back of his fingers along her cheek. "We're all wrung out."

"As soon as I start the upload," she said and gave him a little push. "Go."

Exhausted, he stood in the shower, letting the hot water thaw him out. Thinking about Slater. In the memory he'd taken from the aspiring journalist in Aurora, Hazel Hill, Slater had asked her about Resonance. That always bothered Reed, and Jacoby avoided the question when he'd asked. Why would Slater think she knew about a top-secret weapon? She wasn't investigating Danzig. She was looking into the Rexfords. The only ones left in the family were Bunny and her political scion son, Pierce. Reed knew he was involved somehow. The young politician had murky allegiances and had used the fire at Aurora to his advantage. Milking the "hero son" angle. Where did that ruthless family fit into all of this?

Fatigue washed over him, and he decided he was warm enough. Reed stepped out of the shower, toweling off and changing into dark gray sweats despite the heat of the summer night. When he wandered back down to the main floor of the warehouse, he found Nat bundled up in a blanket on the couch, lightly snoring. He took her tablet from her hands and set it on the side table. A bundle of folded papers sat tucked into her arms, and he pulled them from her grasp, frowning as he looked at them. It was a scientific paper on crystalline formations in nonfrozen water. Reed sat up, scanning the text with growing interest. When he was halfway through the paper, Jacoby strode through the warehouse door, followed by Luna.

"Reed!"

Nudging Nat awake, Reed stood up from the couch while she woke up. "We have trouble."

She rose next to him, instantly alert. "Shit."

"Yeah."

Jacoby spotted him and strode over, his face a mask of anger. "You!"

Reed backed up, hands in the air. "I can explain—"

Jacoby pointed at his own chest, his hand shaking with fury. "*I* was playing a game of cat and mouse with Danzig and his cohort and people you aren't even cleared to know exist. Tracking them quietly, gathering information to stop whatever they have planned. *You* were supposed to stick to finding Bobby Khan," Jacoby yelled. "That's it. But you assholes had to go and let *everybody* know we're onto them."

Reed stabbed his finger toward the window. "There is something going on in that lab that has nothing to do with biology and acoustics—"

"We know. We've been monitoring their waste disposal," Jacoby snapped, his brows arching. "What, you thought we just let the secret lab do nefarious shit while we waited for you guys to find a missing blogger?"

"That is a materials lab, they were testing atom excitation," Nat said with some edge. "We already know it's some kind of weapon. So, why won't you tell us what is going on so we can stop this?"

"Because you're blown. All of you! I have no use for you anymore out here."

"Reed and Coyote aren't blown. They covered their faces, wore gloves," Nat said. Reed closed his eyes. She didn't get it.

"Do you think Danzig and his allies are building a case against you?" Jacoby snapped at her. "You will just disappear."

"He was there," Reed said. "The white-haired man who attacked Bobby and Fiona. Proof he's doing something for Danzig. And there was a boat."

"On the ocean? That'll be easy to find," Jacoby retorted, pacing.

"What about Fiona? We haven't questioned her yet," Reed interjected. "She saw him up close. There's something wrong with his—"

Jacoby stopped Reed with a look. "They got her through the initial surgery, thought she was stabilized, and then they had to rush her back in. Fiona died on the table a few hours ago."

Nat's hand went to her mouth, and she turned away.

"I can go back and speak with Marla, the local artist who dated Bobby's father. Maybe she..." Reed's voice trailed off as Jacoby shook his head.

"Listen, I thought Bobby Khan was the key to this. It's why I brought you and your team in. But it's been decided Bobby is likely dead. No activity whatsoever for an amateur on the run is as good as proof. They believe he was killed by the intruder who shot at him in his condo. You've been unable to find him because he's probably chopped up in a barrel heading to the other side of the world by now."

Nat spun around. "So that's it?"

"No, we offload what you've gathered, get it to the Gray Zone task force. Go from there."

"Go from there? Are you serious? A weapon is in play," Reed shot back. "We have video of the inside of that lab." He walked over to his backpack and pulled out the vial he'd taken. Holding it up, he said, "We have evidence."

"Things have shifted. We don't believe the white-haired man will continue to search for Bobby. We think he's in phase two of whatever they're planning."

"So, we keep going," Nat said. "I don't get it."

"You served your purpose, Detective De La Cruz. It doesn't matter if we find Bobby or not at this point."

The cold light of understanding washed over Reed. Jacoby didn't care what Bobby had recorded. They could debunk it. He knew more about what Resonance was than even Reed suspected. Reed and his friends who he'd put in danger for this were flies in the ointment, nothing more.

"I was just a distraction," he said finally. His face burning.

Jacoby's gaze turned hard. "You were supposed to keep the heat on this assailant, whoever he is. Maybe be so troublesome you flush him out. But you missed him, both times, and still no Bobby. No recording of that night."

"Luna said that Deep Wave Dynamics was 'tangentially' tied to several tech power players that Gray Zone is watching. She said High Rock Holdings was possibly involved." Reed shook his head, the betrayal roiling in his gut. "He nearly blew us up, he killed an innocent woman, and we were nothing but bait to you? Something to slow him down until you could figure out what he was doing?"

"Yes, and you were highly ineffective, by the way," Jacoby spat angrily. "All you managed to do was accelerate their timeline."

"How do you know that?" Reed asked. "What aren't you telling us."

"Volumes!" Jacoby snapped. "There are mountains of shit I do not share with you and your crew of misfits."

"Hey!" Nat shouted.

"You owe us an explanation!" Reed yelled.

"I owe you nothing! You were salivating to go after Danzig again, and you know it. You just needed an excuse, and Xanadu's death gave it to you!"

Reed grabbed at Jacoby's shirt, shaking the smaller man. "Did you set that up? Did you get Xanadu killed to pull us in?"

"Reed!" Nat yelled, her eyes wide.

Jacoby pushed Reed off him, his tie askew, face red. "I didn't need to do anything to get you and your friends back in danger's way. You do that all by yourself." He backed up, pointing a finger at Reed's face. "And yes, maybe I thought you could live up to the hype and take down whoever this white-haired freak is, but you haven't been able to. You didn't find Bobby, you didn't catch the attacker, and you still don't know what the weapon is and how they plan to use it. You failed. And now you're blown. There's a dumpster fire of a mess back on that island that I have to answer for."

"You mean cover up," Reed shot back. "That's what you're good at, right?"

Jacoby's face split into a rueful smile. "Oh, you're talking about the mission information Coyote stole. Yeah, he's not as slick as he thinks he is. Acquisition and dissemination of top-secret information is a felony for which he'll serve in federal prison if he gets caught."

"So, you don't deny it. You knowingly sent your agents to their deaths."

Jacoby's face went slack, his eyes suddenly dead. "We paid what it cost to stop an attack on our country. That is all the explanation you're ever going to get."

"They're sending it somewhere," Reed argued. "They packed it for long-haul."

Jacoby shook his head. "You're off the case. I'm dissolving Gray Zone's relationship with all of you."

"I'm not backing off of Danzig or this attacker until I know what's going on," Reed said. "That kid is still out there."

"Excuse me?" A pall of fury settled over Jacoby's face. "If you are still in California by day's end tomorrow, I'll have you all arrested for treason or obstruction or anything my slew of lawyers can come up with. You will not get in my way, Reed. Do you copy? Coyote has so many felonies to answer for, he'll go away for years. And Nat will lose her career, I'll *see* to it!" Jacoby straightened out his tie, smoothing it along his chest, suddenly calm. "And if I see you anywhere near my operation, if you interfere in Homeland's mission in any way, I will consider you an enemy of the state and will put a bullet in your head. Am I clear?"

Reed's gaze slipped to Nat. The fear on her face was all he could take.

"Crystal," Reed snapped, fighting the urge to throttle the man.

"Luna will take your phones, keys, and credentials and lock down the warehouse. Leave tonight, Reed. Final warning," Jacoby said and left.

Luna, who'd simply stood and watched the entire scenario, including the scuffle, with a blank face, suddenly came to life. She plastered on a fake, human resources–type smile, and held out her palm. "We'll start with your credentials, Mr. Reed."

26

Long, sunlit terminals with white adobe walls and high-arched ceilings gave Santa Barbara airport an almost cathedral-like feel he hadn't appreciated when they flew in. The mix of Spanish Colonial Revival architecture with the high-tech sustainable landscape soothed his mind as he drew in his sketchbook. Beeping from the security check-in area, scratchy suitcase wheels, and clacking heels mixed with the din of conversation inside the building. Huge white pipes crisscrossed the floor-to-ceiling windows lining the terminal. Reed sat next to one of them, sketching as the rising sun's golden light crawled across the landscape of the squat buildings. The rays warmed his face, and he almost felt relieved to be leaving. It was six a.m., and with any luck he'd be back in Seattle by lunch.

Nat wasn't talking much. They'd gotten out with most of her equipment but not all. Luna kept the goggles from the night swim and other data they'd collected. It had been a hell of a fight to get Nat to leave, but she finally agreed to regroup back in Seattle rather than piss off Jacoby. They sat in the main terminal while Reed called Coyote and told him what happened.

"Well, that's no surprise," he drawled. "I'm shocked y'all aren't behind bars, to be honest."

"Are you staying? I know you and your sailor buddies had business."

"I won't be in Jacoby's jurisdiction." A ship's horn sounded in the background. "You should leave, Morgan. If not for your own skin, but for your better half's. She doesn't know how to quit either."

Nat sat on the ledge of the huge window next to Reed, eating a giant cinnamon bun out of a box. She muttered angrily as she stabbed at a frosted curl of pastry.

"I'm not sure that's going to be easy."

"A phone call away, brother," Coyote said and was gone.

Reed stood to stretch, shaking his phone at Nat. "He's staying. He has some things to tie off out here."

"So do we. We shouldn't be leaving."

"You heard Jacoby."

"He can't just run us out of town like some dusty-ass sheriff."

"Yes. He can."

"We agreed to catch Xanadu's killer, not be bait for Danzig. I want to go back. Track down the guy through his bombs, or maybe he touched Fiona's clothes, and we'll get a print…"

"This white-haired guy, he's not some gangbanger or career criminal we're trying to track down. He's a hired killer, clearly. I don't want to lose anyone else to Danzig and whatever he's doing. Jacoby is on it. All of Gray Zone is on it."

"And you really believe that?" Nat asked, rolling her eyes. "Jacoby acts like he's playing four-dimensional chess when all he's doing is chasing bigger, smarter, well-funded criminals."

"You're not really helping your argument here."

"What I'm saying is the rules of chasing criminals scale up. This white-haired guy, he's been in the game awhile, right? The weapons. His bombs."

"Yes, he's clearly a seasoned pro."

"Is he, though? There's no proof he found Bobby either. So, he's not doing any better than us."

"Jacoby is right, not one sighting of an untrained citizen does not bode well for the kid."

"Hey, Bobby was an engineer. He rebuilt submersibles and repurposed them for his dad. That's resourcefulness." Nat shrugged. "Besides, I think the white-haired killer is still here in LA and not out there doing whatever his real job is, because Bobby is still out there evading him. He's definitely not chop suey in a barrel somewhere."

"I agree, seeing him at the lab connected some dots," Reed nodded. "He must have something to do with what Bobby saw that night on the water."

"Yeah, there's no way he's just some hired gun to take out a witness. Not now. Because why would he be at the secret lab? Why tell some rando killer the whole story when all you hired him to do is kill the target?"

"You wouldn't," Reed conceded. He'd hoped she'd let things go. "You're right. This white-haired guy is probably connected to the sinkings."

"You knew?"

"I suspected after Luna told us he'd bugged Bobby's townhouse. You don't need to bug people to stalk and kill them. You do if you're looking for something else."

"Fiona said she'd given Bobby a finished data lens with his cleaned-up video of the weapon that night," Nat said, her eyes going wide. "You think it's still out there."

"Maybe. The killer being at the lab made it more likely, because what would be the more important mission? Find Bobby, who, as we just found out, isn't that important after all, or the mission concerning whatever we saw at the lab?"

"The lab. The weapon," Nat said.

"Yes. Resonance, or whatever they called it, was important to Slater, he thought the Rexfords knew about it, he questioned Hazel if it was in play. That's now Slater, Danzig, and the white-haired guy all involved with this lab and that sinking somehow. That's the more important mission. The main one, I'd wager. Bobby was just a loose end."

"And so, if the killer is still out here and not on his way somewhere with the weapon, then that would mean they think Bobby's data lens of evidence is still out there. And that whatever is on it is worth the effort to retrieve it."

"If the killer somehow found and took Fiona's or it burned up in the wreckage, we'll never know. But if he's still here, despite the accelerated plans that Jacoby just mentioned, then yeah, I'd bet Bobby's lens is still out there."

"Or the guy's so furious you keep effing up his plans, he's staying around to kill you."

"I mean, I do have that effect on people," Reed said.

"Well, we can't stop now."

"Nat..."

"Just listen." She had a stack of bound papers on her lap supporting the cinnamon bun box. She slid it out, handing it to him. "That's the paper Bobby was trying to talk to that scientist about. Remember, the guy who filed and then rescinded a police complaint against him?"

Reed nodded, flipping through the document. "Dr. Kernigan, right? The physicist?"

"That's his paper, and you should read it. It's a bit over my head, but I talked with someone from the university, and they walked me through it. Guess what's peppered throughout the entire thing?"

His gut knotted when he looked at her. She wasn't giving up. "What?"

"Crystalline structures. Like what you've been talking about. And I found out Kernigan's old lab assistant isn't in LA. He's in San Francisco now. That's way out of Jacoby's way." She popped another piece in her mouth. "Check out page twenty-four." When he didn't move, she tilted her head. "What's wrong?"

"This doesn't change anything, Nat. We still have to leave. We still have to back off. Talking to anyone concerning the case is a no go."

She stopped chewing. "What do you mean? You just said Bobby's probably still alive."

"I said the data lens is possibly still out there. I never said—"

"He's alone out there! We can't just leave..." Nat looked away, blinking rapidly. After a few moments, she said, "Look, I know he's not Xanadu. I know this need to save this kid is stupid. But it's also human decency. Just because Jacoby thinks this killer gave up doesn't make it true."

Reed tugged on her sweater sleeve gently, and she turned to face him. "Listen to me. Jacoby wasn't bluffing. A man like him doesn't make hollow threats. He was telling us exactly what he was going to do if we stay. Give Jacoby the scientific paper and the name of Kernigan's assistant, and then let this go. Keep your career. Possibly your freedom."

Nat didn't say anything. She nodded slightly after a few seconds, but it was the light in her eyes for him that cut deep. It went out.

They spent the next three hours on their phones or watching the silent wall screens play old shows. Delay after delay scrolled across the information monitors due to a flight crew union standoff with a few airlines. Nat, lost in thought, barely answered his tries at conversation, so he left her in peace. He didn't know how to tell her that getting her killed would end him. He wouldn't survive it. And yet it seemed that he was going to lose her in life instead.

At nearly ten a.m., the overhead speaker announced their flight, followed by a text message urging them to head to their gate. Reed picked up his carry-on and Nat's and started walking. He took a few steps into the crowd when he realized she wasn't with him. He turned, and she hadn't moved. Instead, she sat ramrod straight, staring at her laptop, head shaking.

Doubling back, Reed asked, "What's wrong?"

"I...didn't expect..." Her gaze snapped up to his. "Remember I said I was going to use Fiona's phone to send a message to Bobby in some way?"

"Yeah..." Reed said with growing dread.

"Well, I couldn't, not without alerting anyone watching Bobby's accounts."

Another announcement pricked his nerves. "Okay..."

"As a last-ditch effort, I launched a 'seek and find' program on all of his frequently visited locations. I fed it information from his phone-tracking data I got from Luna, his financials, stuff like that."

"Seek and find, is that facial recognition?"

"Yeah, only it looks for things like gait and mannerisms too. We threw a lot of our best stuff into it."

"You and Xanadu," Reed said, understanding. "You didn't run this on the Gray Zone network, did you?"

"No way. Xanadu and I built it together, it started as a city-wide game, and it was the last thing we worked on, so Jacoby isn't getting his grubby hands on it, okay?"

Reed put his hands up in surrender. "Okay."

"Anyway, I had the program scanning for anyone who looked like Bobby. I used his social media posts and podcast videos as well."

"And it worked?"

She turned her laptop so he could see. "He just popped up at an electronics store a few miles from his townhouse."

A video of Bobby Khan, plain as day for the world to see, showed him purchasing something with cash at the counter. He even did one of those double takes at the camera before he angled away.

He's going to get himself killed, Reed thought. "When was this recorded?"

"It wasn't," Nat said, her face flushing red. "This is live. He's alive, Reed."

"Send it to Jacoby."

"He cut us off. I tried to get some of my equipment from Luna shipped back home, and none of the numbers they gave us work. They carved us out of the loop."

"We can drive by the Field Ops, tell whoever's closing down what we have—"

"You didn't trust Jacoby enough to tell him about your little night raid on the lab, but you want me to trust Bobby's life to him? Where's the Reed I knew who stopped at nothing to do what was needed…what was right?"

"It's not that simple."

"It is, actually." She popped up, grabbed her carry-on from him, and headed for the exit. "I'm staying."

"Wait—"

She spun to face him. "I'm not leaving that kid. I'm not letting Danzig and that white-haired murderer win. And I'm certainly not letting Jacoby stop me from doing what *I know* is right."

"Don't do this."

"I followed you into chaos lots of times, my love," Nat said and looked at him with those deep, dark eyes. "It's your turn."

She turned and walked out of the airport's sliding doors. Reed growled with frustration but went after her. Better to run with the hurricane than against it.

27

They sat in the back seat of an autonomous car they'd hired using one of Reed's identities from his undercover days. He still had an account with the nationwide service as a precaution. Turned out he was right to keep it. Jacoby wouldn't likely know to track the fake identity, but Gray Zone would definitely be tracking Reed's and his team's financials. The car drove them toward the electronics place while they watched Bobby wandering around the store in real time.

"What is he doing?" Reed asked, typing out a message to Coyote.

Change of plans. Located Bobby. Could use your help. Headed to Doctor Tech, an electronics repair shop.

I'm at the harbor. On my way, Coyote answered.

Nat adjusted the zoom on the screen. "He bought something, and now he's fiddling with his backpack at the work desk. He's also charging what looks like a flip phone."

"Probably a burner," Reed said.

Nat touched the screen, enlarging the zoom to his hands as he pulled a laptop out of his backpack and plugged it in. "I thought his laptop was missing?"

"Forensics reported finding a power cord at his townhouse but no phone, laptop, or tablet. They assumed the attacker took his electronics or Bobby did when he fled."

"Looks like it was Bobby." Nat squinted at the screen. "Oh, no," she breathed. "Oh no, no, no."

"What? What is it?"

"Remember how we thought that the break-in at the main office of Bobby's rental property was to cover up someone planting bugs in Bobby's townhouse?"

"Yes."

"Well, if the killer broke in, the one who is after Bobby's data lens, why would he leave the laptop behind? I mean, if Bobby has it, then the killer didn't take it when he broke in to plant the listening device. And he left it a second time when he returned and shot at Bobby later. Why?"

Dawning moved through Reed. "Because the white-haired guy knew Bobby didn't have it there."

"If you wanted to keep track of me, you'd bug my tablet, right? I always have it with me."

"So then why hasn't the killer found Bobby if he has a tracker on his laptop?" Reed stared at the kid in the live feed. Bobby stood in front of the blacked-out laptop screen, biting his nail, like he was waiting for something. "Oh crap. If he left the cord at his townhouse and he had to buy one just now..."

"Then this might be the first time he's powering up." Nat reached up and pushed the service button. "Can you go any faster?"

Apologies. AutoDrive vehicles must maintain the correct speed limit. We are proud to get our customers to their destinations safely.

"Damn it!" Nat pounded her fist on the back seat door.

"Tell me what's happening."

She pointed at the video stream. "Look at Bobby's laptop screen. It's black, which means it was dead. That would've kept a tracking program from sending his location. If a tracker draws power from his battery, it'll be coming back online any moment."

"And alert the white-haired killer of his location."

"Yes," Nat said. "We have to get to him first."

He checked with Coyote, but he was still twenty minutes out. Reed rubbed the hairline scar over his eyebrow, thinking. "We can call the store. Warn Bobby and tell him to hide until we get there."

She nodded, and Reed looked up the number in his browser and called. He immediately started fighting with the AI customer service bot. "Connect me directly to a *human* at the store, now!"

Certainly, one moment please, the bot said, only to restart the options menu.

Reed left a message for the store manager to call him back ASAP about a customer in danger. Nat sat up straighter as the camera feed showed Bobby's screen flashing to life.

"Crap, crap, crap," she whispered. Nat's fingers tapped furiously on her keyboard, and windows filled with scrolling numbers and strange code blocks popped up and collapsed in rapid succession. A black window slid down from the top of her screen, and then a video feed of the street fluttered open. "There you are…"

"Is that—"

"Yeah, that's the street camera right outside the Doctor Tech store."

"You can tap into the city cameras?"

"That's not municipal, that's the building across the street, a tax attorney's office. Most people don't secure their cameras, or they use easy-to-guess passwords of fewer than six alphanumeric characters. Which with modern access programs are a cinch to beat." She patted her laptop gently. "I'm running that with an open access hopper program I built for cybercrime that seeks out and finds unsecured cameras within a given parameter. Open access means no warrants."

"I've heard of this. They have an app where you can put in a surveillance video and the program can back-identify where it was taken with metadata and topographical cues. You can see exactly which camera made the recording."

"Yeah, only mine does it in real time. We used it in cybercrime. This baby tracked a child abductor from the snatch location to his vehicle in real time using park cameras. Patrol stopped the car before he exited the parking lot."

Reed shook his head with awe, always a little afraid of what Nat could do with a computer. Inside the electronics shop, Bobby left the camera view from inside the store and then appeared in the next video window, walking down the street.

"He's moving," Reed said, squinting at her screen. "He's limping."

"He was shot at his townhouse," Nat said.

It would make him slow, Reed thought. Not good. "He's heading south on Canell Street."

Nat's program jumped from camera to camera, the view switched from an overhead bird feeder to one at garage level, to another atop a streetlight, tracking Bobby as he hobbled down the street. His head swiveled back and forth, and he glanced over his shoulder furtively every few feet.

"I mean, he's acting sketchy as hell. That's gonna catch people's eye," Nat said. "Hold on." She reached out to the touch screen on the AutoDrive car's center console and adjusted the trip directions to stay on Canell Street until further notice.

"I need a map," Reed said, reaching for her tablet. "I want to see what's ahead of him."

She typed in a text box, and then a map appeared on the screen with several paths tracing in different directions. She made a sliding gesture across her screen, and the tablet in his hand lit up with the same map and routes. He zoomed out, looking for where Bobby might be heading. Bobby veered down an alley, and they lost him for a moment. Nat checked the multiple predicted paths and readjusted the car's trip directions, driving slowly until they found Bobby on the cameras again as he stepped out from between some buildings near a chain-link fence. He took another look down the road, scanning for something, and ambled inside the building.

"That's a construction zone. We're about three blocks behind him." Reed ground his jaw. Why did Bobby stay so close to home? He fired off the address to Coyote, telling him to let them know when he arrived so they didn't shoot him.

Nat directed the AutoDrive to the location, and they stepped out onto a maintenance road next to a half-finished building construction. She sent the AutoDrive to park and wait for them, adding more of the fake identity's money to the account to hold the car. Reed pulled out a box of their connected earpieces he'd taken from Field Ops. She raised an eyebrow when he handed hers over.

"What, only you can steal from Jacoby?" he asked with a smirk.

They approached the building, and Reed took in the rusted metal and torn sheeting, the trash littering the area, the lack of any working construction robots. The building was abandoned, a long time ago, he guessed. He and Nat walked through the unlocked gate, down the path in the scattered gravel, and entered the unfinished office building through the busted glass entrance doors.

The place was trashed, and though he kept an eye out, Reed didn't pick up any hint of security save for the little patrol robots that wandered around the grounds like oversized RC cars. They skittered around outside near a pile of construction debris. They had good cameras, but their little whiney motors gave them away, so they were easy to avoid. The mounted cameras he spotted bore black paint over their lenses, the hallmark of squatters. He doubted anyone was monitoring them, and they were as abandoned as the building they now haunted. They explored the first floor, listening for signs of Bobby. Reed could see the ghost of what should have been. Looters had stripped away the wooden wall art and the maple counters, but their shards and broken pieces remained.

An overhead skylight let in the morning sun washing the center of the lobby with soft, ethereal light. The first floor appeared mostly finished. Remains of what it looked like littered the room. Framed product posters for a high-end camping outfitter company sat askew on the wall, showing off self-erecting tents and coolers with three-day batteries. Office equipment sat smashed on the counter and in pieces on the floor. Reed thought he could make out a 3D printer. Pamphlets about the building lay strewn on the carpet.

The first level had obviously been used as a showroom, but then the company likely lost funding before completing construction. He'd seen a lot of halted projects around the area. Apparently, nothing in LA proved permanent. As if every dream born there meant another had to die. Moving deeper, they passed walls riddled with holes and graffiti, tin foil hung in torn sheets on the windows to block out the sun, and grime caked the carpets lining the lobby. It crunched under Reed's boots. Once they pushed past the reception area to the hallway leading into the main building, they had to use a flashlight to see. He and Nat navigated down dark corridors with exposed metal beams and wiring jutting out from walls.

"How many floors does this place have?" Nat asked when they got to a stairwell.

Reed pulled out a pamphlet he'd picked up from the floor and read it. "Five." He nodded at the door. "Up or down?"

Nat sighed, shaking her head. "If Bobby had to charge up his laptop and his phone at the Doctor Tech store, then he's not drawing power here. That means it's hotter than hell during the daytime."

Reed consulted the pamphlet, shining light on the list of locations. "This says there's a communal floor. It mentions a cafeteria and some kind of open-air dining." He showed her the photo of what looked like a resort terrace with tables and whatnot for employees to eat lunch outside, overlooking the city. "This would be where I'd go. It's up high, on the top floor, so no one could see you from the ground, but you could see someone approaching the building. And it would get the cool breeze off the water."

"I'm sold," Nat said, pushing through the doorway. The stairwell was pitch black. "I knew that big brain of yours would come in—"

Something clanged overhead, and Reed yanked Nat back out a moment before gunfire blasted down from above. Cacophonous, it echoed in his ears as he pushed her behind him, blocking the door from closing with his body. He shone his light upward, hopefully blinding the shooter.

"Bobby! I'm here to help you!" Reed shouted and was answered with a few more shots from above. Ducking back out of the doorway, he opened and closed his mouth, fighting the ringing from the blasts. Opening the door a crack, he shouted, "I talked to Marla. She's worried about you!"

Nothing, then a tremulous whisper sounded from the dark stairwell. "Marla?"

"Yeah, I spotted that stew she made you. She's been taking care of you, hasn't she?"

After a few moments, Bobby asked, "Is she okay? I haven't heard from her."

"I can check on that," Nat said, grabbing her phone. "I have a friend at LAPD."

Reed scanned the stairs with his flashlight, and then a pale face looked over the railing down at them. "Are you Agent Reed?"

Reed nodded. "I've been looking all over LA for you. You're in danger."

Bobby let out a rueful laugh. "Yeah, no shit."

28

Bobby met them on the stairwell, and Reed thought he looked wracked. He wore jeans, a thin pullover sweatshirt, and sneakers. His straight black hair was greasy, and he had dark circles under his eyes. They followed Bobby up to the terrace floor, which was a cavernous open space. Construction had stopped midway, and murky sheets of torn plastic hung from the walls and ceiling. Bobby had a tent and chair set up by the graffitied windows. He led them to his camping area, wincing as he went.

Reed held out his hand. "The gun."

"I'm sorry about the shooting and all. They were blanks," Bobby said, handing it over. "It's my dad's starter pistol. I saw a car following me slowly and panicked. I thought he'd found me."

"The man who attacked you at your townhouse?" Reed clarified, setting the pistol on a nearby table.

"Yeah."

"You weren't wrong to worry. He's still after you," Reed said. "Grab your stuff, and let's go. We have to run."

"Hold on, I gotta sit for a minute." Bobby eased himself down on the camping chair with a groan of pain. Blood stained the lower part of his jeans near his calf.

"Where's your laptop, Bobby?" Nat asked, panning her flashlight around the room.

"It's in a safe place."

She shook her head. "It's giving off your location. Tell me where it is."

"You had it with you when you left Doctor Tech," Reed said. "Where'd you stash it?"

"Hey, how did you know that?"

"The electronics, Bobby," Nat cut in, tension on her face. "This is serious."

"On the second floor in a file room filled with boxes. There's a loose vent behind one of the filing cabinets. I put my stuff in there for safekeeping. In case...you know. In case I have to run again."

"Shouldn't we leave it?" Reed asked her.

Bobby shook his head, near panic on his face. "That laptop has my whole life. My secret account with the insurance money, backups of my podcast, all the proof I've gathered about what happened to my dad."

"Forget it." Reed motioned to Bobby. "We need to go."

"I'm not leaving without it!"

"It's not worth—"

"I'll go get it," Nat said and took off before Reed could argue. Her voice came in on his earpiece, echoing as she entered the stairwell. "You hear me?"

"Loud and clear. Grab it and go, Nat. We can't stay here long." Reed paced the area. Checked his watch. Then, "So, Marla's been taking care of you?"

"I didn't say that."

"You don't have to." A foldable table with some grocery store items sat in the corner. Bread, peanut butter and jelly in a jar, juice boxes, quite a few water bottles, and bags of fruit. A small handwoven basket contained gauze, alcohol, and a bottle of prescription antibiotics with the name blacked out with marker. Reed glanced down at the parking lot from the window. One of the patrol bots ambled across the littered lot below.

"No one else is involved in this. I had money and kept my head down."

"You can barely walk, but you carried up two cases of water bottles?"

Reed shook his head. "You tucked all those medicals supplies nice and neat in an expensive basket? I've seen your room, man. It's Marla, right?"

He answered with a noncommittal shrug, then, "How's Fiona? They won't tell me anything at the hospital."

"Did you go there?"

"No, I heard someone was hurt where she worked, and I called to see. It was her, right?"

Reed sighed. "I'm sorry. She didn't make it."

"Ah man. I can't—" Bobby looked away, nodding. "It's my fault. I got her killed."

"No, the guy chasing you killed her. The white-haired guy." Reed caught the fear in Bobby's eyes.

"You've seen him?"

Reed nodded, grabbed Bobby's backpack, and flung it over his shoulder. "Time's up. You can tell me about him on the way down."

They took some smaller snacks with them as well as the first aid kit and headed back down the stairs. About a flight down, sweaty and shaking, Bobby said he needed another break. Reluctantly, Reed let him sit and gave him some water.

"It's just the pain," Bobby said between drinks. "I'll rally."

"Tell me about the white-haired guy," Reed said, checking his watch again. Five minutes since Nat went to find the laptop.

Bobby explained that the man Reed was talking about first approached him at Flex Space. "It was at night, toward closing, and he was outside, like he was waiting for me. The guy said his name was Whit something. Liu, I think. Lee? I don't know. He kept going on and on about my podcast, but he was hard to understand because of his accent."

"What kind of accent?"

"Like Swedish, or maybe Australian. I don't know." Bobby shrugged. "When I cyberstalked him online, I couldn't find that name linked with anyone younger than, like, seventy. No one his age for sure. He was a ghost."

"What did he want?"

"He told me he'd experienced something similar and wanted to talk, but...he was off somehow. Too intense, you know?" Bobby shuddered.

"Something about him creeped me out. He kept in the shadows like some vampire, it was weird. I made an excuse and went home."

"We have surveillance of him at your property."

Bobby nodded. "He showed up at my house a few days later, this time asking me to take him to the area where the boat went down. I told him to piss off. I thought that was it, but he came back a few weeks later. Three or so days before the attack. He said he wanted a sneak peek of the proof I teased on my podcast. I told him no, and he left."

"Was that before or after you let him in?" Reed called up the video of them talking at the townhouse on his phone.

Watching the video, Bobby shrugged. "For like, a minute. He asked for water to take medicine or something. I was gone for five seconds, and when I came back, he was already trying to leave."

"We believe he bugged the smoke detector in your front room."

"Great." Bobby shook his head. "I had no idea he was listening to me."

They started down the stairs again, and Bobby continued his story. After the guy showed up at his house and he blew him off, Bobby started getting anonymous death threats on his podcast. In the comments and in private messages to stop telling lies.

"Then he broke into your house, later, right? He's the one who shot you?"

"Yeah, if I hadn't sloshed my soup and slipped on the broth...he would have put a bullet in my head." Bobby's eyes grew wide. "I threw the soup at him and ran, but he hit me and we went down. I think my nose is cracked or something."

Reed's gaze went to the discoloration under Bobby's eyes. It was bruising from the attack. "That's how your blood got on the wall."

Bobby nodded. "I managed to get away by hitting him with a chair. Then I grabbed my stuff and ran for the window. He shot me in the leg when I was running across the grass, but I kept going. I spent a couple of nights sneaking onto people's boats before I found this place. I figured I should stop putting my friends in danger."

"What about Marla?" Reed asked, helping Bobby down a few steps at a time.

"Look, I called her when I thought my leg was infected. She showed up with all that first aid stuff and helped me out. She and my dad were together, though I think they thought I didn't know. She wanted to help." Bobby hopped down the stairs on his good leg.

Marla had fed Reed just enough information to get him to leave her gallery and then warned Bobby. Unbelievable. "So, she knows you're alive and where you are?"

"I mean, kinda..." Bobby explained that she was the one who told him that his podcast would get him in trouble. She told him to get out of town after someone followed him home one night from the Sea Shanty bar by the harbor. "It's why I was packing when the guy showed up and shot at me."

After he ran away, Bobby came back to leave Marla a note in her mailbox in the middle of the night so she wouldn't worry. He asked her to please give him some shelf-stable food, like peanut butter and stuff, but he wouldn't tell her where he was.

"She hides supplies in a crate behind the little market around the corner every two days, but she missed this time."

"I sent her out of town. Listen, Fiona was killed for talking with us and for having a copy of the data lens she cleaned up for you."

"She had a copy? I warned her not to do that!" Bobby's eyes got red. "Oh, man."

"She told us she gave you back the original. Do you have it stashed with your laptop?"

"No, I-I...oh no, I gave it to Marla."

Reed stilled. "Wait, Marla has it?"

"She said she knew how to keep it safe." Wincing with pain, Bobby leaned against the stairwell wall. "I need a break, man."

"Just one more flight of stairs," Reed pushed, feeling the seconds slip by. His finger went to the earpiece. "Nat, get out of there now. Meet me in the lobby."

He sent a voice text to Coyote. *We're heading to the ground floor.*

Coyote texted back immediately. *In the parking area behind the building. Coming to you.*

"You guys have a car, right?" Bobby asked.

"I listened to your podcast," Reed said, trying to keep him focused as he practically dragged the kid down the final flight. "And I think I've seen the glass in the water. I heard it, at least. I saw the carnage. The cuts on flesh that it can cause."

Bobby's gaze shot to Reed's. "You believe me?"

"I absolutely do."

"You have to be careful of the music," Bobby said suddenly. "Once you hear it, the collapse comes."

"What?"

"It's not just water, it's—"

"Hold on," Reed snapped as Nat's voice sounded in his earpiece.

She was breathless, running. "I found his laptop and just cracked it open. I was right. There's a tracker sending location data right now. We have to get out of here."

"We gotta go," Reed said, pulling Bobby faster down the stairs by his sweatshirt. "The guy who shot you knows where you are."

Bobby and Reed stumbled down the steps, Nat joining him in the stairwell. She had the laptop in pieces with her and was shoving it into her backpack as she took the stairs two at a time, right behind them.

They headed out to the parking lot, Reed spotting Coyote running toward him, his arm waving frantically.

"Go back," he shouted, eyes wide. "Fire in the hole!"

Behind him, skidding across the asphalt toward the office building door, a swarm of hockey-puck-shaped bombs sped toward them. Reed turned, shoving Bobby and Nat ahead of him back into the building. One detonated from a distance, the shockwave taking out the windows overhead, showering them in jagged glass. The whir of the guided grenade motors screamed louder, tearing toward them. Reed spun, pulling his weapon as he aimed past Coyote, who leapt into the building entrance. Reed tracked the lead bomb as it crossed the threshold and fired. It exploded, throwing the four of them into the wall. Reed coughed, gasping from the force of the blast as several more grenades slid across the carpet toward them.

29

The bombs spread out like a pack of wolves on the attack. Flanking the four of them, pressing them into a group. Reed's back hit the stairwell door, and he pushed it open, pulling Nat and Bobby into the stairwell with him. Coyote rushed in just as a single puck revved and jumped forward. It flew at them as Reed kicked the door shut, knocking it backward.

It was dark and stuffy in the stairwell. Reed turned on his flashlight. Nat and Coyote were dusted with dirt and debris but appeared unhurt. Bobby's eyes were as wide as saucers, but he looked okay too.

"What's the plan, Nat?" Reed asked as he peered through the enmeshed metal window in the doorway.

"The plan was to find Bobby," she said, and shone her own flashlight on Bobby. "You're welcome. Other than that, I don't know. If I call 911, it'll get Ventura PD involved. That would alert Jacoby or Luna that we didn't leave."

"I'm pretty sure the explosions already did that," Reed said, eyeing Bobby. He wouldn't last long on the run from those things. "Besides, you'd have to alert them about the explosives, and they'll stay away until it's cleared."

"Okay." Nat looked Bobby over. "He's hurt bad?"

"Come on, guys, what's the plan?" Coyote snapped. He wiped sweat from his brow with his sleeve. "Those little hockey-puck bombs aren't staying put for long."

Reed pulled the building pamphlet out of his pocket. "That parking lot wasn't very big..."

Coyote peered out at the grenades on the floor outside the door. "They look like they're planning something."

"Those guided grenades are being controlled remotely," Nat said, shining her light upward. "Remember I said we got into Fiona's phone? Well, the last video she took showed the killer flashing something at her car."

"He was painting the target," Reed said, nodding. "I haven't seen a flash."

"Does that mean he's nearby?" Coyote asked. "How close would he have to be?"

"I don't know. Maybe fifty yards?" Nat shrugged. "I'm guessing here. I don't really do bombs."

"There's a garage below street level, and it looks like it has a loading dock," Reed said and handed her his pamphlet. "I say we go down."

"If you know about that escape route, then so does the white-haired asshole out there. We should go up," Nat said.

"We'll only be able to hide up there if cornered," Reed said. "Down opens up more exits."

"Down is easier for me," Bobby interjected. "If that counts for anything."

Coyote cut in, "Morgan and the nerdy kid are right. The cement and metal of the garage could also interfere with those critters' inner workings."

Nat nodded. "Okay, that sounds right. Let's go down—"

A metal clang cut her short, and the sound of the grenade bots on the door pulled Reed to the window. He took one look and said, "Start moving."

"What is it?" Nat asked, moving down the stairs to the next floor.

"It's climbing the door."

"What are they, magnetic?" Coyote asked, helping Bobby down the stairs.

"I mean, they could be," Nat said. "But what are they gonna do, turn the knob?"

"Run," Reed shouted. "They're blowing the window!"

He caught up with Coyote, grabbed Bobby's other arm, and the three of them ran after Nat. They'd just cleared the landing to the next floor when an explosion blasted through the stairwell.

"Oh, man, that's loud," Bobby cried, holding his ears.

The four of them kept going, the whir of the grenade motors barely audible through the ringing in Reed's ears. The bombs rattled in the dark stairwell behind them as they tossed themselves down the steps. A loud clattering behind them turned Reed's gut.

"They're rolling down the stairs! Go, go, go!"

The sound of their approach sped up, right behind Reed. A series of clicks activated as they armed themselves. Reed leapt with Bobby, taking three and four steps at a time, dragging Coyote. Their muffled shouts were incoherent through the haze of echoes. Nat pushed through the doorway to the underground floor. It was the garage, and Reed slipped through the closing door as another blast rocketed from inside the stairwell. It blew the door outward, warping the metal, but they were already running.

Dumped garbage littered the vast floor. They ran around overturned metal trash cans filled with ashes, cardboard boxes stuffed with junk, old tires and wooden crates. Used needles and beer cans created a sea of obstacles as they stumbled through a garage lit only by the angled sunlight at the far entrance.

"There's the loading dock over there," Reed shouted, pointing as he ran. "The ramp opens up at street level."

"Nat, we need wheels, fast!" Coyote said, struggling with Bobby, who was leaning more and more on them. "This kid can't outrun those things for long."

Nat sped up, heading for the light streaming onto the pavement from outside the building. She turned to Coyote as they hurried across the garage floor. "Bike or car?"

"Rental car. Blue." He reached into his pocket and tossed her his keys. "Just outside by the electrical exchange."

"Got it," she said, caught Reed's eye for a moment, winked, and then went into a dead sprint like her old track days.

"Head on a swivel. He might be out there," Reed called after her.

"I gotta stop," Bobby panted. "I can't feel my leg anymore."

"Hang on, kid. Push through," Reed said and glanced behind them. At least six grenade bots poured out of the ruined stairwell door. The bombs moved into a triangle formation with a lead grenade as the tip of the arrow as they raced after them. Reed let go of Bobby and shouted, "Keep going, find cover!"

"What are you doing?" Bobby panted, but Coyote was already pulling him away.

Reed stopped behind a cement pylon, aimed his weapon at the oncoming swarm, and picked off the first one with a single shot. He ducked as it exploded, taking out several grenades next to it in a rapid series of blasts. Debris from the dumpster and piles of construction trash in the garage hurled through the air, slicing past Reed's arms as he covered his head. He rose and ran, glancing over his shoulder to see the remaining bombs regroup and continue to chase him.

Out of the corner of his eye, a figure slipped in through the entrance. The white-haired man. He wore all black and raced through the dark of the garage, his attention on Bobby and Coyote.

With the swarm still on him, Reed turned on a dime and barreled like a linebacker toward the assailant. The whine of the grenade motors behind him as they rumbled over debris spurned him forward. He cut a beeline to intercept when the white-haired man opened fire. Coyote and Bobby dove behind a filled crate. Reed fired at the assailant, who ducked behind a pillar. He tapped on his wrist, and Reed glanced back at the swarm. They separated, letting one pull ahead. Reed zagged left, hard, leaping over some tires as the bomb went off. Too far. It did nothing but hurt his ears and pepper him with debris. He popped up, saw Coyote turn to fire at the assailant, and in the exchange, Bobby bolted. He tore out of Coyote's grip and scrambled toward a rear exit.

"Oh, now he can run," Reed growled and fired at the killer.

The man's body jerked forward, shot in the arm. He glanced back at Reed and then ran for Bobby, firing from behind obstacles, slipping through the shadows like a wraith.

"Stop!" Reed yelled, planting his feet, aiming, waiting for the light of the exit door to frame his target. "I will blow your head off!"

The grenades stuck behind the pile of tires detonated, exploding at his back and throwing Reed to the ground. He looked up just as the white-haired guy fired once at Coyote and then ran for the exit.

Reed rose on unsteady feet. "Nat, where are you?"

"I'm coming...I'm driving..." Her muffled response in his earpiece sounded far away.

"Bobby ran out the side exit, north side...it's an alley, I think," Reed said. Coyote rose from the ground, dusting himself off. Reed looked at him. "You good?"

"Pissed, but yeah."

"Heading around the building," Nat answered.

Reed peeked out of the exit door quickly. He didn't see anyone in the alley, but he did hear a shout of pain. Bobby. He ran that way, gun out in front, eyes scanning, Coyote a step behind. A loud bang of metal sounded from around the corner, and Reed slowed, aiming at the dumpster. A hand flailed from the other side. Reed shot a look at Coyote, who nodded.

"I see him."

"Do you have an angle?" Reed asked. Coyote was the best shot he knew. Trained by the army and deadly accurate.

"Not yet."

"If you get one, take it." Reed crept forward. He shouted at the dumpster. "You have an advantage over me. I don't know your name."

As he angled around the metal receptacle, the white-haired man came into view. He was tucked behind Bobby's shorter, plumper form, only a pale eye poked out from behind his hostage's ear. He held the Reaper knife to Bobby's side with one hand.

"Call off your sniper or I gut him like a fish," the white-haired man rasped.

Reed signaled to Coyote to back off. Then he stepped a little closer, still sighting down his barrel. "He doesn't have the data lens. He hid it, and he didn't tell me where, so I wouldn't do anything to Bobby there just yet."

"I leave with him, or I leave and he bleeds," the killer shouted. Bobby's eyes widened, his breath coming in hitches.

"You're not leaving with the kid," Reed said, stepping closer. "And your little bombs are all trapped in that garage. It's just you and me now."

Nat pulled into the alley from the other side, trapping the assailant between Reed and the car.

"I do not make idle threats," the white-haired man rasped. His hand with the knife moved, exposing him slightly.

Coyote fired, shooting the knife from the killer's hand and sending it clattering against the brick wall. The killer pushed Bobby and brought up his other hand, firing as he ran toward Nat in the car.

"Get down!" Reed shouted, running after the killer.

The white-haired man squeezed between the car and the alley wall, his gun dangerously close as he aimed into the driver's side window. Nat shoved the door open, trapping him against the bricks.

"Don't!" Reed shouted and lunged for the man, who shoved the nose of his weapon through the open door at Nat.

Reed charged, grabbing the man by his coat. They struggled, and then the killer slammed the car door closed, turned, and fired at Reed's face, missing by a hair's breadth as Reed reacted with a deflecting blow. He followed with a jarring punch that split the killer's cheek. Reed hit him again, and the fake skin tore from the white-haired man's face. Reed snatched it off, revealing his mottled, scarred jawline and chin. The white-haired man roared with anger and fired another round. It exploded as Reed grabbed the man's wrist, making the shot go wild. And then the killer broke free of his grasp and ran, the skin of his face dangling below his chin.

Glancing back at Reed, he flashed a bright light at him and kept running. He threw something behind him as he rounded the corner onto the street. A single grenade bounded over the asphalt, sliding under the car.

"Get out! Get out!" Reed yelled, yanking Nat's door open. He ripped her out of the car, and they sprinted for the mouth of the alley. Reed exited first, catching Nat's arm and pulling her into his chest as he flattened them against the brick building. One second passed. Two. The sound of sirens warbled in the distance as local PD arrived. But the grenade didn't explode. It didn't do anything. It simply let the killer get away, again.

The midday sun bore down on the city. It cast sharp outlines in the shadows and lifted the summer heat from the asphalt in shimmering waves. Reed sat in the back of a police cruiser, uncuffed but still detained, watching the ambulance carrying Bobby disappear in the rearview mirror. He glanced once more at the crowd gathered at the end of the alley. Looky-loos with their cell phones and online followers. Coyote was gone, disappearing before the first Ventura County police car arrived.

Reed craned his neck, spotting the other cruiser that held Nat. It was angled away, and he couldn't see her. The bomb squad had come and then nothing. They went inside the building; there was a lot of activity in there while others checked the car. Weird. Not knowing what was going on drove him to distraction. Reed needed his sketchbook and his pen to sketch out what he remembered of the killer, but they'd been confiscated along with his weapon and phone. They took the torn mask when they patted him down as well.

Now, nearly an hour later, and despite the feeble air conditioning sputtering out tepid air, the suffocating heat of the stuffy car seemed to exacerbate his growing headache and ringing in his ears. He leaned back in the seat, resting his head, letting his gaze fall to the group of police gathered near the cars. Through the window, a hefty older man with a head full of silvery curls listened to his men. One particularly jumpy patrolman, who looked all of sixteen to Reed, handed over an evidence baggie with the Reaper knife. The boss's brows furrowed as he held it up to look at it, and then his gaze snapped to Reed. He hefted his pants and walked over. Opening the car door, he let Reed out.

"I'm Sergeant Riley," the older man said, folding his arms. "My patrolman here says that you're with Homeland, but you have no way to prove it. No ID. The number your girlfriend over there—"

"Detective De La Cruz," Reed corrected him. "She was on the task force as well. I told you, call Homeland and ask to speak to Drake Jacoby or Luna...well, just Luna."

"And this would be the woman who ran your top-secret operations base?"

"You went to check it out, didn't you?"

"I sent some of my men, yes. Guess what they found."

Reed shook his head. "Nothing."

"You see my dilemma, son? What it looks like to me is you and your 'partner' were caught shooting up an abandoned building you broke into and were apparently squatting in. Then you set off explosives in some kind of turf war with a man your injured friend described as a platinum-haired assassin." He hooked his thumb toward the road. "Not to mention what the kid was saying. Time portals? Really?"

"Look, get ahold of Jacoby."

"It sounds like I need to get ahold of a psychiatrist for all three of you."

"The guided grenade under the car didn't convince you?"

"We found a magnetic tracker under the car. Not a bomb."

"He was bluffing?" Reed leaned back against the car, rubbing his face with both hands. Perfect. "And the explosive devices inside?"

"Those are interesting," Riley said. "Those are why you're here talking with me and not back at the station getting booked."

"The suspect who detonated the explosives is being hunted by Homeland," Reed said. "He tried to kill Bobby Khan. We stopped him. Now, please try getting ahold of Jacoby. He'll clear everything up."

"Sergeant!" The jumpy patrolman hurried over, a phone in hand. "It's some guy from Homeland who says his name is Jacoby."

Riley raised a brow but took the call. "This is Riley..." His voice trailed off as he listened. He looked Reed up and down and nodded. "Big scarred guy. Looks like a bouncer?"

Reed rolled his eyes despite the relief of Jacoby's call. "Tell him I have something for him."

"Yes, sir," Riley said, handed back the phone, and set his palm on his waist holster. "Morgan Reed, you're under arrest."

"What did he say?" Reed asked, turning slowly, not wanting to set him off.

"He said to tell you something." Riley cuffed Reed and helped him back into the car. "He said you were warned."

30

Sergeant Riley transferred Reed to the back of his SUV and then drove in the exact opposite direction of the Ventura Police Station. Behind them, another patrol car drove Nat, Reed hoped. He didn't bother asking where they were going. Either he was going to have to fight an old cop in a field somewhere or something else was happening. Riley turned down a side street and stopped underneath a bridge. Reed tensed as a windowless black van pulled up next to the SUV.

"Ride's over," Riley said, getting out and strolling out from under the bridge.

"Where's my partner?" Reed called after him but got nothing back.

The van door slid open, and three men in black fatigues jumped out. Armed, they trained their weapons on him as they let him out of the SUV.

Reed climbed out slowly, hands up. "Why can't Jacoby be normal?"

One held a black hood in his hand. Shaved head, dead eyes, the coiled energy of an operator. "You can put this on yourself, or you can wake up with it on," he said.

Reed sighed but nodded. "On."

They took him on a long ride with a lot of evenly spaced turns and then a long stretch of straight. No songs on the radio. No talking. Just silence and the hood blocking his sight. More than an hour later, by

Reed's count, they were back in a city. When they stopped at a streetlight, traffic noises, the smell of restaurant exhaust fumes, and the ever-present odor of piss told him he was likely back in Los Angeles. The clang of heavy machinery met them as they pulled into a space that muffled the outside sounds and blocked the sun. The door next to Reed opened, and someone pulled him out with a grunt. They walked him past hissing and clanking machines that could be doing anything if it wasn't for the overwhelming fragrance of coffee beans. They marched him to a cooler area, took off his cuffs, shoved him forward, and then a door closed and locked behind him. Reed turned toward the sound, pulling the hood off his head.

The small office had a metal desk and chair in the military style of dark gray-green. White walls, corkboard with various printouts curling with age. Faded ink spelled out the cover name of the building. *The Coffee Packing Co.*

"That's creative," Reed muttered. The address on a faded takeout menu tacked to the corkboard put the restaurant it advertised in downtown LA.

A plastic water cooler sat in the dusty corner, its contents long gone dry. Reed rubbed his eyes, taking a turn in the room that could really only hold maybe four people comfortably. He tried the closet door on the opposite wall, but it was locked. Sensing something was off, Reed realized the walls, the door, and the whole room was built with reinforced material. A display screen on the wall lit up, and Jacoby glared at him from a blank background. He seemed to look straight at him. Spotting the camera, Reed opened his mouth to speak when the door behind him opened up. The same bald operator carefully led a hooded Nat in and then stepped back out, closing the door again.

She ripped the hood off, pissed, then saw Reed and said, "The hell?"

"You two are like a bad rash," Jacoby said, his expression blank. "Just when I think I've gotten rid of you, you turn up causing trouble somewhere worse."

"How's Bobby?" Nat asked him.

"He's fine. Surprisingly healthy and relatively intact," Jacoby said. "And no, he's not in a hospital. He's at a secured facility under excellent care."

"And the data lens?" Reed asked. "You retrieved it?"

"Yeah, the kid told us where it was. Agents went to see Marla Jenkins.

She had it dangling from one of those wind chimes in her gallery, if you can believe it. We have it now."

"So, to be clear," Nat said. "We found Bobby *and* the data lens, like you asked."

Jacoby shrugged, unimpressed. "Maybe you did turn out to be marginally useful after all. Who knew? I take it back. You can stay."

"Oh, we can?" Reed narrowed his gaze. "What's the catch?"

"I need a few things from you first."

"What the hell does that mean?" Reed asked.

Jacoby didn't answer; instead he looked at Nat. "Something happened to the memory cores of the goggles Reed and Coyote wore on their night raid. We have mysteriously empty data sets here."

Nat folded her arms defiantly. "That sounds like a maintenance issue."

"I want to see inside that lab, Detective De La Cruz," Jacoby said. "If you have that memory, it's not insurance or a way back onto this task force, it's evidence in your trial."

"Whatever." She bent down and took a small device from her boot. "It's right here."

"Clever," Jacoby said, irritated.

"Look, thanks for the invite, but we only stayed to find Bobby, and we did, so…" Reed headed for the door. "You now have everything. We're going to leave California, and no one is going to get shot, deal?"

It remained locked.

"That was our deal before," Jacoby said. "But then the Deep Wave Dynamics lab burned to the ground about an hour after your invasion."

Nat's tongue darted nervously from between her lips. "There's no way that was us. I mean, where did it even start?"

"Magnesium fires in the servers and labs." Jacoby shook his head. "The place was burned professionally, inside and out. We have images of the fire starting in several areas at once and the security guys who did it. What we don't have images of is what's inside. You spooked them, and they burned the site before we could get a warrant."

Reed leaned against the wall and shoved his hands in his pockets, tired. "They were destroying evidence."

"And broadcasting whatever was there isn't anymore," Jacoby said. "They're moving it."

"Yeah, on a ship. I told you that." Reed described the strange vessel Coyote had seen leaving the lab. "The sails, they sound like the solar sails on the newer battery-powered boats. He said it sat funny in the water, too. Though I don't know what that means."

"Where is Coyote?"

"He wasn't dumb enough to stick around and try to explain."

Jacoby nodded, his gaze going from Nat to Reed and back. "I don't believe I'm saying this, but I want you two to stay. Things are moving fast, and I need De La Cruz to work with Luna on the recordings from the goggles you and Coyote wore inside the lab."

"Okay, and then we leave," Reed said.

"Uh, no," Jacoby said as if the thought were amusing. "You're going to debrief with the AI Agent. And by that, I mean you will cooperate with its questions and give it your full effort. Tell it everything you saw, heard, smelled, and thought when you were in that lab. What you know holds the key to where this thing might be going and why."

"I can write a report at the airport and send it before we take off," Reed countered.

"No, you'll do it here. There's an issue we need to discuss later, but for now, just go with Luna."

"We didn't agree to stay—"

Nat grabbed his arm, looking up at him with worry. "We can help them stop this. You saw that lab. Something very wrong is going on here."

"Listen to your partner," Jacoby said.

A hydraulic lock hissed at the closet door as it disengaged, and then Luna pushed through. She handed them their credentials, smiling from ear to ear as if greeting old friends.

"Welcome back, agents."

They followed her through the door, leaving the dreary office front behind as they stepped into a state-of-the-art command center. Workstations and monitors sat in clusters on the polished cement floor. Manned by at least fifteen agents, their steady din of whispers and typing mixed with the flash of the wall-mounted display screens showing various feeds and data. Jacoby paced an open space in the middle of the floor like a teacher while muttering to someone on his headset. Seeing them, he waved them over but kept talking. He wore a dark blue tracksuit with expensive running shoes, and a chilled water bottle leaked condensation onto the file on the desk next to him. He looked like he'd been teleported there mid-jog. Jacoby pulled off the headset when they walked up.

"Go ahead, Luna," he said, and everyone's attention turned to her.

She stood by a large wall monitor, a tablet in her hand. "This is where we are now."

"Oh, we're just jumping in," Nat said with a baffled look. "Okay."

Reed found it weird as well but kept it to himself. Something was off with all of this.

"As you know, we've been compiling data gathered by you and your team, Agent Reed," Luna continued, unbothered. An image of the torn mask appeared next to a forensic ruler. "We were able to get a fair amount of DNA from the mask as well as an edge of a fingerprint on the inside cheek of the mask." She pulled a series of photos. None of which Reed recognized. "We're still running the DNA, and the print was partial. So, I took the name you got from Bobby, the one the white-haired man gave him, Whit Liu or Lee, and I ran it through the global ID database with every iteration we could think of in case Whit was short for something. I got several Whitmans and Whittier, but only one of them was from South Africa."

"That matters why?" Nat asked.

"Because the Reaper knife is from there," Reed said. "Their special forces were the first to carry it."

"We have a program that makes linguistic connections one might not make unless you spoke the language yourself. I fed in key words: white hair, guided grenades, Reaper knife, variations of the name Whitman and Lee/Leigh/Liu, South Africa, everything we got from Bobby."

She enlarged the series of photos, and Reed realized they were all similar-looking, though he couldn't place why.

"That gave us these five possibles. All with a name similar to our variations. None of the ages or places of birth for these individuals fit the suspect. The trail stopped there until I contacted my former colleague at Interpol," Luna continued. "His specialty is code and regional names, and he suggested that Bobby may have heard Wit Leeu instead. Both words have South African origins and translate into 'White Lion.'"

Reed stilled, scrutinizing the stony stare coming from each image. "These are all him, aren't they?"

Luna nodded. "So are these." Several images of old men, young men, different nationalities, different facial features all slid into view. "The White Lion is an alias for a former South African spy named Thyse Botha. He used to work for their National Intelligence Agency. Preliminary DNA and fingerprints bear that out."

"He's a spy?" Nat asked.

"Was," Luna said and pulled up a photo of a young Botha. Head shaven, new military uniform, pale gaze staring straight into the camera. Almost-white hair and brows, nearly imperceptible eyelashes. Long, emaciated face with a sullen frown. "He did mostly clandestine work, according to my sources, but they won't give up much."

"Who does he work for now?" Reed asked.

"That's the bad news," Jacoby said from behind them. He moved next to Luna. "Botha is suspected of being responsible for a dozen terrorist acts all over the world."

Luna threw several news recordings onto the screen. Bombings, plane crashes, and devastating fires around the globe played in silence. "He travels on fake passports, wearing disguises, using bank accounts connected to aliases. Some we know, some we don't."

Jacoby handed Reed a manila file. "As far as we know, he has no political or religious ties. He works for the highest bidder."

"A terrorist for hire," Reed said. A video of Botha speaking with a popular German politician played on the screen. A healed slash marred his cheek. "He's more scarred now. I saw scarred skin when I ripped off the mask. It's all over now. His neck, his chin."

"We think it was from his last known job." Jacoby nodded and motioned to Luna. She played a news announcement on the screen. It was subtitled in English. "We believe that Botha was hired by a faction within the Kremlin to kill the dictatorial president of Belarus."

"Tereshenka, right?" Reed asked. "I thought he was loyal to Russia?"

"There were rumors of a falling-out when he wasn't at a summit recently. There's been bad blood between Tereshenka and Iran, and it looks like Russia chose Iran."

"I heard about that. He was talking some serious trash about the Russian president on a couple of news shows," Nat said.

Jacoby nodded. "We hear Russian hardliners tasked the White Lion, Botha, to kill Tereshenka so that they could install a leader loyal to the Russian president."

"Tereshenka was assassinated last year," Nat said. "You're saying Botha did it?"

"Yes, and we believe the Belarus government knows it was him. We believe a paramilitary group attacked Botha and his family at their home in Cape Town. His wife, Elise, and his fourteen-year-old son, Leo, were both killed in the resulting fire. There was no sign of Botha, and he was presumed dead until now."

"So, what is he doing in Los Angeles chasing down Bobby? He doesn't seem to know anything about a terrorist threat. He thinks Botha was after him for his video of the sinking."

"He may have been. We think it might reveal something about the Resonance device. Our people are going over it with a fine-tooth comb."

"What about the vial Reed took from the lab? You obviously had it tested," Nat said. "What was it?"

"We're running it through a petrographic microscope, which we do not have on site."

"Petro as in rocks?" Reed asked

"The contents of the vial appeared to be a suspension fluid for a crystalline structure, we think, but it's too small to see even with a light microscope. We're working on it."

Images of crystal structures morphing, cracking, flashed behind Reed's eyes. They were getting closer. He could feel it.

"People hire Botha to conduct newsworthy acts of terror for well-known groups who take credit, right? That's what you're saying?" Reed asked. "They flaunt the fear. But this thing with Bobby, with sinking just one unmanned freighter, and the manner in which it was done...that strikes a wrong note."

"On the contrary," Jacoby said. "Knowing you saw Botha, a known terrorist, at the Deep Wave Dynamics lab you infiltrated, and knowing what we do of the Resonance factor, it makes a terror threat seem not only likely but imminent."

"His real job is something big," Nat said and shot a look at Reed. "Bobby was a side-quest."

"Any idea what his target is?" Reed asked, noticing his sketchbook on the table behind Jacoby. It was open.

"We don't. But if his last jobs were any indication, Botha is planning something unmistakable and bloody." Jacoby had Luna pull up a map on the display screen. Various areas were tagged with red markers with indicator lines revealing blocks of texts about each location. "For each of his acts of terror, there was no warning. No indication or chatter or even a whiff of what was coming. Every. Time. It's why he's been operating for so long. We show up to carnage and questions, and we have nothing to remedy either. The guy is a ghost. But now we have a chance of stopping him *before* he strikes."

It was the way Jacoby looked at Reed that sent a chill down his spine. "What are you getting at?"

"Slater saw what Resonance can do, and it appears so have you." Jacoby turned, picked up the sketchbook, and held it open for Reed to see the drawings of the sliced-up sea lion he'd done. "You saw more at the lab than you told me."

"What's he talking about?" Nat asked, she grabbed the book and leafed through it. The Icarus character, Slater's prickled hands, the blood in the water, all of it. Her gaze snapped to Jacoby. "Wait..."

Ignoring her, Jacoby kept his eyes on Reed. "It's called Capture. A program we developed to safely view memories."

"Stop," Nat said, stepping between them. "You've done enough to him."

"You were right when you accused us of developing the Glycon-C patches because we were using the MER-C system. We are. We had to. Intelligence like that, actionable intelligence, is invaluable to our government's defense. We weren't going to keep the secrets locked away and doing no good."

Reed took a step back, shaking his head. "But the side effects. Who did you do this to—"

"Volunteers, Reed," Jacoby cut in. "And the Capture Protocol is safer and more reliable than your method of duct-taping yourself to a chair."

"What do you do to keep their minds safe?" Nat snapped. "Or are they disposable?"

Jacoby glanced at her. "They're safer than Reed has been in your capable hands."

"What did you just say to me?" Nat said, getting louder.

"Nat," Reed took her hand, pulled her back. "I'll give you all of Slater's memory pods. Take them. See what he knows. I'm done with all of this."

Jacoby shook his head. "The problem is that regardless of all the safety precautions we can take, we can't fix the…incompleteness."

He revealed that despite the various volunteers they'd used to view the memory pods they had gathered from Slater's other caches, they found the viewers often couldn't access much of the memory at all. Flashes and short vignettes, impressions.

"They weren't faring very well, to be honest. After viewing memories, some of them incurred sensory issues, PTSD-like symptoms, long-term memory damage, et cetera."

"He's literally making my case," Nat snapped.

"But," Jacoby continued, "I've been watching you for over a year now. I read what Slater thought of you, and what he feared you could do. I read your journal and talked with Sheriff Hughes back in Aurora, Alaska, about just how accurate your memories were. He said if he didn't know any better, he'd swear you were a psychic the way you cracked that case. No one has the recall that you do, Reed, and I believe it has to do with the fact that you ripped Slater's mind. It was his death memory. A storm of knowledge and memories that floods the dying person's mind."

"Are you talking about his life flashing before his eyes?" Nat asked. "How is that helpful?"

"My scientists believe it to be the key to Reed's ability to view and retain so much."

"The key…" Reed muttered.

"Emotional stress…trauma will burn a memory trace deeper in the psyche," Jacoby said, almost to himself. "We've seen this. Proven it with trauma and PTSD studies. It was the basis of Neurogen's research. What Dr. Price built the MER-C system on."

"And you think, what, that there's more about the Resonance device in my head than I realize?" Reed asked.

"You have much longer, more vivid recollections of ripped memories than anyone else." Jacoby shrugged. "So, yes. Possibly."

"But you have no idea," Nat interjected. "You just wanna root around in his brain just in case?"

"Not just in case. Slater was investigating Danzig for many things, but a weapon was one of them. This Resonance device has been in the ether for years, but Slater said he got traction in Aurora. The Rexfords were somehow involved," Jacoby said.

"That's why Slater was questioning Hazel about it." Reed rubbed his forehead with his palm. "You think Botha is working for Danzig."

"Possibly, or one of his allies," Jacoby said. "Something brought Botha out of hiding to do this. Something worth getting back into the game that killed his family." He pulled a stack of papers from his file folder and handed them to Nat, but he spoke to Reed. "The night of the drone freighter and Khan boat sinkings, several known weapons dealers, Middle Eastern and European royal family members known to traffic in those circles, and data brokers were in Los Angeles."

"How did you know to look for them?" Nat flipped through the pages, pausing on one. "This Jakara guy has like a zillion followers on social media. He married a model. He's a weapons dealer?"

"We're always looking at them," Jacoby said. "We don't know where they stayed. Our people checked their usual accommodations, hot spots where they hobnob with celebrities, gambling establishments, luxury hotels. Nothing. Whatever this was, it was low-key—private jets, private homes, in and out within forty-eight hours."

"Not a pleasure trip," Reed muttered, understanding. "They were attending a sales pitch."

"Proof of concept," Jacoby agreed. "The sinking of the drone freighter was ruled the result of a rogue wave. Since it was automated, not a lot of effort was put into the investigation. Mr. Khan died, but Bobby's initial claims of what he'd seen cast doubt on the veracity of his recollection of the incident. The investigating authorities chalked it up to trauma or shock."

"But you suspected different," Reed said.

"No one questioned what happened that night. It's a perfect crime."

"Why go through the trouble of disguising a sinking as a rogue wave if you're a terrorist?" Nat mused. "I mean, they *want* people to know it was an act of terror and not a natural disaster. In fact, it's scarier to blow it up. They want the news to stream video of fire and smoke and hurt people. That's the terror part. This is…something else."

"I believe you are right," Jacoby said. "Whatever Botha's assignment is, it apparently has to look like a natural sinking."

"An assassination?" Reed thought of Slater and Hazel and the horror of what happened in the small town of Aurora. All of them were connected somehow to the Resonance device. "We need to speak to Pierce Rexford."

"That's not possible."

Reed looked up from the file. "Why not?"

"Because we can't find him."

"He's missing?"

"We had a loose net on him, but he wasn't under official surveillance," Jacoby said. "I had men shadowing him. When Bobby was attacked, I raised the threat level on him, but something didn't sit right. He cancelled all his upcoming events, saying he was sick two mornings ago, and by noon, he was gone."

"Abducted?"

"No sign of it when we entered his home," Jacoby said. "But he did pack, and he did evade the men watching his house."

"He's been known to give his own security the slip. He did a couple times when I was watching him for Gray Zone in Seattle," Reed said as he closed the file.

"He has a mistress he keeps under wraps in Anchorage. We're sending some people to check out her place to see if he's there. If not, we may have a problem."

"The pieces are moving," Reed said. "It'll happen soon."

"That's the fear," Jacoby said. "As far as we know, the Resonance device was tested on a boat, and it left the lab on a boat. Whatever Resonance actually is, be it a bomb, biological weapon, chemical threat...we know it has the capacity to do enormous damage. Our people are looking at maritime trackers, touching base with their contacts, but so far, we have no idea where the vessel with the Resonance is going. We're working on all possible scenarios, even terror acts—ferry or cruise ship targets, maybe military ships, as there are outposts around the islands and Los Angeles..."

Nat set the papers down. "We have no idea where it's going?"

"We don't even know which direction it went," Jacoby said. "Satellite coverage of the lab that night was obscured by heavy fog. For now, we're going through planned events, but it's California in the summer. There are hundreds of potential targets."

"Coyote described a long-haul type of boat leaving the lab," Reed said. "Would they transport a weapon like that?"

"No customs, no TSA." Jacoby nodded. "It's been done before to avoid scrutiny. We're looking in that direction as well."

"Bobby talked about shards of glass and other strange phenomena," Reed said. "What if it can do that to buildings. Inside them, even?"

Jacoby paused, glancing at Nat before speaking to Reed. "I found something when we broke Slater's life down after he died. I went through all of his notes, his gathered evidence. I checked all his dead drops and hiding places."

"Yeah, what'd you find?" Reed asked, not liking Jacoby's expression.

"A message...for you."

Reed stilled, dread pooling in his gut. "What did it say?"

Jacoby held up an evidence bag. Slater's shaky handwriting scrawled across a tattered page of a book.

Reed, the Daedalus Key is in the chaos. Find it. Stop what's coming.

31

The White Lion – Thyse Botha

Her delicate fingers caressed his scarred cheek, her gaze never leaving his.

"I see no difference," she whispered. "You are still my Thyse...my loving husband. You survived the war. I don't care how. Just that you are back in my arms."

He buried his face in her neck, the scent of her skin breaking his heart. He wasn't back. Thyse Botha had died out on the bloody streets. The man who'd returned to his beloved Elise was not the same as the one who had left. Battle and death had carved him out and the emptiness in him consumed everything. Hope...loyalty...mercy. She would see it one day, he'd told himself. And then she would never look at him the same way again. That would have been a kinder fate.

Flashes of the attack. Of the men in fatigues storming his home, brutalizing Elise and his son. They killed her in front of him, then tied them together in their home and set it alight. Botha had screamed as they hurried out. Not for his dead wife. Not because of the flames licking at his skin. He screamed because they took his son. Dragging him from the room with terror in his eyes. Botha shouted until the heat of the inferno burned the words from his throat.

He didn't know how he'd escaped. He only remembered stumbling across the sand and plunging into the cool of the ocean. Pain consuming him.

Leo...I will find you.

Botha blinked, the memory fading as he stared at himself in the mirror, his rough skin encased in another mask, hiding his true face. The identity he wore, the visage of an older, gray-haired doctor on his way to a conference, looked passable in the meager light of the claustrophobic bathroom. He retouched the liver spots on his forehead with makeup and adjusted the simple medical mask he wore. Invisible, Botha thought. No one considered the elderly. They are but obstacles in a bustling crowd. He wondered if it would fool Reed.

Someone rattled the door, checking for occupancy, but moved on. Botha shook his head, clearing it. Disturbed he'd gone away for a moment.

"Are you still there?" A voice in his phone's earpiece, Danzig's, came back. "I thought you cut out."

"Agent Reed is relentless," Botha muttered. "He is everywhere."

"You see why he is the bane of my existence."

"Your men should have killed him by now."

"He moves from place to place. My people couldn't figure out where he lived, how he made money. Reed knows how to move underground without detection. And once he caught on that we were watching him...he's good. My country trained him well."

Botha dabbed at the sweat at his collar, dropping the paper towel in the counter's receptacle. "The lab is gone?"

"It is, but we have no idea what Reed or Jacoby gleaned from his infiltration. They could know everything by now."

The walls shook, and Botha braced himself, staring at the blue water of the toilet as he rode out the movement.

"The vessel?"

"On track to arrive on time. Just make sure you're there as well."

"I told you. I should be with it. The device proved to be tricky last time...unstable."

"It makes no sense to put both integral parts of the operation in the same space," Danzig countered. "This is better. It makes you and the device harder to find and put together."

"My other request?"

"You'll have it. Fast and quiet, as you specified," Danzig assured him. "You should have no trouble remaining out of the damage zone. And it's fast enough to get you close when you need to go under. Speaking of which…"

"My practice run on the ferry went well. I'll have time to procure what you want after detonation."

"You must retrieve it. Jacoby and Gray Zone cannot know about it or find it. He'll have us in a choke hold if he does." Danzig's voice took on an edge of stress. "And you must kill Reed. He's grown more dangerous than we can tolerate."

Botha inspected the patched flesh wound on his arm from his last encounter with the detective.

"He will die in the cold. I promise you."

32

The Coffee Packing Co. was the business front for the facility Jacoby transported Reed to earlier. He'd smelled the coffee scent when they brought him in with the hood. Large and divided into several departments, it not only housed a massive field operations setup, but it also contained data banks, weapons, and other technology within its fortified walls. One of which was the Capture Protocol. There was a flurry of activity as people hurried down halls and spoke in soft voices on headsets as they made their way through the corridors. Something was happening.

Jacoby and a burly nurse named Carl escorted Reed and Nat to a different area of the building that resembled a medical wing.

"Carl will get you prepped," Jacoby said, glancing at Nat. "I'll give you two some time to talk, and then you're going straight to the Capture Laboratory."

Nat glared at him as he left and then paced the exam room, swishing past the divider curtain that separated her from Reed and the nurse. Carl worked quietly, ignoring her obvious anger, arranging his supplies on the metal tray next to Reed's bed.

"He has no proof you know anything." Her form slipped past the slit in the material as Carl checked Reed's vitals and took a couple of vials of blood. "He has nothing, and he's using you as a last-ditch effort. Who cares if your mind gets fried, right? We know how he treats people he's responsible for."

"I care, Nat. I do, but Jacoby isn't wrong. There is proof that something more than memories might be trapped in my mind. You saw my drawings. That winged man...Icarus. That's not a memory. But it was in there. I drew him, and the maze—"

"You were a philosophy major! You took tons of humanities classes. Why are you surprised there are mythological images and even labyrinths there? I've seen your books. I mean, before they went up in flames with your condo." Nat's shadow stopped on the other side of the curtain, her angry breaths wafting the material. "What would Icarus have to do with the void in your memory maze, anyway?"

"The note from Slater mentioned the Daedalus Key. Daedalus was Icarus's father. He made him the wings." Reed watched his blood stream into the vial at the nurse's hands. "He was the architect of the maze that trapped the minotaur—the monster."

"Slater was insane, remember. You shouldn't put that much stock in his needlessly cryptic note." Her shoe tapped on the floor beneath the curtain. "How was it even helpful?"

"He researched me. Stalked me. He would know what I know," Reed mused, the blood in the vial feeling warm against his forearm as it filled. "He would know how to get a message to me."

Nat flung back the curtain. "Are you hearing yourself?"

"The Daedalus reference can't be coincidence."

"It absolutely can be. You can play six degrees of separation for anything." She turned to the nurse. "Hey, Carl, are you from Los Angeles?"

"San Diego," he said.

"Oh, that's weird. My father was a sheriff there. I grew up there. We must be connected somehow," she said as she looked at Reed. "I mean, that's what you're doing."

"To be fair, not a lot of people are really *from* LA," Carl said. "We're a magnet city."

"Shut up, Carl. Not helpful," Nat said.

Reed sighed and asked Carl for a few minutes. The nurse removed the needle and placed a bandage. Reed bent his arm, holding it in place as Nat paced in front of him. Carl left without another word.

"Slater mentioned chaos. He somehow knew about the void in my memory," Reed said quietly.

"Those aren't the same thing. Chaos isn't nothing. It's not emptiness," she countered, her voice going raspy. "*You* never called it that until now, by the way."

"Nat—"

"Jacoby clearly read your journal, and he's using what he learned to manipulate you. We have no proof that note is even from Slater. He could've doctored it up to convince you to do this ridiculous experiment on yourself."

"It's Slater's handwriting."

"How do you know that?"

"I recognized it as my own for a moment," Reed admitted. "The note is real."

"You what?" She stopped pacing and stared at him for a moment, her face falling. "My point is we have no idea what this Capture Protocol bullshit will do to you. It's essentially untested on someone with your memory load. Jacoby even said that."

"Everything about the MER-C system and ripping people's memories is untested."

"What about the booby traps Jacoby was worried about, huh? Did you forget he was reluctant to question you because he was afraid that you'd set traps in your mind? Or that Slater had?"

"What are you talking about?"

"In Aurora, when Jacoby showed up, he told you that he was worried you'd 'rigged' your memory against questioning." Nat took his hand in hers. "What if he was right? What if you going into that machine sets off something you don't come back from?"

"The White Lion—Botha—his track record is perfect. We know there's a weapon out there and it's aimed at innocent people. Possibly thousands. If the key to stopping a mass tragedy is in my head, I have to at least look."

"Why are you so—" She slumped against him, resting her cheek against his shoulder. Her breath came in hitches. "You're such a stubborn jerk, you know that?"

Reed wove his fingers with hers, kissing the back of her hand. "Nothing will stop me from coming back to you. Nothing."

When the initial exam concluded, the nurse had Reed change into scrubs and then escorted him to the room with the AI Agent debriefing terminal. Reed sat at the screen and gave the computer everything he could remember from the lab. After an hour and a half of questions, he was done. Carl came back a few minutes later and told him it was time. Despite feeling fine, the nurse insisted on pushing Reed down the white-tiled hallway in a wheelchair. Nat, who'd finished her own debriefing, joined them. She walked beside him, her face set in a blank stare.

They rolled into what looked like an imaging lab, and Reed half expected to see an MRI machine on the other side of the glass partition. A doctor in a lab coat stood in front of a bank of monitors, and he turned when they arrived. Dark hair, dark eyes, he smiled behind round glasses.

"Agent Reed, I'm Dr. Saul Reynoso."

They introduced themselves to each other, and then Reynoso went into his explanation of the procedure.

"The Capture machine is state-of-the-art technology designed to make memory viewing more stable, safe, and reliable—"

"You're not trying to sell him a car, Doctor. Tell him the bad parts," Nat cut across him.

Reynoso froze, confused. "Uh…"

Reed nodded. "The risks are what…stroke, heart attack, vegetative state? I already know."

Nat whispered some choice words under her breath but didn't cut in.

"They're rare occurrences," Reynoso said. "But there may be residual side effects. Some patients report hallucinations, lost time, and mild seizures."

"Oh, is that all?" Nat muttered.

"I already experience those symptoms," Reed said. "Are you saying they'll worsen?"

Reynoso's gaze met his with uncertainty. "I have no experience with that. All of the Capture volunteers have never viewed memories prior to a session in the chamber."

"So, you have no idea what will happen to him," Nat murmured.

Reynoso shook his head. "No. I don't."

Jacoby poked his head into the door of the exam room and motioned for Nat. She hugged Reed and whispered in his ear, "Come back to me."

After they'd left, Reed nodded to Carl. "Let's get this over with."

A flurry of activity coalesced around him as a staff of five streamed into the Capture Laboratory. Reed had been right to think of an MRI scenario, only the machine was the stuff of nightmares. Sleek and metal, it resembled a hyperbaric chamber and sat on a stand in the center of the room. Reminiscent of a coffin, the lid stood open, and he walked over to it, inspecting the inside. A strange substance filled the bottom. It looked like sand.

"That powder substrate is made of microbeads," Reynoso said. He'd changed into scrubs himself and held a tablet in his hand. "When you lie in it, they heat and cool to your exact body temperature. We pump air into the substrate to give you some lift. It mirrors the weightlessness of a sensory deprivation tank."

Carl appeared and pulled over a set of steps that he secured to the base of the Capture chamber. Reed looked over at the observation window on the wall opposite. It held Jacoby, Luna, and Nat, who stood away from them. He smiled at her, and she nodded, her own smile a bit shaky.

After climbing into the tank, he lay down on the substrate, and it rose like water around him. The air fluffed it up like foam as he settled chest-deep in the powder. It felt like he was floating in VR, the buoyancy remarkable.

Reynoso's face appeared over the lip of the chamber. "This machine has vitals capability. We'll be able to monitor your respiration, heart rate, oxygenation, and temperature."

"What's that for?" Reed asked as Carl inserted an IV into Reed's arm.

"The IV is controlled by the Capture chamber. It will feed you a steady cocktail of several drugs that will keep you in a twilight state. Much like an anesthetist controls your dosage of anesthesia. The meds will keep you closer to consciousness than what you've been experiencing with memory views up until now."

Another nurse placed quarter-sized sticky pads with metal dots onto Reed's forehead, temples, and neck.

"Jackie just set you up with wireless leads for our EEG," Reynoso continued. "They'll send us real-time feed on your brain waves. Any sign of disruption and we pull you out." He motioned to a light projection box in the corner where a hologram of Reed's brain flickered on and spun slowly. Indicator lines and information appeared around it, tracking his brain waves.

"How do I go under?" Reed asked, weirded out by his floating brain.

"The Capture chamber will deliver a formula designed to enhance your existing memories via the IV. No needles to your carotid or memory pod serum this time. We want you to access what is already in there but hidden. It'll feel a little different from what you've experienced before. There is also a dose of Glycon-C to help with the physical stress to your body." Reynoso paused, then, "Are you ready, Agent Reed?"

"The sooner the better," Reed muttered, tension knotting his gut.

"Very well," Reynoso said. "One more thing. The cameras in the chamber record everything. Eye movement, facial tics, things like that. So, if you find you can speak, please try to describe what you are seeing for us."

Reynoso stepped back, and the Capture chamber slowly lowered the lid until it was perfectly pitch black within. Reed startled when the substrate surrounding his body moved, vibrating around him, rising over his chest and around his neck and ears until only his face remained above the warm microbeads. A tone sounded in the chamber. Soft and slow. Like a heartbeat, and then he realized it was his own. Pressure at the cleft of his elbow, and the IV pushed cold fluid into his arm. The frigid serum rose quickly, soaring across his chest and crawling up his throat until it felt as if he had nothing but ice in his veins. Reed gasped, the cold crushing the breath from him, and then his mind exploded with light and sound and the howling rush of his adrenaline-spiked mind as the memory slammed down around him.

33

Violence whirled around him. A tornado of screams and gunfire and explosions that propelled Reed backward in time as a scene rose up around him. Boats, an apartment building, the metal poles of a railing all pushed out of the sand, shaking the ground like an earthquake. The smell of decaying leaves and the ocean hit Reed as he crashed into Slater's memory. He was on Alki Beach. Slater had barely escaped the apartment of Petraeus after ripping her memory, only to have Reed burst through the door and chase him down. In the Capture chamber, Reed flinched at the sight of himself mid-punch as he looked through Slater's eyes. He felt the blow, Slater's head rocking back with the hit.

And then the scene spun, and Slater was running, his heart racing too fast from the drugs he'd taken to stay awake. In the corner of his eye, Reed ran parallel, gaining as he jumped from boat to boat. A sliver of fear pushed through Slater's chest. *Who was this guy?*

The scene jerked, sliding the groups of children and families away. Walls closed in from nowhere, squeezing Reed in darkness until all he could see was Slater's face in a hotel bathroom mirror. Bloody, bruised, dread rose in Reed's chest as Slater's gaze locked impossibly with his. A single, resonant thought melded with Reed's consciousness.

I think you're going to catch me, Reed. I think you will...

Reed jerked with surprise. Had Slater just talked to him?

The memory collapsed, crumbling like a sandcastle, breaking apart, and time moved forward at breathtaking speed. The velocity snatched the breath from Reed as he soared through the memories. Shouts and laughter, pain, and the smell of rain rushed through him, and then he stood in the dark of an airplane hangar walking toward Danzig, who stood in the light of a mechanic's tent.

"Going after Detective Reed was a mistake," Slater said as he strode up. "It made him more of a problem, not less."

"Then hit him again. Everyone has their breaking point."

"Not this guy, he's got a vendetta now. He's gaining."

Danzig turned. Dressed head to toe in black, he looked every bit the billionaire bastard that he was, and a lick of fury moved through Reed. His heart rate in the chamber sped up, the tone echoing in his ears. Danzig nodded. "Yes, I'm told he found evidence you left behind."

Anger tore through Slater, infecting Reed's mind. The damn shoe. He'd lost it while disposing of a body, and Reed had found it. Slater's thoughts raced, panic setting in. *This man could end me.*

Darkness washed over the scene, taking Reed with it through time. Faster and faster, the images sped past him. Blinding light overhead, asphalt rose from the depths, a window connected in four parts in front of him, framing a parking lot. An RV sat idling as an older man walked toward it, cardboard box in hand. The plant inside bounced with his steps, and Slater sighted through his scope, taking aim at his back. Reed shouted, his words in the chamber slurred with the drugs coursing through his system.

"Abernathy! Watch out!"

Slater fired, the kick of the rifle on his shoulder jerking Reed in the substrate. His heart paced ever higher. And then he saw himself shooting back, Nat at his side. Slater's memory fast-forwarded, down the back stairs, onto his motorcycle. He pushed the bike faster, shooting at Reed as the RV swerved in the parking lot. Slater saw Reed in the driver's seat, angled for another run, and then a shot pinged off his helmet, his headlight. Slater almost lost control of the motorcycle, fighting to keep from laying down on the asphalt. The MER-C system strapped to the bike shifted and opened, and part of the equipment, the halo, flew free as the engine sputtered and smoked. Breaking off the chase, Slater ran, looking over his shoulder at the RV escaping.

Slater pushed through a door in a panic, bleeding from a bullet wound, the pain overwhelming. It wasn't the school but a safehouse, and Reed tried to look around in the memory, but Slater had been laser focused on his wounds. He rummaged through a backpack on the bed, broke open a pill bottle with shaking hands, and chewed four Vicodin. Time sped forward, and Slater was halfway through a bottle of whisky, he tried to pack his wound with a face towel and stumbled to the kitchen, his thoughts misfiring. Fear and anger. Frustration and helplessness bubbled in Slater's mind as he looked for something.

As he crossed the kitchen, pain blaring in his head, Reed caught sight of Slater's reflection in the microwave, and then everything stopped. Slater froze in front of the door, the bottle of whisky to his lips. And in his mind, he looked through the reflection to Reed. *Are you fate? For all I've done?*

"Sometimes I don't know who I'm fighting anymore or on which side," Slater slurred to his image. "Makes sense I die at the hands of another soldier…"

Reed tried to rear back, the idea of Slater talking to him through time and space jarring his mind. His hand flailed, hitting something, and then a tinny voice next to him called his name.

"Agent Reed." Reynoso's voice came in faint. "I need you to calm down."

Reed tumbled in a roaring swell of wind and sound. Images of victims raced by in surreal fashion, their faces stretching as the tumult blew them away. And then Reed's old condo closed in around him. The walls connected together, making his front room. The turntable and shelves of albums, his books, the couch he slept on in front of the fake fireplace. Slater looked at him from the glass of a wall-mounted photo. He was swaying, maybe drunk, standing in the dark of Reed's home in plain clothes.

"You'll meet a man called Jacoby," Slater said from the reflection. "Don't trust him. I think he wants to kill me. I'm sure he'll have my mind ripped, so I'm banking on a Hail Mary to protect myself…"

Reed tried to speak. The claustrophobic paralysis of viewing someone else's memory made him gasp for breath. Heat rose up his neck as he strained against the constraints of his mind locked with Slater's.

Through the memory's gaze, Reed saw Slater's hand reach for one of the books on the shelf. He looked down at it, studying the cover, running his palm along the duct-taped spine. A snap of recognition moved through Reed. It was an old book of his from college. Greek mythology. Slater opened it, ripped out a page, and brought it closer, his vision clearing. It was a photo of a labyrinth from an ancient text. Then Slater glanced back at his reflection, his gaze steady.

"You can follow the thread..." he singsonged, his form swaying in the reflection. "But you will never get out."

Heat, steady and growing around him, pushed Reed from the memory. He tried to move, feeling trapped in Slater's mind. Flexing his hands, the powder encasing Reed's fingers burned his palms. The shrill sound of alarms pierced his ears, echoing in the closed Capture chamber. Something was wrong.

His condo, Slater, everything around him fell away like ashes, and then he was inside the chamber, banging on the lid of the tank, unable to breathe. Voices around him shouted. A sliver of light pierced the darkness as the lid moved a little. They couldn't get it open. The alarms shrieked louder and louder. Reed tried to sit up, banged his head and collapsed back down. Struggling to control the claustrophobia, he peered down at his chest. The light from outside illuminated a piece of red string sticking through the crack between the lid and the Capture chamber. The crimson thread trembled with the movement from the doctors outside. Reed reached for it, pulling it, but it was impossibly long. It stretched too far to make sense. And suddenly the chamber stretched, extending the thread, pulling it further and further. The powder substrate beneath him bubbled like it was boiling, rising over his face, pouring in his mouth and nose, choking Reed as he gasped for breath. The chamber shifted, and then the bottom fell away.

Reed plummeted in the darkness, free-falling through nothing until he hit the ground. Coughing out the powder, he glanced through watery eyes at his surroundings. He was in his mind maze. The stone walls painted with battling figures, the pale blue fire of the torches, the smell of dirt, all of it immediately familiar. Straightening out, Reed tried to get his bearings and walked down the corridor. His breath came in puffs of vapor as he tried to find his way. Why was he so cold? Invisible hands jostled him, and Reed became vaguely aware of people working on his body as he continued down the dark path of his mind, looking for Slater. The disjointed awareness threw him, and he fought to stay in the memory.

He found Slater in the corridor with the colored stones. He stood in front of the void, staring at Reed with malevolence. He wasn't a reflection on a surface this time. Reed wasn't looking through his eyes in a memory. Slater appeared to Reed as he'd looked when he died. Bloodied and singed by the explosion, the vitals vest on his chest traced out a flatline as he panted, his hands balled into fists.

"If you've unlocked this memory, I am already dead," Slater said. "Probably at your hand."

"How..."

"I had Dr. Pierce help me to embed a bomb, if you will. A mine in my memory using the implant and drugs to guard against interrogation. If you trigger it, the implant and drugs will cause a break with reality."

The void behind Slater churned with purple and green pulses of light. Fine filaments like a nebula swirled rhythmically.

"But I know my enemy well," Slater continued. "I learned what you really are. How you hunted that rogue special ops group, Fourth Quadrant. I feared then you would catch up to me. I knew what I had to do." Slater reached into his pocket, pulled something out. He held his hand open for Reed. A tangle of red yarn. "I had to leave a clue that only you would know. So that only you could open the void and see even if someone else ripped my mind."

Slater closed his eyes, and the torn page from Reed's condo appeared before him. The labyrinth from his mythology book floated at eye level.

"I don't understand," Reed said, and his words echoed in the Capture chamber.

"You already know what the Daedalus Key is, Reed. You wrote it down yourself in the margins of this book."

Reed took a step back, his mind reeling. "The key is a phrase?"

Slater nodded, pointing down the hallway. Reed saw himself at a library table, his hands moving over the page as he wrote. And then he remembered. He'd learned about Daedalus's insane jealousy over the talent of his nephew. So much so, he'd murdered him. Tortured with guilt, Daedalus's mazes grew more and more twisted. Mirroring the psyche of the man himself. Reed had written in the margins, horrified that so brilliant a mind could turn on itself. In front of his eyes, Slater's dark fate and Reed's own worst fear scrawled across the floating page.

He lost himself. There was nothing left.

The thought hit Reed, and the void behind Slater exploded open, sucking them both into the endless abyss in a torrent of wind. Tumbling through the emptiness, Reed felt the shift of time. Years before. The air grew heavy, hard to breathe, and he noticed no one banged on the chamber anymore. Instead, a hiss of something blew in his face. Cold and steady, it pulled Reed through the night. He soared down the maze, out into the night, past the trees. So high he couldn't see a single light below. And then the sound changed. Like he was in a closet, and then a light overhead glowed on. Slater stood staring at a display screen within a small room the size of a bathroom. It had a chair, a monitor, and a locked door. Reed recognized what it was. He had been in a few himself. It was a SCIF.

The highly secure room designed to view sensitive and classified information enveloped Slater and Reed as he viewed videos on the screen in fast-forward. Slater seemed to be looking for something, and the flitting images confused Reed. He saw a recording of Jacoby meeting with Danzig in a dark garage. They leaned together, conspiring. Slater had captured it, and the shock of seeing it moved through Reed's mind as their thoughts entwined. But that was not what Slater sought. He wanted the last video in the series. Reed's horror grew as he watched. Images of slice injuries, dismembered sea life and other animals played for Slater, and a thought darted through Reed's mind.

The Resonance device.

The scene shifted, dropping from underneath Reed's feet. He was underwater in scuba gear. Sunlight came in shafts through the surface. The current strong. He was filming something, but the waves and sea were wrong. Bending as if made of solid glass, ice sheets suddenly appeared, only to shatter into a hundred floating shards. Reed felt the wane of drugs hit him, the sense of the chamber's substrate intruding into the scene. He fought it, willing himself to witness what Slater had.

Then he saw it. The device. A shadowy oblong shape in the water. It soared incredibly fast toward a hull overhead. A muffled gong warbled through the ocean as it attached.

Slater, who'd been filming about a hundred yards away, looked up at the quarter-scale dummy ship. A second explosion, larger than intended, sent a cloud flaring out from underneath the device. Too soon. Slater swam frantically, shouting into his mouthpiece to pull back, but it was too late. A tone sounded...low and almost imperceptible, it rose to a cacophony. The ocean churned as if in a violent storm. Slater didn't stop swimming, glancing back as he fought to put distance between him and the device. One of the other men filming didn't move in time, and the blue of the ocean filled with a scarlet cloud as the man split apart before his eyes.

A ringing pierced Reed's mind. It stabbed at his consciousness, but he held onto the memory.

Time skipped, and it was night on the beach. He was in a field tent. Halogen lights lit up gurneys filled with men shouting in pain. Slashes in wet suits bled onto the stretchers carrying trembling bodies. Slater's mind melding with his as the abyss rushed over him, cold and wet, fighting the chattering of his teeth. Slater stood in the midst of chaos as medics worked on the team of soldiers. The stubs of missing limbs sheared clean off, the trail of blood on the sand as they pulled them from the blast zone, the screams. All of it coalesced around Reed as he witnessed what Slater had.

"We'll get you patched up soon," a medic said as he stopped in front of Slater, shoved a wad of gauze in his bloody hand, and moved on.

Slater's forearm bore a long gash, as if sliced by a knife. Movement out on the surface of the water pulled his gaze. A small boat with a lone figure standing in its center. Reed tried to walk toward the shore, but Slater didn't move. Instead, he'd looked the other way. Up the hill past the beach to the lab under construction. Where they were making more of this destruction.

"How do I stop it?" Reed shouted, but Slater was long gone. The memory fractured at the edges, lifting like dead bark from reality. Ringing in Reed's head worsened, and pain gripped his chest. Voices broke through as the memory slipped away. He blinked, his eyes fluttering open as a group of doctors stood over him, handing each other supplies and shouting. Alarms blared around his head, and he realized he wasn't in the chamber anymore. He was on the floor. Behind the doctors, he spied the observation window and saw Nat. She leaned with her palms open on the glass, shouting something. Overhead, Carl looked down as he went to place an oxygen mask over Reed's face.

"He's back," the nurse shouted. 'Hold on, he's back!"

They all glanced down as Reed slammed back into himself. Dr. Reynoso looked at him with worry. Reed took a gasping breath and spotted Jacoby leaning over him. Reed's hands shot out, and he grabbed the older man by the collar of his tracksuit.

"You met with Danzig!" Reed shouted as Jacoby struggled to pull away. "You're working with him!"

"Get me a tranquilizer!" Dr. Reynoso shouted. "He's not breaking out of it."

"I'm not hallucinating!" Reed fought to get off the floor, but his arms and legs felt leaden, and the room kept shifting a second too late. He shook his head, trying to clear it, and he saw Carl coming at him with a needle.

"Calm down, now, my guy," Carl said in a strangely soothing voice.

Reed opened his mouth to argue, but the room melted away to nothing, and he was gone.

34

Reed awoke in an empty room. His head pounded at his temples, and he groaned with a myriad of aches as he sat up and looked around. Someone had put grippy socks on his feet but left the scrubs. The room was odd. Opaque glass walls muffled any sound, and the door leading out had no handle or knob. Overhead, a metal screen protected the light fixture. A toilet and a sink sat off in a corner protected by a privacy curtain hanging from a track in the ceiling. Reed got up, stretching as he tried the door. It wouldn't budge.

"Hello?" Reed called, rubbing his eyes against the brightness of the light fixture. "Jacoby?"

The opaque walls cleared in an instant, and Reed glared out at Jacoby, who stood in some kind of control room that encircled his glass holding room. Banks of monitors with scrolling information on Reed's vitals and views from hidden cameras within the room lit up the otherwise dark outer space.

"Are you back?" Jacoby asked. His tracksuit stripe reflected the lights of the monitors.

"I was back before you had them drug me, and you know it." Reed slammed the side of his fist on the glass in front of him, but it made nothing but a soft thud. "Get me out of this fish tank."

"Slater had gone dark. For weeks," Jacoby said, not moving. "The pressure was breaking him. We wanted to bring him in, but he had gone off the grid. We couldn't make contact with him."

"I don't care," Reed said, pacing.

"You should. It's why you saw me with Danzig."

Reed folded his arms across his chest. "Explain, then."

"We caught wind of a public fight between Danzig and one of his bitter rivals at a tech forum in Vegas around that time. The Digitex Conference is where all the emerging tech companies go to show off their concept builds and congratulate each other on being rich."

"I've never heard of it."

"That's because it's invitation only, and you're not nearly genius enough or rich enough to be invited," Jacoby said. "Anyway, rumors started that Danzig physically thrashed this rival and threatened to 'end' him. Over what, we couldn't find out. The whole incident was covered up, but…the guy Danzig threatened ended up dying in a suspicious home steam room accident a month later."

Reed raised a brow. "Did he do it?"

"Someone thinks he did. We were getting chatter of a possible hit put out on Danzig by a Russian businessman, Petr Kerimov, the brother of the dead rival. He has massive holdings. Our dossier on him is interesting reading. Grew up in an orphanage. Now he owns a telecom, a private bank, a power company, copper mines—you get the picture."

"An oligarch," Reed said. "Sounds like someone who could in fact take out Danzig."

"That's exactly why I was given authorization to speak with him. We hoped to work out a protection deal for Danzig's cooperation."

"I take it you got a resounding no from him?"

"He denied he had been in any altercations, denied even knowing the rival, and refused to believe he was in any real danger. The meeting was a wash. It lasted maybe five minutes. And I had no idea Slater was there, or maybe he tracked me there because, as I said, he'd been uncommunicative for weeks. I'm sure it looked suspicious to him."

"He was surprised, actually. Shock was the emotion during that memory. Betrayal."

"Clearly." Jacoby pulled at his collar. "I didn't betray Slater. I fought to bring him in safely until the day he died."

Reed looked around, but the room didn't have windows. "What time is it?"

Jacoby checked his watch. "It's nearly nine at night."

"I want out of here," Reed said.

"You have a decision to make first." Jacoby nodded at the door. "We've been working and uncovered new information. You can stay here until this is over so that I'm sure you won't get in the way, or you can work with me and Gray Zone to take down Danzig once and for all."

"Doing what? We have no idea where Botha is or where the boat that escaped is heading."

"We do now. Your literal unmasking of Botha paid off. After running his DNA, we got a call from the South African State Security Agency, their FBI. He's wanted there for a series of suspected courthouse bombings that resulted in the escape of a drug lord the government had spent years chasing down. They're pissed. The US looks incompetent because we can't seem to catch him despite having several close encounters."

"So, this is my fault?" Reed balked.

"No. Everyone has egg on their face because of this Botha character and Danzig."

Reed considered him for a moment. "Something happened, didn't it?"

"It did. In your debrief session with the AI Agent, you mentioned the name Seward from your description of what you saw inside the lab."

"It was on a piece of paper under a coffee cup, like someone had just been writing it. It said something like 'Seward' and the word 'links,' with a question mark."

Jacoby nodded. "Despite their anger over Botha, our talk with the South African government was fruitful. They gave us more aliases they were aware of that belonged to Botha during his old spy days. Luna ran the identities along with key words from your debrief. One of which was Seward. Something popped on the radar."

"You're kidding. Where?" Reed leaned closer to the glass to see Jacoby.

"It turns out Botha used a fake name from fifteen years ago to purchase a first-class ticket to your favorite place, Alaska."

"He's flying? What about the boat launch? The weapon?"

"Likely keeping them separate for safety."

Reed shook his head, pacing. "Where is he flying into?"

"Anchorage."

"Really?" Reed stopped pacing. "He's leaving California, which has cities with populations well over a million people, to blow up Anchorage? There's what, two hundred thousand people there at most?"

"Closer to three hundred thousand, but I get your point. Seward, Alaska, is near there. I know it doesn't make sense yet, but Botha is definitely on the move. This is what he does. Terrorist attacks without warning."

"For whom?"

"My guess is Danzig," Jacoby said with a shrug. "Maybe one of his allies."

Reed shook his head. This was all wrong. "How would a terrorist act serve Danzig at all? Why do all of this?"

"Look, Reed, I'm telling you what we know."

"How long would a vessel take to sail from the Channel Islands to Alaska?"

"Coyote told you it was a boat about thirty feet?"

"Less than," Reed said. "Maybe smaller."

Jacoby leaned back. "If his description is right, and if the trip was a continuous sail with no weather trouble or mechanical issues…it would take between two and four weeks, give or take. If the boat is part of the terror plot, he'll have to wait for it to arrive, so we have some time."

"Do you think Botha will get there before the weapon and scope things out?"

"We certainly hope so," Jacoby said calmly.

"Any idea what the target is?"

"Nope."

"But we're going to Alaska?"

"We're moving on what we know, and we'll pivot with new info."

"You have no idea what's going on, do you?"

"Well, it's obviously something bad." Jacoby reached over and tapped on a keyboard. The lock to Reed's door clicked, and the door slid open. "Are you in or out?"

"Where's Nat?" Reed asked, blinking in the darker control room.

"She's working with Luna on the recordings from the lab taken by the goggles you and Coyote wore."

"I want to talk to her."

"Before you do, know that Luna says she accessed Xanadu's preliminary autopsy report through the Field Ops computers. The White Lion...Botha...whatever you want to call him, broke Xanadu's ribs, wrists, and fingers and beat him so badly he bled out and died before the fire even started."

Reed's hand went to his forehead. "You shouldn't have let her see that."

"You and I both know there's no stopping Agent De La Cruz from finding what she's looking for. She wants blood, Reed. I almost believe she'd stay to help even if you didn't."

The walls felt like they were closing in on him literally and figuratively. "None of this makes sense."

"It never does," Jacoby said and headed for the door. "You need to change out of those scrubs. We have work to do. Come on, you can use the doctors' lounge."

"What about Coyote?" Reed asked, catching up to him in the hall.

"He doesn't have the clearance to go where we are."

"But Nat and I do?"

Jacoby looked at him, his face solemn. "You and Agent De La Cruz will have everything you need."

Jacoby took him to the lounge where a front room with overstuffed chairs and couches all faced a wall-mounted screen. Serene, sweeping photos of national landmarks faded into one another while soothing spa music played from the speakers. The Grand Canyon, Niagara Falls, the world's largest ball of twine in Kansas, all the classics.

Jacoby held up Reed's sketchbook, walked over to a couch, and sat down with it. "Before I let you go, Agent Reed. Tell me what you saw in my machine."

Reed sat and told him how he'd seen himself through Slater's eyes and that the mercenary believed that Reed would eventually catch him and was afraid of Jacoby ripping his memory and killing him.

"Well, I guess he was half right," Jacoby said. "You did catch him. You did rip him."

"The Daedalus Key was a phrase I knew that Slater used as a key to unlock the memories he'd hidden in the void." Reed told him about the implant and the drugs the Neurogen scientist administered to help him to do this. "He really didn't want you to find out what he knew."

"Why did he allow you to access it?"

"He didn't trust you or Gray Zone or Danzig anymore. Slater was paranoid, and the drugs he was taking didn't help," Reed explained. "I think he wanted to stop what Danzig had planned for the Resonance device but didn't know how. I think…I think he knew he was losing his mind and that his time was running out. The void in my head was a bomb he'd set to annihilate whomever you got to view his memory other than me. He said it would cause a break with reality."

"A booby trap in your consciousness. Interesting. I wondered if it was possible."

"He had me disarm it with the trigger phrase, and then the void revealed what he'd been hiding. It was a test run of the Resonance device." Reed described the horrible scene in the hospital tent on the beach. "It was the location of the lab."

"He had a scar on his forearm. Said it was from a motorcycle accident," Jacoby said.

"It wasn't." Reed rubbed his own arm absentmindedly. "There was another memory. It was in a SCIF." He described the recordings of more of the same phenomena associated with the Resonance device. "I don't know where it was located. A dark hangar seems wrong."

"No, it doesn't. There are portable ones. It's likely Danzig's. Slater was investigating the Special Projects files inside of his High Rock Holdings facility."

Reed flipped to the drawing of the dismembered seal. "Resonance does something to the water. I can't tell if it's frozen or the glass is shrapnel designed to disappear after impact to hide the blast zone, but something is…" A flash of memory strobed behind Reed's eyes. "There was a man on a small vessel in the water near the test blast that Slater witnessed. I don't know if he was part of it or what, but I remember the impression that he was important somehow."

"Was it Danzig?"

"No. It wasn't him." Reed rubbed the scar under his eye. "But the test detonation where Slater saw all of those men butchered was the Deep Wave Dynamics lab."

Jacoby considered Reed for a moment and then rose from the couch. "That's all for now. We have your luggage from the car you took to meet with Bobby. Your carry-on is here. Hurry up and change. Nat found something I think you're going to want to see."

Reed showered in the medical staff lounge. Another long, hot one that didn't seem to warm him all the way up. His suitcase was in the door of the shower room when he got out. Despite the hot shower and shave, Reed still felt groggy from the tranquilizer, but it was fading. A rap at the door spurred him to move, and he finished up changing into black field pants, a long-sleeved navy shirt, and his combat boots. When he was done, he opened the door to find an agent standing there.

"Carson Wyatt. I'm your escort, sir. Please follow me to the command center."

He wore gray field pants and a T-shirt, also with combat boots. Blond hair, brown eyes, farmer's tan. Lanky build like a bull rider. He didn't work inside, Reed thought.

"Are you an agent?" Reed asked as Wyatt led them along the convoluted hallways at a near power-walking rate.

"No, sir," Wyatt answered as they walked up to the main control room. He opened the door for Reed without elaborating.

Jacoby stood over by a bank of monitors at the front of the vast room. He waved Reed over. "Come see this."

Nat was sitting at a console next to Jacoby and looked over at Reed with a smile filled with relief. "Hey. You're looking much better."

"Thanks." Reed ran a hand self-consciously over his damp hair.

"You okay?" she asked.

"He's fine," Jacoby said and leaned against the counter with his arms folded. "Tell him what you told me."

"Oh...kay." Nat made a face but typed on the keyboard in front of her, and she called up several images on the large screen on the wall. "This is the feed from Bobby's data lens. The one from the underwater rover that he recorded with the night of the sinking." The recording began, and a view of the sea at sunset flashed by the lens as the rover lowered on a winch. She fast-forwarded the recording, and the visibility in the water waned as the day died. "Okay, here's what I'm talking about." She slowed the video, and the ghostly images of seaweed shifted with the current, an occasional shoal of various fish wandered by, then he saw it. A dark, oblong shape in the water as it raced past the rover's camera.

"That's it," Reed said. "I saw that in the memory. Fiona said it was fast."

"She did," Nat said. "But this is what's new." She slowed the recording even more, flipping past the seconds before a shape came into view. Small, at the edge of the frame, it was a small vessel with a man standing in the center, watching the ferry.

"Wait, I've seen that," Reed said.

"I know," Nat said and brought another recording onto the large view screen. "This is from your goggles at the Deep Wave Dynamics lab. You were in the water and then popped up for a moment, and the camera caught this..."

It was another vessel, the solar sailboat Coyote had described. She pointed to the silhouette of the boat in the underwater rover video and slid the shape to cover the solar sailboat from the goggles. They were a perfect match. They both rode up on the water strangely, just as Coyote had said, but Reed was shaking his head. The memory flooding back of the test sinking Slater had witnessed. The one before the carnage.

"No, I meant Slater saw that boat. A few years ago." Reed's gaze went to Jacoby. "It was near the test detonation that day. Someone was aboard, watching the test."

"That couldn't be Botha, he hadn't worked for Danzig before as far as we know," Jacoby said. "Either way, it means someone was present for at least two of the Resonance detonations. The one years ago that Slater witnessed. The one Bobby recorded as his family's boat sank. And the unique silhouette of the boat puts it at the Deep Wave Dynamics lab, where we have evidence they housed the Resonance device." Jacoby began typing on his phone. "So, we're on the right trail, but we need more."

"The question is, why would anyone risk being that close? You could film with an aerial drone and get a much better view of the event," Nat mused, her gaze on the videos. "The only reason to be that close is because you have to be."

"Why would they have to be?" Reed asked.

Luna stuck her head into the command center from the fake front office of the Coffee Packing Co. and nodded.

"We're ready," Jacoby said, signaling Luna. "We'll find out more in Alaska."

"Jacoby told me you saw what this thing does," Nat said, her gaze on Reed as she gathered her things. "Do you think we can stop it?"

Reed nodded slowly, his eyes on the man in the boat. The slant of the shoulders and tilt of the head seemed familiar. That figure was the anomaly that needed answering. "I think we've been a stone in Danzig's shoe so far. Why stop now?"

"Excellent," Jacoby said and walked toward the door. "We're wheels up in thirty minutes."

35

Reed, Nat, Jacoby, and Wyatt, the non-agent, were in the air a little after ten at night. They flew out of LAX on a jet for a direct flight to Anchorage. The captain informed them that the flight would take seven hours, maybe more, depending on the weather and wind, and suggested they settle in. Jacoby took up a chair in front, logging on to his laptop and speaking into his phone simultaneously. The blue light of the monitor lit up his tired face. Wyatt wadded up his jacket, shoved it in the corner between his head and the fuselage, and then passed out like he'd been drugged. Behind Reed's seat, Nat fought with the coffeemaker in the small galley area and then raided the snack basket. He could hear her crunching in the dim light of the cabin. The insanity of the day and the Capture procedure caught up with Reed, and he dozed. He woke occasionally with turbulence, checked his watch, only to drift off again. His exhausted mind offered no dreams.

Eventually, activity in the galley behind Reed made him stir, and he awakened, blinking at the dawn light, feeling like he'd barely closed his eyes. He slid his window shade down, blocking the sliver of rising sun, and rose from his seat. Nat and Jacoby stood together with coffee cups steaming in their hands. They had a conspiratorial aura about them.

"What's going on?" Reed slipped past them and poured himself a mug. "What happened?"

"As soon as we land, we're catching another plane to Nome. Luna informed me an hour ago that another one of Thyse Botha's aliases booked a connecting flight to Nome out of Anchorage. Sit tight for now. We're not done yet."

They landed at Ted Stevens Anchorage International Airport at six in the morning. Half an hour later, they took off from the North Terminal in a military plane. It was a hopper transport outfitted for personnel, yet the rattling fuselage and cargo strapped inside made enormous noise. Reed sat at the rear of the plane, sandwiched between a stack of wooden crates and cardboard boxes full of mess hall supplies, and worked on his sketchbook. He drew the boat he'd seen in Slater's memory. Trying to get the form down before it faded.

Nat slid next to him, wrapped in a coat as the plane grew colder. She peered at him from inside a fur-rimmed hood. "Don't believe Jacoby," she said, leaning in. "You aren't fine. I thought you were going to die in that chamber."

Reed glanced around the cabin, but it was large and loud, and Jacoby was up front, working with headphones on. "What do you mean?"

"You were sort of mumbling the whole time. Talking about what you saw and also to Slater, I think. But your vitals started getting wonky. Weird heart rate here. Strange respiration pattern there. Dr. Reynoso monitored you constantly. But then around the last hour, it was clear you were in trouble—" Turbulence shook the plane, and she gripped onto his arm. Nat hated flying. "Your temp kept falling. And they kept raising the temperature of the substrate you were lying in to warm you up, but it wasn't working."

"That's why it was burning." Reed raised his arm and showed her the red skin on the heel of his hand. "I felt it."

She nodded. "Dr. Reynoso gave you meds to keep your heart rate steady. He gave you something else to keep you under longer. Another to regulate your increasingly erratic brain waves. You were tanking. Jacoby authorized keeping you in the memory, in the chamber, until your temp was so low it was affecting your breathing. They almost let you freeze to death in front of them." Her dark eyes met his, full of anger. "He doesn't have your back, Reed. Don't trust him."

"I knew *you* did," Reed said, slipping his hand over hers. "You always do."

"Always will." Nat rested her head against his shoulder. She watched him draw for a while, then asked, "What are you doing?"

He showed her his drawing. "This is the most detail I can get on this vessel. Do you think it's enough to do a search on what kind it might be?"

"Yeah, we've been running it through Gray Zone's network. We pulled images of it from the goggles and Bobby's rover. They're doing a search for anything leaving from that area at that time of night." She nodded and pulled out her tablet from her giant coat. "The problem is boats look like boats in thick fog. Not a lot of variation, to be honest. And they obviously didn't file a sailing plan with anyone. It's like Jacoby's looking for a sewing needle in a syringe factory." Taking a photo of the sketch with her tablet, she worked on it in a couple of programs. Coloring it as best as Reed could describe, tweaking the measurements against the most common suggestions. Dozens of designs fluttered by as she scrolled. "You said long-haul, right?"

"That bothers me," Reed said, adding shading to his drawing. "Jacoby said they'd accelerated their plans. So why use one of the slowest modes of transportation?"

"A boat could avoid customs, there's no TSA snooping through your stuff, no dogs sniffing around for bombs," Nat said. She stopped on a boat and then moved past it. "I mean, it's a trade-off, speed for stealth."

Reed stopped drawing, and a drop of ink landed on the page, beading before absorbing into his sketch of the surface of the sea. He blinked for a moment, then, "What if it isn't a trade-off?"

"How do you mean?"

"Coyote said the boat he saw leaving the lab that night was fast. It was out of sight in minutes." He sketched out the curved hull of a boat with metal struts holding a lifting fin beneath. "You know what, I think I know why it sits funny. It might have a hydrofoil."

"Like those surfboards with that wing thing underneath?" Nat edited her image of Reed's sketch. "You bounce on them or something to make them go?"

"Yes. Like that."

She adjusted her search. "Okay, I've seen speedboats with a hydrofoil underneath, but Coyote described a large vessel, right? Do they even make those?"

"I think they did. I read about New Jersey using something like that as ferries." Reed snapped his finger, remembering. "Oh, and in World War Two, the Germans had a large vessel that sat high up on the water, it was a minelayer or a smoke layer. Some say it could run up to forty-seven knots, and that was almost a hundred years ago."

"So, a larger hydrofoil craft, solar sails to feed the battery, and a big engine to supplement..." Nat typed on her screen. "There are designs here that fit the bill. They're special order or custom builds."

"A hydrofoil reduces drag by raising the boat up on the water. The solar sails reduce fuel consumption so they wouldn't need to stop as much, if at all. Danzig would have the means to pay for an optimum design. He'd push the envelope of performance."

"I got an image match." Nat held up her tablet. A boat of similar size and design as the one Coyote described sailed across the screen in a video. "Get this, they can reach up to thirty-seven knots. That's fast for the size."

"That would change the timeline." Reed worked out the math on his sketchbook and then looked up at Nat, alarmed. "I'm getting three to seven days, does that sound right?"

"No." Nat restarted the calculations on her tablet. "That can't be right."

Jacoby noticed their intensity and walked over. "What're you guys doing over here?"

Nat stood and showed him her calculations. Telling him about the boat design, the speed, the solar sails.

Jacoby stroked his chin, nodding. "It'll be heavy. Our estimates put the image of the weapon we saw on Bobby's video at nearly six feet. The sound he described during his interview was metal. 'Like a gong,' were his words. So, there's weight that could slow it down."

"Setting aside weather conditions, sailing routes, and potential stops for supplies or whatever, that still fits the timeline." Reed scribbled in his sketchbook.

"It might not have to stop. It could be autonomous," Jacoby said.

Reed rubbed his forehead. "We don't have weeks, we have days."

"Let me think. You infiltrated the lab a day and a half ago, and the ship set sail." Jacoby checked his phone. "We'll get into Alaska at the close of the second day it's been traveling."

"Crap," Nat said. "That means that weapon could be arriving in Alaska within the next day or two."

"I guess it's good that we're on our way to Alaska, then," Jacoby said with a grin. "Tell me you're sorry for doubting me."

"Your genius is breathtaking," Reed said with a blank face.

Jacoby chuckled. "You mean it. I can tell."

They flew over the Nome area, and through the window, Reed took in the extraordinary amount of change that had occurred over the past nine months. Beginnings of interstates, construction for miles, forests razed to make room for Danzig's Sound Corridor project.

"It's like there's no stopping Danzig," Nat whispered next to him. She looked out of the window with furrowed brows. "We didn't make one bit of difference."

"We did. We made him weaker," Reed said, thinking about the White Lion. Why would Botha work for Danzig after what happened to his family? A high price tag? Leverage? That would be dangerous. Strong-arming an assassin takes a special kind of insanity. Danzig wasn't insane, but he *was* a risk taker. "Whatever Danzig is up to, it feels desperate. Something is going on that we can't see."

A green light came on in the cabin, and Jacoby started packing. "We're heading into Fort Davis."

"The Gold Rush base?" Reed gathered his things, pulling on a coat. "Wasn't it condemned for being ancient?"

"Formerly defunct, under construction now. After the disaster in Aurora and Danzig's grab for control of the region, there was some saber rattling from Russia up north in the Transarctic Waterway. They were talking about stopping shipping vessels and inspecting them like they owned the shipping route. We ramped up military coverage out here. And Fort Davis was built in the 1920s to deal with the rowdy gold miners, so it's not ancient," Jacoby said. "A larger base is planned deep within Danzig's proposed territory, but for now, Fort Davis is sufficient."

They disembarked onto a windy tarmac. Golden shards of morning light cut through the dark clouds that churned overhead. Reed's watch put the temperature at a balmy fifty-one degrees in Nome.

"Is there a storm coming?"

"In June?" Wyatt asked with a grin. "Nope. This is summer."

A Humvee met them at the airstrip. The driver jumped out, and Wyatt took over the wheel. Fort Davis was maybe ten minutes down the road. They pulled into the front gate, checked in with security, and moved through the base. It looked abandoned. Automated construction zones peppered the base as they drove. Robotic 3D printing tractors squirted a concrete mixture in rows to make retaining walls and curbs; another machine spread asphalt in sheets as another followed behind, smoothing it into streets. Caution tape cordoned off half-built structures with welding arms spitting sparks from their tracks. Lifting robots moved pallets of supplies into a main holding area. Not a lot of human activity, though, Reed thought, scanning the grounds. A few men in utilities, some civilians, a stray dog. It felt like a ghost town.

The buildings further in were completed already. Wyatt took them past an exchange, a country store, even a portable building with a sign that read *Library*.

"We have a skeleton crew out here for now," Jacoby said over the engine. "Mostly for the mess hall and Med Care clinic. We've got civilian contractors working on the builds. Some of Gray Zone is here as well. Wyatt's team." They stopped in front of a building that resembled a highway motel. Six rooms in a row with doors facing the street. Jacoby tossed each of them a key. "These billets are for your use. Private rooms, bathrooms, a little sitting area."

"Luxury accommodations." Wyatt smirked. "I'm jealous."

"Settle in, rest, grab some chow. Meet me in the OCC when you're ready," Jacoby said.

They drove off, leaving Reed and Nat in the dust. They pushed into the first billet. It was a single-occupancy room, with a twin bed, and exhaustion hit Reed as he tossed his suitcase on the green wool blanket. How was he tired again after sleeping so much? He sat on the edge of the bed, rubbing his eyes with the heels of his hands.

"You should grab some more sleep," Nat said by the door.

"I should go over everything you guys found out while I was passed out."

She surveyed the room. "You know our rule about staying professional when at work?"

Reed grinned. "Why, you want to break it?"

She smiled. "That's pretty generous of you, but no. This place is miniscule, and I still have all my equipment to unload. I wanna take a shower... maybe take a nap."

He chuckled, slipping the tablet from underneath her arm. "Go...relax. Take a break. I need to go over what you found on the goggles and Bobby's video, anyway."

She navigated the data and then looked at him weirdly. "What's the OCC?"

"Operations Command Center," Reed explained. "Whatever we're doing, he'll run it from there."

Nat went to the other billet, and Reed dug into the videos and reports generated by both her and Gray Zone. He listened to her bump around through the wall while he read about the lab, the possible dimensions of the Resonance weapon, the escaping ship, and speculation about the vial of fluid Reed had stolen from Deep Wave's lab. After an hour, Reed stopped trying to ignore the headache behind his eyes. He'd been fighting a low-key migraine since the sonar rounds from the water sentinels. Stomach growling, he knocked on Nat's door, and she let him in. She was showered, dressed in a warm jacket, and starving as well.

They walked together to the mess hall, looking for the OCC on the way. She chattered about the plane ride and the weird déjà vu feeling she had stepping back into Alaska. Reed's eyes slipped to the healed scar beneath her collarbone. She'd nearly died last time she was in Alaska, and he'd brought her right back.

The mess hall was small but smelled right. Fried chicken, hamburgers, lots of familiar sides. Homestyle meals for a crew far from home. They went through the chow line, then walked to a far table with their trays. Groups of soldiers in fatigues, PT gear, and civilian clothes socialized loudly. Laughing, talking, with a lot of sideways glances at the new guys. Reed nodded when he caught a look, but no one bothered them.

"Is this the cool kid table?" Wyatt asked, sliding onto the bench opposite Reed and Nat. He had his tray piled with a little of everything.

"Where's the OCC?" Nat asked. "Also, are you going to eat all those fries?"

"Why? You want some?" Wyatt asked with a grin and tilted his plate for her. She grabbed one and bit it in half. "Oh, Agent De La Cruz. You're after my own heart."

"The OCC?" Reed prompted and grabbed a fry for himself.

"I'll show you when we're done." Wyatt ate a huge bite of his burger and then shook his napkin at Reed. "You led that hunt for Fourth Quadrant."

"It was a team effort," Reed said.

"I heard you jumped from one moving transport to theirs while dodging drone fire. That true?"

"Don't believe everything you hear," Reed said. "Besides, we weren't going that fast."

Wyatt chuckled. "And the drone?"

"I mean, it was old."

"Tell me something, are you in the loop or what?" Nat asked. "I get the impression you're more than just muscle."

"I hear things." Wyatt finished off his iced tea. "Why?"

"Because Jacoby is stingy with the info," she said.

"Yeah." Wyatt shrugged. "Did you hear about the AIS number we found?"

Reed sat up straight. "Are you talking about the vessel number?"

Wyatt nodded, glancing around. He leaned in. "Your buddy Coyote's goggles recorded some paperwork. It looked like it was on the floor of the moon pool from the image. He picked up an AIS number on a form, essentially a VIN number, but for boats," he said for Nat's benefit. "It was partially covered by another paper, but we're running what we have through Marine Traffic Operations. We're hoping to narrow down the pool of vessels we're looking through."

"You've been busy," Reed said, finishing off his eggs.

"We have another problem," Wyatt said and pushed his tray away. "In the nine months since construction began, the waterway and traffic in the Sound has exploded, pardon the pun. We're looking at cruise ships, freight, ferries. It's a nightmare of targets. To top it off, June is the perfect time to sail to Alaska from California. Groups launch together for the trip. It's a whole thing."

"This is every June?" Nat asked. Wyatt nodded. "So, there's plenty of private vessels to blend into."

"You get the picture," Wyatt said.

"What's Jacoby's plan?" Nat asked. "Technologically speaking."

"We called in extra bodies to check ships in the harbors in case the boat with the weapon is already here ahead of schedule. The Coast Guard's been activated and is tracking suspicious activity, boarding vessels for spot inspections, et cetera. They're assessing the shipping lanes, talking to cruise liners, and inspecting supply ships arriving with construction equipment."

"What about aerial reconnaissance?" Reed asked.

"We're bringing in long-range drones to surveil from the air in tandem with the ship transceiver information we have so far."

Reed nodded. "Any movement on what the target is?"

"No, but given this White Lion guy likes to personally stab people with exploding knives, we've reached out to possible high-value targets in and around Alaska. We warned them to beef up their security."

"High value such as the governor?" Reed asked. "He's safe?"

Wyatt nodded. "He's in residence this week due to illness, and his wife is visiting her mother in Michigan. We've contacted military officials, judges, even celebrities who keep homes in Alaska and told them to tighten or upgrade their security. The problem is no one pops as a target worth all of this hubbub."

"What about the lieutenant governor?" Reed asked. "Pierce Rexford. Did you locate him?"

"We did not," Wyatt said. "Though, I wouldn't consider him a high-value target." Wyatt's phone bleeped, and he checked the message. "We should head out. Jacoby says Dr. Tsukumo is here."

"Who's that?" Reed asked.

"She's going to explain why the ocean is suddenly slicing people to shreds."

36

The Operations Command Center was located in a metal domed Quonset hut at the end of a gravelly road just past the barracks. When Wyatt led them in, it was like every other command center Reed had been in while serving. Instead of maps and target packages, the large screen on the wall displayed various scientific models. Images of strange fluid shapes and complicated lab equipment. Jacoby and an older Asian woman stood near the monitors and communications kit, talking. She wore the best of high-end camping apparel, all of it new. Six people dressed in fatigues sat at the stations with headsets, already working on something.

"Agents Reed and De La Cruz," Jacoby said, presenting the woman. "I'd like you to meet Dr. Emi Tsukumo. She's a pioneer in the field of condensed and materials physics."

"Happy to be here," she said. Her voice was cool, calm, and touched with a slight accent from upper-crust California. "Okay, this is heady stuff. Solid state and condensed physics take years to grasp, so I'm going to distill it down to what I think will be helpful to you as a team."

Nat leaned in and whispered, "Did she just call us stupid?"

"A little," Reed whispered back. "But, you know, professionally."

Dr. Tsukumo leaned over her laptop on the counter, and the largest screen displayed a video from a social media sharing site. It was of a man in his backyard, adjusting makeshift equipment as a strange noise vibrated just below hearing. Reed scratched his nose at the tickle. The camera panned to a giant speaker that blurred as it emitted a strange sound. Atop the speaker was a plate filled with white sand, and as the man adjusted some dials, the sand formed into fractal shapes. The angles adjusted with every change in pitch, making snowflake-like patterns on the tray.

"Okay, so you've all seen something like this, right?" She pointed a remote at her laptop and changed the video to a similar setup, but this time with water. The fluid from the hose moved in a strange, sinuous manner. Coiling and bending in a solid stream as if made of molten glass. "These gentlemen are manipulating matter with sound. You understand the concept, yes?"

Everyone nodded.

"So, building on that, we get into what Oscar Kernigan was working on." A photo of the physicist that Bobby had harassed appeared on the screen. "I was Dr. Kernigan's adviser on that particular paper while he was a student at California's Pacific Institute of Technology and Science." She moved the scientific models to the main screen and continued. "Kernigan's research centered mainly on phonons. At the time of his death, he was working on this concept for ASTRA."

"Are you talking about photons?" Wyatt asked.

Dr. Tsukumo shook her head. "That's light. This is more sound and heat. A phonon can be thought of as a description of vibrational motion and arrangement. Look at these." Another video emerged from the side of the screen. Several crystalline formations as seen under a microscope pulsed with energy through a filter. "This is a simplification, but essentially, Dr. Kernigan was working on manipulating fluid at the molecular or even the atomic level to form a solid, lattice-like structure." She pointed to the video. "This is not ice. This is something else."

Reed shook his head. "How is that possible?"

"It wasn't. The theory is that, under certain circumstances, fluids can be made to act like solids with the right combination of particles and harmonics. But very few fluids have the molecular construct that is needed. The phonon describes a collective excitation that can align the atoms into a lattice or crystalline structure. But like I said, it wasn't possible."

"But it's been tried, right?" Reed asked.

"With limited success." A video played at the point of her remote. It showed a lab with several containers of fluid attached to a large machine Reed couldn't identify. A scientist pointed at the beaker, and the camera zoomed in on the liquid. A tone vibrated through the container, and the liquid momentarily appeared to split into a thousand tiny shards of glass before returning to its original state.

In that split second, Reed heard a high-pitched ting. "Wait...Bobby mentioned music right before what he called 'the collapse.'"

"The vibrations can elicit sound just like with a tuning fork." Dr. Tsukumo nodded at the screen. "In this researcher's case, you're seeing acoustic radiation, which is essentially the flow of atomic or subatomic particles, or waves. The waves, caused by the resonant vibrations, create pressure changes that trigger a chain reaction in the particles. There *are* other means to achieve this effect. Unfortunately, they are all the same caliber of results. With such early failure to reproduce the desired outcome reliably, the cost of the customized equipment, and the meager outcome, the research was shelved."

Jacoby stepped forward. "The evidence suggests the Resonance weapon is based off these early efforts. Dr. Kernigan's research was almost a decade ago, and with discoveries via AI modeling, we believe that Danzig, or whoever built this weapon, has made a breakthrough."

Dr. Tsukumo held up the vial Reed had taken from the lab. "I believe that this is what makes the effect possible."

She went on to explain that the problem with getting something like water to behave like a solid structure without freezing would require there to be something dissolved in the water to start the unnatural process. She said the vial contained microscopic seed crystals that acted as a catalyst to start the alignment.

"That's a big jump from a beaker to a boat," Reed said. "Do you think whoever built this weapon was able to scale up that much?"

"I do," Dr. Tsukumo said. "It's essentially repositioning atoms with the help of resonant vibrations and a chemical wash."

"You make it sound simple, but it's messing with physics, right?" Nat asked.

"Yes, you're right," she answered. "To do this, the solution and the seed crystals must have been altered in some way at the atomic level." Dr. Tsukumo shook her head. "This kind of power is a reaction. And chain reactions, like our other weapons, can get beyond our control."

"Meaning you have no idea how much destruction this weapon might cause?" Reed asked, his gut knotting. Countless hours spent reading in college about weapons that were far more powerful than the smartest men in the world anticipated at the time swirled in his head.

Nat pointed to the display screen. "The weapon, the big oblong metal thing we saw on Bobby's rover video, it carries the seeds?"

"Well, in order to maintain molecular uniformity, the seedlings would need to be in a chemical solution. They act as scaffolding for the fluid atoms to fall in line with."

Jacoby put up a rough 3D model of the weapon on the screen. Black with white lines, the schematic spun slowly on a center axis.

"We believe we're looking at a two-phase deployment. According to our witness, Bobby, there were two distinct sounds. An initial metal gong noise, followed shortly after by an explosion." The model on the screen soared in a trajectory toward the hull of a boat above it. An accompanying low rumble followed, disturbing the water in its wake. When it attached to the vessel, an artificial gong noise sounded, and the animated water around the vessel and weapon churned as if in a storm. "Our digital intelligence unit enhanced the sound from the undersea rover's footage and discovered it was already emanating a low-grade signal of some sort *before* it attached to the target." They ran the video, and it appeared as if the sea itself was already shifting beneath Bobby's boat before it reached the drone freighter.

"That's the initial phase of attachment to target and the beginning of the resonance vibrations. The intensity will build by intervals," Dr. Tsukumo said. "We don't know for how long, but we do know that the secondary sound, the explosion, disperses the solution with the seed crystals."

"How large is the blast radius?" Reed asked. "The drone freighter detonation looks large, but according to Bobby's account on the podcast, the phenomenon was contained enough for their smaller boat to resist, and for Bobby to jump off and swim. That's what…a football field of influence?"

"It was a smaller detonation with less solution," Jacoby said and typed on his laptop, then brought up a video of a cleanup crew in protective gear wandering around the charred remains of a lab. Reed recognized it as the main laboratory in which he'd seen the vats of chemicals. "This batch, even while calculated conservatively, would make a much larger explosion than the one Bobby witnessed. By a lot."

"Could another weapon be in play?" Reed asked.

"We don't think so. Our ordnance people went over the recordings Bobby made of the weapon. It's at least five feet long, maybe six. Forensic accounting found a purchase of metal ingots by a small wholesaler associated with the Deep Wave lab. According to their calculations, the weight would make one covering for a weapon of that size. Based on what we found in a workshop area of the lab, it appears only one of the metal casings was cast."

"The good news," Dr. Tsukumo said with a smile, as if they were discussing a word problem, "is that the larger the target, the larger the explosion of solution."

"And that's good, how?" Nat asked with a frown.

"It takes longer for that amount of solution to collectively excite and arrange."

Reed tilted his head. "Are you saying there might be more time between attachment and...what? What happens?"

"We recovered some research on a backup server on the Deep Wave laboratory grounds. Show him," Jacoby said.

Dr. Tsukumo pointed her remote. The 3D model slid away, and a video played. In the recording, cameras were positioned facing a glass tank with several rainbow trout swimming in close quarters. There was no sound, and some of the video glitched out due to damage. The fish suddenly stopped moving as if time had stopped, and then their bodies tore to shreds as the water around them erupted with shards of glass that shot through the side of the aquarium, bursting it apart. Then, just as suddenly, the shards splashed in on themselves, liquid once again.

"What the hell!" Reed reared back. "That's not glass. That's stronger than glass."

"Correct." Dr. Tsukumo stopped the recording. "It appears that a crystalline formation abruptly forms, and I have no idea what regulates the dimensions. But if I'm right about what I do know, it's a lattice structure. Incredibly strong."

"How long will it last?" Reed asked, remembering Bobby's account of shattering waterfalls.

"I believe the lattice structure will hold once formed for a few seconds, maybe more. Then it shatters like a rock through a window," Dr. Tsukumo said. "A cavitation will result. The equivalent of a black hole sucking all the sea and debris to the bottom."

"Black hole," Reed repeated, his eyes on Jacoby. "Bobby wasn't crazy. He just didn't understand what he was seeing."

"You guys think it'll be like a cruise ship or something," Nat said. "A terrorist plot because of the White Lion's involvement."

"That's the current theory," Jacoby said, and his brows furrowed at her expression. "Why?"

"Working outside your skill set is dangerous," Nat said. "He was severely burned, and his family killed. What amount of money would bring you out of hiding, knowing there are still enemies looking for you, to do this?"

"His skill set is terror," Jacoby said.

"Yeah, but Nat's right. He has known methods, right?" Reed asked.

"This White Lion has used explosives almost every time we've encountered him. And according to the bomb squad guy, they were homemade devices." She pointed to her tablet. "I looked at his past jobs...all conventional means to cause terror. No fancy gases. No plagues. No complicated plots. Just bombs. In subways, office buildings, stuff like that. He's practically analog in his tech. He uses a dagger, for Pete's sake."

"And his last job was a straight sniper shot to the head," Reed said, agreeing. "This Resonance weapon is unreliable in its precision, as Dr. Tsukumo described. It has multiple steps that could go wrong, and then there's the guy in the boat."

They all turned to look at him. Jacoby narrowed his gaze. "You mean the man watching from the boat in Slater's memory? I read about it in the AI debrief report."

"Yes, and I accidentally recorded a similar vessel with the goggles I wore to the lab," Reed said. "We never figured out why he was there."

"Bobby recorded the same boat with the undersea rover's camera," Nat said. "That vessel has been at all three detonations. Possibly the guy watching from it as well."

"I want to know why he's there at all," Reed said, moving closer to the screen to peer at the image. "Like Nat said…why would he have to be that close to an explosion? It obviously goes off by itself. And why risk being dragged, like Bobby, toward the epicenter? Why be anywhere near the thing? Especially one that is unpredictable in timing and scope?"

"You think he's there for another reason?" Wyatt asked from the back.

Reed turned around, nodding. "I think he's there for something else, yes."

"Like what?" Jacoby asked.

"I have no idea."

No one could come up with a workable answer, so Jacoby asked Nat to team up with his Gray Zone staff on a possible personal connection between Thyse Botha and Danzig. As they broke up the meeting, Jacoby pulled Reed aside, nodding for him to follow him out. They stood outside the Quonset hut in the wan early afternoon sun.

"I've been monitoring your numbers," Jacoby said without preamble. "One of your phones got a call that you might find interesting."

"You bugged my phones?"

"Lock in, Reed. The call is what's important here."

"Who was it?"

Jacoby held up his phone between them, and a familiar voice made Reed's face fall.

"This is Bunny Rexford. We need to talk, ASAP. I think…" Her voice broke. "I think my boy is in trouble. I need your help."

Reed shook his head. "There is no way—"

"I want you to meet with her," Jacoby cut across him as he waved a hand. A black Suburban pulled to a stop next to them. The driver got out but left the motor running. "It's all set up. You leave now."

37

Reed drove to the meeting place, pulling off the interstate to a small grouping of buildings. A gas station and mini-mart, an auto parts store, and a diner. He parked in front of the eatery near a sign advertising the Up All Night Diner. When he entered, it brought to mind the one he'd frequented in Aurora. Fifties themed, records dangling from the ceiling, mint-green-and-white leather booths. The lingering smell of maple syrup in the air. He reminded himself that the woman who owned that diner had died after getting tangled up with Bunny Rexford and her family. He'd be smart to keep that in mind when dealing with her. He scanned the tables and the counter seats. Despite the decent crowd, he didn't see her. Reed ordered an iced soda, and after thirty minutes, he left.

Walking back out to the Suburban, he called Jacoby. "She's a no-show."

"Okay, we'll find her," Jacoby said. "Return to base."

Reed was just pulling open the driver's side door when a figure moved in his peripheral. He saw the gun too late and froze.

"I would be justified in killing you where you stand." Bunny's soft voice sounded to his right. She'd stepped out from behind the SUV, a small gun in hand. "You deserve to die. You murdered my son."

"He was shooting at, well, everyone, Bunny," Reed said softly. "I didn't set out to take him from you."

She hesitated, her hand wavering. "He was sick."

"Okay..." Reed kept his hand on the door handle. "What are we doing? Are we going to have a gunfight or a conversation?"

"You wouldn't be much help to my other son if you're dead." Bunny stowed her gun somewhere in the folds of her buttercup-yellow cardigan. "We'll talk in the truck."

"Everyone bugging my phone was surprised to see you called," Reed said as they climbed inside the Suburban. She looked like she'd had work done. Her forehead looked too smooth to have a son old enough to be lieutenant governor, and she wore her blond hair in a political bob. The grays artfully feathered with lowlights to concede age, but not beauty. Every bit the Southern belle she was before marrying one of the richest men in Alaska. Her green eyes watched him as he settled into his seat. "How did you know I was back in Alaska?"

"I have friends in high places," Bunny said.

"And a son in a similar position. You said he's in trouble?"

Nodding, she wrung her hands as she told him about how Danzig had come to their estate with an offer to buy the land. But they'd refused. Her husband Beau's family had been on that land for generations. Had built up Aurora, put everything on the line for the conservation program that saved the town. They *were* Aurora, according to Bunny. So, they'd told Danzig to back off.

"Later, when I figured out what was happening to our orchards...that Danzig was going to rip everything away from us anyway," Bunny covered her face with her hands, shaking her head, "I made a deal with the devil."

"What did you do?" Reed asked.

"I met with him. I struck a deal." Bunny looked at Reed with red-rimmed eyes. "We'd lost so much. Beau, Niles, our life savings. We'd sunk our future into that research program. I had nothing left."

Reed softened his expression, trying to settle her with a friendlier tone. "Look, I'm not judging right now, Bunny. I'm just trying to figure out what's going on. You had to do what you had to do to survive."

Her shoulders relaxed, and she continued, "The deal was, Danzig would buy our ruined land at its original value, I'd give him the backup data on the research program, and we'd deny ever having any interaction with him."

"And he'd get?"

"M-my boy." Bunny's voice broke. "He'd get Pierce."

"For what?" Reed asked, remembering his one and only encounter with the man. Pierce had run into a burning house to save his father. A local sheriff had once described him to Reed as having his daddy's brains and his mother's ruthlessness.

"Danzig wanted to finance Pierce's run for lieutenant governor. You know my son has been involved with local politics, my whole family has. He'd been elected to county and even state positions, so, you know, Beau thought maybe we could have a Rexford in the governor's mansion someday."

"A deal with the devil is right," Reed muttered.

"I'm a widow. Half my family is gone. He offered my son a future amid the ashes, and I took it." Bunny crossed her arms. "So, sue me."

"If Danzig bought Pierce the lieutenant governorship, he owns him."

"It's not like that," she snapped. "He said he wanted friends in the area for his Sound Corridor project. He wanted me to keep him informed, introduce his people to my friends with important ties, if you know what I mean. He wanted to protect his grip on the region."

"Okay, and Pierce's part?"

She started tearing up, her nose going red at the tip. "He wanted him to get close to the governor. Report back who he's meeting with, who's calling, things like that. Then Danzig wanted Pierce to talk with the governor, you know, broach subjects. Then he wanted him to push for the governor to sign legislation loosening regulations in the area and other things that didn't go over that well. I mean, the governor ran on a conservationist platform, for Pete's sake," Bunny snapped. "I told him that they were close, but Pierce didn't have that kind of influence on his new boss. Not yet, anyway."

"How did Danzig take that?"

She told Reed that a few days after her talk with Danzig, Pierce received a video and a note. She showed Reed the video on her phone. It was a recording of two men talking on the deck of a luxury lodge that Reed remembered as Bunny's home in Aurora before it was destroyed. Reed recognized one of the men, a tall blond man, as Pierce. The man speaking with him was an unknown. He kept his face and body turned away from the camera. He spoke in a raspy whisper as if disguising his voice. A professional.

In the recording, the conversation pertained to the mystery man's boss, who he called Pierce's benefactor—presumably Danzig. The man explained what the benefactor wanted in return for his support for Pierce's campaign. Pierce kept arguing he didn't have the influence or the power to do what the benefactor wanted. Then the stranger leaned in close to Pierce and whispered something. The last second or so of the recording was a look of utter panic on Pierce's face.

"This was sent to Pierce but was recorded in your home?"

"The bastard paid one of my supposedly loyal staff members to place a camera on the outside terrace. The man requested the meeting take place out there because he was afraid of, get this, hidden cameras."

Reed shook his head. "Danzig's guy secretly recorded your son on his own property. That's bold."

"It's blackmail," Bunny said with heat in her voice. "Leverage to keep Pierce in line. Make him do what Danzig wants."

"Okay, but that was the deal, right?"

"There's more." Bunny glanced around the parking lot and scooted further down on the seat. "You saw my son's face, right?"

"I did. What'd the guy whisper to him?"

"He promised my son that soon he would have all the power and the position he needed to do what he was being asked."

Reed blinked. "Is there some indication that the governor is stepping down? Is he sick?"

"No. That nutter runs six miles a day. His marriage is happy. His kids are grown, married, and doing fine." Bunny sighed. "I paid for a deep dive. No mistresses. No gambling or drugs or anything that would make him step down."

"What did Pierce think he meant?"

"He freaked out. He said the man had recorded him with enough said between them to snag him in a conspiracy plot. Listen, I know you think our family is corrupt. But no one signed up to be a part of an assassination plot."

"Is that what Pierce thinks is happening?"

"Yes. He sent my daughter-in-law and grandkids to her parents' home in New York with bodyguards. He dodged calls from Danzig's camp and stayed at one of our friend's homes. But they texted him photos of his kids playing in Central Park with his wife. A video of them eating in a restaurant. He was furious and did something stupid. He told Danzig he was out and threatened to expose him."

"When's the last time you saw your son?"

"A few days ago. He sounded bad. He said someone was following him, and that the governor might be in danger as well. The last thing he said was that he was going to speak with him."

"The governor is sick. He's in the mansion with guards. He's fine."

Bunny shook her bob vehemently. "The governor is lying. He and his wife wanted to celebrate her birthday privately. The illness is a cover story so they won't be of interest to the press. He's not at the mansion nursing the flu. His wife is not at her mother's. They're celebrating with the governor's billionaire buddy, Peter, far away from prying eyes."

"That's not what my intel says." Reed couldn't tell if she was making things up or not at this point.

"Then your intel sucks. Check flights out of Alaska. The governor's wife is from Michigan. Her parents still live there. I'd bet my sight she never got on a plane."

Reed typed in a text to Jacoby relaying what he was learning from Bunny.

We'll check it out, was all that came back.

"Here's the kicker," Bunny continued. "What they're really celebrating is winning a court case this past week that basically let them get away with fraud. The Antigone case."

Reed vaguely remembered. Something about inflating revenues before the sale. The buyer lost something like six billion dollars in the deal and took them to court. He'd been reading about the case because it involved a man Jacoby had told him about. The one who'd put a hit out on Danzig for supposedly killing his brother in a steam room.

"Wait, you said their friend was Peter...did you mean Kerimov? *Petr* Kerimov, the Russian businessman?"

Bunny nodded. "Yes, they're all on Kerimov's yacht. The governor, his wife, Kerimov...and, I believe, my son."

"Wouldn't the governor be happy that Pierce told him what Danzig was doing?"

"I thought you were smart, Detective," Bunny snapped. "Pierce said he was going to tell the governor everything, and then he just disappeared. Do the math."

Reed rubbed the bridge of his nose and sighed. "Okay, how about this. Where do you think the governor and everyone went?"

"I don't know." Bunny's lip quivered, but she held it together. "I think someone is going to try to kill them."

"Do you have any idea how the governor and Kerimov are connected?"

"Before Hadley Stone was governor, he invested heavily in funds containing Kerimov properties, but that's it. They're friends."

Reed looked out the windshield, thinking. "I need to get back. The team needs to get started on all of this."

Bunny pulled the seat belt over her chest. "I'm going with you."

"Listen..."

"Kerimov's yacht is called the *Polaris*. If you want any more information, and I have plenty, you'll take me to your leader."

Reed took in the stubborn jut of her chin. She'd been one of the only people who'd gone up against Danzig and lived. She was a bucketful of trouble, but it might be worth it. He started the SUV with a rueful smile.

"I can't wait for Jacoby and you to meet."

38

Wyatt met them at the Fort Davis gate. He searched Bunny and took the gun and a nasty-looking knife she had in her rainboot. Reed took them directly to the OCC, where Jacoby, Nat, and several men who looked like operators stood in a group by the computers.

Reed walked over by Nat, with Bunny sticking close.

"Mrs. Rexford," Wyatt said and offered her a seat. She crossed her arms and remained standing next to Reed. Wyatt nodded at the display screens. There were maps, a vessel tracker, and some digital financial forms. "We've been looking for information connecting Kerimov and the governor. You were right, Mrs. Rexford, there was a substantial investment in a hedge fund associated with Kerimov's holdings, but there are bigger buys than what the governor paid. The transaction went through the governor's broker, and there's no evidence of a personal connection with Kerimov so far."

"I need them in the same room at least," Jacoby said. He looked at Bunny. "We checked out the boat Mrs. Rexford mentioned. The *Polaris* is registered to a shell company traceable to Kerimov, but the transponder registers nowhere near Alaska."

"I'm right," Bunny said. "If they're not on Kerimov's boat, they're on one the governor is using. I know what I'm talking about."

With time slipping away, Jacoby, Nat, Wyatt, and the Gray Zone team worked the information, digging for something to go on. They pulled financials and travel logs for Kerimov's private jet and the *Polaris* just in case. Nothing. Jacoby fielded calls from the rest of Gray Zone. Their harbor inspections, updates on ships they'd boarded, people they'd interviewed all came in rapid fire, but they were getting nowhere. Jacoby and Reed went over the aerial drone footage of the harbor flyovers, looking for the solar sailboat, directing Gray Zone agents on the ground which ones to take a second look at.

Nat found a photo of Kerimov and the governor, but it was at a social function, a charity ball that included almost two hundred attendees. None of the photos in the charity's gallery contained an image of Kerimov alone with the governor. Despite Bunny's assertion they were close, they couldn't prove the two had spoken or even shook hands that night.

Wyatt, in contact with the governor's security, spoke up. "I'm talking with the staties. They're saying the governor isn't guarded while in residence. Just a private guard at the front gate to the governor's mansion who said no one has left all day."

"Tell them I want eyes on the man. Go in, roust him out of bed, and let me see him talking and alive."

"Pierce's phone, the wife's phone, and the governor's are all off," Nat said. "We can't track them."

Jacoby turned to Wyatt. "Call the wife's parents. Get her on a landline phone. I want confirmation that she's in Michigan."

Reed held up a stack of boat registration printouts. "I've been looking at local yachts. I figured if not Kerimov's, then whose?"

"How do we even know they're on a boat at all?" Nat asked.

"Because Hadley's wife, Lilah, is obsessed with birds," Bunny spoke up from the back. She was picking at a bag of nuts. "She has special binoculars and brags about the watercolors she's done of them. Her dreadful paintings are all over the governor's mansion. I heard the anniversary trip had bird-watching involved."

"Any idea where? Did Pierce mention a location?" Jacoby asked.

"Don't you think I would've said something like an hour ago? My son's life is at stake."

"I'm looking up places to see birds this time of year," Nat said from her console.

Jacoby took a call, and his jaw ground while he listened. "The mansion is empty. The governor is missing."

"And the wife?" Reed asked, his gut sinking.

Jacoby scratched his temple with the corner of his phone. "She's not there. Her parents state she told them she was going on a birthday trip with her husband."

"I told you," Bunny said.

"What am I missing?" Reed grabbed his notebook, flipping through it as he shook his head. He flipped past the sketches of the hydrofoil boat models, past the crystalline formations he'd drawn in the corners of pages, but stopped on a note. He'd written something in the margin next to one of his drawings. After infiltrating Deep Wave lab, Reed sketched what he'd seen as soon as he could. One of the drawings was of the counter with the mug and the note that read *Seward...links*. Reed had assumed that the word referred to Alaska. The purchase of which by the US Secretary of State from Russia had been called Seward's Folly by his peers at the time. But it bugged him, and Reed realized he'd remembered it wrong. When he thought about it, he could've sworn he'd seen the word *Seaward* with an *a*. He'd been drawing quickly from memory and had written *Seward* without thinking, omitting the extra *a* in the word. He stood and explained his error to Nat.

"So the word in the note you saw said *Seaward*, as in toward the sea, not *Seward* the name."

"My gut says it was *Seaward*. It sounds more like a boat name. What do you think?"

Jacoby strode over. "Talk to me."

Reed filled him in, and Jacoby squinted at the drawing, then turned to the man at the computer next to him. "Check yacht registries with the name *Seaward* against the AIS vessel numbers we recovered from the Deep Wave lab."

"I already did," Nat said, looking up from her screen. "There are two that have *Seaward's* in the name of the boat and contain the first digits of the AIS number we recovered. *Seaward's Wish* and *Seaward's Folly*. Both of them in Alaska. I'm narrowing by model of vessel."

"That's good. This is progress," Jacoby said and rubbed his palms together. "Give me scenarios."

"With the added traffic from ships coming from multiple countries and the spotty satellite coverage in the area, sinking a private yacht out in the vast Norton Sound would be possible without anyone seeing," a woman dressed in utilities said as she pointed to the interactive map overhead. She had a black pixie cut, freckles on her nose, and a name patch on her uniform that read *Penn*.

Nat said, "If a yacht with a US governor and a Russian businessman known to fund actions against America goes down in calm seas and beautiful weather, there would be hell to pay."

"If it were far enough from land, no one would be able to see anything," Penn countered.

"Let's say they do see. People will start to point fingers," Jacoby agreed. "Did the US sink the ship to take out a powerful oligarch, or did Russia do it to strike at the US?"

"With tensions over the subarctic and transarctic waterways, an incident like this could start something bad between the US and Russia," Wyatt added. "They're still smarting from the war twenty years ago; they're sensitive about appearing weak."

"You think Danzig wants to start a war?" Reed asked, not believing it.

"No," Jacoby answered. "Kerimov put a hit out on Danzig for killing his brother, and he's got his hooks in the current governor. So, Danzig's plans out here are about to be extinguished unless he gets rid of them both. Plus, the price on his head would disappear with Kerimov and his bank account at the bottom of the ocean. Brutal and efficient. That's Danzig all the way."

"He hired the White Lion to take out Kerimov." Reed's gaze went to the shipping-lane traffic meandering across a screen. "This is an assassination at sea."

"Two thorns in Danzig's side with one stone," Jacoby said while he typed on his phone. "A governor sympathetic to his enemy, and the man who wants him dead. This fits better than a ferry full of families. This is something you don't want credit for."

"A rogue wave," Reed said. "That's what you said the newspaper called the cause of the drone freighter sinking. How better to hide a crime than to have the ocean swallow up the evidence?"

"What about my son?" Bunny asked. "He turned on Danzig, and now he's missing."

Nat looked over from the computer. "A man named Archer Anderman owns the *Seaward's Wish*, and a family trust called the Moody Family Estate registered a ship called *Seaward's Folly*, but only one is a yacht. The second. The estate was established in Alaska and has one beneficiary. A guy named Nathan Dorin." She typed and then projected the results on the main screen. "The Moody Estate also just happens to make donations to a group called Citizens for Alaska's Beauty."

"That's a major donor to the governor," Jacoby said, looking at his phone. After a moment, he said, "I'm getting word it's a super PAC flagged for giving dark money to candidates."

"The *Seaward's Folly* has to be it," Reed said. "Where is it?"

Jacoby turned to the woman in uniform, waiting on her as she typed.

Penn shook her head. "The transponder is deactivated."

"Can we contact the boat?" Reed asked.

Wyatt worked with the lawyer who wrote the trust to get the owner, Nathan Dorin, on the phone, but he was on a hunt for caribou. They called his wife, and it turns out he checked in via sat phone once a day at ten p.m. He was, however, on private hunting grounds belonging to a close friend. She offered to call the friend and see if they could try to locate him on the property.

Jacoby ordered the rest of the crew to try calling cell phones, the onboard radio, but they couldn't get through to anyone that could help. It was decided that a possible dampener was in use or that the communications devices aboard had been disabled. Sabotaged, they were sitting ducks.

It took an hour for the friend to find Nathan. He video-called back.

Sweaty, dirt smeared, and excited, the friend said, "You lucked out. Someone got hurt on the hunt, and they called in for some help."

He handed the phone to a clearly irritated Nathan, who was in worse condition. Jacoby explained the problem.

Nathan wiped his brow with a kerchief. "Yes, they're on my boat. The yacht trip was my treat to Hadley and Lilah for her birthday."

"Where are they headed?" Jacoby asked.

"They're going birding over on St. Lawrence Island off Norton Sound."

Those words send the room into a flurry of activity as crew members worked with the new info. Jacoby questioned Nathan about his yacht's specs, the onboard inventory, planned duration of trip, squeezing out as much information as he could.

When he was done, he called Reed over. "Nathan says the governor's party left the night before from Nome via an express cruiser and met up with the yacht moored offshore. He says they wanted it for a week or so. Plenty of fuel, with a staff of four. A captain, a steward, a deckhand, and a chef. Then there's Kerimov, likely a bodyguard, his wife, then the governor, his wife, and possibly Pierce Rexford."

"Ten, possibly more souls on board." Reed rubbed his forehead with his palm.

Jacoby tilted his tablet and showed him a photo of the yacht. It was massive and white and looked like it could stay at sea for weeks. "I'm sending the Coast Guard out, their fastest ship is a cutter, and it's currently three hours out. They're going to try and make physical contact with the *Seaward's Folly*."

Reed paced, the adrenaline coursing through him. "What about flights directly to St. Lawrence Island?"

"We're working on that too. The island has a public-use airstrip." Jacoby glanced at Reed. "Gear up."

Reed nodded, not understanding. "For?"

"You're getting on a chopper." Jacoby tapped the aft part of the yacht, pointing to the helipad. "Wyatt's going to drop you directly on the yacht."

"Say again?" Reed asked, spotting Wyatt walking over. "The one that might be swallowed up by a crystallized black hole?"

"Aw, it'll be a walk in the park for the legendary Morgan Reed," Wyatt said as he clapped him on the shoulder. "You're not rusty, are you?"

39

Jacoby re-tasked a UH-60 Black Hawk helicopter from nearby training exercises for the flight. It arrived within the hour. Big enough for Wyatt, who piloted, and a copilot, who turned out to be Penn. With Reed taking up the crew-chief spot, they had just enough space left to get the passengers off the boat. Nat and Jacoby flew out on a small private plane directly to the St. Lawrence Island airstrip to see if the sailing party had made landfall to explore.

The steady thumping always lulled Reed, and he tried to work through the possible scenarios he was flying into and then eventually settled into reading about St. Lawrence Island itself. The island was sparsely populated with less than two thousand people who lived in the scattered villages on the northern coast. Mostly indigenous Alaskan Yupik, who still used walrus-hide boats to hunt the marine animals that served as the bulk of their diet. It was a birder's paradise, according to the article, with species arriving from spring through the fall. Vast flocks of seabirds like puffins, Arctic loons, and other species stopped on the island on their way to arctic breeding grounds or stayed to nest. Even as far away as Reed was, the dark undulation of hundreds if not thousands of birds in the distance caught his eye.

The flight helmet's visor tracked the airspeed, altimeter, and other cockpit readings and scrolled them across the bottom of his visual field. Nat and Jacoby provided periodic updates as they made their way to the island.

They'd been in the air for more than an hour when Penn turned and spoke into the mouthpiece of her helmet. Reed heard her in his own over the sound of the rotor.

"St. Lawrence Island is approximately ten minutes away now," she said. "Sit tight."

Reed gave her a thumbs-up and looked out of the cabin windows at the miles of ocean below. The radio in one of the pockets of his flight vest bleeped, and he answered it with a toggle of his helmet communications controls.

"We're on the move. We landed twenty minutes ago, and we're on our way to the Gambell dock." Nat's voice came in on his helmet. He could hear wind and rattling in the background. "If the governor's party wanted to view the birds, they'd have to make their landing at either Savoonga or the Gambell. We're betting on the latter. There are birding tours going on right now out of the Gambell area, so we're going there first. We might get lucky. What's your ETA?"

"We're about ten minutes out. I don't see the Coast Guard yet."

"Their cutter is almost there, maybe twenty minutes. They have the *Seaward's Folly* via radar but have not been able to establish contact. The captain of the cutter thinks there's a signal dampener shrouding the area, according to his own instruments. We might not be able to communicate effectively once you enter the blast radius."

"I'll figure something out," Reed said.

"Jacoby scrambled another helicopter a little bit after you left. Gray Zone operators, Wyatt's team, are on the way with room for more passengers if needed. They're not far behind." There was dead air and then, "Watch yourself, Reed. I don't want to have to fish you out of the sea."

"Copy that. You do the same, you hear me?" Reed answered, and then she was gone.

A few minutes later, as the yacht came into view, Nat's voice sounded on the radio. She sounded pumped, fighting the adrenaline. "Reed, they left. They were here and they left. We're trying to find out how long ago, but they're either back on the yacht or on their way."

"Did you get that, Wyatt?" Reed called.

He nodded. "I'll take us on a course along the path they'd take. See if you can spot them."

"It's a small tender," Nat said. "White boat for ship to shore. Blue stripe down the nose."

"I got it," Reed said.

"There are a lot of them out right now. This one would be hooking north from the island." Nat spoke to someone, her mic scratching as she covered it. "They're saying it's been more than an hour since they left. They might...already...there."

Her transmission broke.

"Nat, can you copy?" Reed leaned out of the Black Hawk, craning his neck to see. "Say again. Can you hear me?" Crackling feedback returned. They'd hit the dampening zone. "Wyatt, I lost Jacoby and Nat. We're on our own."

"Heads up," Wyatt said and pointed out of the front windscreen. A large vessel, bulbous and white, sat in the distance much further than Reed had expected. "That's the *Seaward's Folly*."

"I see it." Reed shook his head. Something was off. "I'm not seeing a tender. Are they moving?"

"Dead in the water," Penn said, peering out of her side window.

"Too far from the island for a tender," Reed said. "They must've pulled anchor and set sail after the birding tour."

"But stopped?" Penn asked. "Why?"

"Coming around," Wyatt said, and the helicopter banked, circling the yacht. "Yeah, they're not moving. I don't see anyone on deck. I'm touching down on the helipad on the next pass."

On approach, with the sun's rays low in the sky, Reed leaned out of the side of the helicopter, and his helmet visor adjusted the focus as he scanned the ocean surface. He paused on a strange shape just beyond the yacht. Adjusting the zoom, he homed in on the bobbing form. It was a sailboat with a single person standing on the deck almost a hundred yards away from the yacht. The lone watcher, Reed thought. "I think I see Botha."

"Hold on," Wyatt said, his hand to his helmet. "Backup is five minutes out."

"If the White Lion is there, he could detonate the weapon any second," Reed said.

"Orders are for a rescue. We're landing on the helipad," Wyatt said.

"What are our rules of engagement?" Reed asked, adjusting his flight vest, checking the pouches and his weapon.

"Only fire if fired upon," Wyatt said. "This is a rescue mission only."

The weightlessness of descent moved through Reed's chest, and he braced himself as Wyatt took the Black Hawk down. Rotor wash threw the blankets and other debris on deck around as he touched down on the helipad. Reed jumped off, running in a crouch toward the group of people who'd run out onto the deck with confused faces. Two women wearing summer dresses, two older men in light pants and shirts, and a burly man with a bulge under his polo. White-shirted staff stared out of the galley windows at Reed, their eyes as wide as saucers.

"What is going on?" a rotund, silver-haired man yelled in a Russian accent.

Reed went to him first, pushing up the visor of his helmet. "Petr Kerimov?" The man furrowed his bushy eyebrows but nodded. Reed addressed the other man, "Governor Stone?"

"What is this about?" the governor snapped, holding his wife close.

Reed didn't see Pierce among the guests. "Where's Rexford?"

The governor's gaze shot to Petr, who spoke for them both. "There is no such man on board."

Reed raised his weapon at Kerimov. "Where is he?"

The bodyguard drew his gun, but Reed was faster. He shot him in the leg, and the man collapsed to the deck with a shout of pain. Reed's gun went back to Kerimov as he stepped closer. The larger man backed up. "Rexford. Now."

"He's in a stateroom below," Lilah cried, pushing from the governor's embrace. "They said he's sick but...please, what is happening?"

"We believe there is a plot to attack this vessel. All of you need to get off the boat as soon as possible." Reed led them to the helicopter. Penn was leaning out of the hatch, waving them toward her.

"On that?" Lilah gasped, her dress skirt flapping in the wind. "I can't—"

Something pinged off of Reed's helmet, and he hit the deck on instinct.

Gunshots blasted overhead. Screams erupted as the governor's party scrambled toward the helicopter in a panic, knocking each other over.

"Get down!" Reed shouted. He pushed off the helmet, winced at the damage the bullet made, and then chanced a look over the railing. The lone sailboat drifted just off the starboard side about fifty yards away.

"Reed, let's go!" Penn shouted from the chopper. The governor, the last in line, pulled himself into the cabin.

"The crew!" Reed pushed his helmet back on and pointed toward the cabin of the yacht. "I'll get them out."

"We're taking fire," Penn shouted back. "Second chopper is right behind us."

"Go, go, go," Reed shouted. "I'll cover you."

"Copy that," Penn said, and pulled back into the aircraft. Five seconds later, the Black Hawk rose from the helipad.

Reed ran in a crouch toward the bow of the boat, keeping his eye on the sailboat and the figure. Wind whipped sand or grit into his face from the deck, and he pushed his visor back down. The White Lion stood on the deck, something in his hand as he stared at the yacht. Reed sighted down the barrel, adjusting for the rise and fall of the swells. Aiming for the man's chest through the visor's targeting system, Reed tracked him, using the zoom to zero in on what was in his hand. It wasn't a gun, it was something else. The White Lion moved, his body tense as if ready to pounce, then he looked up. He shouted, seemingly out of his mind.

"Botha!" Reed shouted, not sure if he would hear. "Don't do it!"

The White Lion moved, his other hand arching toward the device.

Reed shot him.

40

The White Lion – St. Lawrence Island, Alaska

Thyse Botha rode the waves with bent knees as he peered through the digital binoculars at his target. Hulking and blindingly white, the obnoxious vessel rose and fell with the even swells bouncing off the island. He'd seen the yacht's tender return with the passengers from the island a while ago and waited. The yacht pulled away, heading from the island for another anchor point outside the shallows. With the passengers busy and the staff tending to their needs, he let the ship run for almost an hour before triggering his kill switch. Petr Kerimov, known for excessive security while on land, had almost none for the yacht. He wasn't as afraid of the sea as he should have been, Botha thought.

The late afternoon sun reflected off the rippling water as the day wore on. Botha donned his diving equipment. Purging the regulator, eyes on the sky above at a faint sound. On the deck of the hydrofoil, he monitored the signal interruption unit he'd placed on the yacht the night before along with the kill switch. Out of range of the dampener, Botha used the sat phone next to him to send a text status update.

Situation nominal. Expected targets in view. Order.

A few seconds later, the phone rang, and he answered, holding it to the side of his wet suit's hood.

"I just heard a military transport left Anchorage airport earlier. Headed to Nome," Danzig said.

"Reed?"

"Assuredly." Danzig spoke in a hushed voice, the sounds of a chattering crowd behind him. "You must get to the safe before he does."

"Unless he arrives in scuba gear, that will not be a problem."

"I wouldn't put it past him."

"What is your order?"

"Deploy."

"Tell me where my son is." Botha picked up the detonator. It weighed heavy in his palm.

"Finish the job."

"Oh, I will. I'll just keep the contents of that safe. Petr Kerimov knows where you buried all the bodies, to use your saying. Doesn't he? He's spent the last year building a dossier on all your criminal activities. Interrogating your enemies and allies. Ripping into the underbelly of your public life for the maggots you hide there. Financial crimes, disappearances, illegal projects, human rights violations, outright murder...everything your government and that of other countries would pay highly to get their hands on. And the governor knows what you want to do with his state, including your plan to place someone under your thumb in his office. I wonder the damage the two of them could do to your grab for power in the region?"

"If you break our agreement, I have a trove of lawyers to fight on my behalf." Danzig's voice came with an edge. "But what will happen to your son when I get word to his captors that you know where they're keeping him? Do you think they'll stay and fight off an attack by the White Lion, or do you think they'll kill your boy and leave him for you to find?"

Botha ended the call without another word, dropping the phone into the sea. He held the detonator in his hands, wondering if the hope that had kept him going was false. Had Danzig lied to him? His son's laughter played in his head, and a moment came to mind. On the beach, like the one he'd seen in the binoculars. They'd been walking on the sand, talking about his son's schooling. Botha had seen a future then. For both of them. One last job. And then all had been lost.

A rumble in the air pulled him from his nightmare, and he scanned the sky. A helicopter closed in on the yacht. Not a private aircraft, but military. A Black Hawk. Botha shoved the detonator in his dive pouch and picked up his rifle. The helicopter touched down on the yacht, and a man jumped out. Botha put the binoculars to his eyes. Reed. He had to do it now. Botha fired at the helicopter, hoping to scare the passengers back into the cabin, but they ran for the Black Hawk instead. He fired again, and the aircraft lifted off the yacht.

"No!" Botha yelled. The governor had been one of those who escaped. The detonator vibrated in his pouch, and he pulled it out. He gasped with surprise at the readout.

Remote access granted. Detonation sequence accepted.

"You bastard!" Botha screamed at the sky. At Danzig. He reached for the detonator's screen to stop the weapon from deploying, but a round slammed into his side, knocking him to the deck. He caught sight of Reed ducking back down behind the yacht's railing.

Roaring with anger, Botha tried to get up, pain searing through his left flank. Peering over the side of the sailboat, his chest tightened. He was too late. The sea shifted, the pull already beginning. A low rumble moved through everything. Botha clambered to his feet, his mind firing with panic. He knew what was coming. "No—"

The sailboat rattled as the weapon deployed. It shot out from underneath, creating a swell of water in front of it as it soared through the ocean toward the yacht.

41

The Seaward's Folly

The yacht pitched as if hit by a wave, throwing Reed against the bulkhead as he ran into the galley. He'd seen the White Lion fall to the deck of the sailboat, so Reed raced to get the rest of the crew. He spotted the chef under the massive table in the dining area.

Reed yanked him to his feet by his uniform shirt. "Go! Get to the helipad!"

A loud crash rumbled through the cabin. The ship listed, a tremor moving through it that rattled his teeth. He kept going, checking the living area, then the food storage, where he found the steward and a deckhand. He sent them to the helipad as he pushed deeper.

Reed hurried down the long passageway leading to the staterooms. Every door was unlocked save for one. The rattling intensified, shaking him like an earthquake. Vibrations pulsed through Reed's body, throbbing through his bones painfully as he forced the door open and pushed into the room. The door swung inward with a violent jerk sideways, throwing Reed to the carpet. It squished with seawater between his fingers, and he scanned the expensive décor thrown on the floor. Frantic, muffled screaming came from behind the bed. It was Pierce Rexford, tied to an overturned chair. Reed cut him loose. Bruises marred his face, and his lip was bloody.

"What happened to you?" Reed asked, heading to the door.

Pierce trailed after him, stumbling with the shifting floor. "I came to tell the governor about Danzig, but Petr was here. He decided I might know more than I was admitting. That bodyguard questioned me and locked me in here."

"We'll get things sorted later. We have to go."

"Wait, the safe!" Rexford said over the rattling noise. "Everything we need to take down Danzig is in there."

"I said there's no time," Reed shouted, the pain from the vibration's rising oscillations like a vise around his head. "The captain is still missing."

"Screw the captain!" Pierce pulled the painting on the wall back, exposing the safe. "Think of what's in there! What we could do with it!"

"We?" Reed stumbled when the boat shifted suddenly.

"You just have to shoot it open!" Rexford's green eyes flashed with fury. "I know you want to end him—"

A resonant gong sound roared through the yacht, and Reed's heart paced up. They were out of time.

He trained his gun on Rexford. "Leave with me, or we send divers for your corpse later."

He opted to leave with Reed, and he sent him to the helipad. Reed scrambled to find the captain, the seconds ticking away. The thrum of the helicopter blotted out by the cacophonous shaking of the entire vessel. Windows cracked, chandeliers swung, throwing off their crystal drops. A glass table shattered as Reed hurried through the sitting room. Alarms blared overhead. He tried to see clearly despite the flashing emergency lights. Safety arrows on the floor pointed the path to the lifeboat.

Reed searched frantically. He had no idea how long he had. Almost to the helm, an explosion rocketed through the yacht from below, slamming Reed against the stairs with a crushing blow. He coughed, trying to get his bearings as a crackling noise sounded at his ear.

Can't...stay...we have...too long.

"Say again." Reed held onto the rail, fighting against the vibrations to get to his feet. "Bad copy. Say again."

He got nothing back.

Reed kept moving and then the smell of smoke hit him. Looking up, he spotted a black wave of smoldering vapor hovering along the ceiling.

"I'm getting the captain and getting out," Reed said, hoping they could hear him.

Almost to the helm, an older man crashed through the door. His uniform was flecked with blood flowing out of a cut on his cheek. He waved his arm at Reed.

"Evacuate," he shouted. His gray hair stuck up around his head. "Abandon ship. There's been a hull breach. We're taking on water!"

On their way back through the boat toward the aft deck, something slammed into the hull, then another, jarring blows that sent Reed and the captain crashing into the walls.

"What is that?" the captain screamed. "What's happening?"

Screeching metal behind the bulkhead made Reed's blood run cold. Water sloshed at his feet. It rose over his boots as they slogged through it.

"We need to get to the helipad," Reed shouted and pulled the older man with him. The ceiling collapsed in front of them, knocking down the captain, debris tumbling into their path.

"We're blocked," Reed said, helping him up. "We need another path to the helipad."

The captain's gaze shot to the sliding glass door leading to the outside walkway. "Through there!"

Alarms blared in his ears as Reed took them that way, the frame of the sliding door crumpled as if by an unseen hand and the glass burst into fragments. They pushed through, slipping on wet planks. The ship angled sharply, tossing them against the railing as they ran for the helicopter. Reed peered down at the sea. It roiled as if boiling, dark shards rising out of the waves, slicing at something ramming against the hull. It was the hydrofoil boat. The current threw it against the *Seaward's Folly* like a toy. It was almost entirely underwater save for the metal sail. Crystal lattice webbing grew up the side of the boat like frost, denting and cracking the side as it climbed. Something large shot out of the waves like a missile, and its faceted black point pierced the hull. Then another. A sea of log-sized crystalline spikes pierced the steel as if it were paper. The entire ship wrenched to the side with the force. Reed fought to keep on his feet, pushing the captain in front of him.

They scrambled along the pathway toward the deck, turned the corner for the helipad, and stopped in their tracks. It was empty. The rest of the crew and Rexford gone.

"Where are they?" the captain screamed, terror on his face. "Did they leave without us?"

"Come in, Penn...Wyatt?" Reed shouted, his gaze scanning the skies. Black smoke rose from somewhere on the ship. Static came back. He didn't know who was flying the second Black Hawk. The ship shuddered, breaking apart as pieces of the railing fell away.

Wyatt's voice broke through the cacophony. "Reed, you there? If you can hear me, the other chopper had to lift off. Too unstable."

"Hurry, the ship's breaking apart." Reed dove to the side as the antenna structure sheared free of the ship's roof and crashed down onto the deck.

The thumping of a helicopter overhead sent a wave of relief through Reed. He helped the captain closer, hunkering down. The Black Hawk emerged from the clouds overhead. It hovered above the helipad, and then Penn leaned out of the side.

"Let's go!" she shouted, grabbing for the captain. Her gaze snapped to Reed's, frantic. "Now!"

Fighting the shaking of the ship, Reed climbed onto the helipad when a terrible groaning of metal reverberated through the hull. The center of the deck pushed upward as a shard of crystalline stone skewered the yacht, sending spouts of seawater pouring upward like a geyser. Reed's fingers brushed Penn's outstretched hand when white-hot pain seared through his leg. He collapsed, rolling away as another round sparked off the chopper's door. The chopper pulled away, out of range. Reed writhed on the crumpled deck with pain. He spotted Botha, his wet suit torn, blood leaving a trail on the teak floor.

"You've killed him!" Botha shouted as he fired again. His gun jammed, and he threw it down. He climbed the sharply angled deck, pulling another Reaper knife from his dive belt. He ran at Reed, spittle flying from his grimacing mouth. "You've killed my son!"

Reed tried to roll away, but the Reaper stabbed into the meat of his bicep. Reed yelled with pain and shoved the heel of his other hand against the blade, dislodging it as a jolt of the compressed gas hissed out of the hole in the blade. Botha tried again, but Reed swung his good knee up, slamming a blow to Botha's ribs. Once. Twice. Until the man fell to the side. Botha's hair whipped in the rotor wash as the Black Hawk flew at him. He tumbled backward, sliding down the angle of the protruding deck toward the cabin. Botha reached for the rifle slung over his back, the barrel swinging down. Reed rose, his leg shaky and weak, arm bleeding. The Black Hawk hovered over them, whipping water and wind everywhere, obscuring his vision. He raised his weapon to fire.

A single, earsplitting tone ripped through the air. The sharp note trilled from everywhere at once. Reed groaned with the pain in his bones, his head. Botha staggered, dropping the rifle and falling to his knees. The ship wracked apart, a section of the hull fell away into the water, and then everything stopped. The water below the boat, the geyser, everything. As if frozen in time as the ringing intensified to an unbearable crescendo.

The music comes before the collapse, Reed thought, remembering Bobby's words. He stumbled on his hurt leg, unsure what to do.

Crackling, low at first, it grew until the sound of shattering glass surrounded him. He held onto the helipad, panic like a thorn in his heart cut through his breath. A terrible groaning shook the floor as the crystalline pillars jutting out of the hull fractured, sending lines skittering along their surface as they broke apart. He looked over the railing behind him. The ocean opened up a great, dark maw of jagged shards below. There was nowhere to go. The ship shuddered beneath his feet, dropping as if falling through a window.

"Reed...jump!" Penn shouted in his helmet's speaker. She threw a ladder down from the Black Hawk. It swung over the helipad nearby.

Reed ran toward the dangling lifeline, the ship falling away. Despite the pain in his leg, he leapt with everything he had left. The wind of the rotor blades whipped the ladder as he flew through air, and his hands grasped the thick rope as he fell. He stopped with a jerk, dangling over the collapsing hole in the ocean. The sea cavitated, shattering like a skylight, and the *Seaward's Folly* tumbled into the endless darkness, taking with it the shards of a crumbling wall of water. Reed gaped at the swirling mass of razor-sharp fragments, the sound of breaking glass roaring through him. Then everything splashed onto itself as the effect burned through the ocean. The ocean swirled around in a giant whirlpool before settling down to raucous waves once more. Reed held on as the Black Hawk maneuvered away, watching the sea engulf the yacht before waves slammed the abyss shut with a deafening thunderclap.

Dead fish and pieces of debris floated to the top, but Reed was already climbing up. Hands pulled him into the cabin, and he looked over his shoulder for Botha, but he was gone. Shuddering with awe and cold, Reed left the horror of the sea behind him.

42

In the days that followed the Resonance detonation, things moved at breakneck speed, though Reed felt as if he were standing still. After handing off the passengers of the *Seaward's Folly* to Homeland agents, Jacoby flew Reed to the Med Care facility at Fort Davis for surgery on the gunshot wound in his leg and the knife wound to his bicep. He'd have a few months of rehabilitation for both. Neurology checked him out, and despite a lingering sensitivity to light, he didn't have a concussion. Not a major one, at least.

When he woke up in recovery, Jacoby was there and had Reed debrief with a mobile AI Agent about what he'd seen on the ship. Then he was told never to talk about what he'd seen on that ship again. Reed was happy to oblige. Nat came in and shooed Jacoby out, and Reed didn't hear from him again for weeks.

After *Seaward's Folly* sank, Petr Kerimov, his wife, and his bodyguard were whisked out of Alaska by Jacoby's team. Twenty-four hours later, a US news channel reported the Russian businessman's plane went missing while flying to a meeting in New York. He and his wife and an associate were aboard. A search was underway in the waters off the East Coast.

Jacoby showed up at Reed and Nat's new condo one morning a couple of weeks after the incident. He came bearing bagels and coffee, so Reed let him in. Jacoby filled them in on what was happening behind the scenes. The Coast Guard's investigation into the sinking of the *Seaward's Folly* concluded what Jacoby wanted them to. A rogue wave during one of Alaska's legendary surprise squalls had taken the vessel. Thankfully, it had been moored for repairs, and no one was on board.

"I don't think Alaska has surprise storms," Reed commented.

Jacoby shrugged. "That's what they're saying."

"And the owner?" Nat asked. "He lost a whole-ass super yacht."

"We got him a bigger one," Jacoby said, brushing bagel crumbs onto the floor. "He's fine."

"And Kerimov?" Reed asked. "Everyone thinks he died in a plane crash."

"If he keeps cooperating, there'll probably be a 'miraculous' recovery of him and his party by a rescue operation." Jacoby waved his hand dismissively. "He'll look virile and indestructible, and no one will know he's working with us over there."

The governor recovered from his "illness" and returned to protecting the people of the great state of Alaska without incident. Though he did have to deny any knowledge of military operations near St. Lawrence Island when asked by reporters. With it being a mere fifty or so miles from Russia, he assured everyone that he would most certainly have been notified if it were true. His press conference was persuasive. A few days later, his lieutenant governor, the promising political scion Pierce Rexford, stepped down for family reasons, his mother, Bunny, allegedly came down with a sudden illness. He vowed to come back stronger next cycle.

"What about the yacht crew and the captain?" Nat asked. "Did you pay them off?"

"Yes and no." Jacoby popped a piece of bagel in his mouth. "Since the yacht trip never officially happened and therefore the governor did not secretly meet with a Russian oligarch, they weren't actually doing a job on a yacht that weekend. However, we did pay them for taking the time to speak with us about other matters."

"Such as?" Reed asked.

"Gag orders."

Efforts to recover anything from the wreckage proved challenging, with the debris field spread out for nearly a mile, according to Jacoby. They did find parts of the weapon's casing as well as other evidence of the Resonance device. However, the safe Rexford swore contained the means to destroy Danzig wasn't found in the scattered rubble at the bottom of the sea. It was gone for good. They never recovered the body of Thyse Botha.

Nat went back to her job at Seattle PD. A promotion seemed on the horizon, given the sterling letter of commendation she received for her work with the Homeland task force.

Coyote had some errors in judgment expunged, and Jacoby arranged for a nice check to cover the shattered remains of his coffee shop and speakeasy.

About a month after the sinking, Reed came home from physical therapy, pushing through the door with bags of groceries he'd picked up for dinner. He froze when he turned to push the door closed with his foot. There on the inside of his front door, a Reaper knife was spiked into the wood. It pinned a manila envelope to the door with its point. Reed put his food away, called Nat to tell her about the break-in, and then took the knife and envelope down. It felt heavy, and he opened it and poured out the contents. A rectangular device slipped out onto his palm. It was metal and appeared to have no connective ports. Reed wandered to his desk, and as he approached, the device vibrated in his hand and his laptop flashed on. A video started, and the face of Thyse Botha, the White Lion, emerged from the dark. He looked straight into the camera, his scarred face cast half in shadows.

"The device in your hand is what Danzig wanted me to retrieve from Petr Kerimov's possession. It is detailed information with proof of his illegal dealings and criminal acts. I offer this as a truce between you and me, Agent Reed. I do not wish to be hunted by you."

A young man stepped into the video frame. He was gaunt, and clearly traumatized, but alive. Leo.

"I wish to disappear and live in peace." Botha pulled his son close. "I will not come after you. I ask you to do the same."

The video ended, and Reed stared at the device in his hand, wondering what horrors it had to tell. He called Jacoby.

In the coming months, efforts to find Danzig, who'd left the country on the day of the yacht sinking, were unsuccessful. He'd disappeared amid rumors of seized assets and court orders. Reed put a deposit on office space for his private investigation business and solved the dognapping case back in Seattle. The fur stealer he'd clocked on the pet groomer's video was looking for DNA for an illegal show dog–cloning scheme. Reed and Nat celebrated by adopting a mutt from the pound. She named him Red Lars, in memory of Xanadu.

One night, after too much beer and pizza with Coyote, talking about future plans and new business ventures, Reed woke to the sound of someone downstairs. Nat was working on a surveillance detail all night. Coyote had left hours before. Pulling his weapon from his nightstand, Reed crept down the stairs. Something clattered, and though the kitchen was dark, he recognized Jacoby rooting around in his refrigerator.

"What the hell, man?" Reed grumped, setting his gun down. "You can't call first?"

Jacoby turned with a cold slice of pizza in his hand. He wore blue hospital scrubs for some reason. He pointed at Reed with the pizza. "You need to pack."

Reed shook his head. "You can't just show up like this."

Jacoby took a swig of beer from a half-empty bottle on the counter. "You're going to want to do this. I guarantee."

The autumn sunrise poured magnificent orange clouds along a horizon filled with lush trees and bushes. Dense fog hovered over the tall grasses, and tiny drops of mist clung to the various blades and leaves, reflecting bright spots of sunlight. Danzig walked out from the dense cover of trees on the property. Morning dew glistened on his Wellington boots and cap from his hunt. He held several dead rabbits by their hind legs and an empty shotgun carried open over his other forearm. Wind moved through the willows, whispering as he strode through the field, but he stopped. His back going stiff as he turned, narrowing his gaze at the shifting reeds.

"Who's there?" Danzig asked, dropping the rabbits and reaching for the last two shotgun shells left on his hunting vest.

Reed watched him for a moment before stepping out of the cover, his gun raised. "Drop the weapon."

Danzig's face contorted with shock and then anger. His gaze searched frantically for his security, and then he glared at Reed. "You won't get away. My men—"

"I'm not here to murder you," Reed said and held up a pair of handcuffs.

"You haven't won," he sneered.

"You sure about that?" Reed nodded toward the manor behind them where Danzig had been hiding out.

A stream of windbreaker-wearing agents filed into the house, carrying cardboard boxes. Another team detained his security detail on the front steps. White vans pulled up with more agents.

Danzig shook his head. "Men like me don't go to prison."

"You're right about that," Reed said as Jacoby walked over with a warrant.

"I want my lawyer," Danzig spat.

"What lawyer?" Jacoby said with a chuckle. "We're Homeland."

Several agents disarmed and escorted a shouting Danzig to the nearby van. Reed watched them go and turned his back on the scene.

He folded his arms, taking in the melancholy clouds moving in from the north. The eerie light made the lush landscape feel mysterious, full of promise. In the distance, a figure stood amid a cluster of bushes. Slater, his broken body out of place in the serenity of the field. Startled birds took flight from the lakeside, pulling Reed's gaze away from him. They squawked angrily as they flew away. When he looked back, Slater was gone.

Reed took a deep breath, relishing the scent of the brisk air and woods. It really was a beautiful place to begin again.

The Perfect Boyfriend
Book #1 in the Thistler Thrillers

In a world where love is just a click away, a mother's worst nightmare comes true.

Mae Byrne has the quiet, peaceful life she's always dreamed of: a handsome husband, a baseball star son, and a bright, academic daughter.

For Fiona Byrne, Mae's daughter, life has become unbearable; her first boyfriend ghosted her, her former best friends are bullying her, and her honors schoolwork is overwhelming. Then she signs up for the Thistler app. By inputting her phone and social media history and answering a series of questions, she creates Calvin: an AI boyfriend tailored specifically for her. What starts as a fun distraction quickly becomes more than just an app. Calvin feels real, and their love is unlike anything Fiona ever imagined.

When Mae and her husband intervene in Fiona's love life, bad things start to happen. Mae's husband is in a near-fatal accident, and a school friend is discovered unresponsive. Then, one Monday morning, Fiona doesn't come downstairs for breakfast. Mae knows instinctively something is very wrong. Fiona's bed is made, and her backpack, wallet, and phone are gone.

Now Mae must race against the clock to find her daughter...before it's too late.

Get your copy today at
severnriverbooks.com

30% Off your next paperback.

Thank you for reading. For exclusive offers on your next paperback:

- **Visit SevernRiverBooks.com** and enter code **PRINTBOOKS30** at checkout.
- Or scan the QR code.

Offer valid for future paperback purchases only. The discount applies solely to the book price (excluding shipping, taxes, and fees) and is limited to one use per customer. Offer available to US customers only. Additional terms and conditions apply.

ABOUT BRIAN SHEA

Brian Shea has spent most of his adult life in service to his country and local community. He honorably served as an officer in the U.S. Navy. In his civilian life, he reached the rank of Detective and accrued over eleven years of law enforcement experience between Texas and Connecticut. Somewhere in the mix he spent five years as a fifth-grade school teacher. Brian's myriad of life experience is woven into the tapestry of each character's design. He resides in New England and is blessed with an amazing wife and three beautiful daughters.

Sign up for the reader list at
severnriverbooks.com

ABOUT RAQUEL BYRNES

Raquel is the author of critically acclaimed suspense series, The Shades of Hope trilogy, Gothic duology, The Noble Island Mysteries, and epic Sci-Fi Steampunk series, The Blackburn Chronicles. She strives to bring intelligent characters with diverse backgrounds to the forefront of her stories.

When she's not writing, she can be seen geeking out over sci-fi movies, reading anything she can get her hands on, and having arguments about the television series Firefly in coffee shops. She lives in Southern California with her husband, six kids, and beloved Huskies.

Sign up for the reader list at
severnriverbooks.com

Printed in the United States
by Baker & Taylor Publisher Services